What Readers Are Saying About
The Key on the Quilt

"In a richly textured novel about the sting of betrayal and the power of truth, three women discover what it means to love and be loved. Equally tender and stirring, *The Key on the Quilt* is not to be missed!"
—Tamera Alexander, bestselling author of *A Lasting Impression* and *The Inheritance*

"Whitson's *The Key on the Quilt* is much deeper and richer than the usual historical romance. I devoured it in one gulp and couldn't put it down. No one immerses me in a story world like Whitson. Highly recommended!"
—Colleen Coble, author of the Lonestar and Rock Harbor series

"From the opening line, *The Key on the Quilt* held me captive. Three women, their lives connecting in a hard place, must each learn lessons about the power of love and truth. As their faith grows, so will yours. Don't miss this excellent novel!"
—Robin Lee Hatcher, bestselling author of *Belonging* and *Heart of Gold*

"Love, grace, forgiveness, a captivating setting, and a compelling story await you in Stephanie Grace Whitson's *The Key on the Quilt*. An excellent read with well-drawn characters you won't soon forget, and a story you wish would never end."
—Judith Miller, author of the Daughters of Amana series

"Stephanie Whitson never fails to deliver a novel that reminds us all of our weaknesses and rejoices in our strengths. History doesn›t change who we are, and the women in this poignant novel give us new insight into what it means to be forgiven—and loved."
—DiAnn Mills, author of *Attracted to Fire*

"*The Key on the Quilt* is a romance that showcases hope, tenacity, and the strength of the human spirit. Highly recommended."
—Nancy Moser, author of *An Unlikely Suitor*

"Stephanie Grace Whitson›s name on the cover of a book makes it a must-buy for me. I discovered her novels over fifteen years ago, and her writing has grown even richer and deeper with the years. *The Key on the Quilt* grabbed me from the very first line and contains perhaps her most unique storyline and characters to date. An unpredictable story of redemption and hope, this one will have a place of honor on my "keeper" shelf."

—Deborah Raney, author of *Beneath a Southern Sky* and the Hanover Falls series

THE KEY
ON THE QUILT

The Quilt Chronicles

STEPHANIE GRACE WHITSON

BARBOUR
PUBLISHING

Dedicated to the memory of
God's extraordinary women
In every place
In every time

ISBN 978-1-61626-442-0

eBook Editions:
Adobe Digital Edition (.epub) 978-1-60742-790-2
Kindle and MobiPocket Edition (.prc) 978-1-60742-791-9

All scripture is taken from the King James Version of the Bible.

For more information about Stephanie Grace Whitson, please access her website (www.stephaniewhitson.com), her blog (www.footnotesfromhistory .blogspot.com), or her Facebook author page. Contact her at Stephanie@ stephaniewhitson.com or write P.O. Box 6905, Lincoln, NE, 68506.

Cover design: Müllerhaus Publishing Arts, Inc., www.mullerhaus.net

Published by Barbour Publishing, Inc., P.O. Box 719, Uhrichsville, OH 44683, www.barbourbooks.com

Our mission is to publish and distribute inspirational products offering exceptional value and biblical encouragement to the masses.

ecpa Member of the
Evangelical Christian
Publishers Association

Printed in the United States of America.

CHAPTER 1

April 1876
Dawson County, Nebraska

If it wasn't for the occasional night when he tried to kill her, Owen wouldn't be a bad husband. Jane Marquis risked a sideways glance at him. Moonlight and shadows revealed an all-too-familiar expression on his weathered face, as Owen guided the wagon across the spring prairie toward home.

Doing her best to suppress a shiver, Jane ducked her head and closed her eyes. *Oh. . .God.* It wasn't much of a prayer, but it was the best she could do. God hadn't seemed interested in answering her prayers for some time now. When the wagon lurched, she grabbed the edge of her seat with her right hand, lest she be thrown against him.

From where she lay sleeping in a tangle of quilts in the wagon bed, Rose whimpered. She stirred but did not awaken as the wagon lurched back up out of the ruts on the trail. *Thank God for that.* If only Rose would sleep through until morning. By then it would be over. Owen would smile and tease her from across the breakfast table, and everything would be fine.

Owen had never so much as raised his voice with Rose. He was

5

good with her. Always had been. In fact, it was Rose's need for a father that had finally convinced Jane to overlook the one or two incidents when he'd been a little rough on her, back when the two of them were courting. After all, it had only been a couple of times. The rest of the time, he'd been exactly what any woman in her right mind would want—successful, handsome, and fond of the child he'd be getting in the bargain of marriage to a young widow.

It shamed Jane to think of it, but the truth was *handsome* had done a lot to win her over. After all, he could have had any one of a number of single women in the county. Just about everyone had been surprised when Owen Marquis turned his considerable charms in the direction of the widow Jane Prescott, Jane included.

He'd never said a word about thinking her pretty. That didn't really matter, Jane told herself. Still, she liked to remember the catch in his throat that first night when she let her thick chestnut hair down. She liked the feel of his rough, work-worn hand at her narrow waist. No, she wasn't beautiful in the way some would think. . .but Owen had chosen her, and for a while he had seemed to be the answer to her prayers.

It was true she didn't love him the way she'd loved Thomas, but then a woman only got one of those in a lifetime, didn't she? Besides, she had to think of Rose, and Owen had been fond of Rose from the start. He'd even promised to see to her education, and that was important. It wasn't often a man agreed on the matter of educating a woman. Jane liked that about him. In fact, she almost took it as a sign that this was the man to fulfill Thomas Prescott's dreams for his only child. She told herself it wouldn't be hard to learn to love Owen Marquis.

It had all seemed so logical only two years ago. But now as Jane clung to the wagon seat beside a husband as tightly wound as a strand of new barbed wire, she wondered at the way she'd ignored all the signs: signs that through the mountain of a man who was Owen Marquis there ran a vein of violence he could not—or would not—control. And now. . .now she felt like some poor creature caught in a closed trap. Not killed, only forced to remain tethered to the very thing that would eventually bring about its demise. Owen was like that—shiny and sleek on the surface like a new trap, but with jagged teeth that bit down when Jane unwittingly tread on this sensibility or that feeling, on this opinion or that belief.

He was always quick to repent. At first, that had given her hope. He'd even wept over the faint bruises resulting from late-night confrontations. Every time, Jane took him in her arms and promised to forgive and forget and proved her sincerity by giving herself. But as the months went by and Owen didn't change, Jane began to concentrate less on forgiving and more on trying desperately to avoid doing anything that might displease him. And wasn't that the irony of it all tonight? The very thing that had painted jealous rage on Owen's face—an innocent dance with Dr. Zimmer—was something that, absent Owen's drinking too much at the social over at the Bar T, likely would have pleased him.

How many times had Jane heard Owen praise Doc? How many stories had she heard him tell about the man's fast thinking and how he'd saved this cowhand's life or that rancher's child? Owen trusted Max Zimmer. Appreciated him. And Owen himself had once said there was no better way to show a man your trust than to let him dance with your wife. He'd even encouraged Jane to dance with this visiting dignitary or that bloated politician. So she'd taken it upon herself to grant the doctor a waltz tonight, thinking Owen would see it for what it was—a wife supporting her husband by showing kindness to a trusted friend.

That wasn't how it had played out, though. Jane had known before she and the doctor took the second pass around the dance floor that she'd made a terrible mistake. The look on Owen's face—thinking back on it sent a brand-new river of dread flowing over her. This time Owen noticed her shiver.

"Cold, darlin'?"

She started at the sound of his voice. The edge to his mellow purr set her skin to crawling. She managed a murmured "I'm fine," but he ignored it, pulling her across the wagon seat with one arm, which he clamped around her.

"There now," he rumbled. "Thas better, hunh?" He squeezed harder.

"Much," Jane agreed, wishing his breath weren't heavy with whiskey, wishing she could somehow keep her voice from cracking with fear, wishing she could manufacture a way to take Rose and go so far away that Owen wouldn't be able to follow them.

"You jus' put your head on my shoulder and catch a wink or two. We need ta talk, but it can wait till you put Rose ta bed."

Jane did what she was told. She leaned into him. But she did not sleep.

September 1876
Lincoln, Nebraska

A person learned a new vocabulary in prison, and for Jane Prescott—she'd done away with the name Marquis the minute she'd arrived here—the most important phrase was, "learning to do the time." At first, she spent a lot of time just standing at the tall, barred windows, staring off toward the west. Then one evening when the sun was setting and Jane was watching a spectacular sunset, wondering if Rose would forget how the two of them used to watch the sky, Agnes Sweeney sidled up to her and said in a gravelly voice, "You stand there much longer, you're gonna grow roots."

Jane didn't even look at her. Only shrugged and kept staring west.

Agnes turned her back to the window and leaned against the bars while she stared at Jane. "You got to learn to do the time."

Jane frowned and glanced her way. "Am I bothering you?"

Agnes shook her head. "Don't bother me one way or the other. But the way you're staring west, I'm thinking you got somebody out there you care about. Maybe they care about you; maybe they don't. Either way, you got to learn to do the time, or you ain't gonna live long enough to find out." She jabbed a finger at Jane's waistline. "You ain't been eatin'. Dress hangs on you. Fit right smart when you come in."

Jane put her hand to her waist. She hadn't really noticed, but Sweeney was right. She could pinch at least a couple of inches of the gray waistband between thumb and forefinger. *Gray.* They all wore gray, a color she'd always avoided, thinking it made her look washed-out. She shrugged again.

"Here's the thing. I done time down Texas way. Now *that* is hard time. The thing is, sooner you learn to cope with the truth of where you are, the better chance you got of surviving it. Miss Dawson's an angel compared to the witch of a matron in Huntsville. Food here's better, too. Exceptin' for you, we ain't violent offenders, so you find a way to just 'do the time,' and you'll be all right." She nodded toward the west. "No way to tell if they'll still be waitin' when you get out. My man said he would. But he didn't. Either way, whether you do the time hard or easy, it's mostly up to you."

Jane didn't suppose Agnes Sweeney would ever realize that she just might literally have saved another woman's life with those few words of hers. Thinking on Agnes's words, Jane had realized that she already knew quite a bit about "learning to do her time." Essentially, that was what she had done to survive marriage to Owen. And that had been very hard time. From what Jane could tell of prison life so far, Agnes was right when she said that whether or not the time was hard or easy would be mostly up to her. She decided to do what she could to make it easy.

At first, Jane thought making her time easy meant being what people expected when they learned she was here for manslaughter. When the moment seemed right, she let the others know she was doing "ten years for killing my husband. He deserved it, and I'd do it again, so leave me alone." No one bothered her after that.

Then a few months into her sentence, Dr. Max Zimmer came to visit.

October 1876
Lincoln, Nebraska

Max Zimmer just wasn't the kind of man people expected to visit a woman in prison for killing her husband—even if the charge was "only" manslaughter. Lean and ruggedly handsome, the doctor had turned heads wherever he went back home. Jane had never let herself think about it while she was married to Owen, but some nights when she lay in the dark in this place, she wondered if her life might have been different if Zimmer had arrived in Dawson County a few years earlier than he did. She remembered his hand at her waist during that one dance and the kindness in his gray-green eyes and thought that surely that hand would never be raised against a woman in anger. Whether it was those eyes or his kindness or something else, when Jane was summoned to the barred door and heard that Dr. Max Zimmer had come to visit, her pulse quickened.

The visit began well. The doctor sat across from Jane at the plain oak table in the visitor's room and said he was going to petition the governor for a pardon. He insisted that if Jane had only allowed him to keep a proper record of the bruises and that cracked rib, no judge in his right mind would have handed her ten years. Then something odd happened. As Zimmer sat there, making his case, Jane realized that looking into those gray-green eyes was going to make the next few days after he left really hard. The longer he talked, the more panicked she felt at the prospect of going back up those stairs to the third floor and hearing the door clank as it locked her back inside.

Finally, she cut him off in midsentence. "That's not going to change anything, and we both know it. The judge was a friend of Owen's, and Owen didn't allow me to visit, so I never did make friends of the neighbors. No one is going to believe anything but that it was exactly what it looked like. I wanted the ranch and plotted to get it. Owen found out, confronted me, and we fought. I got hold of his gun."

The doctor stood up while Jane was rattling off the story that had come out in court. He actually reached across the table as if to take her hand. The guard stepped forward. Jane pulled her hands into her lap and leaned away. "Just leave me be."

He shook his head. "I won't. I can't. You don't belong here."

Jane saw the guard's expression transform into a barely concealed sneer. She swallowed and looked away. "The only thing I want from you is for you to hang on to that little trunk until I get out and send for it." She cleared her throat. "Don't come back. If you do, I won't see you." She turned toward the guard. "Take me back. Please."

After that visit, he became *Max* in her thoughts, and the memories and longings and the dreams his visit resurrected were a torment. She lost her appetite again. She worried about Rose. And she prayed. But still, God was silent.

The other women's teasing didn't help. They hadn't seen much, but they'd flocked to the windows to watch whoever had visited Jane Prescott head back into town. Seeing a lone man astride a handsome gray was enough. And then Adam Selleck, the guard who'd monitored the visit, added to her troubles with snide comments about her "handsome lover."

She began to fear she'd give up the truth one day. What if she talked in her sleep? Terrified at the prospect of who might be hurt if that happened, she crawled inside herself and stopped talking, hoping the others would take her silence as a sign she was a hardened criminal. She convinced the matron, Miss Dawson, to stop bringing her the letters Max wrote. "Send them back," she begged, even as she blinked away the tears she hoped Miss Dawson didn't see. She would keep writing Rose, but that was all. Rose would keep her alive—not some false hope involving Max Zimmer's championing her case and getting a pardon.

Max didn't come back, and toward the end of the first year, Jane realized with a jolt one morning that most of the time life wasn't unbearable. She and the other eleven women shared a decent, dormitory-style bedroom, dining room, parlor, and bath on the third floor of the prison's castle-like central building. The windows might be barred, but they let in plenty of light. The food was adequate. Truth be told, the hardest thing about the place was the monotony. There just wasn't enough to do.

The men had all kinds of industries. From dormitory windows that looked down on the yard inside the walls, the women could watch them filing from here to there, a human chain created by each man's right hand on the shoulder of the man in front of him. They worked in the brick kiln or the clay kiln or for Great Western Stone Cutting. The buildings along the western side of the compound housed a woodworking shop and the laundry, among other things. But here on the third floor, the women had hand-sewing, mending, and reading. They never went outside. The days were long, the nights longer.

Agnes Sweeney had been right about Miss Dawson, though.

The matron was in a position to make life miserable if she had had the mind to do so, but Mamie Dawson had no such mind. She was firm but fair, and beneath her serious exterior, Jane saw evidence of true kindness. In another life, the two of them might actually have been friends.

Most of the time, Jane was able to take Agnes's advice and concentrate on doing her time as easily as possible. Every bell and every sunset marked a few less minutes until she'd be released and be able to try to rebuild a life for herself and Rose. She couldn't quite imagine what that life would be like. Rose would be a young woman. When tempted to worry over it, Jane told herself, *Just get through today.*

No one must ever know the truth about that night when a drunk Owen Marquis raised his hand against her for the last time. Justice demanded payment for Owen's death, and Jane would pay it. She got past Max's visit and the resurrected emotions and spun a cocoon around herself. She did the time, one long day at a time. And then, toward the end of the first year, a postcard arrived from Flora that threatened to snuff the very thing keeping Jane's flickering hope alive. *Rose has mourned her loss and is happy with me as her new mother. It is not wise to stir up memories of the tragic past.*

Jane kept writing for a few months, but every letter came back unopened. Finally, she asked Miss Dawson if the returned letters could be kept for her in the prison safe along with her other personal items. Miss Dawson agreed to see to it, and Jane stopped writing. The cocoon grew darker, but still she managed to slog through the days. God might not be listening anymore, but something in her would not let go. She couldn't imagine what her purpose on the earth was, yet she clung to hope. She would survive and get out. She'd find Rose and. . .something. Most of the time her daydreams ended with finding Rose. Lacking knowledge of what Rose looked like now, she envisioned a younger version of herself. That would do for daydreams and fantasies. She'd deal with reality when the time came. For now, all she could do was the time.

Fall 1876

Mama! Mama, *no*! Papa! Papa, *stop!*" Nine-year-old Rose Prescott flailed against the darkness, fighting whatever it was that held her in bed. Her heart racing, she tried to kick herself free.

Aunt Flora's voice sounded through the fog. "Rose. . .Rose, honey, wake up. You're having a nightmare."

Arms encircled her, and Rose inhaled the comforting aroma of lavender as Aunt Flora held her, rocking back and forth, back and forth on the bed. "Shhh, sweet girl, shhhh now. . .you're safe. Safe with Aunt Flora."

Clutching at her aunt's sleeve, Rose began to cry, whimpering for Mama, wishing the bad dreams would go away.

"I know, sweetheart, I know. They will. You're safe now. No one can hurt you."

"Not me," Rose murmured. "Not me. . .Mama." Finally, she gathered the courage to open her eyes and peer over Aunt Flora's shoulder toward the golden glow of the lamp in the window. The lamp they lit every night, just in case Mama came looking for Rose. So she'd know where to look. Aunt Flora said the angels would bring Mama right to Nebraska City, and Mama would see the light in the window and come for her.

Aunt Flora began to hum softly. Finally, weariness took over. Rose relaxed, clutching Aunt Flora's sleeve with one hand and the doll quilt Mama had made her with the other.

CHAPTER 2

Early April 1880
Brownville, in Eastern Nebraska

Ian McKenna, whatever are you talkin' about?!" Ellen laughed as she looked down the length of the new, cherrywood dining table to where her husband sat, waiting for her to answer his question. He had to be joking—didn't he?

"You'll like it in Lincoln," Ian said. "We'll get Jack his own horse to ride from home to school. It's less than three miles. In a few years, he can attend the university instead of going away. You can't tell me you haven't already started dreading his leaving home."

Blast those blue eyes, anyway. Using their only son to persuade her—even if it was true that she'd already started to complain at how fast Jack was growing and how he'd be leaving home in the blink of an eye. Ellen dreaded the day more than she'd let on. Something about that little grave off in Missouri made her unwilling to think of Jack growing up and leaving home. Ian was right. The idea of the university just a short ride away made the offer almost appealing.

"There's a new house," he offered. "Two stories. Brick. Reminds me of Belle Rive a little. In fact, the ladies of Lincoln will likely envy you the parlor and the wide porch. We can screen it in.

You'll entertain in style."

"Belle Rive," Ellen said, allowing just the slightest bit of the Southern drawl she had worked to eradicate back into her voice, "wasn't in the shadow of high, stone walls sportin' guard towers." Ian just sat there, tugging on his mustache, waiting for her to acquiesce. *What would my parents say? How could I possibly write home and tell them Ian McKenna's latest idea of providing for his family was hauling them to Lincoln, Nebraska, so he could be the warden at the state penitentiary?*

"Two years," Ian said and extended two fingers. "If you hate it after two years, I'll quit. As for living in the house across the road, give it six months, and if you hate that, we'll get something in Lincoln—although it won't be nearly as grand. And you'll have to put up with an absentee husband now and then if I can't make it home every night."

Taking a deep breath, Ellen pushed herself away from the table and stood up. She crossed the room to look out the windows at the freshly turned earth just outside. She had a lovely garden planned for that spot—as exact a copy of the garden at Belle Rive as Nebraska's comparatively harsh climate would allow. Thinking on that garden brought back such memories.

No one, least of all herself, had expected Ellen Sullivan of the Lexington Sullivans to marry someone she'd only known for a few weeks. Her family had not approved, not one little bit. When her father threatened to disown her "over that Yankee," Ellen threatened to elope. On the last day of August in the year of our Lord 1861, sixteen-year-old Ellen Sullivan and her beau stood on the front steps of Ellen's childhood home just outside Lexington, Kentucky, and promised to love and cherish one another until death.

When, little more than a year later, Ellen's husband donned his new blue uniform and left her on their farm in Missouri, Ellen refused to agree to her family's pleas that she return home to Kentucky. Firm in her resolve to support President Abraham Lincoln's Grand Army of the Republic and equally firm in her resolve to keep the vows she had made to follow Ian McKenna wherever he went, Ellen wrote home that death might take Ian from her, but nothing else would, least of all a little skirmish over a state's right to secede from the United States.

Death almost did separate Ian and Ellen, but not in the way the young wife feared. In 1864, it slithered into the McKenna's bedchamber along with the moist breeze of a summer night while Ellen labored to give birth to her first child. He lurked in the corners of the room, and at one point hovered over the bed, expecting to see Ellen's soul depart her body. But another Spirit won that night. Another Spirit seen not by Ellen and not by the doctor, and certainly not by Ian who, home on temporary leave, knelt by the bed and watched his wife's pale face and prayed. But Death heard that Spirit's voice. *The days are written. Today is not that day. Begone!* And so Death slithered away, leaving behind not only an exhausted woman, but also a redheaded baby girl they named for Ellen's mother.

Ellen expected things to settle down once Ian had fulfilled his duty to President Lincoln by serving in the Fourth Missouri Volunteer Cavalry. It was not to be. Only six months after their baby girl survived the battle to be born, she succumbed to a high fever brought on by only the Lord knew what. Ellen grieved alone while Ian was off riding into the face of the good Lord only knew what. In 1862, grief and a longing for her husband's arms occupied Ellen's mind far more than either the Free Homestead Act or the Pacific Railway Act. Until, that was, the war ended, and Ian came home.

He was still the love of her life, but he, too, was forever changed by the things he'd endured. "I can't be a farmer," he said. "I just can't. It's too—" He broke off. Shook his head. He didn't have words for a lot of things these days.

Ellen put her hand on his arm. "What is it you want to do, darlin'?"

They packed up and headed west, and Ellen's only regret in the matter was leaving the little grave in the churchyard. If her father's threat to disown her and a visitation from Death had not separated Ellen from the love of her life, then neither would Indians or rattlesnakes or any of the myriad horrors she had heard talk of among the other women whose husbands had caught the same fever as Ian.

As it happened, however, Ian McKenna's westward fever was less about land and more about helping good people bring law and a semblance of order to Brownville, Nebraska, a bustling river city upon which dozens of riverboats a day spilled their contents and through which hundreds of wagons a week departed on their way to live their respective dreams farther west. Not long after the McKennas arrived in Brownville, Ian was elected sheriff. And Ellen gave birth again, to another redheaded child, this one born squalling, and flailing strong arms and pudgy legs. They named him Jack.

To her great surprise, Ellen loved Nebraska. She loved the sound of the whistles that announced the arrival of yet another boat; she loved the never-changing scenery that rolled by the front door of their modest home every day, and after nearly twenty years, Ellen loved her husband more than ever. So as she stood at the window, looking out on the place where she'd planned to plant her garden that spring, she envisioned scraping a bit of earth into her palm and then turning it over and letting it go. Much as a woman releases the earth over the grave of a loved one, Ellen released the dream of planting her garden in Brownville. She would not, however, give over her Brownville garden for a square of untamed prairie—at least not without a question or two. "Why can't we get something in Lincoln right away?"

Ian moved to stand behind her. Wrapping his arms around her, he pulled her close and nuzzled her neck before whispering in her ear. "Well, I suppose we could. But I promised myself that if I survived the war, I'd never waste one more minute of my life than I absolutely had to waiting to see you again. Lincoln is nearly three miles away, and I'm selfish." He nuzzled her neck again. "I want you closer." Caressing one of the auburn tendrils curling at her neck, he traced the line of her bare shoulder along her décolletage toward—

"Stop that!" She batted his hand away and turned around. As she looked up at him, she felt her cheeks warm.

"I love you, Ellen Rebecca Sullivan McKenna," he said, as he took her hands in his. "Just try it for six months. Please." He kissed first one palm, then the other.

"I know what you're doing," Ellen said, glowering up at him. "Jack's gone for the evening and you want—you want—"

"What?" He laced his finger through the loosened curls at the back of her neck.

"You want to use your—wiles—to convince me."

With his free hand, he caressed one arm, then lifted it to kiss the inside of her wrist. "How am I doing?"

She pulled free. "Meet me upstairs," she whispered. "I'll let you know. After."

Spring 1880
Dawson County, Nebraska

Max Zimmer's heart thumped when he saw the state seal on the envelope. *From the Office of the Governor.* He tucked it into his breast pocket and tried to distract the combination postmaster-storekeeper by pointing to the row of candy jars lined up on a shelf in the display case across the way. "I'm out of horehound over at the office. I'll take half a pound."

Hiram Comstock followed Max across the store and, opening the sliding doors at the back of the display case, grabbed a handful of the individually wrapped candies and dropped them into the basket attached to the scale atop the counter. Peering at the numbers, he grunted and reached for a couple more pieces. "Looks like you've got some mighty important mail there," he said as he reached for a small sack and bagged the candy. "You finally listening to reason and thinking about running for office?" He held on to the bag while he waited for an answer.

Max shook his head. "Not a chance. I'd be a terrible state senator. I've no patience with all the ballyhoo that goes on up in Lincoln." He reached for the sack. "Don't mean to be rude, but I've likely got an office full of patients waiting."

Hiram glanced through the storefront window toward the doctor's office on the opposite side of the town square. "You keep emptying that candy jar at this rate, you're gonna have to raise your prices." He grinned as he handed over the bag.

Max headed for the door. "Naw. . .candy's worth its weight in gold. Best incentive there is to ensure the little ones' cooperation with the doctor. Mothers think I have some kind of talent with children." He grinned. "There's no talent to it. I bribe them." With a wave, he exited the store, then cut across the town square and rounded the courthouse. Widow Mabry had obviously preceded him to the office. A sign reading THE DOCTOR IS IN beckoned, and Max could see that the chairs lining the front window were all occupied.

Skirting along the side of the emporium, with which his building shared a wall, he ducked beneath the overhang that sheltered the clinic's back porch. Glancing around, he finally opened the envelope. He'd been writing letters to judges and the governor since the day Jane Prescott was sentenced. At times he'd been tempted to believe

Jane had been right that one time he'd visited the penitentiary. Maybe he was wasting his time. But he couldn't forget her, and he couldn't give up. Sometimes he wondered why. Maybe it was the unforgettable scene when young Rose's aunt came to take her away. Certainly Jane's refusal to say anything negative about Owen Marquis at the trial had left an impression. And that dance. Max had gone over and over it in his mind and finally come to rest at a place where he felt culpable. Maybe Owen did have reason to be jealous, but if he did, it wasn't for anything Jane had said or done. She was everything a man could want in a wife, and loyal beyond reasonable expectation. But Max had loved that dance. Maybe more than he should have. Maybe Owen had sensed it.

As he looked down at the letter, a knot of emotion rose in his throat. He gazed toward heaven and called out a triumphant "Thank You!" Folding the letter, he tucked it into the inner pocket of his coat, patting the place where it lay over his heart. As he grasped the doorknob and went inside the clinic, his mind raced through everything he'd need to do to get away. Patients to see. . .an announcement in the paper that he'd be gone for a few days. . .packing to do. . .and a train ticket to Lincoln. He had an audience with the governor. A chance to appeal for Jane's release.

She would have to see him now.

CHAPTER 3

April 7, 1880

J ane started awake. As the moments ticked by, she realized she'd been awakened by silence. Nights here usually included snuffles and snores and the sounds of women rearranging blankets, or on occasion, muffled weeping. This night was different. Ominous. As Jane lay still, listening to that quiet, she realized that beneath it hummed a wire of tension.

"Hmpf—"

"SHHH!"

"Hunh—*hunh*?"

Words. Murmurs. From the opposite end of the room. Another grunt, this time loud enough that it sounded like a protest. And then. . .nothing. Nothing but the unmistakable sound of bare feet padding. . . *Toward me*, Jane thought. She pulled the blanket away from her face and glanced over her shoulder.

Pearl Brand was out of bed, likely the cause of the grunts and protests, and. . .*she was looking straight at Jane*. A chill ran up her spine. Pearl was the first woman Jane had encountered in this place who truly frightened her. She was different from the rest of them in some fundamental, terrifying way. Whatever Pearl had been up to in the predawn darkness, she now knew Jane was aware of it.

Convince her you didn't see anything. Didn't hear anything. Sleepwalk. With a shrill cry of terror, Jane threw her blanket off and, jumping out of bed, stumbled toward the cold stone wall just a few feet away. Pressing her palms against the wall, she began to sway from side to side, blubbering, "Out. Out. Let me *out*, do you hear? Let. Me. OUT!"

Raucous laughter sounded as a beefy hand clasped her shoulder and shook her. A cloud of putrid breath carried the words. "Having a nightmare, Janie? Don't like the accommodations? Want to speak to the *manager*?" Pearl laughed, but there was no mirth in the sound.

Jane wheeled about and blinked, rubbing her eyes. "I—I—I was—" She hung her head. "I was asleep."

"You were sleep*walking*," Pearl corrected her.

"I'm sorry." Jane gulped. "Did I wake you? I'm so sorry." Even Agnes Sweeney backed away from Pearl. Jane mimicked Agnes now. She didn't challenge, made no eye contact, gave Pearl no reason to think she posed any kind of threat. Looking down at the gray stone floor, she rounded her shoulders and tried to become as small and nonthreatening as possible.

As Pearl loomed above her, Jane's heart rate ratcheted up several notches. She had definitely heard something a few minutes ago. Something not good. Obviously, something involving Pearl. It took everything in Jane at that moment to keep her gaze down, to keep herself from looking toward the locked door. Where was the guard? Why wasn't he checking on them? Couldn't he hear? The sun would be up soon. Any minute now, they would hear a key rattle in the door, announcing Miss Dawson's arrival. *Please. God.*

"Can I—?" Jane pointed at her rumpled cot. She could feel Pearl looking her over, sense the hulking woman's small, dark eyes get even smaller as Pearl peered at her. What was she looking for? Evidence

Jane had heard—what? Jane didn't know what she'd heard. She only knew she'd awakened to *something*.

Giving Jane a little shove toward her narrow cot, Pearl turned away. "Get your beauty sleep, princess."

Jane slipped back into bed and once again pulled the blanket up over her head, but not before noticing that every other woman in the dormitory lay with their backs to the part of the room Jane had avoided looking at. The part of the room where whatever Pearl was up to had taken place.

———⚬———

When Mamie Dawson had promised Jesus she would love every lamb He sent her way—including those who'd wandered from the fold—she'd never expected Him to take her quite so literally. But here she was, a matron living in an apartment on the premises of the state penitentiary, spending her days among a flock of wandering sheep the likes of which even her overactive imagination could never have dreamed into existence.

Stretching and yawning, Mamie padded barefoot from her bedroom into the large parlor that still tended to surprise her when she considered its relative opulence compared to the apartment she and Minnie kept in Lincoln. Passing through the parlor, she went into the kitchen and put a pot of water on to boil, then paused long enough to look out the tall, narrow set of windows toward the west. The sky was still indigo there, but on the opposite side of the apartment, the eastern sky was more of a pale blue. Soon it would be streaked with pink, and by then she'd have dressed and made her way down the stairs to the second floor, through turnkey, and onto the secure side. For now, though, she would enjoy the quiet before her workday began. Teacup in hand, she made her way back to the parlor and into the turret just off the northeast corner of the room. Setting the tea on the table beside her Bible, she settled in her rocking chair and bowed her head.

Lord, I'd be grateful if Pearl Brand would behave herself today. And if she doesn't, then help me to bear up and show me how to handle it. I don't like admitting it, but she frightens me. Please protect us all from whatever it is I see in those dark eyes of hers.

Help me know what to do for Vestal. Please let her time come easy on her. . .and make me brave when I ask the warden about the situation. Make him brave, too, because it'll take courage for him to say yes, what with him being new and needing to please the governor and all. Please make a way.

I thought Jane Prescott was doing better, but this business with Vestal seems to be making it hard on her. Should I intervene? Should I try to find that Flora person who wrote that postcard? What about Jane's daughter? Why doesn't someone bring her to visit? And why'd that doctor who visited when she first got here give up on her? I just don't know where to start with all of that, Lord, but I hate seeing Jane so heartbroken. She seemed to be doing better for a while, but now I think that was just her learning to hide her cares. I wish I could get her to trust me with her burden. Of course that doesn't matter nearly as much as her learning to trust You.

Mamie prayed for a long while, naming each one of the women in her care as she talked their problems—and her problems with them—over with the Lord. She'd learned that, if she prayed often enough for each one by name, the Lord eventually granted her grace to love them all. Even Agnes Sweeney who, until Pearl's arrival, seemed to be the blackest of the black sheep. Agnes was beginning to come around. Pearl—well, she was another matter entirely.

As the eastern sky began to show tinges of pink, Mamie rose to dress, continuing her conversation with the Lord even as she donned unmentionables and a simple gray skirt and waist, even as she bent to button her sturdy, black ankle-high boots.

As she closed her apartment door and locked it behind her, a thought came to mind, almost as if the Lord was talking. *It IS a flock, Mamie. It just isn't the flock you expected Me to give you.* That, Mamie thought as she descended to the second floor, was the understatement of a lifetime.

Years ago she'd ended several restless nights of internal struggle and walked the straw-strewn aisle of the revival tent one Reverend Joseph Weaver had pitched near Salt Creek. She'd stood in front of a hundred of God's saints and told them she was finished wrestling with God. "I am a sinner, but I am putting myself in God's hands and trusting Him to forgive me. I am asking Him to be my Lord." Mamie had hiccuped—something she always did when feeling emotional— and then looked at the Reverend Weaver as she concluded, "The fields are white unto harvest, and I will go wherever He sends me."

The next day, Mamie followed Reverend Weaver and five other born-again sheep into the saline waters of the meandering creek. Emerging from the baptismal waters, she shivered with joy and not a little fear about to which fields God might send her. Part of her hoped Reverend Weaver would see fit to propose so that she could labor in the fields to which the Lord sent *him.* But if he did not, there were fields all over the world where a saint could work out her salvation with fear and trembling, as the Good Book said to do.

Two young women from Lincoln had gone north to work among the Dakota Sioux in recent years, while a third sailed for the Sandwich Islands—wherever they were. But nothing quite so glamorous as laying down one's life in exotic places seemed to be in God's plan for Mamie Dawson. Nor, for that matter, did marriage. At least not yet. Mamie still hoped the Lord was working on that one.

Motion on the other side of turnkey pulled her out of her memories and back to the day at hand. . .and a suppressed sigh of regret. Why did it always have to be Martin Underhill waiting to escort her upstairs? She'd protested this practice from the day the new warden had enacted it. She didn't need a male guard looking over her shoulder every time she unlocked the ward in the morning. She had things well in hand.

"I know you do, Miss Dawson," Warden McKenna had said with a smile. "Please don't take this as anything more than what it is—a desire to keep you and the ladies in your care as safe as possible." *Ladies*. He'd called the women inmates *ladies*.

As the guard at turnkey admitted Mamie to the secure side, Mr. Underhill began to babble about his horse. Again. "Lovely spring morning," he said, as they headed upstairs. "I could hardly keep Bessie in hand on my trip out from town. She pranced about like a half-broke filly."

By the time they reached the top of the stairs, Mr. Underhill had stopped talking about his horse and progressed to his other favorite subject. The weather. As they bypassed the empty set of rooms constructed for Negro women, a childish thrill rippled up Mamie's spine as she saw who'd been on post outside the female department overnight. "It's good to see you, Mr. Selleck," she called out. "It's been so long since you had the post up here, I'd begun to wonder if something was wrong."

"Just taking a little holiday to Omaha," Selleck said with a smile that almost made Mamie start to hiccup.

She knew it was ridiculous, but she couldn't help it. The man made her feel like a schoolgirl with a crush. He probably knew it, but he seemed to enjoy bantering with her—even though she didn't think she was very good at it. He always had a new joke to tell, and he noticed things about her that no one else did; if she changed the part in her hair, or if she added a bit of lace to her ensemble.

Mr. Underhill didn't give her a chance to say a word. "Tom's courting in Omaha," he sputtered. "And a right fine lady she is, too. President of the Women's Missionary Society and sings in the choir at the Baptist church."

Selleck chuckled even as his pale eyes sought hers. "Well, Martin, I don't know as I'd call it *courting*." He changed the subject, nodding toward the dormitory. "No trouble in the henhouse last night."

Mamie thanked him and wished him well with his friend in Omaha. She hoped she sounded sincere, but she couldn't help the twinge of regret accompanying the man's departure. *Such a handsome man.* So much so that she felt downright intimidated in his presence sometimes—in a thrilling way.

The bell rang, signaling the arrival of breakfast. Mamie started, then reached for the key to the dumbwaiter. Mr. Underhill retrieved the rolling cart they served from, even as he groused about Adam Selleck's lack of respect for the women. There was no love lost between Martin Underhill and Adam Selleck, but Mamie wasn't inclined to step into that situation, and so she asked Mr. Underhill to retrieve breakfast while she roused the women.

Martin shook his head. "You're supposed to have a guard with you."

"And I do," Mamie snapped. "You'll only be three steps behind me. Mr. Selleck said things were fine. Please, Mr. Underhill. Just unload the dumbwaiter for me. I'll leave the outer door open. You can close it when you come in with breakfast." She bustled off without waiting for his answer. Unlocking the first door, she made her way through the combination parlor/workroom, past the bathroom, and toward the second locked door in the apartment that led into the dormitory where the women slept. Calling out a greeting to the ladies, she unlocked the second door and stepped inside.

And that was when she noticed the body on the floor.

CHAPTER 4

Mamie let out a shout that roused the women from their cots, even as she crouched beside Vestal Jackson's still form. Mr. Underhill appeared, seemingly out of nowhere. Having abandoned the breakfast cart, he placed himself between her and the rest of the women. Mamie sent a fleeting prayer of thanks heavenward, even as she told him there was no need for the truncheon he'd pulled from his belt. The second she felt Vestal's blood pulsing through the veins at her wrist, she stood back up. She was about to send Mr. Underhill to rouse the prison doctor when Vestal groaned. Scanning the room, Mamie waved Jane Prescott over.

As Prescott knelt down, Vestal clutched her hand, begging and gasping, "My baby. Don't let them take my baby, Jane."

Prescott said nothing, only settled beside her and murmured meaningless comfort while gently stroking Vestal's hair back out of her face.

No one's taking your baby. Mamie longed to say those very words. Instead, she told Vestal to hush, that Mr. Underhill would go for the doctor. New terror washed over Vestal's thin face.

"What about Dr. Mason from town?" Mr. Underhill murmured.

Mamie glanced his way. *What an odd thing to say.* Odd, only because it came from him. It was no surprise Vestal didn't want the resident

30

physician. No one would. The man was notoriously fond of strong drink, and Mamie had intended to bring the matter up with the new warden soon. But for Mr. Underhill to be so. . .perceptive. . .was—

"Bessie would love the run," he said. "We could have him here within the hour." He took a step toward the door.

The terror on Vestal's face eased. "Dr. . . .Mason?" Her hopeful tone dissolved into a groan as a reddish stain seeped into her prison gown.

Lord, no. Vestal may not be a good girl, but You'll recall defending one about to be stoned to death. . .and this child she's carrying deserves a chance. Don't You think so? Show me what to do, Lord. Help!

"Let me in there." Agnes Sweeney lumbered to Vestal's side. With a grunt, she knelt down beside Jane Prescott and, with absolutely no apology and no ceremony, leaned down and positioned one ear on Vestal's rounded belly, frowning slightly as she listened.

"Have you had experience as a midwife, Mrs. Sweeney?" Mamie asked.

Agnes only shrugged as she lifted the edge of Vestal's nightgown, looking for the source of the blood. Grunting again, she reached for Jane Prescott's free hand. "She's been stabbed in the leg." She positioned Jane's hand over the growing red stain and ordered her to press down, then glanced up at Mamie. "Needs stitching, but it'll keep." She nodded toward Mr. Underhill. "If he hurries."

Mamie glanced at Mr. Underhill. Was that compassion on the poor man's misshapen face? It was hard to tell. More than once, Mamie had seen a child duck behind a mother's skirts at the sight of Martin Underhill's too-large nose and too-wide forehead, his weak chin and the bulging eyes that looked off in different directions. Minnie said he shuffled along the city streets, looking no higher than the belts of passersby. Yet, for all his physical anomalies, Mamie knew that Mr. Underhill had gifts. He was a fast runner, and he prided himself in owning a fine—and fast—horse.

"Say the word, and Bessie and I will be halfway to town before the prison doc even wakes up."

"Go, then," Mamie said and moved to unlock the door even as she spoke to the women. "I'll be right back." She and Mr. Underhill hurried past the abandoned breakfast cart and across the parlor. She let him out.

"It'll be all right, Mamie. You'll see."

It had better be. Even though Dr. Mason had kindly offered to attend Vestal's confinement, no one expected an emergency, and Mamie hadn't had time to get Warden McKenna's approval. If the warden's seeming kindness didn't extend into his view of the female department budget, she might be risking her job to call a doctor from town. Ah, well, she'd worry over that another time.

Her heart pounding, Mamie headed back into the dormitory. What she saw there brought her up short. She wished the people who wrote newspaper articles assigning labels like "villainess" and "deranged" to incarcerated women could see this. The "depraved shadows" in Mamie's care had lifted Vestal onto a cot. Jane Prescott stood at her side while Agnes Sweeney dipped a cloth into a basin of water on the small table at the head of the cot, wrung it out, and laid it across Vestal's forehead. Susan Horst tucked a pillow beneath Vestal's knees, and when Vestal grimaced and announced another birth pang, the three women murmured encouragement.

Mamie gazed around the dormitory, feeling a renewed sense of care for her wandering lambs. But then—she frowned. Told herself she'd miscounted. Counted again. And tried to suppress a shiver.

Pearl Brand was missing.

—⁓—

The alarm bell.

Ellen McKenna jumped to her feet, leaving her trowel stuck in the freshly turned earth of her backyard garden. Mama's okra seeds would have to wait. With the back of one gloved hand, she lifted the wide brim of her sunbonnet away from her face and peered toward the limestone building across the road. Her gaze ran along the top of the cellblock toward the guard tower. Expecting someone to be aiming a rifle down into the yard to stop something horrible, she was surprised to see that, whoever the guard was, he wasn't aiming anything. In fact, he was waving at someone down below.

Frowning, Ellen hurried down the freshly turned furrow toward the house. Thank God Jack was already on his way to school in town. Whatever was going on inside those walls, he was safe. Her heart pounding, she scurried up the back stairs and inside, pulling her garden gloves off as she went. Dropping them to the floor, she untied her bonnet and hung it on the hook just inside the back door before heading toward the parlor where Georgia was descending the front stairs.

"The bell," Ellen said, her voice trembling. "Do you think someone's escaped?"

Georgia went into the parlor and drew the drapes open, peering out the window. She shook her head. "No'm. They'd be out on the walkway with their guns. And Mr. McKenna would have sent guards our way." She didn't seem any more worried by that alarm bell than she would be if something boiled over on the kitchen stove.

Ellen joined her. What could be the problem? She glanced at Georgia's regal profile. "I'm glad you're here. It makes me feel safer."

Georgia kept her eyes on the building across the road even as she smiled her thanks. In a moment, she glanced Ellen's way. "Would you like me to go over there and see what's caused the alarm?"

Ellen thought back to Ian's explaining his feelings about this new job. "People are made in the image of God, and I refuse to believe that any human being deserves to be thrown away. But don't mistake all of that for softness. I'm sworn to protect, and I'll do whatever it takes to fulfill that part of the job."

Thinking back on Ian's promise, Ellen relaxed a little. Whatever had precipitated the alarm, it couldn't be anything horrible or there would be a lot more going on up there along the wall and in the guard towers. Ian would have sent someone over to the house. Still. . .

Georgia read either Ellen's mind or her expression, for she started for the door. "Can't hurt to check in at Mr. McKenna's office."

As the two women descended the front porch stairs into the morning sunshine, a lone rider appeared on the horizon, coming from the direction of town. He'd just dismounted and tied up at the hitching post when Ellen and Georgia reached the stairs.

"Was that a breakfast bell or an alarm I heard a few minutes ago?" the stranger asked.

"Alarm bell," Ellen said and led the way inside. One of Ian's clerks—the one Ellen liked least—stood up when she and Georgia opened the office door.

"The warden's not here," he said, glancing up toward the ceiling. "Some kind of ruckus up on the third floor. Underhill's offered to go to town after Doc Mason. Guess the one we've already got isn't good enough for 'Miss Dawson's lambs'." Sarcasm tainted the man's voice as he said the last phrase.

At the sound of Ian's voice behind her, Ellen whirled about, relief flooding through her at the sight of him standing in the doorway across the hall, asking one of the clerks to pull an inmate's file. The stranger who'd just come in with Ellen introduced himself.

"Max Zimmer." He shook Ian's hand. "Dr. Zimmer, actually. We had an appointment, which you're obviously too busy to keep. Someone mentioned a doctor. Can I help?"

"There's been a stabbing in the female department," Ian said. "The wound isn't serious, but the victim was expecting a child and she appears to have gone into premature labor. If you're willing to help—"

The doctor nodded. "Happy to."

"As to supplies—"

"No need to worry over that. My mentor said a doctor should never be more than five minutes from his medical bag. I've always tried to follow his advice." He tipped his hat to Ellen and Georgia, and with a promise to be right back, exited the building.

Ian smiled down at Ellen. "I won't pretend not to be amazed that you came over, but I'm pleased you did. I'm sure Miss Dawson will appreciate your help. I'll trust you to direct the doctor through turnkey, and I'll have someone waiting to escort the three of you upstairs." He called out to turnkey. "Tell Underhill we've a doctor. No need to be Paul Revere today." He bent down and kissed Ellen's cheek, then headed into the clerk's office. All Ellen wanted to do was go back across the road where it was safe. But here came the doctor bounding in the door, black bag in hand.

"Has either of you ever attended a confinement?"

"G–Georgia has a great deal of nursing experience," Ellen stammered.

"I'm no midwife," Georgia said, "but I've helped a dozen or so babies into this world."

"Excellent," the doctor said and headed up the hall.

Ellen took a deep breath. Ian had told her that the warden's wife over in Iowa served as the matron to the female department. The doctor clearly assumed she could be counted on. This was no time to disappoint. With a little shrug, she motioned for Georgia to follow her and headed after the doctor.

———

As Vestal groaned her way through another contraction and Agnes kept pressure on the wound, Jane tried to murmur encouragement even while she wondered where in tarnation the doctor was and why Pearl Brand had chosen Vestal as a victim. When the contraction passed and Vestal lay back, Jane muttered the question.

Agnes Sweeney looked at her like she thought she must be nearly as dumb as dirt.

"Why do you think? Because she's the least likely to be able to defend herself, that's why."

"I heard. . .something," Jane said. "I should have—"

She broke off. Shook her head as a sense of shame descended. *What's happened to me?* She'd been downright pugnacious as a girl, ready to defend the underdog, even if it meant getting into scraps. Had Owen beaten that out of her for good? She'd never forgive herself for hiding beneath a blanket while Pearl Brand hurt someone.

Agnes snorted. "Who *didn't* know something was going on? You think we're deaf?"

"Then why—?" Jane glanced around at the others. "Why didn't you do something?"

"Didn't know it was Vestal," Susan Horst offered. She shrugged. "Just thought it was more of the same."

"More. . .what?" Jane frowned.

Agnes rolled her eyes. Shook her head. She looked down at Vestal. Something passed between the two women. Agnes looked up at Jane and said, "Vestal don't want to say, and that's her business."

Jane couldn't imagine strong-willed, stubborn, downright sassy Vestal Jackson having nothing to say. Whereas Jane had made it her goal not to cause anyone trouble and never to draw attention to herself, Vestal caused Miss Dawson no end of frustration. But even Miss Dawson couldn't resist the charm lying just beneath the surface of Vestal's sass. The two bantered back and forth in a way that reminded Jane of sisters who annoyed one another on the surface but, when it came right down to it, grudgingly admitted mutual respect.

Jane looked away from Vestal and the group of women, wishing she could escape this moment with a woman about to give birth to a child she could not keep. She'd tried to keep her distance in recent months, even as Vestal babbled on and on about how active "he" was (she was certain the baby was a boy). . .how he kept her awake at night turning somersaults inside. . .how he didn't mind the breakfast gruel but objected strongly to the tough meat. Something about Vestal's condition had drawn the other women together in recent weeks, as if they were a flock of birds guarding a single nest. But not Jane. Jane kept her distance.

Reaching out to say, "I understand," would have brought Aunt Flora's betrayal too close to the surface. *I'll read Rose every letter,* she'd promised. *I'll send you a new cabinet portrait every year on her birthday. I'll bring her to visit. We can come for Sunday services. I'll explain it so she won't be harmed. Goodness, doesn't the warden's own family come to services? Rose wouldn't even be the only child there.*

Jane had wondered over Aunt Flora's lies for weeks. How could someone do that? Smile and make promises she never intended to keep? Jane hadn't received a single letter, let alone a cabinet portrait of Rose. What had Flora told Rose to explain her mother's disappearance? Did Rose think she was dead? Jane could recite that final postcard. *Rose has mourned her loss and is happy with me as her new mother. It is not wise to stir up memories of the tragic past.* Not even a letter. Two sentences scribbled on a postcard.

Jane had found a way to survive the betrayal, but she wasn't willing to open that wound. . .not even to help Vestal Jackson. Not even when she learned that Miss Dawson's sister—whose name was Manerva, although Miss Dawson called her Minnie—had "made arrangements" to have Vestal's baby taken in at the Home for the Friendless. Not even when Vestal's saucy attitude transformed to a sadness that cast a pall over every woman in the dormitory—with the exception of Pearl Brand, who didn't seem to have one drop of compassion, one drop of motherly instinct, one drop of. . .*womanliness* about her.

And now Vestal had been stabbed. . .and her baby. . .Jane closed her eyes and willed the threatening tears away.

Vestal, her dark eyes wide with terror, sucked in a breath and began to groan. "When's the doctor coming?"

Someone shouted from out in the hall, and Miss Dawson hurried to unlock the outer door. Jane heard. . .a woman's voice? She looked up. What was the warden's wife doing here? And that man. . .and those gray-green eyes. Suddenly, it was as if everything in the dormitory had receded into the distance and a glass dome lowered over Jane's head, closing out everything but the sound of her own heartbeat and the sensation of the blood pulsing in her temples, as a blush crept up the back of her neck and spread across her cheeks.

Max Zimmer.

CHAPTER 5

In a panic when Max caught her eye and smiled, Jane looked toward the far corner of the dormitory where everyone except Agnes, Susan, and she had gathered. It was as if someone had drawn an imaginary line between the scene by the door and the women over there. Jane wished she could join them, but Vestal would not let go.

The warden arrived. Jane heard enough snatches of his conversation with Max that she knew the plan had been to take Vestal across the hall to the unoccupied Negro dormitory to deliver her baby. But that was before they realized Pearl Brand was missing. Vestal's confinement was little more than an unwelcome distraction in light of a possible escape, and the warden had taken steps to remove it. "I'm having a wagon hitched and brought to the front door. She'll be transported to town." He glanced at Max. "I'd be grateful if you'd agree to ride along."

Before Max had a chance to respond, the warden's wife spoke up. "Bring her to the house."

Jane and Agnes exchanged amazed glances. Everyone had felt a bit wistful over the loss of the former warden's wife—mostly because of pie. Once a month, she'd hosted a Ladies Aid meeting in her home. Each member brought one or two pies with them, and after their meeting, those pies were delivered to the guard's dormitory and to the "friendless women" on the third floor. While Jane hated being thought of as friendless—even if it was true—that home-baked pie was a welcome treat. Apparently, Mrs. McKenna neither belonged to the same women's group nor baked pies. In fact, so far she'd acted as if the female department didn't exist. And now she was offering her house as a birthing clinic?

The warden seemed just as surprised as everyone else. In fact, he looked about ready to say no, but then Mrs. McKenna put one dainty hand on his forearm and said, with what Jane thought sounded like steel-edged sweetness, "You cannot expect a woman about to give birth to endure a wagon ride into Lincoln." And with that, she waved for her maid to follow her as she said to Miss Dawson, "Have her brought to the house. Georgia and I will make preparations."

Miss Dawson quickly agreed, and the warden went to the door and gave orders for a cot and two guards to bear it—and Vestal—across the road. From the look on Vestal's pale face, it was obvious she didn't know whether to be relieved or even more frightened. But then Max began to talk to her in that soothing voice of his, and she lay back while he examined the wound on her leg and reassured her it wasn't much and he'd take good care of her.

After a brief exchange with Miss Dawson, the warden motioned for Jane to follow him into the parlor. Jane had braced herself to be questioned about her knowing Max Zimmer, but the warden didn't mention Max. "Miss Dawson tells me she would have appointed you trustee last month, but that you declined."

Jane glanced back toward the dormitory. "I didn't mean any disrespect. Miss Dawson's nice enough. I just don't want. . ." She paused. "I just want to mind my own business, sir."

"I'd appreciate it if you'd look me in the eye, Mrs. Marquis."

"Prescott," Jane said quickly. She met his gaze, hoping she wouldn't be punished for talking back. Was that kindness in his eyes?

"I–I'm not using that other name. If you don't mind."

He nodded. Seemed to be thinking through something. When was he going to ask her about Max? But again, he had something else on his mind. "Normally, I'd assign a guard and the matron to accompany Miss Jackson and the doctor over to my house and be done with it. But I need Miss Dawson here right now to help me with this Pearl Brand business." He paused. "So I'm asking: Will you do the job of a trustee even though you refused the title? Would you go with Miss Jackson and stay with her for the duration?"

Jane wanted to say no with everything in her being, and the desire had nothing to do with Vestal or the birthing—and everything to do with Max Zimmer. What was he doing here? He didn't seem to have let on that he knew her. Should she tell the warden? Vestal hollered again. The poor thing shouldn't have to go through this alone—she just shouldn't. Knowing that she would likely regret the decision, Jane nodded. "Yes, sir. I'm willing."

"Do I have your word that you won't try to escape?"

It was odd having a warden ask a woman serving time for manslaughter for her word. As if he could trust it. Why would he do that? She shrugged. "There wouldn't be any point." Would he still believe her when he found out about Max? The first visit had happened on the other warden's watch, and Max hadn't contacted her since. So unless one of them told him—and she wouldn't—the warden would have no reason to know. For her part, she was going to pretend she'd never seen Max Zimmer.

Apparently satisfied, the warden nodded. "All right, then."

Together, they went back into the dormitory where Miss Dawson reached out and squeezed her arm. "Thank you for your kindness to Vestal."

Jane shook her head. "I'm not—kind. I'm just not willfully cruel. Vestal's frightened. She shouldn't be alone. Even an animal deserves company when it's suffering."

Was she out of her mind? What had she done? And why had Ian allowed it? Not half a minute after Ellen so confidently offered her home as a medical clinic, she began to have doubts. As she and Georgia headed out of the facility, Miss Dawson caught up with them.

—ɯ—

Glancing behind her toward the ward, the matron said, "It probably doesn't seem like I know what I'm doing, what with one of the women missing and all." She lowered her voice. "I expect I'll lose my position over it, and I won't blame your husband one bit." She took a deep breath. "I just want you to know that I'll be forever grateful for your help with Vestal. She's—" She paused. Shook her head. "She's brokenhearted over the idea of having to give that baby away. Your kindness means a great deal."

Ellen didn't quite know what to say. "Don't give me too much credit. It seemed the thing to do to help my husband."

Miss Dawson nodded. "The warden's sending another woman along, and I wanted you to know that you don't have to be concerned that she'll doing anything. . .untoward. She's been exemplary in every way since she's been here. In fact, if I didn't know better—" She broke off. "I just wanted you to know there's nothing to fear from either Vestal or Jane."

Ellen glanced past her toward the space beyond turnkey. "And the one who's missing? Pearl Brand, is it?"

Miss Dawson hesitated. Pursed her lips. Cleared her throat. "She'd be a different story. But you've nothing to fear from her, either." She gestured about her. "She's here somewhere. Couldn't have gone far. We'll find her."

"Godspeed," Ellen said, "and thank you for your. . .reassurance." She made her way toward home, not certain whether hearing Miss

Dawson's appraisal of the two women who would soon be inside her house was comforting or not. Ian had nice things to say about both Miss Dawsons. Ellen had only seen Manerva at chapel services on Sunday. She had a dressmaking establishment in town and relieved her sister on weekends, but both women seemed nice enough. As to competence—well. How *did* one account for losing track of an inmate?

In spite of Miss Dawson's reassurance, Ellen's doubts grew with every step toward home. Ah, well. Two guards and the doctor would surely be able to handle any trouble. She rubbed her arms to rid them of the goose bumps prickling her skin.

Georgia spoke up. "It was the right thing to do. There's two guards coming along. What could happen?"

—⁓—

Jane had done her share of pressing her cheek against the tall, narrow dormitory windows to watch the warden's house go up across the road. After all, other than the magazines people brought to "encourage the women," the warden's house was the only piece of "normal life" any of them had had a chance to encounter since entering the prison. Oh, a committee of women came out on Sundays, but something about them made Jane uncomfortable. For one thing, a couple of them seemed more interested in eyeing the more attractive guards, like Adam Selleck, than in worshipping or encouraging the inmates.

Thanks to Owen, Jane knew not to take smiles at face value. Thanks to Aunt Flora's betrayal, she was wary of any supposed kindness, and she wondered what price she would pay for Miss Dawson's apparent good opinion of her and the warden's apparent good opinion of Miss Dawson's opinion. The possibilities—in light of Max's role in today's events—made her tremble.

Momentarily blinded by the sun, Jane stumbled on the top

stair just outside the front door. If Max hadn't grabbed her arm, she would have fallen headlong down the entire flight of stairs. When she flinched, he let go.

"Are you all right, Ja—?" He broke off, swallowing the last part of her name.

Jane glanced at the guard to see if he'd heard Max almost call her by name. His face revealed nothing, but then he was like that. Jane stayed as far away from both him and Adam Selleck as possible. She couldn't quite say why, but none of the women on the ward seemed to like either man, and she was no exception.

"It's bright out here," she said. "We don't get outside. I'm fine." Which was a lie. She wasn't fine at all, but Max wasn't the reason at the moment. Her eyes swept the horizon. There was too much sky. Too much. . .everything. The enormity of the landscape frightened her.

Again, the question surfaced. *What's happened to me?* Her heartbeat ratcheted up with every step away from the penitentiary. She, who had always loved to stand outside as the sun set, taking joy in the unbroken view all the way to the horizon—she couldn't bear the thought of all this. . .space. She felt almost dizzy. To steady herself, she reached for Vestal's hand and forced a smile. "Feeling better?"

Vestal swiped at her lips and croaked assent. "Pains have eased some."

Max spoke up. "I'll see that you get a drink of water as soon as we get inside." Jane sensed rather than saw him look her way. "A drink of water for both of you. It'll help calm your nerves."

Jane glanced up at him, then quickly looked away. She wished she hadn't come. Returning to what everyone called "the castle" couldn't happen too soon as far as she was concerned. She'd told Max she wouldn't see him if he came to visit, and she hadn't changed her mind. Why was he here? What made him think she would change her mind? If Vestal ended up being transported to Lincoln, she was just going to have to handle that part of it on her own. Jane would find a way to hold herself together for a few hours, but it was going to take everything she had.

She wondered at the near-panic she was feeling over being outside. What would she do when she was finally released? If she felt this way now, what would it be like after a few more years? Drawing inside herself had seemed like the only way to survive. But now, with her heart racing and perspiration crawling down the back of her neck, she wondered. Had the cocoon been a bad idea?

—⁓—

Once they got to the house, the guards kept Vestal out on the porch while Mrs. McKenna and her housekeeper "arranged things" inside. Jane wanted to stay with Vestal, but Max waved her inside to help. She entered feeling like an intruder, even more ill at ease when she caught her first glimpse of the fine things furnishing the warden's new house. The aromas of linseed oil and new paint filled the air—or was she overly sensitive to aromas she connected with high-toned living?

While they all moved dining-room chairs away from the table— the doctor was going to use that for his exam table—the housekeeper said something about a mattress in the attic. She nodded Jane's way. "The two of us could bring it down while the doctor washes up."

Jane trailed up the stairs after the housekeeper, unprepared for her exposure to a world that sent her whirling back in time just as surely as if the past few years had been a dream. When she stopped dead in her tracks at the top of the stairs, the housekeeper glanced back.

"Is everything all right?"

45

Jane started. "Y–yes. I just"—she nodded toward what was obviously Warden and Mrs. McKenna's room—"that quilt. . ." She forced herself to look away, but just inside the next room was yet another wonder.

The housekeeper smiled. "Mrs. McKenna brought most of that fabric home with her from the Centennial."

Jane nodded. She knew. She had to bite her lower lip to keep from crying over the memory it evoked. She and Rose had lived above a dry goods store for the two years after Thomas died—before Owen. The owner and his wife had attended the opening of the Centennial Exposition in Philadelphia, and when they came back, Mrs. Carr had purchased a bolt of commemorative fabric. *A centennial print*, she'd called it. Rose had called it *the George Washy*. Jane had made her a doll quilt with it, barely finishing it before. . .leaving. . .for Lincoln. Blinking back threatening tears, she lifted the hem of her plain gray skirt and followed the housekeeper up the steep, narrow stairs and into the attic, where they retrieved a somewhat limp mattress covered with a red-and-brown ticking.

"Needs fresh straw," the other woman murmured as she and Jane carried it back downstairs. "But it's better than nothing."

As they traversed the second-floor hall, Jane stole another glance at the exquisite appliqué quilt adorning the McKennas' bed. Red-and-green pomegranates danced across an ivory surface framed by the most exquisite swag border Jane had ever seen. *Love Apples.* Thomas had teased her about the name when he first saw their wedding quilt. And that first night, when he drew it aside and pulled her toward him. . .

Jane cleared her throat. It didn't matter that the warden trusted her. It didn't matter that Vestal wanted her. This had been a mistake. *Please just let Vestal's baby come. Let this be over. I can't bear it. I can't do this.*

Mrs. McKenna spread a clean sheet atop the straw tick the minute Jane and the housekeeper had it positioned atop the table. The older woman had said it needed straw, but when Vestal settled atop it, she sighed with pleasure. Jane smiled, too. No one else in that room realized how luxurious that straw tick would feel compared to what they were used to over in the ward. There they slept on bags of corn husks freshened every six months.

While everyone else bustled about, Jane stood in the corner of the room, her hands clenched behind her, afraid she'd mar the elegant wall covering if she moved closer to the wall, even though she longed to lean against it for support as she tried to get control over her memories and hold back the tears threatening to slide down her cheeks.

When Mrs. McKenna's housekeeper touched her on the shoulder, Jane jumped.

"I'm sorry, ma'am," the woman said. "I didn't mean to startle you. I thought maybe you'd help me haul water in?" She nodded toward the back of the house. "I asked the guard, but he reminded me he's no slave."

Oh, how she longed to get away from this room, from Max's presence. Yet Jane hesitated, nodding toward the front porch where the other guard lurked. "They won't want me outside," she said, then added quickly, "not that I'd mind—I mean, I'll do whatever you want me to, I just—they might think I'll run."

The woman arched one dark eyebrow. "Will you?"

"Of course not."

"That's exactly what I'll tell the guards if they protest." She offered her hand. "Name's Georgia. And you're Mrs. . . . ?"

"Jane. Just Jane."

"All right then." Georgia lifted her chin and called out to the doctor. "Jane and I'll be going out back. We'll bring you a drink directly, Dr. Zimmer. I'll get some water to boiling, too."

Vestal had been resting quietly, but just then she gasped. With a grimace, she endured a contraction. "Just a little one," she said, then looked up at Max. "I—I tend to take a good while," she said. "Never had pains come on this early before, though."

Max looked up from the table where he'd been arranging a frightening array of instruments. "How many times. . . ?"

"Three." Vestal practically spat the word out. Then the contraction ended, and she lay back. The unspoken and obvious question hung in the air. Vestal turned her head to one side and closed her eyes. "One lived to be two. The others. . ." She shook her head.

Max moved to her side and put a hand on her shoulder. "I am so sorry."

When he smiled, Jane's heart lurched. She'd forgotten about that dimple.

CHAPTER 6

The room felt claustrophobic, and it had nothing to do with its arrangement. As Max tried to reassure Mrs. Jackson, he glanced toward the doorway leading into the kitchen where Jane stood, her hands clasped in front of her. What had happened to her? Where had the lovely woman with the rich laugh and the quiet strength gone? What had happened to the fire he'd seen when she stood up that day and ordered him out of the visiting room? She reminded him of a nervous colt, wary lest anyone get too close.

Mrs. McKenna brought him back to the task at hand. "What would you like us to do next, Dr. Zimmer?"

The leg wound. Best to treat it first. He asked Vestal's permission to lift the hem of her gown so he could examine the cut on her leg. As the gown cleared Vestal's knee, the light coming in the parlor window faltered. He looked up just in time to see a flash of blue. Frowning, he smoothed Vestal's gown back into place, then excused himself and headed onto the front porch. The guard was leaning against an upright in a very good imitation of a man at ease.

"I don't believe I got your name," Max said.

The guard turned around then. "Something you need, Doc?" He nodded toward the house. "You want me to come in and make sure the hens stay in the henhouse?"

Max flexed his hands to keep from making a fist. "What I want," he said in a low voice, "is for you to stay as far away as possible and not be disciplined by the warden for dereliction of duty." He paused. Swallowed. Cleared his throat. "Miss Jackson may be your *prisoner*, but as long as she is here in this house she is my *patient*, and I will not have her privacy violated." He pointed to the parlor windows. "I need the light, or I'd close the drapes. But I'd better not see you staring in on us again. Is that clear?"

The guard smirked and gave a halfhearted salute. "Crystal clear, Doc." He ambled over to the far end of the porch and slouched against the railing. "How's this?"

—~~~—

Whatever the guard said in response to Max's dressing-down, it wasn't satisfactory. Jane could see that when Max stepped back inside, his clean-shaven cheeks still red with emotion. He swiped his palm across the sharp angle of one jaw, then marched toward the back of the house to speak to the other guard.

While he was gone out back, Vestal reached for Jane's hand. "Here comes another one," she grimaced. "A good one."

When Max returned, Mrs. McKenna suggested that Georgia stay and help the doctor while she and Jane got the water. She glanced Jane's way. "If that's all right with you?"

No one talked to inmates that way. Jane didn't even answer, just nodded and prepared to follow her through the doorway. It was impossible not to admire the polished wood floors in the hall, the turned spindles on the stair railing, the gleaming kitchen. Jane almost complimented the house, then thought better of it. Making small talk probably wasn't wise. Anything she said might be taken as her paying entirely too much attention to things that were no concern of hers.

Mrs. McKenna had the luxury of a well right outside the kitchen door. Actually, Georgia probably benefitted more from that pump than anyone. Mrs. McKenna didn't seem like the kind of woman who hauled water very often. In fact, she'd fit right in among the fashion-plate models for *Demorest's* magazine or *Harper's Bazaar*.

Jane glanced over to where the second guard lounged in the shade of the combination carriage house and barn. Did Mrs. McKenna realize just how closely he was watching her from beneath the brim of his stained hat?

Apparently oblivious, Mrs. McKenna set her pail down and reached for the pump handle. "I'll pump," she said and began to do just that. Now that it was just the two of them, the warden's wife seemed to feel an obligation to fill the silence. "Thank goodness the men didn't have to go down too far before they struck water," she said. "The apartment in the central building was lovely, but I'd just gotten the earth turned over for a flower garden back home in Brownville when Mr. McKenna decided—" She broke off. Her cheeks reddened. "I'm sorry." She reached for another pail. "I didn't mean—" She gave a nervous little laugh. "I didn't mean to be so insensitive to your. . .situation."

The poor woman was embarrassed. Jane nodded toward the dark square of earth just past the barn. "You've a big garden planned."

Visibly relieved at being handed a topic of conversation, Mrs. McKenna nodded. "My husband thinks it's ridiculous, what with the trustees raising so much food just across the way, but. . ." Her voice sounded wistful. "I don't suppose they'll be growing okra, now, will they?" She shrugged. "That's what I was doing when the alarm sounded. Planting okra." She sighed. "I haven't any idea whether there's any hope it'll grow."

"It'll do fine," Jane said. "One of my neighbors grew a mess of it every year. She used to bring gumbo to our quiltings. It makes my mouth water just to think of it." The silence that met the statement sent a chill through Jane almost as harsh as if she'd stepped beneath the cold stream of water gushing out of the pump head. Who did she think she was, anyway, discussing gardening as if she were still a lady?

The pails filled, Jane bent to heft the two largest ones, but Mrs. McKenna intervened. "I know I look like I'll break, but I won't." With a soft grunt, she bent and hefted a pail of water, then returned to the topic of gardens. "Do you think I should put a fence up? Georgia wants chickens, but we hear coyotes every night."

Jane didn't think the guard, who'd found an excuse to leave the shade by the barn and follow them to the house, needed to hear her making small talk with the warden's wife. When he offered to take Mrs. McKenna's pail of water, Jane glanced his way. Again, a warning sounded. Yet another guard who bore watching.

"No thank you," Mrs. McKenna said. "We'll be fine. You feel free to go back and lounge in the shade."

Was it her imagination, or was the comment laced with a touch of sarcasm? Jane ducked her head and bit her lip to hold back a smile. Back inside, Mrs. McKenna filled a pitcher and glasses of water while Jane poured the rest into the huge iron pot atop the oven. "You're right about the coyotes," she said as she worked. "It takes a sturdy fence to keep them out. Or a big dog. If you put the chicken yard next to that garden, it'll make it easy for whoever does it to put up a fence around the whole thing. Your maid will have fat, sassy hens if she lets them feed on Nebraska hoppers. That'll save your garden."

Mrs. McKenna gazed through the kitchen window toward the garden space. Jane went on. "The same trustees who built the barn could probably build you a chicken coop. They'd most likely be glad to fence in a yard, too." She paused. "The time goes slow, sometimes.

It helps to have work." She slid the pot of water back off the burner and stood back. "Ready to heat things up, ma'am." Seeing the question on Mrs. McKenna's face, she explained. "I don't imagine anyone cares to have me building a fire."

Mrs. McKenna's face turned red. "Oh. . .I—I suppose. . . ." She lifted the cover off the stovetop, got the fire going, and then slid the pot in place. Just then Vestal yelled Jane's name.

Georgia appeared in the doorway.

Mrs. McKenna frowned. "What is it? What's wrong?"

Georgia shook her head. "Baby's turned wrong. Coming out feet first." She glanced at Jane. "You squeamish?"

"I don't know."

"Guess we'll find out," Georgia said. "Follow me.

—⁓—

Sometimes it seemed like the good Lord just wasn't quite paying attention. Not that Mamie would have said anything quite so heretical out loud, but she couldn't help but think it, now could she? What else could explain the situation today?

The Lord Himself had said that when a child asked for bread, a father didn't give him a stone, so why had Mamie been given Pearl Brand to mind, just when Mamie herself had been in the middle of a season of especially faithful, fervent prayer, asking for all kinds of things that were definitely in the realm of bread when it came to the women on the third floor.

She wanted to serve these women. She wanted to show them God's love. She wanted. . .so much. And yet, here Mamie was in the middle of a crisis, at the mercy of a new warden, and looking like she hadn't done her duty.

If that weren't enough, she had to put up with Martin Underhill again, for it was Martin the warden appointed to "keep Miss Dawson apprised of the situation" while that handsome Mr. Selleck, who could just as easily have been given the task, was sent off to join the search for Pearl Brand.

Perhaps it was just as well, Mamie thought as she remembered the way Mr. Selleck's golden hair curled around the back of his uniform collar. The man could be a distraction. Still, the entire situation put her ill at ease and out of sorts. So much so that the fourth time in an hour Mr. Underhill showed up at the barred door to the dormitory and called for her, Mamie almost snapped at him in front of her charges. "What is it now, Mr. Underhill?"

Underhill waited for Mamie to come to the door before saying quietly, "Warden McKenna wants to question each of the women. Said to have you decide who's to go first." He paused. Swallowed. "Least likely to most likely."

Mamie frowned. "Least likely to most likely *what*, Mr. Underhill? I am not a mind reader."

The man blushed. "Least likely to most likely to be in cahoots with the one that's missing. He said I should escort you over." Another guard arrived on the third floor and headed their way. "J. B.'s here to mind the ward while we're gone."

With a sigh, Mamie turned around and called for petite, half-blind Ivy Cochran, then spoke to the other women. "The rest of you might as well begin your sewing stint while Ivy and I are with the warden."

"What about breakfast?" Agnes Sweeney called out. "Don't seem right us getting stuck with cold oatmeal and colder coffee on account of Pearl Brand's foolishness."

J. B. scowled as he retorted, "Don't seem right I should have to stay on duty on account of some fool woman, either, but here I am. So git to doin' what Miss Dawson said and quit harping. You'll get lunch soon enough." Taking up a stance by the door, the guard put his back against one of the walls and folded his arms across his generous stomach, then nodded at Mamie. "Go on now, ma'am. I'll handle the ladies."

Muttering her thanks, Mamie waved for Ivy to follow her. Thinking they would be going downstairs to an office, she was surprised when Mr. Underhill led the way across the wide hall to the empty ward.

Mr. Underhill glanced at Ivy and lowered his voice. "He wants the ones he's talked to kept separate from the others. Guess he figured this would make things easy on you, it being just across the hall and all. They can stay here with you while I shuttle the others over to be questioned. You'll just have to tell me who to bring next."

It did make sense, but Mamie hated the idea of half a day or more of this nonsense. It would put everyone in a sour mood, likely for the remainder of the week, and there was no telling how long it would take to reestablish a sense of routine. *If it's all the same to You, Lord, I'd just as soon You led someone straight to wherever in the world Pearl Brand is hiding. And then let them put her in the hole for a good long while.*

It was going to be hard not to resent Pearl after this. On the other hand, that might not be an issue. Did the warden's questioning each of the women himself mean he had lost confidence in Mamie? Did he believe she'd missed some hint of trouble brewing? Maybe she had. Maybe she'd been wrong to look at the job as a calling. Well, there would be plenty of time to think about all of that. *Don't borrow tomorrow's trouble;* wasn't that what the Good Book said?

Taking a deep breath, Mamie followed Mr. Underhill across the twenty or so feet of hallway separating the two wards that were, essentially, mirrors of each other. Just inside the door, Mr. Underhill jerked sideways and stumbled into Mamie. When he stomped her foot, she cried out, barely managing to keep from crushing Ivy as the two slammed into the wall just to the right of the door. She heard the air go out of the poor child and saw Ivy's face go white.

With a cry of protest, Mamie whirled about to face Mr. Underhill. Her cheeks blazing, she opened her mouth and said—nothing. For there was Pearl Brand, standing behind a chair in which an unconscious Warden McKenna sat, his legs splayed out in an unnatural pose, a bluish lump showing just at the hairline on one side of his forehead.

Pearl kept the warden in the chair with one thick arm about his neck, even as her free hand held the tapered end of an ominous-looking, homemade weapon against the tanned flesh just beneath the man's jawline.

"Don't move," she said, glaring at Mr. Underhill. "One sound. One word and—"

"I s—see that," Underhill stammered. "Y—you're the one in charge here. What do you want me to d—do?" As he spoke, he sidled toward where Mamie and Ivy cowered against the cold stone wall.

Pearl nodded at Mamie and Ivy. "Tie them up. And gag them." She sneered at Mamie. "Guess it'll be *silent* prayers today, Dawson."

Mamie could feel Ivy trembling. She reached for her hand and gave it a squeeze.

"And then?" Mr. Underhill said.

"And then we'll have ourselves a game of checkers," Pearl snapped. "What do you think, Frankenstein? That's what they call you behind your back, y'know. *Frankenstein.*" She spat on the floor, then tightened her grip on the warden's neck even as she gestured with the weapon. "Just do what you're told."

"I don't believe I can," Mr. Underhill said, and before Pearl reacted to the odd comment, he launched himself through the air.

CHAPTER 7

Martin's crossed forearms hit Pearl Brand just above the arm with which she held the homemade weapon to the warden's throat. The force of the blow knocked the weapon from her hand. She staggered back.

Mamie jumped toward the warden's slumped body, barely managing to break the man's fall as he slid out of the chair and onto the floor. She glanced behind her at Ivy and shouted, "Get the guard from the ward!"

Just as Ivy skittered along the wall and out the door, a loud crack sounded from the other side of the room as something made contact with—Martin! Pearl had managed to recover her weapon. Martin rolled away from her, but she still made contact. He got to his feet, the weapon protruding from a spot dangerously close to his heart.

A potent mixture of rage and fear launched Mamie at Pearl. Grabbing Martin's truncheon from the loop just above his hip, she landed a blow. A crack echoed in the room. Pearl cried out and fell back, clutching her arm, and finally. . .finally help arrived.

Mamie staggered back, truncheon in hand, as J. B. bent to check on the warden and others rushed into the room, some taking Pearl Brand in hand, others surrounding Martin Underhill.

"I'll take this now, ma'am."

Someone was talking to Mamie, but it sounded very far away. "Here, now. Sit down. That's it, ma'am. Head down for a moment. Breathe now. Just take some deep—"

Mamie shoved the hand away even as she spun about on the chair to look in Martin's direction as she heard him calling out. "Let me up, do you hear me? Where's Mamie? I don't care about that—it's nothing—is Mamie all right?"

Swallowing, Mamie croaked an answer. "I'm here, Mr. Underhill." Her voice sounded reed-thin. Weak. She took a deep breath. Grasped the chair back and forced herself to stand. Her knees quaked, but she held firm, and her voice had new strength when she called out to him again. "I'm right here, Mr. Underhill. I'm fine."

The guards who'd gathered around Martin's prone body pulled back so he could see her. He lifted his massive, misshapen head, and met her gaze. And then his eyes rolled back in his head, and he fainted dead away.

—⁓—

The sun climbed upward from the horizon and hung high in the sky, and still, even though it was Vestal's fourth confinement, still, she labored on. Max had long since transformed the gaping wound along the top of her thigh into a neat red line. He'd done the unthinkable, too, grasping the footling and trying to right the baby for a normal delivery, apologizing all the while to Vestal for the pain he was causing her.

The more Jane saw of him, the more she longed for the end of the day. She didn't want to be drawn to this man—or to anyone else, for that matter. Mrs. McKenna was a good woman. Georgia treated Jane as an equal. And she didn't want any of it. At least not now. Normal emotions would just make her miss normal life, and that was not wise in light of the years ahead. But as the day wore on and the three people in the house continued to show Vestal compassion, it got increasingly difficult for Jane to stay in her place—the safe place she'd created for herself. The place *apart*.

Mrs. McKenna seemed especially affected by Vestal's predicament. Early in the afternoon, she stationed herself at Vestal's head, whispering encouragement and patting her brow with a cool cloth, while Georgia came and went with the grace and efficiency of a practiced, able nurse.

For her part, Jane sat to one side of the table-turned-examining-table, alternately holding Vestal's hand and reading to her from a prayer book Mrs. McKenna had produced: "O God of peace, who hast taught us that in returning and rest we shall be saved, in quietness and confidence shall be our strength: By the might of Thy Spirit lift us, we pray Thee, to Thy presence, where we may be still and know that Thou art God; through Jesus Christ our Lord. Amen."

Of course Mrs. McKenna meant well, but as Jane read, she wondered if God had any interest in what was going on in this place at this moment. She wished she could go back to the barred room across the road. It was too hard being in the middle of another woman's agony over a child. She prepared to read another prayer.

Vestal grasped her hand. Wild-eyed, she said, "Stop reading it. . . . Oh dear God. . .please stop. I know you mean well, Jane. . .but I can't stand it. . . . God gave me over a long time ago for what I done. . . . I only want—" She writhed in pain. "I only want Him. . . ." She tilted her chin up toward the ceiling and cried out. "Please, God! Love my baby! Please don't punish him for me. . . . Jesus! God! Please!"

Jane closed the book of prayers and laid it aside with a sense of relief. She didn't dare look at Mrs. McKenna. Instead, she glanced at Max, hoping to see evidence that Vestal would soon give birth. Instead, she saw concern. When he met her gaze, she couldn't suppress her own quick intake of a terrified breath.

"What is it?!" Vestal moaned. "Tell me what—"

"It's time, Mrs. Jackson," Max said.

"Vestal," she gasped. "You call me Vestal."

"All right. You're doing a good job, Vestal. It'll be over soon." He picked up the forceps. Hesitated. Laid them down and said, "I need you to walk."

Vestal gasped, "I can't. . .possibly."

"We'll help you." He directed Georgia and Jane to help Vestal sit up. Once they'd done so, he locked his arms in place below Vestal's bosom, pulled her off the table, and stood her up. She groaned as Max, Jane, and Georgia propelled her down the hall toward the kitchen and back again. While they walked, Mrs. McKenna wheeled her claw-footed piano stool into the room—atop a sheet she'd spread over her carpet. When Vestal screamed a protest at walking more, they positioned her on the stool. Jane and Georgia held her upright. Vestal writhed and moaned as Max crouched down before her, speaking encouragement in a surprisingly calm voice.

Mrs. McKenna stood to one side, yet another clean sheet draped across her forearms, ready to receive the baby.

"I. . .can't. . . ." Vestal groaned.

The poor woman couldn't even hold her head up. But then her body tensed, and she yelled her way through another contraction. "I can't—can't—can't—"

Max raised his voice. "But you are, Vestal. Do you hear me? You are!"

Time seemed to stop. Vestal bore down, weeping and moaning, Mrs. McKenna leaned forward, Jane glanced at Georgia, and together they leaned forward ever so slightly to help Vestal push. . .and then. . .life gushed into the world. Max laughed aloud as he plopped a squirming, screaming infant into Mrs. McKenna's outstretched arms. His laughter died when he returned his attention to Vestal.

Jane saw the sheet beneath the elegant piano stool turn crimson.

—∞—

Ellen cuddled Vestal's impossibly tiny newborn next to her, not caring that doing so would likely ruin her dress. Feeling helpless, she looked on as Dr. Zimmer swept Vestal into his arms and returned her to the feather tick atop the dining-room table.

"Don't you give up on me, Vestal," he said. "Do you hear me? You've a darling baby girl. She's tiny, but she's got a very good chance. You've done well by her. Now you must do well by yourself." As he worked, the doctor kept up a running commentary. "Are you listening to me? Do you hear me? Georgia's here, and Jane's right beside you. Mrs. McKenna is just now taking the baby in to get her cleaned up. We're going to warm some blankets in the oven for her, and she's going to be just fine. She'll be back with you very soon."

While he directed his commentary at Vestal, Dr. Zimmer was obviously telling Ellen and the others what to do. Georgia dealt with the sheet and the piano stool while Ellen headed into the kitchen with the baby, lowering the oven door even as she gathered the sheets around the infant to keep her as warm as possible. Georgia came in and stirred up the fire as Ellen knelt on the floor, holding the baby close to the warmth emanating from the stove.

When Georgia returned from taking another bowl of clean, warm water into the other room, Ellen looked up at her solemn face and said, "Take Jane with you back upstairs. Get some things out of the trunk. The key's in my jewelry box on the dresser."

Georgia tilted her head. "You sure?"

The baby in her arms mewled softly, squirming and burrowing close. Ellen blinked back tears. Nodded. "I'm sure."

Georgia swept out of the room.

—⁂—

Jane had followed Georgia halfway up the front stairs when the doctor called after them. "Do you have any surgical experience, Georgia?"

Jane looked over at the willowy housekeeper just as the woman put a hand on the stair railing, seemingly to steady herself. "Some. If you mean stitching."

"Good. I need extra hands." He spoke again to Vestal. "Now, Vestal, you stay with us. There's some repair work here to be done, but it's nothing I can't handle and nothing for you to worry over." He raised his voice and pointed the next words toward the kitchen. "Mrs. McKenna's just now bringing your little girl back in here. You listen to those baby sounds, you hear?"

Jane glanced toward the kitchen just as Mrs. McKenna appeared in the doorway. Were those tears on her cheeks? All that was visible of Vestal's baby was a tiny shock of red hair peeking out of the dishcloth Mrs. McKenna had used to swaddle her.

As the doctor worked, Mrs. McKenna held the baby close to Vestal's cheek. "Feel that?" she murmured. "That's the very breath of life, Vestal. She's already punched me with her tiny fists. She's a fighter. You fight, too, now. You hear?"

As the doctor directed Georgia to position Vestal's legs so that he could repair the damage done when the baby tore her way into the world, Mrs. McKenna glanced up to where Jane waited. Then scooping the baby up again, she pulled her close and headed up the stairs.

—⁂—

Warden McKenna regained consciousness with a roar that Mamie thought likely to be heard halfway to Lincoln. He blurted out a couple of swear words even as he pushed himself to a sitting position. Scowling, he felt the bump on his head, then the place under his jawline where Pearl's weapon had pricked the skin. He ordered J. B. to help him into the chair he'd slid out of not long ago and then began to fire questions.

"The prisoner?"

"Captain just took her to solitary. She stabbed Underhill."

"How bad is it?"

J. B. shrugged. "Not too bad. All Underhill seemed to care about was Miss Dawson."

Mamie's cheeks flamed at the words, even as she realized they were true. Martin had risked himself for. . .well. . .not *only* for her. Ivy and the warden were in danger, too.

The warden didn't comment. He raked his fingers through his hair and shook his head, wincing with the effort even as he looked up at Mamie. "You're all right?"

She nodded.

One of the guards stepped forward. "Not meaning any disrespect, sir, but you've had a blow to the head. It might be a good idea to let the doctor—"

"I will," the warden said. "Just as soon as I know what all's gone on here." He reached up to feel the bump on his head again. "I'd be obliged, Miss Dawson, if you'd sit for a moment and tell me what I missed." He glanced around them. "Obviously it was something. . . of note."

Mamie described the scene she and Ivy and Martin had come upon. "He launched himself across the room before Pearl had a second to react. It was. . . ." She paused. "Very quick thinking, sir. And very brave, to my mind."

The warden nodded. Grasping the back of the chair for support, he stood up, wavered momentarily, then seemed to recover. "I'll have more questions, Miss Dawson, if you'll make your way to my office in about half an hour." He glanced at the captain. "For now, though, let's check in on Underhill." At the doorway, he paused and waved for Mamie to precede him. He gave orders for the women's ward to be attended in Mamie's absence and then followed her to the stairs. They descended to the second floor together.

As Mamie turned right to go through turnkey and toward the warden's office on the free side, the warden turned left toward the door that opened onto the yard and the collection of buildings inside the walls, among them a square building that served as an infirmary and hospital for the men. She hesitated. Thought of Martin being treated by the prison doctor. The man was, to her mind, a quack. And Dr. Zimmer was just across the way at the warden's house. Without giving it another thought, Mamie hurried past the door leading into Warden McKenna's office and out into the sunshine.

—◊◊◊—

At the top of the stairs, Mrs. McKenna handed Jane the baby. "I'll be right with you," she said and went into the room with the pomegranate quilt. Jane made a point of minding her own business, facing the windows instead of peering after the woman. Swaying back and forth, she hummed softly to the infant nestled in her arms. It seemed less than a minute before Mrs. McKenna reappeared in the doorway. Back at Jane's side, she removed a potted fern from atop the trunk positioned below the windows and set it on the floor. Kneeling before the trunk, she unlocked it and lifted the lid.

The faintest scent of lavender accompanied rustling sounds as Mrs. McKenna picked her way through the assortment of things inside. Packages tied with ribbon, damask and lace, small boxes, and a beautiful china doll all accumulated beside the potted fern until, finally, baby things. Two knit caps, a pair of impossibly tiny stockings, and a stack of diapers. Three flannel blankets, five dainty gowns, one of them with pink flowers embroidered along the hem. Mrs. McKenna paused for a moment when a pink-and-white nine-patch crib quilt came into view. She hesitated, then pulled it out of the trunk and spread it across her lap, running her palm over the surface. Was Mrs. McKenna really going to part with all those lovely things for Vestal? Surely not.

She looked up at Jane. "Have there been. . .arrangements to clothe the child?"

"I don't know." Jane glanced down at the baby. "She arrived sooner than expected."

"I thought Ian said you all sew as part of your work."

"We mend." Jane nodded down at the pile of baby things in Mrs. McKenna's lap. "But we've no supplies to make anything like that." She paused. "Miss Dawson had an idea a couple of years ago to get us to making things for the babies and children at the Home for the Friendless. Some of us were excited at the prospect. Thought they might even bring in a machine or two. But it didn't happen. I don't know why."

Mrs. McKenna frowned. "You sew entirely by hand?"

Jane shrugged. "We have nothing but time. Besides, why spend money on something that makes things easier for. . .people like us?"

Mrs. McKenna set the baby things—crib quilt included—aside and began to return the other items to the trunk. She closed the lid and put the fern back in place. "Ian—Mr. McKenna—says the shops have requirements. I think he told me every man in the cooper shop is expected to make something like seven barrels a day. The men who don't are disciplined. How would the women feel about that? I mean, if they had the ability to do more, more would be required, wouldn't it?"

Jane gazed at the pomegranate quilt in the bedroom, then back down at the baby quilt. For some reason, she decided to speak her mind about this one thing. "I can't speak for anyone but myself, ma'am." She nodded toward the bed in the other room. "Mine didn't have a swag border on it, but I was proud of it, just the same." She looked down at the baby and murmured, "I miss making beautiful things."

Someone rapped on the front door. Mrs. McKenna led the way downstairs, the baby things folded over her arms.

CHAPTER 8

At the foot of the stairs, Ellen handed the baby things off to Georgia and opened the door to an obviously frazzled and out-of-breath Miss Dawson jabbering news of an "incident" and asking to speak to Dr. Zimmer. Ellen's mind connected three words. *Stabbed. Warden. Doctor.* Speechless, she turned toward the dining room and Dr. Zimmer, even as she felt her knees buckle.

Miss Dawson grasped her arm and guided her to back up and sit on the stairs. "Just take some deep breaths, dear. The warden's all right. You did hear me say that, didn't you?"

Ellen swept a curl back off her forehead with a trembling hand. "Y–you said he'd been stabbed."

"Just nicked beneath the chin," Miss Dawson said as she turned toward Dr. Zimmer. "It's Mr. Underhill I'm worried about." Quickly, she described what had happened with Pearl Brand.

Again, Ellen's mind shut out everything but news of Ian. Someone had attacked Ian. Knocked him out. And then held a knife—or something—to his throat. A *woman* had nearly done what neither Rebels nor bank robbers in Brownville could. A *woman.* Ellen glanced at Jane Prescott and Vestal Jackson, and for a moment all the kindness that had been growing inside her toward the women living over on the third floor faded.

"Please, Dr. Zimmer," Miss Dawson was saying. "You know—" She broke off. "He saved the warden's life. Probably mine and Ivy's, too." She paused. "He deserves good care."

The doctor stood up and, taking a pillow, tucked it beneath Vestal's knees and covered her back up. "I've done what I can here right now." He spoke to Georgia as he handed her the brown vial he'd just taken from his medical bag. "Laudanum if she needs it, but I'd prefer not if it can be avoided." Rinsing his hands in the bowl on his instrument table, he grabbed a towel and bolted out the door.

Ellen stepped out onto the front porch and told the guard about what was happening. "Miss Dawson will stay here until we receive further instructions from the warden. I'd appreciate it if you'd join us inside, now." The guard nodded. With him stationed inside the front door, Ellen summoned the other one from out back. *One at the back door, one at the front.* The idea that they would be able to hear anything that went on in the house made Ellen feel safer—in spite of their less-than-gentlemanly behavior earlier. She asked Georgia to make coffee for the men, then realized that no one had eaten all day and decided they'd "have a little lunch" as well.

Georgia got to work, slicing cold roast beef and bread and making sandwiches, humming while she prepared the food. Ellen returned to the sickroom, where Miss Dawson had taken a seat beside the barely conscious Vestal Jackson. Jane Prescott had spread one of the flannel blankets across her lap and was dressing the baby, crooning softly as she worked. Ellen's fears subsided as she looked around the room. There was no Pearl Brand waiting to hurt anyone here.

Poor Jane Prescott had looked longingly at the quilts upstairs and wished for a chance to make beautiful things again. Ellen realized she'd never so much as considered that there might be women across the road who even knew how to do fancy work. *But then you haven't really considered them at all, have you?* For the first time, she felt guilty about that.

Poor Vestal—giving birth only to have to let the baby go. *Do others over there have children? What's happened to them while their mothers are here?* Ellen couldn't remember seeing any children come to visit on Sundays after chapel services. How did a mother stand being separated from her child? On the other hand, how would a mother stand having her child see her in this place?

Poor baby—born early and soon to be separated from her own mother. As Ellen looked at the infant, her head now covered with a cap she'd knitted for Daisy, she swallowed and looked away. *Poor Daisy*, not all that much bigger than Vestal's baby. . .left behind in Missouri in an obscenely small grave marked by a simple stone.

Ellen blinked away her tears. Cleared her throat. Glancing into the kitchen where the guards sat eating, she offered to sit with Vestal while Miss Dawson had something to eat.

"That's very kind of you, Mrs. McKenna, but I believe I'll stay right here."

Jane Prescott declined to eat as well, preferring to tend the baby and stay by Vestal's side.

Ellen stayed, too. She went to the front windows and looked out for a moment before turning around and asking, "What's to happen now?"

"Why, he's to get better, that's what," Miss Dawson said quickly. "There just isn't anything else to even consider." Her voice wavered, and she broke off. Then she said with more hope than confidence in her voice, "Dr. Zimmer will know what to do."

"I sincerely hope the best for your friend," Ellen said, "but I was actually referring to"—she nodded at the infant, then gestured toward a sleeping Vestal Jackson—"the things at hand."

Miss Dawson sighed. "Of course." She shook her head. "More

sorrow and pain, I'm afraid. My sister, Manerva, has been making inquiries as to a wet nurse. Of course we didn't expect to need anyone so soon." She paused. "Which reminds me. . ." She glanced toward the kitchen where the guards sat and, lowering her voice, asked, "Would your housekeeper help me with the binding?" When Ellen frowned, Miss Dawson explained. "It will go much better for Vestal if we bind her now to discourage. . ." She cleared her throat. "To discourage nature taking its course."

It took Ellen a moment to realize that Miss Dawson was talking about Vestal's body preparing to feed her baby. She frowned. "But couldn't—do they have to be separated right away? It seems wrong to put the baby at jeopardy if you're still trying to locate a wet nurse. The baby hasn't done anything wrong. Why should she be punished?"

Miss Dawson smiled. "I agree, Mrs. McKenna. Would you care to take the matter up with your husband?"

Ellen glanced through the windows toward the penitentiary again. All the "right" answers came to mind. It wasn't her decision to make. It wasn't her place to interfere. It wasn't any of her business, really. But then the baby began to cry. Vestal stirred. Jane Prescott leaned close and murmured something, and even in her exhausted state, Vestal did what any mother would do. She reached up to fumble with the ribbons holding her nightgown closed, and held out her arms for her baby. In that moment, although she didn't realize it, Ellen McKenna's life changed.

She knew what people said about women in prison. Knowing had kept Ellen away from the female department for weeks. Those women were evil. Deranged. Less than women, really. But here was Vestal Jackson, suckling her baby, a faint smile on her pale face, even as tears coursed down her cheeks. And Jane Prescott, biting her lower lip as her cheeks flushed, and she swiped her own tears away.

I miss making beautiful things, Jane had said upstairs. Ellen wondered what else Jane missed. Perhaps she, Ellen McKenna, was meant to find out. *"I was in prison, and ye came unto me."* Was it Jesus or Paul who'd said that? Either way, it was something God smiled on. She stepped away from the window and answered Miss Dawson's question.

"As a matter of fact, yes. I will take it up with the warden."

—⁓—

Late that evening, Ellen stood at her bedroom window, staring toward the starlit horizon. Ian stepped up behind her. Placing one hand on each shoulder, he pulled her back against him. "Please, Ellen. You have to understand. There's nothing else to be done until Miss Dawson's sister can make arrangements. But long term, it's just not possible." He hooked a curl at her neckline. Pulling it aside, he bent to kiss the uncovered spot.

She shrugged him off. "That baby girl deserves our protection and care."

"And she'll have it. Miss Dawson said her sister speaks very highly of Dr. Mason, who provides care for the inhabitants of the Home for the Friendless. The baby will be in good hands."

"She's already in the best hands possible," Ellen insisted. "She's with her mother."

"And eleven other inmates in a maximum security penitentiary. Would you have her grow up there?"

Ellen turned around and looked up at him. "You could petition the governor for a pardon."

Ian frowned. "And who have you been talking to, to come up with that idea?"

"Miss Dawson said it happens, sometimes, at other institutions. Of course we couldn't have a forthright discussion about it, not with Vestal and Jane Prescott hearing everything we said."

"Thank goodness you at least knew that much."

She turned back around to face the window. "I didn't know how to explain any of it to Jack when he got home from school."

"I didn't have much luck with that after dinner, either." Ian paused. "And I don't like the idea of him—or you—seeing me as someone who'd willfully hurt the innocent." He cleared his throat. "I am not unsympathetic, but the truth is Vestal Jackson is responsible for her circumstances. Someone was hurt when she stole that money, Ellen. They could have died. As it is, she's lucky she isn't serving time for manslaughter."

"But Vestal—"

"Vestal? It's *Vestal* now?"

"She said she would have paid back every cent. She was *hungry*." Her voice dropped. "I remember being hungry when you were off with your regiment. And if it hadn't been for our neighbors, I would have done whatever it took to feed our baby. In Vestal's case, the baby died anyway."

"That child didn't starve. She had the ague."

"And she was weakened by hunger, or she might have survived. It seems so cruel. Cruel beyond the crime. Which Vestal admits to committing." Ellen paused. "And since when do we put women who are going to give birth in prison, anyway?"

"No one knew she was. . .in the family way when she was sentenced."

"Why wasn't she released when it was discovered?"

Ian was quiet for a long time. When he finally spoke, he said gently, "You've taken a sudden and very personal interest in Vestal Jackson's story. They all have one, you know. And most include logical explanations as to why they had to do what they did. Or why they're innocent."

"She doesn't claim innocence." A combination of anger,

frustration, and desperation brought tears to Ellen's eyes as she said, "What if that little cherub *dies*, Ian? How will you ever live with yourself?"

He let go of her then. Left her at the window and retreated into the shadows. She took a deep breath and brought back the gentle Southern drawl he loved as she said, "I didn't want to come here, Ian. Truth be told, I've hated nearly every minute of it. But I haven't complained. Because I love you. You're brave and kind, and you really do believe that every human bein' was made in God's image. I didn't know how I felt about any of it until today. But today I saw something that made me realize that yes, they are prisoners, but they're also—"

"Misunderstood?"

She brushed the sarcastic comment away with a wave of her hand. "Don't try to make me sound like those sops who come to the services on Sunday in the guise of serving the 'poor and lowly,' when all they really want to do is flirt with the guards." She paused again, just long enough to recapture the soothing tone she wanted him to hear. "No. I do not say they are misunderstood. But still—" She broke off. "Like I said, I don't really know how to interpret all the new feelings flowing through me. I do, however, know about mothers and babies.

"Vestal Jackson committed a crime. She should serve her sentence. But to take the baby away?" She shook her head and took a deep, wavering breath. "You weren't there when I lost our little girl, Ian. You don't know—" She went to him and stepped back into his arms, weeping quietly. "Don't do this, darlin'. Please." She paused. "I asked Miss Dawson who would eventually raise the baby. She didn't even know. She said it would be difficult. People tend to think that children from questionable backgrounds are tainted, somehow. That they won't be normal because of 'bad blood.'"

She leaned her head against his chest, reveling in the warmth of him even as she said, "The baby's going to be in an institution either way. Which is better: a ward with a wet nurse and strangers, or a ward with her own mother? And how much will she remember? Vestal doesn't have that much longer to serve, does she?" She looked up at him. Kissed the place where that awful woman's weapon had pricked the skin. Traced the line of his jaw with her finger.

"And now who's using their wiles to get their way?" He covered her mouth with his own.

—◆—

Tears dampened Jane's pillow as she lay in the dark staring toward Vestal, who'd fallen asleep with one arm curled about the baby. Miss Dawson had been exactly right earlier today when she answered Mrs. McKenna's question about what came next. *More pain.* The child might be here for a few days, but Miss Dawson's sister was "making arrangements." Everyone knew what that meant. Vestal wouldn't even name her own child. She'd cried herself to sleep. But Vestal wasn't the only one swimming in dark waters of pain and longing and regret tonight, nor was Jane. Muffled sobs echoed through the dormitory.

Jane had lingered at the windows long past sundown, hoping in spite of herself to catch sight of Max as he headed back toward town. The moon came out, and still there was no sign of him. Jane hoped that didn't mean something terrible concerning Mr. Underhill's condition. The gangly, awkward Mr. Underhill was one of the few people in this place who expressed kindness and compassion. All the women appreciated him. But however sincere Jane's concern was for Mr. Underhill, her thoughts soon returned to Max.

She'd told him she wouldn't see him, but now she'd spent the day with him. He'd be back, wanting to see her about—whatever it was that had brought him here. What would she do? Would she be strong enough to refuse a meeting? More important, what would Warden McKenna do with the knowledge that Dr. Max Zimmer and Jane Prescott had once been friends?

When she finally retreated from the window and slipped beneath the coarse sheets on her cot, Jane's thoughts whirled from Max to Rose to Owen to the trial to Pearl Brand to Vestal's baby, and back again, in a dizzying rhythm that rocked her emotions and finally wore her out. Rolling onto her back, she counted *in*-two-three, *out*-two-three, willing her breathing to even out, trying to make her mind go blank. She envisioned the endless prairie, the hot sun, the far horizon, the relentless space. But Max invaded the space.

Careful, Mrs. Prescott. She remembered the sound of his voice and the feel of his hand on her arm as he reached out to steady her, to keep her from falling down the stairs. *To keep me from falling.* And here she was, hours later, in danger of falling into. . .something.

She must not want his kindness. Must not want *him.* Lying alone in the dark, Jane swore at his smile and his gray-green eyes, his faithful friendship, his soothing voice. She mustn't want any of it, for wanting *that* would make bearing *this* impossible.

The baby whimpered, and in the darkness Jane whispered concern.

"It's all right," Vestal replied. "We're fine."

And they were. The little girl was strong. Her suckling echoed in the dormitory, along with Vestal's contented murmurings. Jane imagined every woman in that dormitory lying awake, listening to the very normal sound of a mother feeding her child in a place that was far from normal, as they tried to rise above waves of regret over their own lost hopes. She had no idea what those regrets might be. She'd made it her mission not to know, not to care. . .to merely exist in this place until finally she could go to a new place and create something for herself and Rose.

Today had brought that someday hope to the surface. Uninvited. Too far in the future. Too impossible. There was more to regret about today than seeing Max Zimmer. She wished she'd never seen the inside of that house and Ellen McKenna's beautiful quilts. She wished she hadn't been reminded of missed quiltings and lost time, of things entrusted to friends and trunks filled with memories.

Tonight, the longing for those things felt as strong as it had her first night here. So strong she hurt. Her stomach ached. Her chest felt tight. She turned on her side and curled up. . .but that only made her remember Thomas encircling her waist and pulling her against him in the night. Turning onto her stomach, she peered over the edge of the cot toward the bare stone floor.

Max Zimmer should just go away.

CHAPTER 9

Max paused at the top of the administration building stairs, looking up at the night sky. Every inch of him ached. He was bone tired, both from the challenging confinement and the evening spent wrestling with the prison doctor over how to treat the wound Pearl Brand had inflicted on a guard. He wished the warden hadn't asked him to look in on Underhill, but how could he say no? He needed to be in the man's good graces when he came back tomorrow.

The warden had been distracted enough not to press Max about the reason for the missed appointment. Thank God he'd let it go when Max said, "I'll come back tomorrow. It's nothing that can't wait." Now, as he retrieved his horse from the prison stables and mounted up for the ride back into Lincoln, he tried to work out a reasonable excuse for his failure to say something about knowing Jane.

It was certainly true that everything had happened quickly. That might serve as reason enough for the first part of the day. But once Vestal's baby had been safely delivered and the women had returned to the secure third-floor quarters, things were well in hand. Underhill was in no real danger, and the physician on staff was finally sober by the time the warden looked in on things in the infirmary. Max had had plenty of opportunity to explain himself.

But he hadn't. And he wasn't quite sure why.

Instead of urging the horse into a lope and heading for town, he sat staring up at the third-floor windows, thinking about Jane. She was rail thin. Not sickly, exactly, but not healthy, either. Was she not eating, or didn't the state feed prisoners very well? Maybe he'd ask the warden about that. As a physician. When he thought back to that one dance with her and the way she smiled up at him, the pallor on her thin face today made him. . .what? What, exactly, did he feel?

Taking a deep breath, he clucked to get the horse moving up the trail toward the dim glow in the distance that was Lincoln. Still he thought of Jane. Some things about her hadn't changed. Her gentle manner with Vestal and the baby reminded Max of the way she'd always been with Rose. But the inner calm she'd seemed to have was gone, and Max didn't think he was the main reason. He'd done his best to telegraph the message that he wasn't about to reveal their connection. Still she'd seemed on the edge of fear for most of the day. As if she didn't quite know how to behave in the real world anymore.

First thing tomorrow, he'd ride back out here. Surely after today she'd agree to see him. He'd never forgotten, never given up, never stopped demanding justice. Neither should she. Especially not with a new warden at the helm and a new governor in office. If that wasn't a recipe for hope, Max didn't know what was.

Urging the horse into a lope, he made plans for the morrow. He would smooth things over with the warden and convince him to sign a written recommendation for a pardon. Then he would keep his appointment with the new governor. He would make both men listen and convince them of what he believed to be true. The only thing Jane Prescott had ever killed was a rattlesnake that threatened Rose one day.

Mamie gave in to her insomnia and sat up in bed. The night was so quiet she could hear the prairie grass below her windows rustle in the wind. Her stomach growled. With a sigh, she threw the covers back, felt her way into the slippers at the side of her bed, and made her way through the parlor. Moonlight spilling in the turret windows reflected off the muslin squares marching across the top of a quilt draped over the back of her rocker. Making a shawl of the quilt, she stood at the narrow turret window, staring at the warden's house across the road and thinking back over the day's events.

Be thankful unto him, and bless His name. . .Give thanks unto the Lord for He is good: for His mercy endureth for ever. God had a way of reminding her of phrases from the Good Book that applied to the moment at hand, and tonight was no exception. She'd learned long ago that going down a list of what she thought of as "thankfuls" was one of the best ways to banish worry. And it seemed that, in spite of the day ending well and no one being permanently harmed, she still had a lot to worry over.

It took some thinking to untangle the blessings from the fabric of a day that looked downright tattered at first glance. She should have recognized that Pearl Brand was a danger. *Thank You that she didn't do serious damage.* The idea of facing the day when Pearl was released from solitary made her shudder with fear. *Thank You that the warden doesn't seem inclined to do that anytime soon.* Matrons had lost their jobs over smaller disturbances than the one today. *Thank You that the warden's already said he doesn't plan to fire me.* She couldn't bear the idea of taking Vestal's baby away. *Thank You for sending a good doctor around just when we needed him.* Her laxness could have gotten the warden killed. *Thank You that Martin is such a brave man.*

Martin. Heaven help her, she was thinking of the man by his given name. She must never call him Martin to his face. *Why not? He called you Mamie more than once today. And you didn't mind.* Mamie sighed. Try as she would, she could not bring herself to be thankful for Martin Underhill's obvious interest in her. Mr. Selleck's handsome smile flashed in her mind. *Why are you being so. . .earthly minded? The Bible clearly says that it isn't the outward appearance that matters.*

"Thank You, Lord, for putting up with me. I know I'm shallow, but. . ." Surely God wouldn't answer years of prayer with a man people called Frankenstein behind his back, would He? *Forgive me, Lord. I can't help it. You're going to have to take charge of the matter of Martin Underhill. I realize there's a good man behind those odd eyes. But Lord. . .*

Shivering against the cool night, Mamie pulled the quilt closer and headed into the kitchen. She lit a lamp on the table, murmuring to herself as she heated water for tea. She would think about Martin another time. Or not at all. Perhaps her assumptions were another case of her overactive imagination rearing its head again—a repeat of her nonsensical musings about her and the Reverend Weaver. Goodness. For an old maid she could spin fantasies.

The truth was that much more than her thoughts about Martin Underhill and her concerns about Pearl Brand were keeping Mamie awake tonight. Tonight's vigil was about the things she hadn't seen. She'd been a matron for four years. . .but she hadn't *seen*. She'd missed a lot more than just Pearl's potential for violence. She'd missed Agnes Sweeney's potential for caring until Agnes came to Vestal's side. She'd missed Jane Prescott's potential for tenderness until she saw her care for Vestal and her baby. And worst of all, she'd missed something that should have been obvious. Something she hadn't thought about until she saw how nervous and on edge Jane Prescott was at the warden's house and how, the minute the door closed locking her back in, her shoulders relaxed. *I've missed thinking about how they're going to do once they leave this place.*

Would they ever be able to shake off the past and find a way back into the world?

She called them *lambs*, and in spite of Adam Selleck's handsome smile, she resented his tendency to talk about "hens in the henhouse" and "mares in the stable." Oh, she knew the twelve women weren't *innocent* lambs, but still. One day they would all leave, and what would the future hold? Jane Prescott had returned to the evening routine behind the walls with obvious relief. And that seemed. . .wrong, even if the world did think of female inmates as being less than women. Mamie had never believed that, but given the opportunity to defend her own beliefs, she wouldn't have had much evidence. Until today.

Today's crisis had revealed the women behind their names and their sentences. Yes, they had done bad things, but they had the potential to be more than caged birds. They were still women. As Mamie waited for the tea to steep, as she pondered what she thought she'd seen today, she wondered what she should do about it. How could she remind them of who they were apart from the punishment? Was there a way to lift them above their crimes and somehow set them on a new path? She hated the idea of Jane Prescott—and Vestal and every single one of the women she'd been praying for all these months—cringing with fear at the idea of freedom. That wasn't justice.

Teapot in hand, Mamie retrieved a china cup and saucer and settled into the armchair at her kitchen table. As the golden stream of hot tea arched from spout to delicate teacup, as she inhaled the soothing aromas of bergamot and lemon, the idea that Jane Prescott now drank bitter coffee from a tin mug every morning gave Mamie pause. What was it Mrs. McKenna had said as they left the house to return to the third floor? Something about Jane's noticing the quilts on the beds and saying she missed making beautiful things.

Mamie bowed her head. *Forgive me, Lord. I've fallen short. You put me here for something beyond what I've been doing. There's more work to be done. Show me how to do it. Show me what You want.* In one motion, she lifted her head and stood up. She didn't have an answer yet, but she would begin her search in the best place she knew to find answers. Retrieving her Bible from the turret room, she brought it into the kitchen and sat back down.

Everything about their lives will change when they leave here. Should we be focusing on what happens after they leave instead of being content to punish?

It was an absurd notion. No one believed in efforts at reform, at least not once a woman ended up here. These women were hopeless, weren't they?

"*You. . .were dead in trespasses and sins. . .fulfilling the desires of the flesh and of the mind. . .by nature the children of wrath. . . . But God. . .rich in mercy, for his great love wherewith he loved us. . .raised us up together.*" Mamie read the passage over and over again, struck by two words. *But God.* The passage spoke of terrible acts of sin, *but God.* Because of God's free gift of redemption, the same passage rang with hope. God loved sinners. He promised hope. If God hadn't given up on Mamie Dawson, how could she give up on those women just past turnkey? How could she be content to merely lock them in and hope for the best?

Mamie sat back in her chair, thinking. Muttering to herself. Praying. And finally, she realized that she couldn't just lock them in and hope for the best. God expected more of her, and with His help—and the warden's cooperation—she would give it.

If this is Your voice, Lord, show me what You want me to do. Show me how to help them learn how to be. A familiar passage came to mind, and she opened her Bible to Proverbs 31. "*Let her own works praise her in the gates. She seeketh wool, and flax, and worketh willingly with her hands. . .she shall rejoice in time to come."* Mamie had always concentrated on the parts of that passage that spoke of husbands and children. Somehow it had always made her feel a sense of loss. Now she wondered if it might show her a way to serve the women on the third floor.

Retrieving pen and paper from the desk in the parlor, Mamie reread the passage. *"Who can find a virtuous woman?"* There was a very long list of all the things a woman should do, a woman society would "praise in the gates." Mamie knew she couldn't change hearts. Only God could do that. *"Begin with the virtuous works. Help them do the right things. . . . Leave their hearts to Me."*

Mamie scribbled until dawn, and still she wasn't finished. When she finally sat back, she had several pages of notes. Ink blotches. Crossed-out words. And more than likely, a good amount of faulty reasoning. Still, it was a beginning, and the ideas borne on the night air, somehow inspired by the events of the previous day, gave her a new view of her unlikely work. The sudden realization that some of her thoughts this night echoed the words of one of the missionary ladies from China who had spoken at a church meeting last year gave her goose bumps.

Of course predawn discoveries supported by a combination of reason and scripture wouldn't matter one bit if Warden McKenna listened and laughed. Or—what would be worse—listened, nodded, seemed to be in agreement with her. . .and did nothing.

—⚬—

Ellen cherished the predawn moments when she and Ian lay in each other's arms beneath a pile of quilts, content to revel in their nearness until the skies blushed with morning light. She loved the feel of his whiskers on her skin and the lingering scent of bay rum from the pomade he used to tame his obstinately curly hair. And this morning as Ian roused and pulled her close, the preciousness of every single blessing brought unexpected tears. *Forgive me for not being grateful.* She kissed the back of his hand before pressing it against her cheek.

"You using your wiles again, Mrs. McKenna?" He nuzzled her shoulder. "Because it's working."

Ellen rolled onto her back, so she could look up into his eyes. "I'm realizing how blessed I am. And regretting how hard I've made it on you lately, what with grumbling about the garden and the house and—" His hand moved. She caught her breath. "I'm going to try to do better."

He grinned down at her. "Have I complained?"

"No. But I haven't exactly taken it upon myself to be a model warden's wife, have I?"

He shrugged. "I'm sorry if I've made you feel—"

"You haven't." She paused. "But yesterday. . .being around those two women. . .it changed how I think about things. How I think about *them*. It made me think that I should do. . .something."

Ian slid from under the covers and reached for his long underwear. She moved closer and put her palm on his back. "I didn't mean to send you skittering out of our bed."

He spoke without looking her way. "I can't make a decision about Vestal Jackson's baby until I've talked to some people, Ellen. I heard what you had to say on the matter, and I'm not unsympathetic, but—"

She patted his bare back. "Did I mention the baby? I'm not some harpy intent on nagging you to get my way. I'm saying that yesterday reminded me of how blessed I am." She took a deep breath. "And if you approve, I'd like to speak with Miss Dawson about how I might be of use. One of the women mentioned how much she misses making beautiful things. Apparently she used to go to quiltings."

He turned to look at her. "Are you telling me you want to start a quilting bee across the road?"

Ellen shrugged. "I don't know. I'm hoping Miss Dawson might have some ideas."

He smiled. "I have a meeting scheduled with her this morning. I'll tell her you'd like to speak with her."

"Doesn't she get Saturdays off? Invite her to tea."

Ian nodded. "Tea on Saturday. I'll let her know. Anything else?"

"Not a thing. Unless—" She batted her eyelashes, bared one shoulder.

"Georgia's made apple fritters!" Jack's voice sounded from the hallway.

Ian groaned softly even as he bent to kiss her on the cheek.

"Sounds wonderful!" Ellen called in the general direction of the bedroom door. She tucked her shoulder back inside the gown and reached for the wrapper draped across the foot of the bed, chuckling as Ian groused about "that boy's confounded timing." Blowing him a kiss, Ellen headed downstairs.

CHAPTER 10

Mamie affixed her key ring to the loop at her waist and smoothed her collar. With a last glance in her bedroom mirror, she headed into the hall where the notes she'd made in the night waited on the silver tray by the door. Adjusting her glasses, she scanned the list again and said a prayer before putting it back down. *If I've lost my mind, please somehow keep me from presenting this to Warden McKenna today.* She'd have to come back this way to reach the warden's first-floor office on the free side. She'd grab it then.

As she took the familiar path down to the second, through turnkey, past the chapel on the secure side, and then up the narrow stairs to the third-floor female department, Mamie thought of Martin Underhill. He was always waiting for her on weekday mornings, whether he'd had the night watch or not. He might be sweeping the floor or polishing doorknobs—as if either of those were part of a guard's regular duties. He'd made it his habit to help Mamie unload the dumbwaiter that brought breakfast up from the basement kitchen. And it had annoyed her no end. This morning, though, realizing that Martin had been ordered to rest for the next few days and was likely still in the infirmary, Mamie was shocked to realize that she would miss him. *Well of course you will. If there's one thing the female department needs today, it's reassurance that we have things in hand and they are safe.* Martin might not be pretty, but he did have a way about him, a kindness that none of the other guards—

"Morning, Ma—Miss Dawson."

How long had he been waiting? Hopefully he'd been sitting in that chair, but now he'd risen to stand, grinning in that crooked way of his as he teased, "Running a bit late, I see."

As he spoke, the first bell of the day rang out, and Mamie realized he was right. They usually had the dumbwaiter unloaded by now. "What on earth do you think you're doing?"

He looked perplexed. "Well. . .what I always do. Helping you serve breakfast."

She bustled toward the dumbwaiter. "You were supposed to rest for the next few days."

"Aye." The great head nodded. "The doctor advised it. But he didn't *order* it. I'll rest after we see to the dozen." He paused. "Really. I'm fine."

"Is that so? I don't recall your skin being this particular shade of gray in the past."

He grinned again. "I had no idea you'd noticed my complexion, gray or otherwise."

Was she blushing? Unbelievable. She swept past him. "You should attend to your health. I'm certain the guard on duty is completely adequate to help me dole out a few bowls of gruel and some dry toast." *Vestal's portion must be increased. She should have milk.* She would mention it to Warden McKenna.

Martin followed her toward the dumbwaiter. "I thought it might help if things get back to normal right away." He offered a shy smile. "As normal as they can be at least—now there's a baby and all."

Mamie had, of course, been thinking the same thing. "Business as usual" would reassure everyone. Martin's realizing it was a bit surprising, though. "I can't deny that I've been concerned about what effect yesterday's—events—will have."

"Exactly. The baby aside, they've got to be wondering about Pearl Brand's coming back on the ward." He shook his head again. "I don't mind saying that if the warden decides to do that, I hope you'll refuse it. Tell him you've an obligation to keep the others safe."

Mamie started to retort that she was well aware of her obligations, but Martin must have sensed what was coming.

"Not that I think you need a reminder," he said quickly. "It's just that. . ." He swallowed. "I worry about you, Mamie. That Brand woman, she's a hard nut."

Martin Underhill had been on duty here since the day the penitentiary opened back in '76. Mamie knew she would do well to heed his warning.

He misinterpreted her silence. "I didn't mean you don't know—" His face turned red. "What I meant to say was—"

"You meant exactly what you said. And I appreciate your concern."

"You do?"

"Of course." A second bell sounded. Mamie unlocked the dumb-waiter door, but when Martin winced with the effort of working the pulley, she shooed him away and did it herself.

While Mamie transferred the steaming pot of oatmeal from the dumbwaiter to the serving cart, Martin reached for the bowls and spoons. He grunted when he hoisted the coffeepot but managed to fill the twelve tin mugs with the sludge that passed for coffee. Grimacing when the smell of burned beans assaulted her nose, Mamie helped push the cart toward the door leading into the dormitory.

The second the night guard—Mamie thought his name was Peterson—caught a glimpse of Martin, he headed for the stairs, offering little more than a gruff "nothing to report" on his way past. But then he turned back. "Heard you were in the infirmary," he called to Martin. "Heard you got stabbed. . .by a woman."

Mamie opened her mouth to deliver an angry retort at the sneering tone, but Martin gave a little wave she took to mean *don't*. He glanced back. "Kind of you to show concern," he said. "Doc fixed me up."

Peterson laughed. "Well, you stay alert. Selleck says the little half-blind one packs quite a punch." His snickering echoed off the high ceiling as he made his way to the stairs.

Vestal Jackson's baby was awake and demanding breakfast. Before Mamie could say anything about Peterson, Martin tilted his head and smiled. "Isn't that a blessed sound." He looked down at Mamie. "I'm praying the warden lets the baby stay," he said. "Can't see as it would do a bit of harm. In fact, the little mite would probably do a lot of good."

Mamie sighed. "I don't hold out much hope for the warden's allowing that." She paused. "And it's going to break Vestal's heart."

"You stand firm." Martin swept one palm over his balding head. Took a deep breath. "No child should grow up thinking his own mother didn't want him."

In spite of being weary both in mind and body, Max spent a restless night. He was up at dawn, peering at himself in the mirror above the washstand in his hotel room, trimming his mustache, cleaning his nails, doing everything he could do to both occupy himself and make sure he looked every inch an upstanding citizen. The warden had likely had little time or interest in evaluating him yesterday. Today would be different. . .and some aspects of the difference set Max's teeth on edge.

After a breakfast of black coffee and toast, he walked over to the Windsor stables, asking once again for the powerful gray gelding that thrust its nose over its stall door and whickered in his direction.

The livery owner chuckled. "Don't recall him saying 'hello' to a customer before."

"We have an understanding." Max smiled.

"Oh really?"

"He takes the bit, and I hang on."

The livery owner shook his head. "You sure you don't want something with a little less vinegar?"

Max shook his head. "We do fine." He pulled a sugar cube out of his pocket and offered it to the gelding, who licked it off Max's palm and crunched, bobbing his head up and down.

Minutes later, as the powerful gray reached the edge of town, Max gave him his head. The animal lunged forward and ran full-out until the castle-like turrets of the penitentiary came into view up ahead.

Max reined him in with difficulty, then forced him to close the remaining distance at a walk. He continued past the main door and down the length of the east wall, then back again, cooling the animal down and trying to calm his own nerves. Finally, when the horse's breathing had returned to normal, Max dismounted and tied the reins to a hitching post before taking a seat at the base of the stairs leading up to the entrance. He was still sitting there when the warden came out of his house and crossed the road on his way to work.

"You're up early," McKenna said and held out his hand. "I don't think we even had time to introduce ourselves officially yesterday, did we? If you'll follow me inside, you can remind me of the purpose of the visit you had scheduled."

Max shook the man's hand. Might as well get it over with. At least if the guy sent him packing, they were already outside. He swallowed. "There's no easy way to say this. I have a confession. . .and an apology." The warden said nothing, just waited. Max cleared his throat. "The appointment was to make an appeal for a pardon for one of your inmates."

McKenna frowned. "None of my clerks recognized your name as a regular visitor. I had them check."

"I haven't visited her for a long time. She essentially kicked me out and told me not to come back."

McKenna frowned. "*She?*"

Max nodded.

He folded his arms across his chest. "I'm waiting."

"It's Jane Prescott."

The man's gaze narrowed. "As in the woman you spent the better part of the day with yesterday *in my home?*"

"As in the woman who agreed to stay with a friend in trouble. . .and who didn't so much as acknowledge she'd ever seen me before. And for the record, I did the same. We never spoke. I don't think we even made eye contact." Max paused. "I should have said something. But I was caught up in the moment—concerned for my patient. . .and. . ." He shrugged. "And it was a poor decision on my part."

The warden took his hat off. He ran thumb and forefinger along the crown, re-forming the crease. He stood there for so long Max wondered if the man was ever going to say anything. When he did, it was three words. "Walk with me." He set off down the stairs and along the east wall. Max hurried to catch up. "I assume the new quest for a pardon is precipitated by the idea that I just took over a job for which I have little experience."

Max frowned. "If you mean am I trying to pull the wool over your eyes, the answer is no." He paused. "I've been writing letters to try to get a hearing with the governor for four years. The new governor finally agreed to listen to what I have to say."

"When's that meeting?"

"Tomorrow afternoon."

"And it wouldn't hurt to walk into that meeting with a letter from the warden stating the sterling qualities of the misunderstood and unfairly punished Mrs. Jane Prescott."

Max stopped short. "This looks bad. I know that. But not nearly as bad as the idea you've a good woman locked up whose only child is growing up without her mother." Max met the warden's gaze and held it. Finally, he said. "She's my friend. Read her file. Talk to her. Judge for yourself."

"I'm not a judge, Dr. Zimmer. I'm a warden. I don't decide. I just administer the results."

"But sometimes you advocate for pardons," Max said. "And a pardon isn't even the only way. Last year they released two women. 'Time off for good behavior' or whatever they called it. I'd stake everything I have on your getting a good report from your matron if you ask what she thinks of Jane." He paused. "She's no danger to society. She never was."

McKenna took his hat off. He glanced toward the sun. "I've a 10:00 a.m. meeting with Miss Dawson," he said. "Make your case."

As the two men made their way inside to the warden's office, Max talked. He related what he'd seen and heard about Owen Marquis in the short time he'd known the man before the shooting. When he mentioned the bruises he'd seen on Jane's face and the time she'd come to him about pain in her side that turned out to be a cracked rib "from a fall," McKenna's eyes narrowed and a muscle in his cheek flexed.

"Go on," was all he said.

Max went back to the night Marquis died. "I saw stark fear on that woman's face when we'd taken no more than one turn around the dance floor. Minutes later, Marquis practically dragged her out of the room to go home. Rose had fallen asleep, and I carried her to the wagon for them. Jane thanked me, they drove off, and the next thing I knew Marquis was dead and Jane was on the stand admitting to a crime."

They were just inside the administration building door. Instead of going into his own office, McKenna headed into the clerk's office across the hall. Max heard him ask for Jane's file. He emerged, file in hand, and led the way into his own office. "This is going to take more than a few minutes," he said, opening the file.

"I can wait."

With a nod, McKenna began to read. Max didn't know how to interpret the expressions that flitted across the man's face. At times he frowned, at others he seemed surprised. Once, he flipped back through the assortment of papers as if he needed to double-check something. He motioned to the water cooler in the corner without looking up. "Help yourself to a drink."

Max drank a dipperful, more to occupy himself than for any need to slake thirst. Finally finished reading, McKenna got up and opened the two windows behind his desk. He got himself a drink of water, then crossed to his office door and asked the clerk outside to bring a coffee tray up from the kitchen. Finally, he sat back down and, leaning back in his chair, said, "Tell me your version of all of this again. Start at the beginning. When you arrived in the area, how you met the Marquises." He paused. "But I only want to hear what you *know* from firsthand experience. I don't care what you think or how you feel. Just tell me what you know."

Just when Max began, a knock at the door announced the arrival of the coffee tray. As the assistant set it on the desk, he glanced at Max and spoke to the warden. "Ten minutes until you're expecting Miss Dawson, sir."

McKenna nodded. "Thank you, Conrad. Just knock on the door to tell me she's here. I won't keep her waiting long."

With a nod and another look Max's way, Conrad left. McKenna filled two tin mugs with coffee. Max took a sip, grimaced, set the mug back on the tray, and began again. "My practice had been open maybe a month when Marquis came roaring into the office one day with Rose in his arms. He'd been teaching her to ride. The pony bucked, and when Rose went flying, her hand caught a nail on one of the corral posts. I stitched it up with Marquis looming over me threatening to shoot me if 'his little gunslinger' ended up with so much as a scar." He paused. "If I gave you the impression that Owen Marquis was pure evil, I shouldn't have. From what I heard—" He broke off, before McKenna, who'd raised his eyebrows in an unspoken warning, could say anything. "Everything I know from being around Marquis and Rose indicates he was fond of her. While I was putting in those stitches, he kept her distracted talking about how well she was doing at learning to shoot and how she shouldn't worry about Mama—that once Mama understood things, she'd be proud, too. Rose hung on every word. When he praised her, she beamed."

Max wove the story as best he could. It was hard to stick to what he knew from personal experience, but he thought he did a fairly good job. He'd seen Jane's bruises. He'd treated the broken rib. He'd seen her change from a confident woman who smiled and laughed to little more than a silent shadow trailing Marquis wherever he went. A knock on the door sounded the matron's arrival, and Max stopped. He looked at the door.

"Finish what you have to say," McKenna said. "Miss Dawson won't mind waiting a few minutes, especially if she knows we're discussing the fate of one of her favored lambs. I'm new at the job, but that's one thing I do know for certain."

Max shrugged. "I think I've pretty much said everything I know."

McKenna nodded. Took a sip of coffee, which, amazingly enough, he seemed to be savoring. Taking a paper out of Jane's file, he closed the folder and laid what was obviously a newspaper account atop it, then slid it toward the edge of his desktop. "I owe you a sincere thanks for what you did for us yesterday," he said to Max. "And I'll be expecting a bill for your services." He held his hand up. "Don't say the polite thing. Just make out a bill."

Max nodded. "Happy to."

"I assume you're hoping Mrs. Prescott will change her mind about letting you visit, especially in light of yesterday."

"I don't expect she'll change her mind."

"But you hope she will."

"Of course. The governor's agreed to listen to what I have to say. That's good news." *Please God, let it be good news. . .and not false hope.*

McKenna stood up. "I'll tell the clerk to send the request upstairs. You can wait for Mrs. Prescott's answer in my outer office." He smiled. "Take the coffee with you. It's an acquired taste, but another half cup and you might find yourself liking it."

Max very much doubted that he was ever going to like stuff that, in his opinion, tasted like someone had boiled a pair of old socks in the water before making coffee. Still, he smiled, said "thank you," and reached for the coffee mug.

"One more question before you go."

"Yes, sir?"

"How long have you been in love with Jane Prescott?"

CHAPTER 11

T aking a deep breath, Mamie grasped the shining brass doorknob and gave it a twist. The minute she stepped inside the warden's first-floor office, his assistant, Mr. Conrad, smiled a greeting and stood up to rap on the door leading into Warden McKenna's private inner office. He motioned to one of the chairs lined up along the windows facing the road. "He said to knock when you arrived and to tell you he wouldn't be long." Conrad lowered his voice to add, "That doctor fellow's in there. He was waiting on the front stairs when the warden came to work this morning."

Mamie perched on the edge of a chair, paper in hand. Mr. Conrad returned his attention to the stack of paperwork on his desk. Whatever he read in the next envelope he opened made him stand up and excuse himself to take something across the hall to the clerk's office.

Mamie glanced out the window toward the warden's house just as Mrs. McKenna emerged from around the west side, watering can in hand, and began to water whatever was growing along the porch. Mamie had been too preoccupied both going and coming yesterday to take any notice of new plantings. *New plantings.*

She'd just crossed to retrieve a pencil from Mr. Conrad's desk when the warden's door opened. Mamie started. "Mr. Conrad had to take something across the hall," she said. "I was just making a note." She hastily did so on the paper she'd brought with her, as Dr. Zimmer greeted her and then asked about Vestal.

"She's a bit pale this morning," Mamie said. "But she ate a good breakfast, and the baby seems to be doing very well." She paused. "She hasn't complained of undue pain. That's a blessing."

The doctor nodded. "Glad to hear it." He glanced at Warden McKenna. "I don't know anything about how things are run, but Mrs. Jackson should be on bed rest for at least a few days. If the food is rationed out, she should have more as long as she's nursing a child. And milk. Is milk available?"

"It will be if you feel it's advisable," the warden said. He motioned for Mamie to join him in his office as he said to the doctor, "Tell Conrad I've approved your request. He can knock on my door if he has any questions."

Whether it was the impressive furnishings or the masculine aroma of cigar smoke in the office, something about the warden's office had always intimidated Mamie. She perched on one of the three oak chairs opposite his desk, feeling like a supplicant on trial. The warden surprised her when, instead of taking his place on the opposite side of the massive desk, he offered to serve coffee or water. When Mamie chose water, he took a tin mug off the coffee tray on his desk and crossed to the water cooler in the corner, then set the full mug in front of her before taking a seat. As he settled he asked, "Are you recovered from yesterday?"

"The women ate a hearty breakfast. I think they're all just as relieved as I am to have the matter of Miss Brand handled—at least for a while."

When Mamie mentioned Pearl's name, the warden nodded, even as he touched the place beneath his chin where Brand had held the sharpened piece of wood. "I imagine we all feel a sense of relief about that." He paused. "But I was actually inquiring about you, Miss Dawson. How are *you*?"

Mamie swallowed. "Embarrassed, but fine."

"Embarrassed?"

"I failed to realize the extent of the threat. That failure could have had catastrophic results."

Warden McKenna pointed to the paper in her hand. "I do hope that isn't a letter of resignation."

"Goodness, no!" Mamie faltered. "I mean—you said you wouldn't require it."

He smiled. "Not only do I not require it—I won't accept it." He took a sip of coffee, then touched the wound beneath his chin again. "I'm the one who owes an apology. I've been so taken up in other matters since arriving here, and you've been so efficient in your handling of things, that I've virtually ignored the female department. I am sorry."

"There's no need—"

"Yes," the warden interrupted her. "There is. It's a small department, but I shouldn't have ignored it. Or you. I realized just how thoroughly I have done so last night when Mrs. McKenna began asking me questions about Miss Jackson, Mrs. Prescott—and you. None of which I could answer to her satisfaction."

Oh dear. What had happened yesterday before Mamie got over to the house? "I'm so sorry," she said quickly. "I didn't imagine either of those two would cause problems."

"They didn't. In fact, their model behavior was exactly what inspired Mrs. McKenna to ask her questions—and make some interesting observations."

Mamie couldn't help wondering what Mrs. McKenna's "observations" had involved. But the warden didn't continue on that subject, and Mamie felt it best to let him guide their meeting. . .as long as she got a chance to present her plan.

The warden took a sheet of paper from atop the stack at his right and scooted it to the edge of the desk, turning it about so that Mamie could see the list of the women inmates' names. Next to each name he'd written their crime, their sentence, and their expected date of release.

"Being in charge of women prisoners is new to me. In my entire time as sheriff in Brownville, I had exactly one encounter with a woman guilty of a crime. The poor thing was clearly deranged, and my deputy brought her to the insane asylum here in Lincoln." He paused. "My wife's questions and observations pointed out my personal lack of experience. It's clear I have a lot of thinking to do. I came here hoping to make some changes for the better, but changes must be based on a sound philosophy. Hence the questions I'm about to ask." He took another sip of coffee. "What would you say is the purpose of the penal code in America?"

"Sir?" Mamie frowned.

He gestured around them. "Why are we here? To protect society, to punish, or to rehabilitate?"

Mamie thought for a moment before answering. "I suppose there'd be no argument with the idea of the first two. The high walls and the bars are clearly intended to do both."

The warden nodded. "And when I was running a jail, no one stayed long enough for me to think about the third. But here"— he pointed to the list again—"they're going to be here for a while." He took a deep breath. "Everything society believes about the 'fair sex' is challenged by the very fact that we even *need* a female department. Women aren't supposed to be criminals. Many people think the explanation for women criminals is mental unbalance. Do you agree? Did a form of insanity cause yesterday's attack? Have we given the women in the female department too much freedom?

Is a dormitory arrangement a bad idea?"

"Which of those questions do you want me to answer?"

The warden laughed. "Point taken. Start with the first one. Is Pearl Brand deranged?"

Mamie thought for a moment before saying, "You're asking me why people sin." She shrugged. "The Bible says it's in our nature. But we don't all yield to the same temptations, do we? One person cowers and goes hungry. Another breaks into a store and steals." She pointed to Vestal Jackson's name. "Each one has her own story and her own reasons for doing what she did. Maybe they're telling the truth. Maybe they're lying. I imagine some don't even know the reason behind their behavior." She swallowed. "And then there are the ones like Pearl Brand, who seem to enjoy evil."

The warden pondered that for a moment. "Are we agreed that she should remain segregated for the foreseeable future?"

Relief flooded through Mamie. "We are." She paused. "The more I question the *why* of this place, the more confused I become."

"Fair enough. We aren't going to solve the problem of evil today."

Mamie nodded. "For someone in my position, I feel the better question is: now that they have done something that has brought them here, what do we do?"

"Exactly the question at the heart of Mrs. McKenna's and my discussion last night. What do we do with them? Even the murderess is going back into society at some point. What Mrs. McKenna had to say could argue for the merits of rehabilitation—although she didn't phrase it quite that way."

His smile made Mamie wonder exactly what Mrs. McKenna's points had been—and about whom. The warden continued. "Protecting society once the legal system has determined that a wrong has been committed and must be punished is the part of my responsibility everyone seems to agree upon—at least in principle.

But that's a short-term response to the problem of crime. I wonder if we can't do more. As it applies to your department, Miss Dawson, we might ask the question: where do we want these women to be in five years—or fifteen? Can we have a positive effect on their future in society?"

Clearing her throat, Mamie unfolded the paper in her hand. "I think we should try. If we don't provide the tools for them to change, then our effectiveness in protecting society lasts only as long as we keep them here."

"For someone who has no philosophy of penology, it seems to me you've given this a great deal of thought."

"Not in the way you mean. I've prayed a lot, though."

He tilted his head. "I beg your pardon?"

"The Creator knows what's going on in their hearts and minds. I ask for His guidance." Mamie hurried on. "I expect you're wondering why the Lord didn't warn me about Pearl. The truth is, I think He did. I just didn't pay attention. I knew there was something. . .different about her. The others were afraid of her from the day she stepped onto the ward. I should have done something."

"You should have come to me."

Mamie nodded. "Yes. I suppose so."

"But that takes us back to the fact that I haven't taken time for the female department. And again, I apologize. I won't make that mistake twice. In fact, we should establish a regular meeting time. Shall we say Monday mornings at ten?"

"I'd welcome it."

The warden tapped another name on the list. "Pearl Brand's name raises the subject of the women's capacity for violence." He took a newspaper from the stack and put it next to the list. The circled headline read NEBRASKA v. MARQUIS. "What about her?"

Mamie shook her head. "I don't believe there's a drop of venom in Jane Prescott's entire body."

"Have you read that article?"

"Yes. And I stand by what I just said. She isn't dangerous. She's tended to stay to herself, but I've noticed she's quick to help where it's needed. She notices things like Ivy Cochran fumbling for her fork at a meal. Agnes Sweeney struggling with measurements when they're sewing. Things like that. She hasn't made any efforts to make friends, but she's not unfriendly."

The warden pondered that for a moment. Finally, he said, "All right. Let's leave that for now. Tell me what you've written on that piece of paper."

Mamie unfolded it. Took a deep breath. "I would like to emphasize that I am not a Pollyanna. The Bible tells us to be as gentle as doves. But it also says we are to be as wise as serpents. I try not to let my Christian concern turn me into a fool. Not everyone can be reformed. It takes desire on the part of the person to want to change."

"All right," the warden said. "Let us assume that you have some women who want to change. What then?"

It really was happening. God was opening a door. Mamie didn't hesitate to step through it. "We've already protected society by bringing them here. We're protecting them by isolating Pearl for now. As to punishment, their being here *is* the punishment. It's been months since most of them have so much as stepped outside. Their days are long and monotonous. They're separated from their families, have likely lost any friends they might have had, and you and I both know that the shadow of this place will hover over them wherever they go for the rest of their lives. You said it yourself. Society attaches many labels to women who've been incarcerated. *Deranged* is one of the kindest."

The warden nodded. "Agreed. Please, go on."

"If we agree that their being here is the punishment, then it is not our job to further punish. When Dr. Zimmer said that Vestal should have milk, you immediately agreed to it. You didn't withhold something she needs in order to punish her further. But our current arrangement does punish the women more than necessary. They need fresh air. Daily. Dr. Zimmer told me that Jane nearly fell down the stairs yesterday. It's been so long since she was out in the sun, it nearly blinded her. That's not healthy."

"Your remedy?"

"Let them take the air every day. Not on the yard—that would cause untold issues with the male convicts." She paused. "I noticed Mrs. McKenna watering flowers this morning." She turned the paper over and pointed to the scribbled drawing. "Let the women plant flowers at the entrance. It would get them outside, and it would beautify the grounds."

"What about security?"

"The guards in the towers will be able to see them. It shouldn't require any changes, other than making certain they're aware of the daily schedule." She paused. "You could have male trustees dig the beds."

"All right." The warden nodded. "Next?"

"The next items on my list are more about rehabilitation and the answer to your question about what happens when they leave. Ivy Cochran needs her vision corrected. She's illiterate, but if she could see, perhaps she could learn to read. Agnes Sweeney doesn't seem to know basic arithmetic. I could go on down the list of names, but the point is, how can we expect them to succeed once they leave here if they can't read or do sums? We have some reading materials that have been donated, and my sister Manerva has proposed midweek Bible lessons, but what good is any of it for women who can't read?"

"Point taken."

Mamie took a deep breath. "These issues aside, I think the most difficult thing for them revolves around the fact that they just don't have enough to do. I'd like to start an industry. Even two sewing machines would make it possible to produce any number of things."

"Scissors make excellent weapons."

"So do hammers and stonecutting tools, and dozens of other things the men have access to every day to keep their industries going." Mamie paused. "Not a single one of these women is guilty of a violent crime—except Jane and Pearl. You're keeping Pearl in solitary confinement, and Jane—as I said, Jane isn't a threat to anyone."

"Adam Selleck has said he thinks Agnes Sweeney bears watching."

Mamie frowned. "Agnes is brusque. And Mr. Selleck—not to speak ill of him, mind you—but he teases the ladies. Nothing out of order, but Agnes doesn't like it. I don't think she likes *him*, actually."

"We'll come back to the plans for an industry in a moment, but since Selleck's name has come up, I'd like to ask your opinion of something. He should have heard the attack on Vestal. Can you think of any reason why he didn't?"

Oh dear. The very thing she'd dreaded. Mamie hesitated.

"Have you ever seen a guard asleep in his chair when you came onto the floor in the morning?"

Mamie shook her head. "No, sir. Never. They grumble and complain about how boring the post is, but they're always waiting, eager to leave when Mr. Underhill and I come to fetch breakfast."

"Underhill." The warden murmured the name. "He's a good man."

"One of the best."

"I'm going to promote him."

Mamie smiled. "He's certainly earned it."

The warden was quiet for a moment more. Finally, he took a deep breath and said, "All right. Daily fresh air. Flower gardens at the entrance. School. A sewing industry." He paused. "That's quite a lot, but it all seems reasonable."

"It—does?"

"Don't sound so surprised. Everything you've said makes sense. Why shouldn't we try them all? I'll assign Underhill to think through the security issues, and we'll have another meeting and get things going." He reached for the newspaper article about Jane Prescott's trial as he asked, "Is there anything else on that list of yours?"

"Nothing else written down, sir, but there is something else I was hoping to discuss." Mamie's heart pounded when he nodded. "I'd like you to consider letting Vestal keep her baby."

"Impossible."

The abruptness of the answer took her aback. She swallowed. "May I ask why?"

"Because, as I told Mrs. McKenna when she raised the same idea, we aren't the Home for the Friendless where destitute mothers and children are allowed to reside together."

"Then petition the governor for a pardon for Vestal."

"And release her to. . .what?"

"I'll find her a place to stay. A position somewhere. Minnie might be able to use her in the shop." *Minnie will kill you for not talking to her first.*

The warden had just opened his mouth to reply when someone knocked on the door. When it proved to be Mrs. McKenna, Mamie tried to excuse herself, but the warden waved for her to wait, even as he bent to kiss his wife on the cheek.

Mrs. McKenna spoke to Mamie as she reached up to inspect the dark bruise at the warden's hairline. "Dr. Zimmer mentioned someone keeping an eye on my husband in regards to headaches or vision problems connected with this." When the warden winced and pulled away, she frowned. "And *do* you have a headache, you stubborn old goat?"

The warden caught her hand, then bussed her palm. "I'm fine. You can go back to watering flowers and planting okra."

She turned toward Mamie. "And did he remember to invite you to tea on Saturday?"

"He did," the warden said, "although he hadn't quite gotten around to it yet." He grinned. "You'll be pleased to know Miss Dawson has been presenting her plan for improvements in the female department. It includes flower gardening, instruction in reading and arithmetic, a sewing industry, and more. Overall, it's brilliant."

Mamie could feel herself blushing at the praise. "I don't know as I'd call it 'brilliant,' sir, but if that means you're going to approve *everything*, I'll accept the praise." She hoped he understood that Vestal's keeping her baby was part of her proposal.

Mrs. McKenna spoke up. "I'm told that my predecessor was known for her pie. I'm no pie-maker, but I'd like to think there's something meaningful I can contribute to the. . .work. If that's even the right word."

"I should probably warn you, Miss Dawson," the warden cautioned, "that once Ellen gets a bee in her bonnet about something, she has a way of taking over."

"Ian McKenna!" she scolded, then turned to Mamie. "I don't really know what I'm offering. . .except that yesterday, because of Vestal and Jane, something changed in the way I feel about this place."

CHAPTER 12

When Jane finally got word she had a visitor the day after Vestal had her baby, the dread that washed over her had very little to do with whatever had brought Max Zimmer to the penitentiary. There was half a floor of relatively empty space and a poorly lighted, narrow stairway between them and the visitors' room, and Adam Selleck had come to fetch her.

"You must have made some kind of impression on the man for him to be back out here so early today," he purred. "Way I heard it, he was waiting on the stairs when the warden came across the road this morning." He winked. "What say, princess? You granting audiences today?"

Disgusting as some of his coarse talk was, Jane had always thought Selleck harmless—until that exchange between Vestal and Agnes yesterday morning resurrected the memory of a host of unexplained sounds in the night. Jane didn't want to jump to conclusions, but she didn't want to be alone with Adam Selleck, either. Her heart began to pound. The thought that she might be able to convince Max to plead Vestal's case with the warden won out over her dread of Adam Selleck. She had to speak to Max about Vestal. And so she nodded. "I'll see him."

"All right, sweetheart." Selleck nudged J. B., the guard who'd been on duty all night, and made a crude remark about the doctor's "special interest" in the female department.

J. B. unlocked the door, and Jane stepped into the hall. It took all of her self-control not to pull away when Selleck slid a hand beneath one arm, ostensibly to "take her in hand." It was the first time she'd been touched by another human being in a long while, and it made her skin crawl. And then, as Selleck grasped her upper arm, he pressed against her breast with the back of his hand. She jerked free.

"Well how about that," he taunted. "There's fire in the old gal, after all." He reached for her again.

J. B. cleared his throat. "What say I escort the prisoner downstairs, Selleck, and you wait for Miss Dawson." He put his hand to his mouth and coughed, then tucked a finger in his shirt collar and tugged at it. "Been feeling like Job most of the morning. Thought it'd get better if I ignored it." He coughed again. "Got a fever coming on. I'd owe you if you'd spot me, so I can go over to the infirmary." He nodded at Jane. "I'll drop her on the way, get someone to mind the visiting room, and let Dawson know you're up here." Selleck relented when J. B. rubbed his forehead with the back of his hand and said something about a terrible headache.

Handing his keys over, J. B. nodded toward the stairs. "Get going," he said to Jane. He coughed again, but with every step down toward the second floor, he seemed to feel better. Just before they got to the visitors' room, Jane thanked him. J. B. nodded. And then they were at the doorway, and she was looking across the room at Max. . .and steeling herself against the kindness in those gray-green eyes. She slid quickly into the chair J. B. indicated, her hands in her lap, her fingers interlocked. J. B.—apparently feeling suddenly and completely well—went to the far end of the room and stood in a military "at ease" position, his back against the wall.

"I didn't know if you'd agree to see me," Max said in a low voice. "I'm grateful you did."

"I'm surprised the warden didn't banish you from the premises when you told him." She paused. "You have told him we know each other?"

Max nodded. "I rode out early. He wasn't very happy with the news, but I think he believes that it all just happened. Unforeseen circumstances, and all that." He glanced toward J. B, then asked about Vestal and the baby. "I just spoke with Miss Dawson, but you were with Vestal in the night. Do you think she's really doing all right?"

"She's tired, but seems amazingly well. As for the baby? Hungry." Jane allowed a smile. "We're all fairly well wrapped up in it." She hesitated. "Vestal's so terrified they're going to take the child, she won't even name her." She might as well get it over with. She blurted out the request. "Do you think you can convince the warden not to do that? Is there some reason—some medical reason—it would be a bad idea? I'm not asking you to lie. But it *was* a hard birth. Wouldn't it be better for the baby if—"

He didn't even let her finish. Simply nodded and said, "I'll do my best."

"You. . .will?"

"Of course. You're in a better position than anyone to know if Vestal's a fit mother, and obviously you think she is." He paused. "But I do have to ask—because of the stabbing. Will a baby be safe up there?"

"Vestal has done some bad things, but she's not an evil person. As for the rest of us, the baby seems to be helping us all remember a softer side of ourselves."

"But doesn't remembering make it harder?"

Jane took a deep breath. "If Vestal gets to keep the baby because of. . .you—" She broke off. "It would be nice knowing I did something like that. Something to help. But I am *not* asking you to lie."

"I'll do what I can."

Jane thanked him, and for a moment they sat in awkward silence. Finally, he said, "Don't you want to know why I came out here in the first place?"

"You're smiling, so it must be good news. Is it about Rose?" Jane's heart thumped. Had Flora changed her mind? Was she coming to visit? No. There'd be no reason for Max to know about that.

Max frowned. "Why would you think. . . ?" He studied Jane for a moment. "Haven't you been seeing Rose all along? I thought Flora promised to bring her for visits. Surely you've been getting letters."

Jane shook her head. "She decided that kind of contact would be too. . .difficult. Too confusing for a little girl." She told him about the last postcard, blinking back tears as she murmured, "I'm sure she meant well."

Max's face flushed. "You haven't had any news in four *years*?" Jane shook her head. "Why didn't you tell someone?"

"Who would I tell? Who would care?"

He jabbed his own chest with his forefinger. "Me. You could tell me. I care. In fact, I'll go to Nebraska City. I'll find out—"

"No!" She leaned forward. "Don't." She glanced at J. B. and forced herself to sit back and lower her voice. "I've had a long while to think about it, and maybe Flora was right. Maybe it is better for Rose this way." She swallowed. Forced herself to give words to the fear she'd barely let herself think, let alone talk about. "If anyone causes a stir, she could just. . .disappear. Make sure I never saw either of them again." She slid one hand, palm down, across the table toward him, beseeching. "Please. Don't do anything. Don't say anything to Flora or anyone." She sat back, tugging at the too-short sleeves on her gray waist. "When it comes right down to it, Flora's probably right." Tears gathered in her eyes. Embarrassed, she tried to brush them away. "I don't want to talk about this anymore." She changed the subject. "You'll really try to help Vestal?"

"I will." And then he changed the subject back to Jane. "I'm meeting with the governor about your case tomorrow. I'm going to present—"

"Don't. Don't say it. I don't want to know."

She might as well have slapped him. He brushed his cheek with one palm before saying, "Why in tarnation not?"

"Because I can't afford hope."

"But you're hoping to help Vestal. You're fighting for her to keep her child. Why won't you fight for yourself and Rose? I don't understand."

She took a deep breath. "I know you don't. You don't have to. But please believe me. I am fighting for myself—and for Rose—with every ounce of strength I can muster." She looked over at J. B. "I'd like to go back to the ward now, please."

Max stood up when she left, and she almost did the normal thing. She almost put her hand on his arm and thanked him for coming. All the way back to the ward she wondered. If she'd done that, if she'd stepped close. . .would he have put his arms around her? *That is a dream you had better put away.*

Back up on the third floor, Adam Selleck was still on post outside the dormitory. At sight of him, Jane folded her arms across her chest and held on tight until she was back inside the bars. Safe. For now.

—⟋⟍⟋—

As Max stood in the doorway of the visitors' room and watched Jane and the guard retreat toward the stairs, his mind raced. He could understand Jane's fear that Flora might run off, but the way she refused hope didn't make any sense. Taking a deep breath, he gave up trying to decipher Jane's thought process and focused on her request that he influence the warden to let Vestal's baby stay with its mother. Was there precedent for anything like that in any United States prison? Max had no idea. *Maybe Nebraska can take the lead.*

From what Jane had said, there wasn't any reason not to let Vestal keep her baby. At least not as long as Pearl Brand was kept in solitary. Of course the warden might have other ideas about it all. *I don't care what you feel or what you believe*, he'd said earlier. *Tell me what you know from experience.* As a doctor speaking about the matter of a woman and her newborn child, Max knew a lot from experience. Hopefully, the warden would listen. But first, Max had to convince the man to write a letter to the governor about Jane. He had to convince him that his interest was purely in seeing justice done for someone who'd been an upstanding member of the community; had never done anything wrong but marry a violent man; was a wonderful mother; and shouldn't spend ten years in prison because she'd defended herself against only God knew what. It had nothing to do with the warden's ridiculous notion that he, Max Zimmer, was in love with Jane Prescott.

When the guard at turnkey hollered at him, Max started, then went through the process of transferring from the secure side to the free side. Still, he looked back toward where he'd last seen Jane. She looked so forlorn, so thin. How he wished he could have held her in his arms for just a moment. Humans needed that kind of thing. And that was a medical fact that had nothing to do with romance.

CHAPTER 13

Ellen had just exited Ian's office to head home when Dr. Zimmer emerged from the stairwell up the hall. She called a greeting. "I hope your patients are doing well today?"

"I hear they are, although I haven't seen them." He nodded toward the office. "Actually, I was just heading in to see your husband—for the second time today—on that very subject." He cleared his throat. "I spent our first meeting this morning apologizing."

"Whatever for? You saved the day yesterday."

"Thank you, but while I was, as you say 'saving the day,' I was also neglecting to inform you or him that I was here to ask your husband to support my petition to the governor for a pardon for Jane Prescott." He paused. "But I got caught up in the emergency, and then. . .then I just didn't." He put his palm to his heart. "I sincerely apologize. I've no use for liars, and yet by not speaking up, I committed what a pastor I know calls a 'sin of omission.'"

Ellen saw nothing in the handsome man's open expression but embarrassed honesty. "And when would you have done so, Dr. Zimmer? Before kneeling to check on Vestal's condition yesterday? While you were helping her bring the baby into the world? During surgery, perhaps?" She smiled. "I'm grateful you were willing to help and grateful I had the sense to offer the house instead of forcing that poor woman to endure a wagon ride to town."

"If she'd been subjected to the jarring, I don't know what would have happened. It was hard enough on her as it was. I've lost patients who endured less."

Hearing the doctor say that sent chills up Ellen's spine. "Well then, let us thank God that things went as well as they did. I will admit I'm surprised that you would know—and champion—a female inmate."

"My practice is in Plum Creek. I knew the entire family. Owen, Jane, and Rose."

"Rose?"

"Jane's daughter."

"She has a daughter." Ellen murmured the words, trying to absorb the idea. "Where is she?"

"With Jane's sister. I've been trying to get a pardon since Jane was sentenced. The first governor refused. This one's agreed to a brief meeting on Monday. I'm hoping your husband will help me make the case that Jane is no danger to anyone and that her child—" He broke off. "I'm sorry. It's probably highly improper for me to be dragging you into this." With a nod, he headed toward Ian's office.

Ellen stopped him. "I'm afraid Ian was called away. Something about another disturbance with that woman who caused all the trouble yesterday." She paused. "I wonder if I could interest you in lunch over at the house? We can leave word with Mr. Conrad as to where you are." She smiled. "In fact, you can turn your horse into a stall in the barn. Fresh water and feed for the horse, lunch for you."

"How can I say no?"

Ellen stepped into Ian's outer office and left word. Dr. Zimmer was waiting for her at the bottom of the stairs. They crossed the road, and while the doctor fed and watered the horse, Georgia made lunch. It wasn't long before they were seated on the front porch where they could watch for Ian, savoring roast beef sandwiches and iced tea.

They chatted about the weather and the way the prairie was beginning to bloom. Ellen did everything a good hostess should before dabbing at the corner of her mouth with a lace-edged napkin and making her own confession. "I suppose I should admit that I didn't invite you to lunch merely for the sake of hospitality." She folded her napkin, pressing the crease with her fingertips as she said, "I have a medical. . .situation I'd like you to advise me about."

The doctor put his sandwich down. "Should I get my medical bag?"

Ellen laughed. "Goodness, no. Let's call it a hypothetical situation. In your medical opinion, what would be the ramifications of a mother's newborn being taken from her and placed in an orphanage? Would you think—medically speaking—a case could be made for that to be an unwise move?"

The doctor swallowed. He took a gulp of tea. "Knowing more particulars would of course be helpful, but assuming the mother is able and willing to perform her duties, I'd have to say the child would be much better off—from a medical standpoint—in the care of its mother."

Ellen looked off toward the penitentiary and murmured, "Exactly." She smiled. "And now for the real question: are you willin' to say that to my husband?"

Dr. Zimmer grinned. "Great minds run in the same channels, Mrs. McKenna. I was already going to do exactly that. When I met with Jane this morning, she was much more interested in convincing me to come up with a medical argument for Vestal's keeping the baby than she was in discussing her own situation."

"Well isn't that. . .kind of her."

"She is kind. She knows the heartache involved. Her separation from Rose is unavoidable. Vestal's might not be."

"If you don't mind my asking, how old is Rose?"

"She was eight when Jane. . .when she went to live with her aunt Flora. I just learned today that apparently the aunt's promises to bring Rose to visit haven't been kept. She's broken off all contact. Jane hasn't seen Rose in four years."

"But that's terrible!"

Dr. Zimmer nodded. "I can't imagine it. I offered to try and do something, but Jane said not to." He sighed. "It almost seems as if she resents my attempts to get her pardoned."

"Why would she?"

"She's afraid to hope. The last time I tried, I failed. She says she's found a way to handle 'what is' and I should let it be. She wants me to help Vestal if I can, but she insists I leave her situation alone."

"She doesn't seem. . .hard, if that's the right word."

"She isn't. She's a good woman who was caught in an impossible marriage to a violent man. I don't know what happened the night Owen died, because I wasn't there, but I saw the aftermath." He looked away. Shook his head. "A ten-year sentence doesn't make any sense at all. It's as if the judge expected Jane to just lie down and let that son of—" He broke off. "And again, I must apologize. I tend to get 'riled up,' as they say, in matters pertaining to Jane."

Ellen reached for his empty plate. "She is very fortunate to have a loyal friend. Now. . .can I tempt you with a piece of raisin cream pie? Georgia just took it out of the oven."

Raisin cream pie was the doctor's favorite. Excusing herself, Ellen headed toward the kitchen, cutting two pieces and sliding them onto dessert plates while Georgia rinsed the lunch dishes.

"He was already planning to speak to Ian about the baby— because Jane Prescott asked him to. Apparently they were friends— or at least acquaintances—before." Ellen paused. "It all seems so strange. Who'd expect a woman in prison to have a friend like Dr. Zimmer?"

"There's more to most people than meets the eye," Georgia said.

"Do you think I'm being foolish to get involved this way?"

"In helping a mother keep her child? I don't mean any disrespect to Mr. McKenna. He's a good man. But to my mind, the only foolishness in the whole affair is that he needs convincing."

Ellen put a fork on Dr. Zimmer's plate. Then she smiled. "Wrap up another piece, won't you? Ian just loves your raisin cream pie. It can't hurt to take a piece across the road."

Georgia chuckled. "Pie can go a long way toward getting a man to see reason."

For Mamie, Friday flew by in a wave of baby cries and coos, chores and more chores. Agnes and Susan suggested laundry facilities in the bathroom so they could wash and hang diapers to dry. Together they came up with a system, but not before more than one guard grumbled about hauling "enough water to float a battleship" up to the second floor. When Martin heard the complaints, he suggested Mamie carry the baby down to the kitchen.

"What good will that do?" Mamie groused.

"Maybe none. On the other hand, I know at least one of those cooks has a soft spot for little ones. He's been hand-feeding a litter of kittens. He'd enjoy seeing the little nubbin'."

To Mamie's amazement, when she followed Martin's suggestion and carried Vestal's baby girl down to the basement kitchen and Martin mentioned the grumbling about hauling water to keep the baby in clean diapers, the cook named Harry Butler suggested they send diapers down to him via the dumbwaiter. "I can boil 'em on that stove back in the corner. Nobody uses it for cooking now that we got the steam vats."

"Won't the staff complain?"

Butler shrugged. "And who will care if they do? Not me."

Back up on the ward, Mamie announced the possibility of instruction in arithmetic and reading and was gratified when half a dozen women said they'd welcome a chance to "do some learning." She and Jane Prescott—who seemed thrilled at the prospect of sewing more—surveyed the parlor with an eye to installing sewing machines.

Late in the afternoon, Martin and J. B. asked her to pace off the outlines of the flower beds so the trustees could get to digging. Finally, as the sun dipped below the horizon and still Mamie had not met with Martin to discuss the security measures that would be needed once the women began a sewing industry, Martin offered to forgo supper to work on it.

"I won't have you skipping meals to help me," Mamie said.

"Then let's talk over supper." When Mamie hesitated, he added, "No one has to know. I mean—I realize you wouldn't want anyone thinking—" He ducked his head. "Never mind. I was just trying to think of a way you could have a nice weekend without worrying over things. We can have our meeting at a more respectable time." Head bowed, shoulders rounded, Martin turned away. He reminded Mamie of a puppy that had learned to expect boxed ears or a swift kick.

Mamie called his name. When he looked back, she heard herself inviting him to join her for supper. "I'd suggest my apartment, but I don't think either of us wants that being noised about. The kitchen, perhaps? Do you think Mr. Butler would mind? He's already doing above and beyond."

"Mind? Harry's a good sort. He'll put out a feast."

"Then I'll meet you in the kitchen as soon as I've sent the

women's trays down the dumbwaiter and gotten them settled. Shall we say seven?"

She would have thought she'd told the man he'd just won the finest racehorse in the land. He nodded and headed on downstairs, but a joyful whistle echoed up from the stairwell. *Oh dear. What if the kitchen staff think. . . ? What if they noise it about?* Mamie realized she didn't care. When it came to gentleman friends, a woman could do worse than Martin Underhill.

—⁂—

As it turned out, it wasn't much of a meeting. Once again, Martin surprised her. He arrived in the kitchen with a folder in hand and a security plan that seemed to solve all the questions the warden could possibly pose. Harry Butler served up roast pork and sauerkraut, potatoes and biscuits, and, much to Mamie's amazement, drinkable coffee.

At the close of the meal, which they ate at one end of a long table marred with the scars of years of knives peeling and dicing, carving and cutting, Mamie took a last sip of coffee and, with a satisfied sigh, thanked Martin for putting things in order in such an efficient manner. He mumbled a response, bobbing his head and blushing. Mamie stood up to go. "If I can organize the rest of my lists with half the efficiency you've displayed this evening, I believe the warden will be duly impressed at Monday morning's meeting."

Martin, who was helping Harry by feeding one of the orphaned kittens with an eyedropper, looked up at her. "What lists are those?"

"The lists of things I'm praying the Lord will provide through donations. Sewing needles, fabric remnants—that kind of thing."

"Scissors," Martin said. "Pin cushions, too. And you'll be wanting more measuring tapes, I suppose."

Mamie nodded. "Yes. And flower seeds for the beds out front."

"You having the trustees dig in any manure?"

"I hadn't thought of that."

"I'll see to it." He grinned. "One thing we have around here is plenty of manure." He stroked the kitten's tiny head with a gnarled forefinger, then lifted it to his shoulder, laughing when it nuzzled his neck and began to purr.

"I said you need to keep that one," Harry called from where he stood at the stove, stirring a pot of boiling diapers.

Martin shook his head. "And what would I do with a kitten? Can't keep it in the dormitory, don't spend enough time in town." He smiled at Mamie. "I could help you with your other lists. If you want."

"I don't want to impose."

"On what? My getting beat at another game of cards? Adam Selleck's making fun of the way I walk? Someone hollering at me for—" He broke off. "Well, now, that was wrong. I should be counting blessings instead of rocks."

"Rocks?"

A blush crept up the man's neck. Even his Adam's apple turned red. "Oh, that's just a saying I have. There's a reason but it's not fit to tell. It means I shouldn't complain." He reached up to touch the kitten's paw. "Anyway, I don't mind helping. My penmanship isn't as nice as yours, but I could copy lists well enough. As many as you need. You don't even have to stay down here if you don't want to. I'll take care of it and bring them up in the morning. Or whenever you say."

"I'm not about to let you risk your eyesight making lists in this pathetic light." Mamie waved at the flickering lamp on the table.

"Whatever you say, Mamie." He transferred the kitten from his shoulder to one cupped palm, laughing when the tiny creature curled onto its back, one paw flailing the air in a lazy wave.

Mamie gathered up her folder of papers and plans and called out her thanks to Mr. Butler for "putting up with me."

"I'll walk you home," Martin said, and returned the kitten to the rag-lined box where three other balls of fur lay in a tangle of paws and tails. The kitten protested with a mew, but finally settled in.

And Mamie decided it was nice to have someone "walk her home."

CHAPTER 14

Mamie spent all of Friday evening after Martin "walked her home" working on her lists. She would need at least a dozen copies to share with the presidents of several Ladies Aid Societies in town. With Minnie's help, Mamie hoped to begin gathering things up within a few days. The list included much more than sewing supplies. They would need readers, arithmetic texts—and a teacher. She began to think she was asking a lot of the good Lord. But then wasn't He just the one to ask? Didn't He often supply "above and beyond all that we ask or think"? She wasn't positive, but she thought it said exactly that somewhere in the New Testament.

"Well, Lord. You said to let my requests be made known." She paused. "I've never taken You quite so literally. If I'm being foolish, please forgive me. But there it is." She sat back, as if waiting for God to read the list over her shoulder. Was it silly to ask God to supply three packages of number ten needles and eight pairs of sewing scissors? When it came to sewing machines, was it wrong to specify a brand?

At some point, she decided that after tea with Mrs. McKenna she would drive into Lincoln and speak with Dr. Zimmer—assuming he was still in town and she could find him. There had to be some medical reason why it was wrong to separate mother and child.

Martin had mentioned something about a fine horse the doctor had rented from a certain livery. The livery might know where the doctor was staying. If only she could catch up with him before he left town. She would stay at Minnie's Saturday night and distribute her lists to the ladies at church on Sunday. And then she would trust the Lord to move hearts toward a group of women most of them wanted to forget.

By Saturday morning, an overwhelmed and exhausted Mamie was sitting at the kitchen table, wondering how she would stay awake through tea with Mrs. McKenna, when she heard a key in the apartment door lock and a familiar voice calling a much-too-cheerful greeting.

"Toodle-*oo*-hoo, Mamie, it's you-know-who."

It was going to be one of *those* days. Cheerfulness personified. As Minnie swept into the apartment kitchen, Mamie groused, "Land sakes, you scared me to death."

"Is it going to be one of *those* days? I thought you'd be glad to see me. Especially after the week you've had! Shall I exit and creep back in like a mouse?" She pulled her gloves and hat off and retreated into the hall.

Minnie didn't know the half of it, but Mamie was too tired to go into it. With a sigh, she got up to get her sister a cup of tea. She filled Minnie's hand-painted china cup and added two lumps of sugar. Setting the cup across from her at the small kitchen table, she sat back down to eat but could only stare at the oatmeal in the bowl. She had no appetite.

Minnie settled opposite her. "I hope you aren't coming down with something. Isn't that always the way? A girl gets a day off, and that's the day her health goes. I'm scared to retire from the shop for fear the Grim Reaper will take note." She frowned and ducked her head, trying to force Mamie to look at her. "Hellooo. Mamie?

Anybody in there?" When Mamie still said nothing, Minnie sighed. Shook her head. "I am so glad I'm not the smart one. You're always pondering the mysteries of life. And they always seem to depress you." She jumped up and moved to the window, sipping her tea as she looked out.

"*You're* the smart one," Mamie said. "You just won't admit it." She poked at the oatmeal with her spoon. "If you doubt it, consider our paths through life. Mine led here. You have a successful business in town and no need to worry over whether or not one of the women you interact with on a daily basis is going to stab someone."

Mamie heard rather than saw Minnie set her cup and saucer on the window ledge, but shortly thereafter she felt her sister's hand on her shoulder. "Mamie Dawson. You stop that right now. *I* attach feathers and ribbon to buckram frames so that homely women can look in the mirror and pretend they look just like the fashion plate they saw in *Demorest*'s latest edition. *You* show compassion to women the world has forgotten about. Which do you think is most worthy in light of eternity? Not that a Minnie Dawson creation isn't the next best thing to heaven," she joked. With another pat, she twirled away toward the kitchen to refill her cup. "Tell me what I need to know to shepherd your lambs today. And where are you off to, by the way?"

"Tea with Mrs. McKenna. Then—"

"Tea with the warden's wife?" Minnie interrupted. "You must have made an impression through all the drama!" She slipped back into her chair. "What's she like? Is she sickly? Is that why she's been hiding away in that house?"

"Minnie!" Mamie's stern voice was all that kept her sister from going on and on. "Mrs. McKenna is lovely."

"Well, of course she is. I know that. With a husband like that? My goodness, doesn't he look good enough to—"

"Please, Minnie."

"You are *such* an old maid at times. But all right. I'll hush."

"Mrs. McKenna is. . .interesting."

"And?"

"Southern."

"And?"

"And you'll likely meet her soon enough, and then you can judge for yourself. She seems to be taking a new interest in things over here." Mamie went on to summarize her plans for the female department and the warden's approval.

Minnie patted the back of her hand. "I am so proud of you."

"Will you still think it's wonderful when I tell you I need your help?"

"What kind of help?"

Mamie held out a copy of the list she'd spent half the night making. "I need everything on that list. Will the ladies in town think I'm being. . .greedy?"

Minnie perused the list. "To ask for needles and thread?"

"Keep reading."

Minnie's smile grew as she read. "Goodness, sister. Is the moon on here?" She looked up. "I'm teasing. It isn't excessive. It's a beginning designed to change lives."

"Lives most people don't give a fig about."

"All you can do is ask. And pray. Which, if those bags under your eyes are any indication, you've been doing the better part of the night."

Mamie sighed. "The warden pointed out that sewing involves tools that make excellent weapons. I suppose everyone in town will think the same thing."

"And I suppose the men are cutting stone with their fingernails?"

Mamie chuckled in spite of herself. "Exactly." But then her mood changed. "You haven't heard the latest. You remember me telling you there was something. . .different about Pearl Brand?"

Minnie's voice was stern. "Mamie Dawson. You are not to blame for what happened, and I won't sit here and listen while you criticize my sister."

Mamie frowned. "What do you know about what happened?"

"Martin Underhill is out front with another guard overseeing the digging of flower beds. He told me all about it."

"Vestal could have died. She could have lost her baby."

Minnie slipped into the chair beside her and took her hand. "But she didn't. You acted quickly, and everything turned out just fine." She squeezed her hand. "Mamie, you're a blessing to those women, and I think they know it. Why don't you?" She took a bite of Mamie's oatmeal, made a face, and plopped the spoon back into the bowl. "No wonder you don't want breakfast. I've never understood how you can eat this stuff." She took another sip of tea. "Listen to me. I'm five minutes older than you, so show some respect for my more mature view of things. *No one blames you for anything that happened this past week.* Mr. Underhill told me how brave you were and how the warden thinks you're going to revolutionize the female department for the better, and—"

Mamie shook her head. "That man. Did he tell you the doctor told him to rest?"

"He looked fine to me. Happy, in fact." Minnie smiled. "Underneath that weathered exterior, he really is a very nice man." She grinned. "And the way he talked about *you*. I was the perfect audience for his soliloquy on my intelligent, capable sister." She plopped her teacup down onto the saucer. "Now get dressed and get out of here. It's time you got to know the warden's wife—so you can tell me all about her. Not to mention what that gorgeous house looks like on the inside. I'm assuming you were too distracted to pay much attention the other day."

Mamie didn't respond, merely got up and went to dress. She'd just buttoned her chemise when Minnie appeared in the doorway. "There's a new resident at the Home for the Friendless. A woman with an infant. Both quite healthy from what I know. Might be willing to take on another baby." She paused. "And I can see that isn't good news in the least."

Mamie shook her head. "I don't think I can stand by and let that happen, but I don't know if I'm strong enough to say I *won't* put up with it. It would mean my job, just when we're starting something that has the potential to be truly meaningful." She sat down at her dressing table and took up her brush, but instead of dealing with her hair, she sat looking at Minnie.

"I need help at the shop," Minnie said. "But it would break your heart to give this up, and we both know it. Like it or not, this is your calling." She paused. "Is the warden's mind truly made up?"

Mamie sighed. "He said he was 'making inquiries.' I don't know what that means. He also told me he doesn't have any experience with women in prison. So why doesn't he just listen to *me*?" Minnie stepped into the room. Taking the brush, she began to brush Mamie's waist-length hair. Mamie closed her eyes, reveling in her sister's loving touch.

"We'll think of something," Minnie said. "Maybe you should 'make inquiries' of your own this morning with *Mrs.* McKenna. Didn't Martin tell me she provided some lovely baby things?"

"I don't know that the warden would appreciate my going behind his back."

Minnie shrugged. "Suit yourself. It was just an idea." She twisted Mamie's hair into an elaborate chignon.

Mamie pretended to scold. "It's tea and a drive into Lincoln, Minnie, not a ball at the governor's mansion." She turned her head sideways to look in the mirror. "And how on earth do you manage things like that so easily?"

"It's the consolation prize from God for His giving all the brains to my twin." Minnie laughed, hugging Mamie from behind. "Now go forth and have a nice day. That color suits you. And you must tell me who makes your hats, Miss Dawson."

"You are incorrigible."

Minnie batted her eyes. "Aren't I just?" She snatched up the matron's keys and attached them to her belt, pausing at the door long enough to say, "You'll figure something out for Vestal and her baby. You always do."

—⁓—

It took some effort for Ellen to keep her mouth from dropping open when Miss Dawson appeared at her front door, parasol in hand. The woman Ellen thought "plain" had transformed herself into a fashion plate with an elegant updo. The hat on her head was in the latest style and a perfect complement to the beautifully tailored, pin-striped walking suit, obviously cut from very fine cloth. "My goodness, Miss Dawson, I feel positively dowdy next to you."

Miss Dawson blushed at the compliment. "The benefit of having a sister who owns a dressmaking establishment. Minnie rules my 'town wardrobe.'"

Ellen motioned her inside. "I always admire the *Manerva* display windows in Lincoln. She does have a way with color."

Miss Dawson chuckled. "She does. And the fact that I insisted on dark blue for this ensemble caused no small amount of friction between us." She smoothed her skirt with a gloved hand. "Minnie insisted that claret was just the thing. I told her I didn't want to look like a bottle of wine walking down O Street."

Ellen giggled. "Not to slight your sister, but the blue does bring out your eyes." She led the way into the parlor where a silver tea service awaited alongside a tiered tray boasting an array of elegant pastries. While Miss Dawson settled on the upholstered settee, Ellen began to pour tea. "Do you miss living in town?"

Miss Dawson shook her head. "Minnie was always the popular one. I've no patience for small talk and tea and—" She broke off. "What I meant to say was, a prison matron isn't exactly at the top of the guest list for social events."

Ellen settled back, teacup in hand. She didn't have much patience with small talk, either, but here she was engaging in it—albeit with a purpose in mind. "How long have you been matron?"

"Since the female department opened."

"Did you have experience with. . .this kind of work?"

"Goodness, no." Miss Dawson laughed. "I thought God was calling me to missionary service." She paused. "Sometimes I think my position is proof of a certain verse in the Bible."

"The one about going forth and making disciples?"

"I was thinking more along the lines of 'He who sits in the heavens laughs.'"

Ellen nearly choked on the bit of pastry in her mouth and suddenly, she and Miss Dawson were laughing together. "I know what you mean about feeling like you're the object of a celestial joke. When I was a girl dreaming about the future, I knew three things for certain." She counted off on her fingers. "I was never marrying a Yankee, never leaving Kentucky, and never moving to a farm. The next thing I knew I'd married a Yankee and moved to a farm in Missouri."

Miss Dawson grinned. "When Minnie and I were young, we were going to marry brothers and have at least six children each. And here we are. The closest Minnie has gotten to having children is the volunteer work she does at the Home for the Friendless. As for me, well, I mind adults who never learned to play well with others." She shook her head. "Sometimes I tell myself I'm not doing one bit of good."

"And yet you stay."

"Once in a while, I get a glimpse of something in one of them....I can't even explain it. I just know this is where I'm supposed to be, at least for now."

Ellen nodded. "I think I know what you mean about that glimpse of something." She took a sip of tea. "I don't mind telling you that, even though I suggested it, I was frightened when Vestal and Jane came through my door. But then, something changed. Vestal became just another woman desperate to have a healthy child. When Jane saw my quilts upstairs and said she missed making beautiful things, I realized I'd never thought about the inmates as *women*. All these weeks I've lived right across the road, and I just didn't think—" She shrugged.

"You just didn't think. . .what?"

"Well, that's it. I just didn't think." She paused. "Now it seems I can't *stop* thinking. Especially about Vestal and Jane." She set her cup and saucer down, folded her hands in her lap, and leaned forward. "Tell me what I can do to help."

Miss Dawson set her cup and saucer down as well. "I'll have a much better idea about that after I've been in Lincoln this weekend. I've an entire list of things needed to implement the programs the warden's approved. Minnie's very active in several benevolent societies in town. She's provided a list of contacts, and I'll be making calls this afternoon. She's even said I might ask to say a few words at one of the churches tomorrow morning, although the idea of standing in front of a congregation makes me shudder. I'll probably leave that to Minnie for another Sunday."

Ellen spoke before she could change her mind. "I'm an example of someone who's had her mind changed for her. What if I came with you?" She paused. "If you think it would help, that is. I don't mean to—" She shrugged. "I'm not all that fond of small talk, myself, most of the time."

Miss Dawson's smile seemed genuine. "You wouldn't have to say a word. Just your presence would suggest the warden's endorsement. It might really help. . .and I'd love having the company."

"Then it's settled. I'll have Jack hitch up my little mare—as long as you don't mind having a chauffeur?"

"Not at all," Miss Dawson said. "You can leave me in town, and when Minnie drives in tomorrow evening, I'll use her rig to return to my apartment out here."

"But then Minnie won't have her transportation in town."

Miss Dawson smiled. "I'll work it out with one of the guards to drive it back in when the shift changes. It's no problem, really."

"And so," Ellen said, "two women who don't particularly care for making small talk are about to spend an afternoon doing just that."

Miss Dawson raised a gloved hand and extended a forefinger. "But it's small talk with a purpose."

Ellen mimed meeting someone new. "Good afternoon, Mrs. Whosits. How *do* you get those peonies to bloom so profusely? Do you happen to have an extra pack of number ten needles?"

Mamie joined in. "Minnie tells me you are one of her most faithful customers. She only wishes more of her regulars had your exquisite taste. Now, we could send someone out tomorrow afternoon to get that sewing machine out of your way—you never use it, do you?"

Laughing, Ellen headed for the stairs. "Help yourself to another pastry or a cup of tea or both. I'll have Jack hitch up the rig and be ready in no time."

CHAPTER 15

Late Saturday night as Ellen turned the little roan mare named Jenny into a stall at home, she could have sworn the mare sighed with relief. "You rest easy, girl," she murmured, as she pulled the stall door closed. "Jack'll be right out and give you a nice helping of oats and some fresh water." The mare shook her head and snorted, then dropped her head and began to snuffle the fresh straw.

Making her way from the barn toward the house, Ellen paused on the back porch steps to look up at the night sky. She was tired, but it had been a wonderful day. Who would have thought the potential for friendship lay right across the road? She and Mamie had ended up having fun begging donations. They'd laughed themselves silly more than once after retreating from someone's front door to the buggy, and Ellen had almost accepted Mamie's offer to stay in town when it got later than they expected. As if they were girls.

"Jack and I were about to send out the troops."

Ellen turned to see Ian silhouetted in the kitchen doorway, Jack's mop of red hair showing just past his father's shoulder.

"I promised the horse Jack would bring her a treat," Ellen said. "But first, tell me about the fishing."

Jack ducked past Ian. "A two-pounder," he said. "We had him for supper." He rubbed his stomach. "And it was good." Planting a kiss on Ellen's cheek, he slipped past her to see to Jenny.

Ellen crossed the porch and stepped into Ian's outstretched arms. He kissed her on the top of the head. "Good to have you home. Nothing's right when you aren't here, you know." He untied the ribbons that fastened the neckline of her cape, then waited for her to hand him her gloves and bonnet, and followed her inside. "Georgia's turned in, and I hate to inform you there is not one crumb of pie left. I hope you weren't expecting a piece."

Ellen chuckled and led the way through the kitchen and up the hall toward the front of the house. "With the two of you unsupervised for an entire evening? I wouldn't be surprised if what Georgia had planned for Sabbath-day breakfast had already been consumed."

Ian hung her cape and bonnet on the hall tree by the front door, depositing her gloves on the silver tray. Following her into the parlor, he settled in his chair and asked, "Dare I ask how the day went?"

"We met with some resistance and some success. In spite of her horror of speaking in public, Mamie is going to accept an invitation to present her project to the ladies at First Presbyterian in the morning. Apparently the church has a very active Ladies Aid Society and is quite missionary-minded. The pastor's wife, Mrs. Irwin, invited her to speak." She lowered her voice. "Apparently Mrs. Irwin's brother is incarcerated out West somewhere. He doesn't communicate at all. Mrs. Irwin said she'd help us. In fact, she invited us in. She looked at Mamie's list and said she knew where we could get a nice sewing machine for very little money. She wants to donate funds for the purchase."

"Sounds like the day went well, to put it mildly."

"Oh, there's more." But just then Jack came in and wanted to talk fishing, and so for the better portion of the next hour, Ellen set aside her own day and reveled in her son's. When the men resumed their ongoing chess game, she went to her writing desk and began to jot down all the ideas and projects she and Mamie had discussed as they made the rounds in Lincoln. Finally, Jack retired, and Ian came to read over her shoulder.

"The Female Department Improvement Committee?"

"Once we get up and running, the name could change. There's only the four of us for now. Mamie, her sister, Mrs. Irwin—she said to call her Louise—and me. After Mamie sees what kind of a response she gets from the church ladies tomorrow, we'll have a better idea of how to proceed." She looked up at him. "But Mamie and Louise wanted me to be sure and ask you something right away."

"I'm listening."

"Who's going to be in charge of the budget? And how much have you set aside to get things up and running? Miss Dawson seemed to think she would be expected to solicit donations for everything. I told her I was certain that since you approved an industry for the female department, you must have had a plan for funding. So how much do we have? Because I think we can make an excellent case for *four* new sewing machines. Louise thinks that, if the women want to quilt for hire, she can supply them with plenty of work. That would create two industries. We'd charge a penny for each foot of quilting thread that goes into a piece—" She broke off and laughed. "Well, I know that look. Am I going too fast for you?"

"I haven't seen you this excited about anything since Jack said his first word." Ian tugged on a curl at the nape of her neck. "I love the way the lamplight makes your skin glow."

Ellen took a deep breath. She laid her pen down and, standing up, put her hands on his shoulders. "Tell me you love the way I organize."

He grinned. "I love the way you organize. And yes, we'll come up with a budget. I don't expect Miss Dawson to do it all on donations, but I have to consult the bookkeeper about a few things before giving you a figure. If you'd like to come to the meeting at ten o'clock on Monday morning, you're more than welcome. I'm assuming that since you're calling her 'Mamie,' you and Miss Dawson have reached an understanding, and she won't mind."

"I think we've reached more than an understanding," Ellen said. "We've started a friendship." She paused. "And I've offered to teach reading—unless you object. We thought we'd do that first thing in the morning, three days a week to start. I'll walk over as soon as Jack leaves for school. That's assuming, of course, that when Mamie presents the plan, any of the women sign up."

"Sign up?"

Ellen nodded. "We want them to take it seriously. If they commit, then they promise to attend every session and complete the required work. There will be a written agreement they have to sign. Of course at first they'll only be able to make their mark, but the premise is the same. They need to take it seriously, and if they don't abide by the rules, then they won't be allowed to attend."

"You really want to do this?"

"I want to try. It's only until there's a more qualified teacher in place. Did I mention we're going to present a paid instructor for consideration as part of next year's budget?"

Ian laughed. "You didn't, but I'm not surprised. I'm the one who warned Miss Dawson about what happens when you get a bee in your bonnet, remember?"

"There are no bees in my bonnet, Mr. McKenna." Ellen stood on tiptoe and kissed his cheek just as Jack came back inside, bade them good night, and headed up to his room. Ellen nodded toward the stairs. "I'm exhausted. Let's retire."

Ian blew out the lamps, checked the doors, and followed her up the stairs. "Fishing with Jack gave me time to think through some things—and some of Miss Dawson's plans and how they all fit into what I thought I wanted to accomplish when I took this job. I've decided something Miss Dawson said the other day is exactly right. Just being in prison is the punishment. As long as an inmate's behavior doesn't require something more, we have neither the need nor the right to punish any further than the state has already mandated."

He talked all the way up the stairs and into the darkened bedroom. When he perched on the edge of the bed, Ellen knelt and helped him pull off his boots, then went to the dresser and began to take down her hair. He talked a while longer about his newly solidified philosophy regarding his job and how Miss Dawson had made suggestions for improvements just when he was formulating his own argument for the changes he wanted to make and the future he saw for the institution. His mellow voice filled the room as he talked. Try as she would, Ellen was having trouble paying attention. She did her best to murmur just enough response to let him know she was listening.

"And I know this is all so much babble to you, but it's led me to feel like I can properly defend what I've decided."

Hairbrush in hand, Ellen turned around to face him. "About?"

He stood up and started to unbutton his shirt. "About Vestal Jackson's baby."

Ellen's heart lurched.

"Did you know Miss Dawson took the child down to the kitchen, and old Harry Butler offered to boil diapers?"

"Who's 'old Harry Butler'?"

"Friend of Martin Underhill's." Ian chuckled. "The two of them are hand-feeding an abandoned litter of kittens. With eyedroppers."

"Can we have one or two? There's evidence of mice in the pantry again."

"I'll ask. Anyway, Butler takes one look at what he calls 'the lit-tle nubbin'—referring, of course, to Vestal's baby—and between him and Underhill and Dawson they've figured a system for using the dumbwaiter as a diaper service." He chuckled. "And so it seems that everything's fallen into place."

Ellen had disrobed and slipped into bed, but she was wide awake now that the conversation had turned from philosophy and toward practical things like mousers, diapers, and babies.

Ian slipped into bed and turned to face her. He stroked her temple in a gesture she loved, raking her hair back from her face and tucking it behind one ear. "I've got an argument all prepared if I need one, and it's reasonable. I can defend my decision."

"Which is?"

"The baby stays."

Ellen gave a little cry of joy and kissed his cheek.

"I'll tell Vestal before the chapel service in the morning," Ian continued. "If she isn't strong enough to come down, Manerva Dawson can let her know."

"Tell Jane Prescott," Ellen said. "Let her carry the news."

"Why?"

"Because I think it would mean a lot to her." Ellen slid closer and, with a sigh, put her head on Ian's chest. He kissed the top of her head, and she fell instantly asleep.

—⁓—

On Monday afternoon, Max Zimmer stood on the capitol balcony overlooking Lincoln, his mind awash with conflicting emotions. He went back over his presentation to the governor on Friday, his conversation with the judge he'd just waylaid in the courthouse hallway, and the letter the warden had written. In the end, he blamed the warden's letter. It was lukewarm at best. Oh, it said that Jane Prescott had been a model prisoner. She'd caused no trouble and "didn't seem to be a danger to anyone." There had been no complaints against her for the entire time of her incarceration. But that was the best Warden McKenna could come up with. He'd fallen short of personally recommending a pardon, and when Max pressed him about it, the warden had cut him off, almost angry.

"The state is indebted to you for stepping in during an emergency and performing admirably, Dr. Zimmer, but that does not mean you can tell me how to do my job. I don't deny that you've made some interesting points, but none of those points erases the fact that a man is dead and Mrs. Prescott has owned responsibility for that death. My letter stands as written."

And so, for want of a better letter—at least that was how Max saw it—the governor had "taken things under advisement" and "would respond after he had time to review the case."

The judge Max had just talked to at the capitol building said there wasn't anything more to be done. Max should be grateful for the promise that things were under review. He should advise the inmate of the status of things and go home. He should, under no circumstances, harass the governor, and at this point any further contact would be seen as just that—harassment.

Max looked out over the growing city. Walkways stretched away from the capitol building like the spokes of a wheel. Young trees had been planted on the grounds and here and there in town, but beyond the buildings, all was treeless plains. A body of water shone to the west, glimmering silver in the gray light of a day that promised rain. Lightning flashed along the distant horizon, but the storm was still too far away for Max to hear the resulting thunder. Off to the north, the red granite walls and green mansard roof of the one building that comprised the fledgling University of Nebraska rose up out of the prairie. From his place here on the gentle rise where the capitol stood, Max could see for miles. . .yet he felt trapped.

How was he going to face Jane? She'd told him she couldn't bear false hope, but he'd been so sure that this time things would work out differently. He'd bullied his way back into her life and forced her to listen. He'd encouraged her to hope, and now what was he going to do?

Suddenly, he turned his gaze toward the east. It was only fifty miles to Nebraska City. A relatively short train ride compared to the ride back to Plum Creek. *I can still give her good news.* He might have to tell her the pardon wasn't a sure thing, but he could find Rose. If Rose was happy and healthy, that would mean a lot to Jane. If he found something else, he would fix it. If he couldn't fix it, Jane didn't need to know. At least not now. What was the name of that Nebraska City doctor he'd run into at the Medical Society meeting last year? Bowen. That was it. Dr. Aurelius Bowen.

Hurrying back to the main level and out the front door, Max made his way past the picket fence surrounding the capitol grounds, past the livery where he'd rented that fine gray gelding, and toward the hotel. He extended his stay in Lincoln indefinitely and then ran for the train to Nebraska City. Just as the train pulled out of town headed east, the skies opened. Yet Max smiled as he looked out on the sodden landscape.

CHAPTER 16

Rain poured from the sky for the entire fifty-mile trip to Nebraska City, but just as the train slowed to a stop beside the station, the clouds parted and the sun came out. Max stepped onto the siding and ducked beneath the station overhang, looking off up the street. Steam rose from the teams hitched along the thoroughfare as the wind drove the aroma of soaked animals and wet wood through the air. Grabbing his hat before it blew off, Max ducked into the station and inquired as to the location of Dr. Bowen's office.

"You feeling poorly?" the stationmaster asked.

Max shook his head. "No. I'm a colleague. I met the doctor at a Medical Society meeting last year."

The stationmaster nodded, then surprised Max by coming around the counter and leading him outside to gesture as he spoke. "Straight ahead. You see that building that juts out from the rest? Well, that's not it. But if you turn right just after that and go to the next block over, then take a left, you'll see a yellow house with a nice rose arbor. That's not it, either. But you keep going and up a ways on the left, you'll see the doc's office. On a corner. Door set under a black awning. The doctor's name's etched on the glass set in the door. Kinda fancy." The stationmaster pulled a watch out of his vest pocket. "You might want to hurry. If he isn't busy, Doc Bowen closes up around four o'clock. Usually has an early supper at the Monarch Hotel, now that the missus has passed." He squinted over his spectacles at Max. "You knew the missus passed?"

"No. I'm sorry to hear it."

"Poor woman suffered something terrible. Now it's the doc who suffers."

"Dr. Bowen's unwell?"

"Suffers from 'widower's plague.' Plagued by every single woman within twenty miles wanting a husband." He crowed with pleasure at his joke as he slapped Max on the back. "You married, Doc? No? Want to be? I can see you're thinking on it by the way you hesitate. Must have someone in mind. Well, you take it from me. Beware the women of Otoe County. They are a persistent bunch."

"I'll keep that in mind," Max said. The stationmaster retreated behind his counter, but the man's talkative nature gave Max an idea. He followed him back inside. "Does Nebraska City have a directory? You wouldn't happen to have a copy, would you? You know what I mean. It's a printed listing of—"

Before Max finished the sentence, the man had slapped what appeared to be a small pamphlet on the counter. "Population seven thousand. Five doctors but always room for one more, if that's what you're wondering."

Max nodded. "As a matter of fact, my current situation is far from ideal. I'm hoping Dr. Bowen might have some words of wisdom." While he talked, Max was flipping through the pages of the directory, trying not to be obvious as he located the name and made a mental note. *Flora Ward. 126 11th Corso.* "What's a *corso?*" Max pointed to a name on the opposite side of the open page.

The stationmaster laughed. "Yeah. Can you imagine a better way to confuse the witnesses? Corsos and streets, all in the same place."

Thunder rumbled. Max went back to the doorway. Gathering

clouds had obscured the sun. "If I don't finish my business before the last train out, what hotel—"

"The Fisk."

"But you said the doctor dines at the Monarch."

"Monarch for supper, Fisk for rooms. And neither one pays me to say that."

Max thanked the man and headed off. Halfway to the first boardwalk, his pants were spattered with mud. If boardwalks didn't extend all the way to the doctor's office, he wasn't going to make any kind of professional impression.

—⁓—

Yellow house, rose arbor, and the number *126* painted in black letters above the front porch steps. Could it be? The rain had been hard on the rosebushes climbing along the top of the picket fence, but the petals scattered all along the walkway wafted a welcoming aroma as Max made his way up the street, doing his best not to be obvious as he looked the house over. It could use a coat of paint, but otherwise it seemed fairly well tended. Ornamental railings and cornices made it almost seem like something out of a fairy tale. He was nearly past the house when the front door opened, and a girl stepped onto the porch. Max's heart thudded. She was the right age. She had something rolled up under her arm, and when she settled on the swing, she unfurled it. A patchwork quilt. She tucked it around her legs and opened a book. From inside, a woman called for Rose.

"I'm out here on the porch, Aunt Flora. It's stopped raining."

Movement in the doorway sent Max on his way. Rose might not recognize him, but Flora might. He didn't think Jane's fears about her taking the girl and disappearing were reasonable. Then again, why test those waters? Turning his collar up against the damp, he continued on down the street, relieved when Dr. Bowen's office came into view. He'd just stepped under the awning when it began to rain again. At least it was a gentle rain. The kind of rain where a good book and a porch swing could be especially inviting. He glanced back toward the yellow house, smiling at the notion that he would have some comforting news to soften the rest of what he had to tell Jane this week.

A bell attached to the back of the door announced Max's arrival in Dr. Bowen's office. The front waiting room was empty. Looking down, Max grimaced at the clods of mud dropping off his boots onto the worn, but spotless floor. The minute the doctor appeared in the doorway, Max apologized. "I'm afraid I've ruined your floor. I'm sorry."

Bowen waved the apology away. "Thought I was finished for the day." He removed his glasses, wiping them as he said, "You don't look particularly sick. Can it wait?"

"I'm not here as a patient. I'm here for advice." Max took his hat off. "Dr. Max Zimmer. We met last year."

"I remember," Bowen said with a nod. "You rather energetically defended a new treatment for compound fracture. Something developed in Germany. I told you it was unwise to so quickly replace tried methods with new-fangled ideas."

"Yes, sir, you did."

"And then you told me about some doctor's wife who'd saved a rancher's leg following the new protocol out in some county. I can't remember." He tilted his head. "And how is the West treating you these days, Dr. Zimmer?"

"Well enough." Max shrugged. "I'm contemplating a change— but I hasten to clarify that I'm not contemplating setting up a competing practice here."

"Why not? You have something against Nebraska City?" Bowen didn't wait for Max to answer. "I suppose Simon over at the station gave you his 'widower's plague' speech." The doctor produced an overcoat from what must have been a hook just the other side of the doorway and began to shrug into it. "Don't listen to him. Have you had supper? I've a regular table over at the Monarch since the missus passed. Don't want to keep them waiting. Hate cold mashed potatoes. Care to join me?" He didn't really wait for an answer, just headed out. Max put his hat back on and followed in the doctor's wake.

"The stationmaster said I should eat at the Monarch but get a room at the Fisk."

"Probably good advice," the doctor muttered. "You could also hang your hat with me if you don't mind a little dust. I've a housekeeper, but she's farsighted and refuses to wear her spectacles."

"I wouldn't want to impose."

"If it was an imposition, I wouldn't have offered."

And so it was that Max ended up seated opposite Dr. Bowen at the Monarch Hotel, savoring a plate piled high with roast beef and mashed potatoes and enough gravy to nearly float the biscuit riding atop the mess of food. Between bites, Dr. Bowen regaled Max with the merits of Nebraska City to the point that Max realized he really was thinking of moving to the eastern part of the state. "Plum Creek just doesn't feel like home. I've been there for about six years, but I don't feel settled. I don't honestly know why. They're good people—mostly."

Bowen slathered butter on a biscuit. "You got any stories about late-night visits from Doc Middleton? Clandestine surgeries performed by lamplight to remove a lawman's bullet?" He grinned. "I may be an old codger, but I like a good dime novel as well as any boy."

Max smiled and shook his head. "Sorry, no exciting stories. I've been there—oh, wait—there was one case. But by the time I got to the scene, the rancher had passed on. The whole county was up in arms over it for a while." He paused. "Violence in a family does that. Folks never forget. Especially when there's a child involved."

Bowen nodded. "Nothing worse than a tragedy that threatens a child." He took a deep breath. "Those are the cases that make the job difficult. Not all of them have unhappy endings, though."

"Now that you mention it"—Max hoped his casual manner was believable—"it seems to me there was a Nebraska City connection with the case I'm talking about. Rancher's name was Marquis? The child's aunt came to the rescue."

"You're talking about Rose Prescott," Bowen said.

"That was it." Max nodded. "The child's name was Rose."

Bowen shook his head. "Horrible tragedy for any child, losing both parents. I know the aunt. Wonderful woman. Took Rose in and has raised her as if she were her own. The poor child had nightmares for months, but she's doing fine now." Bowen smiled. "Time heals wounds, especially for the young. Rose is proof." He set his fork and knife down. "Hope you saved room for dessert. This place has the best gooseberry pie you've ever eaten."

—◊◊◊—

Aurelius Bowen was a lonely man with a thriving practice, and he seemed to take Max's appearance as a sign that he should consider taking on a partner. So Max spent Tuesday morning assisting in Bowen's office before heading back to Lincoln on the afternoon train. He was hoping to learn more about Rose, but the topic didn't resurface. From what Dr. Bowen had said, what he'd suspicioned was true. Flora Ward had guided Rose to believe her mother was dead. He wouldn't tell Jane that, at least not until she was free and they could do something about it.

As he headed for the train station to head back to Lincoln, he walked past the yellow house again. A small black dog came tearing off the porch and charged the fence like a guard dog bent on destruction. Max could barely keep from laughing at the fur ball's intensity. The only sign of human life was a young girl's voice calling an apology from an upstairs window.

"Don't pay him any mind, sir." She didn't wait for Max to respond, just scolded the dog with the improbable name of Zeus.

"Not a problem," Max called, and hurried on his way, alternately thrilled at having another tidbit of information for Jane and worried that Rose would recognize his voice or his face. Then again, if she'd been encouraged to forget her own mother, she'd have no reason to remember the man who stitched up her hand once a long, long time ago.

Mr. Simon, the stationmaster, tried to pry more information loose before Max climbed aboard the train. "Heard you spent the morning helping Doc Bowen."

Max smiled. "Thanks for the recommendations. The Monarch served up a noteworthy supper last evening."

"But you didn't stay at the Fisk."

Max paid for his ticket without answering.

"Doc Bowen answer all your questions about Nebraska City? You going to join his practice?"

"Hard to say."

"It isn't hard at all," the stationmaster said. "Not if you like a place."

"What's to dislike about Nebraska City?"

The man harrumphed. Shook his head. "Best evasive answer I've had in quite a while." He grinned. "You have yourself a nice train ride, Doc. Hope the rails bring you back our way sometime."

Max thanked the man and headed out onto the siding, looking toward Lincoln and trying to plan what he would say to Jane tomorrow. Wondering about his own future. Dreading, rather than anticipating his return to Plum Creek.

—⁓—

It was raining again that Wednesday when Max slogged back out to the penitentiary with news that was part burden, part joy. Jane would be disappointed about the way things had gone with the governor, but he could tell her about Rose, and that would help. When Underhill brought her down to the visitors' room, Max thought she looked lighter, somehow. Something in the way she held herself reminded him of the woman he'd danced with. Even when she sat down opposite him, she seemed more sure of herself. When he asked about Vestal and the baby, she smiled. A real smile.

"Warden McKenna drew me aside after the chapel service Sunday morning. Vestal didn't go. She's feeling amazingly well, but I think she was afraid to stir up anything among visitors, especially with the warden still deciding what he would do. Anyway. . ." She smiled again. "The baby stays until she's weaned."

"And that's good? That isn't very long."

"It's just long enough. Vestal will have served her sentence by then. They won't have to be separated at all." She paused. "First thing Vestal did when I gave her the news was look down and say, 'You hear that, Grace? You're staying with Mama.'" Jane nodded. "When she came in Monday morning and heard the name, Miss Dawson said the baby could be a reminder. Prison walls can't keep God out. He can rain 'grace notes' into a life whenever and wherever He chooses."

"God bless Miss Dawson," Max said. "She's obviously helping everyone see their circumstances in a different light. I can see that you feel better."

Jane shrugged. "It's not like I've discovered the secret to life. It's just something to think about. A different way of looking at things that happen. Maybe. I haven't—" She shook her head. "I haven't thought it through, but Miss Dawson does seem to have a way of insisting that hope isn't always a fool's game." She smiled. "In Vestal's case, it would seem she was right."

Seeing her smile, seeing that new light in her eyes was so good. Max delayed the subject of the pardon. "And how does everyone else feel about having baby Grace around?"

"No one's going to be completely transformed because Vestal had a baby. But things are different. God hasn't given up on the human race as long as there are babies. Grace is a reminder of that. At least that's how I think of it." She paused. "I'm just so glad Vestal doesn't have to—you know."

Max did know. And so he spoke into that silence in a way intended to fill Jane with even more hope and joy. The governor had said "not yet," but he hadn't said no. He was looking into her case. "It's good news, Jane. He didn't say no. Still, I dreaded coming back out here today."

"You didn't need to dread it. I expected a no."

He cleared his throat. "Well, I didn't. And I wanted to give you something more to go on. So I did something. . .brash." He told her about going to Nebraska City.

Something flickered in her eyes. The half smile disappeared. "I told you not to do that."

"Yes, I know. But then I realized that I'd spoken with a Nebraska City doctor at our Medical Society meeting just last year. All I did was stop in to say hello to him. We had dinner together, and in the course of the dinner. . ." He related the meeting and the result. "I didn't ask specifically. There are no red flags waving in Dr. Bowen's mind. I'm sure of it." He smiled. "I walked past the house, Jane. It's a lovely little cottage. And I saw Rose." He drew a word picture of Rose on the swing, the book in her hands, the patchwork quilt tucked about her legs. "What she's been led to believe about you is wrong. Someday she'll know the truth. But for now, I wanted you to have that mental image. She's lovely. Healthy and happy and doing well."

He'd expected the good news about Rose to cover over the bad news of the delayed pardon. He'd planned what he would say and how to say it so that it would soften the blow. Help Jane to feel better about things. Instead, as he talked, the woman across the table seemed to deflate. She closed her eyes and sat, motionless except for the rise and fall of her waist as she breathed. The woman who'd been so happy about the news concerning Vestal Jackson's baby—who'd smiled at the notion of grace notes and God—was gone. A pale replica stared back at Max.

She cleared her throat. "Are you finished?"

"I—I guess. Don't you want—?" Frowning, Max met her gaze. Something he saw kept him silent. He waited.

She took a deep breath and shifted her focus to a place just to his right, looking past him as she spoke. "My world was shattered when Thomas Prescott died. Rose was only two years old. How would I go on? But then, in time, Owen Marquis looked my way. For a while, I thought he was God's way of setting Rose and me on a new path. Proof of what Miss Dawson calls God raining 'grace notes' into a life." She gave a low, sad laugh. "Imagine. I thought Owen Marquis was a 'grace note.'" Bitterness sounded in her voice. "I was a fool, and I've paid for that mistake every single day for four years now. In spite of everything, I've hung on. Because of Rose."

Her voice wavered. "Rose gives me reason to hope." A tear trickled down one cheek. "Flora sent a postcard that first year." She recited the words. "'Rose has mourned her loss and is happy with me as her new mother. It is not wise to stir up memories of the tragic past.'"

She swiped through the air with one hand. "Just like that,

she erased me. I don't imagine it was all that difficult. I can even understand why she did it—in theory. It would be easier for Rose if I were dead. Why try to explain reality?"

She brought her hands onto the table, lacing her fingers together and then twirling a nonexistent ring around her ring finger as she continued. "At first, I thought the idea that I had been erased from my daughter's life would kill me. But it didn't. I'm still here. Still serving the sentence. Still doing the time." She looked up at him. "In Miss Dawson's terms, you might say I've held on to believing in grace notes." She took a deep breath.

"Enter the well-meaning Dr. Max Zimmer. The man I danced a dance with that fueled the hellish night that ended everything. He wants to be the knight on the white horse, vanquishing the dragon and saving the damsel in distress." She shook her head. "Never mind that the damsel has begged him to leave her in the tower. Dr. Zimmer knows a better way."

Jane leaned forward. "I asked you to leave it be, Max. I *begged* you. But you wouldn't listen. You couldn't just let it be. You had to go looking for Rose. Bring me news of her sitting on Flora's front porch, reading in the rain, cuddled beneath a patchwork quilt." Her voice wavered. She swallowed. Swiped at the tears cascading down her face.

"Did you think that would comfort me? Did you think it would be helpful to know that my child has forgotten all about me? Did you think it would cheer me to know how beautiful she is? To be reminded that someone else braids her hair and sees her school reports?" She spoke through sobs. "Did you think it would be a comfort to imagine her cuddled beneath a quilt I didn't make for her, to think of her standing with her class at the end of the school year, giving her recitation while her eyes search the crowd for *Flora*?"

Her fingers curled against her palms, and she brought two fists down on the table before her. "Do you have any idea how many ter-rified nights and endless days it took me to learn how to be in this place?" She started to say something more, but then apparently thought better of it.

Her voice was calmer, almost emotionless as she went on. "You've just set a banquet before a starving woman, describing every course in detail. I can see the luscious dessert, imagine the tart strawberries combining with the sweetness of the cake and the whipped cream in my mouth. I can smell the aroma of the roast turkey. Imagine the spices in the dressing. Taste the champagne in the crystal flute." She paused. "You've reminded me of the banquet. . .and left me starving." She sat back. Her voice held no emotion as she croaked, "I'm glad you feel better for having gone to Nebraska City. Good for you, Max. But please, if you care about me at all, stop being kind. Because you're killing me."

She didn't jump up and ask the guard to take her back upstairs. She didn't even swipe at the tears spilling down her cheeks. She just sat, weeping quietly.

Max closed his eyes. He took a deep breath. Finally, he slid his hands, palms up, across the table toward her. Beseeching. "Dear Lord in heaven. Jane. . .I didn't think. . . . I'm. . . I just didn't think. Can you ever forgive me?"

When Jane reached out, Max expected Underhill to intervene. *No contact with the prisoner.* He did move, walking to the door and, with his back to the room, leaning against the doorjamb as Jane linked fingertips with Max. He sat motionless, for fear she would jerk away.

"I forgive you," she croaked. "But please. No more." She slid her hands into his and held on. "Miss Dawson says these walls can't keep God out. I want to believe that. But all the hope I have strength for is the hope that He will get me through today." She looked up at him.

151

"Please. You have to let it be."

He nodded. When Underhill called a greeting to someone in the hall, Jane snatched her hands back. Max cleared his throat. "I've been thinking I might move, but I don't know where. Not far. Just—not Plum Creek anymore." He stood up. "I'll make sure Warden McKenna knows where to find me so you can retrieve your trunk when the time comes. It's safe. You have my word on that. If you ever need me—" He broke off. "I won't bother you again. I promise." He waited for her to look up at him, but she never did. She was still sitting at the table when he brushed past Underhill and made his way toward turnkey.

Back outside, he unhitched the gray gelding, but when he moved to mount up, the horse danced away. Max stood with the reins in his hands. When the horse stepped close again, Max leaned forward and rested his own forehead against the gray's, battling a brew of anger, regret, and something else he didn't dare name. Finally, taking a ragged breath, he mounted the horse and headed off toward town. This time, he didn't pause to look up toward the barred windows holding Jane captive.

Prison walls can't keep God out. Jane said she wanted to believe that. So did he.

CHAPTER 17

Mamie started awake when something hit her foot. It took her a moment to reorient herself. It was Wednesday night, and she'd just fallen asleep in her rocking chair. Nodded off over God's Word. Awakened to the same hitting her foot when it slid off her lap. Completely unacceptable. Both the nodding off and the losing hold of her Bible. As she bent to pick it up, someone knocked at the apartment door.

If it's all the same to You, Father, I'd appreciate being able to turn in early tonight.

Groaning, she put her Bible back on the small table at her left. Rising, she stretched, then hesitated. She'd taken her shoes off. Whoever it was knocked again. Well, they would just have to deal with her stocking feet. Maybe they wouldn't notice. "Coming," she called toward the door as she passed through the parlor, ducking quickly into the bedroom to peek in the mirror and to straighten her collar and smooth back her hair. With a last glance, she headed into the hall and opened the door to. . .Martin.

"What is it?"

"Sorry to bother you, but there's something—something important."

She didn't disguise the weary sigh. "All right." She stepped aside.

153

"If you'll just wait while I get my shoes."

"You don't need shoes." Martin's face turned red. "I mean. . .unless you. . .well, yes. I see what you mean. I suppose we should—"

"I'm not needed upstairs?"

He shook his head. "Why, no, Mamie. Not that I'm aware." He glanced behind him. Scratched his nose. "There's just something you need to know. About Jane Prescott."

Jane. Her part in Vestal's confinement seemed to have changed her for the better. And then. . .well, for the last couple of weeks it had been as if that flickering light had gone out. "What about Jane?"

"I'm the one who brought her down to see Dr. Zimmer that Wednesday. I thought maybe she'd bounce back, but she hasn't. So. . .I thought you should know more."

Mamie waved him inside. He hesitated. "I appreciate your concern for my reputation, Martin, but my feet are killing me and, frankly, I just don't have the energy to care what anyone might think at the moment. So please come in. I'll make tea and you can tell me whatever it is you think I need to know." She didn't wait for an answer, just closed the door behind him and pointed toward the kitchen on the left. Martin turned left while Mamie turned right. Retrieving a pair of knitted slippers, she pulled them on and hobbled back into the kitchen.

"You sit down and put your feet up," Martin said. "I can make tea, and you need the rest. Goodness, you've been practically galloping through the days recently. It's no wonder your feet hurt." He headed into the kitchen, then reappeared at the door, red-faced. "That was awful bossy of me, Mamie. If—"

"At the moment, Martin, I am more than willing to be bossed." She pulled an extra chair out and propped her feet up. "The teapot is on the stove. I always keep it filled with water so it's ready whenever I want it. There's several tins of tea. I like them all."

"I'm partial to Earl Grey."

"So am I. Good choice. Tea ball is—"

"In the sink. I see it. And cups on the shelf here." He appeared in the doorway again, glanced at the table, and answered his own question. "I see you've got the sugar bowl out already. Do you take cream?"

It was odd having a man in her kitchen. Having him be so efficient was even stranger. But then again, Martin was a surprising man. Organized and highly intelligent—people mistook his being quiet for low intellect. Kind and sensitive—people would expect someone who'd been treated so badly himself to be angry and hostile. And now—good in the kitchen. When he set a steaming cup of tea before her, she said, "I suppose you cook, too."

He sat down opposite her, smiling and shaking his craggy head. "Not a bit. Harry Butler and the state of Nebraska get credit for keeping old Martin Underhill alive."

"That's *Sergeant* Martin Underhill," Mamie said, smiling.

True to form, he deflected the conversation from himself and back to her. "I hope you're going to be able to slow down one of these days. I've been worried about you."

"What on earth for?"

"Like I said, you're mostly galloping through the days."

"Well, there's a great deal to be done to get things organized. Starting everything at once might not have been the wisest move, but then again, don't they say to strike while the iron's hot? I want to take every advantage of the warden's support for as long as it lasts."

"You've made a friend of Mrs. McKenna," Martin said. "I think you can count on the warden's support for the foreseeable future."

She smiled. "It was very good of the Lord to use Vestal's desperate circumstance to change Ellen's heart. Her reading instruction has so much potential to make things better for the women."

"Everything you're doing is good, Mamie. Just don't wear yourself out doing it."

"You're here about Jane."

Martin nodded. "Adam Selleck was doing his usual the other day—you know how he is. Anyway, he said something about one of the 'hens' turning into a scarecrow. Made me angry at first—you know I don't like him much—but then I noticed what he meant. Jane's awful thin." He cleared his throat. "I don't like to speak out of turn. I tell the guards all the time that when they're on post in the visitors' room, they should forget anything that was said the minute they walk out the door—unless, of course, they hear a discussion of an escape plan." He paused. "So I'm breaking my own rule just being here right now."

"You're the furthest thing from a gossip I've ever known, Martin. Please tell me whatever you think might help me understand—and help—Jane. I've thought she seemed terribly depressed, but I'll be honest. I just hoped it would go away. I've been so busy. . .but that's no excuse for ignoring a problem. She hasn't complained about being ill. What do you think the matter is?"

When Martin tried to grasp the teacup by the handle, it was clear his huge fingers weren't going to accomplish that. Instead, he palmed the entire cup as he lifted it to his crooked mouth and took a sip. "Well, of course you know the doctor told her the news about the pardon. She brushed that aside like it didn't matter one bit. But then he told her he'd gone to Nebraska City and checked up on her daughter. That's what made the change. It was like she crumbled away while he talked."

Mamie frowned. "If there's a problem with Jane's child, something should be done. Why do you suppose she hasn't talked to me about it?"

"It's not that. He had a good report. The girl's doing fine. But that woman in Nebraska City that's keeping her? She's let the girl think Jane is dead."

Mamie put her feet back on the floor. She sat up straighter. "No wonder Jane's melancholy."

"Well, that's the thing, Mamie. It seemed she already knew. She even recited a postcard she'd received."

Mamie tried and failed to remember a postcard that might have had a nasty message on it. "What did it say?"

"I can't quote it exactly. Something about Rose 'mourning her past,' and how it wasn't good to 'stir up memories' of the tragedy. And that she was happy with that other woman as her new mother."

Mamie shook her head. "I never saw that postcard." She paused. "But if Jane already knew that was going on and she expected the pardon to be turned down, why is she having such a hard time?"

"She said she'd learned to do her time, and now here he came reminding her of everything she was missing. She said it was as if she'd just arrived all over again, and that if he didn't quit talking about Rose it was going to kill her." He paused. "I hear a lot of emotional talk when I'm on post in the visitors' room. Usually I don't pay it any mind. But—" He took another sip of tea. "She mentioned you."

Mamie frowned. "Me?"

"Said that she'd been trying to believe what you said about prison walls not keeping God out." He shook his head. "But now it's like she's fading away. Just when things are getting better up on the ward in so many ways, it's like she's lost hope." He leaned forward. "We've got to do something, Mamie."

From the look on his face, it was clear Martin wasn't finished. "What aren't you telling me?"

He hesitated. "Something about the way she talked about the past, something just doesn't feel right."

"Obviously something isn't."

"No, not that. I mean the way she talked about the trial. About what happened." He swallowed. Shook his head. "Mamie, I'm not sure she did it."

"The judge was certain. So was the jury."

He shrugged. "It wasn't much of a trial. She took the blame and that was that. She checked in here ten days after Marquis died."

"You think she's protecting someone?"

"I don't know. I just—everything I've seen and heard leaves me asking questions. I do know she needs help. I don't know if she'll take it, and I'm sorry to put the burden on you, but she needs help." He glanced out the window. "It's nigh on to dark. Time I headed downstairs. Patch'll be raising a ruckus."

"Patch?"

He gave an embarrassed smile. "The cat. Crazy little thing seems to think she owns me. Won't let Harry feed her. Waits for me." When Mamie moved to get up, he waved her to sit back. "You enjoy that tea. I'll let myself out."

"Martin." Mamie called his name just as she heard the door creak as he opened it.

"Yes, Mamie?"

"Thank you for telling me about Jane."

"Yes, Mamie."

She started to tell him he was a good man, but thought better of it. "Good night, Martin."

"'Night, Mamie. You get yourself some rest, now, y'hear?"

Mamie finished her tea. Intending to go back to her rocker, she detoured into the bedroom and changed into her nightgown. Once in her nightgown, she decided she'd just lie down for a minute before going back in to finish her Bible reading and prayer time. The next thing she knew, it was dawn.

Things were changing for the better in the female department, but Jane couldn't bring herself to care. She lay awake at night replaying Max's last visit, lost in a morass of conflicting emotions she couldn't seem to sort through. He'd kept his word. He hadn't come back. She should be thankful for that, shouldn't she? Part of her felt relief, but then things got confused. As long as she could picture Max in the office in Plum Creek—and demand that he stay there—she'd rarely thought about him. Now that she didn't know where he was, she couldn't seem to stop.

Maybe thoughts of Max were just her way of avoiding thoughts of Rose. . .with a new mother, and Jane all but forgotten. Even if she managed to fall asleep, let little Grace so much as peep and Jane jolted awake, thinking about those wonderful days when Rose was a baby and Thomas was alive. Had it really happened, or was she remembering a novel she'd read—someone else's love story?

She tried to distract herself from the downward spiral. Sometimes it worked. For a while. She sat in on Mrs. McKenna's lessons just to have something to do. Helping Agnes and Susan Horst work through their lessons for the next day took up more time. Those two had taken a fierce interest in learning, as if they'd been thirsty for a very long time and just discovered the only thing that would slake that thirst. Jane was happy for them. She just couldn't seem to catch the same enthusiasm. . .for anything.

She didn't even notice she hadn't been eating much, until one morning when she went to button her skirt and it nearly slipped off her hips. Embarrassed, she looked around, hoping no one had seen. After breakfast, she took a dart or two right through the waistband as soon as Miss Dawson produced the sewing supplies. She didn't think Miss Dawson saw her do it, and she was glad. She didn't have the energy to cope with concern directed her way. There were no grace notes falling on behalf of Jane Prescott, and she didn't want anyone trying to convince her otherwise. The idea just made her tired. And then a grace note plopped down beside her—in spite of her attempts to dodge it.

It was the afternoon the guards delivered four sewing machines to be lined up in a row beneath the windows on the west side of the parlor. Mr. Underhill was supervising instead of hauling. Jane supposed that was because he was still healing from his encounter with Pearl Brand. Or maybe it was that he'd been promoted. People called him Sergeant Underhill now. Jane didn't think he liked it. Nor, she observed, did Adam Selleck, because Underhill's promotion meant he was actually in authority now, a reality that obviously galled Selleck no end.

Jane didn't take pleasure in much of anything these days, but she did like knowing that someone like Martin Underhill was in a position to control Adam Selleck's more prurient tendencies. If only Underhill would realize that Selleck's verbal assaults were just the tip of an iceberg that someone needed to shatter. But that wasn't Jane's concern. As long as Selleck didn't try anything with her. As she watched the sewing machines slide into position and noticed the way Selleck leered at Ivy Cochran, Jane realized that there was something she did still care about. If she could feel disgust for Adam Selleck, maybe there was hope for her yet.

"Mrs. Prescott?"

At the sound of Mr. Underhill's voice, Jane started.

"I'm sorry, but Miss Dawson said I should maybe talk to you about something. There's a problem up here on the third floor, and I've got a solution, but Miss Dawson doesn't want to be bothered. She said if I could get one of you ladies to take it over, she wouldn't object. Said she'd clear it with the warden." As he was babbling,

Underhill was reaching into a bag he'd carried in with him. Jane had assumed it was sewing supplies, but then the bag moved. . .and mewed. Underhill thrust his hand in. When he withdrew it, his hand encircled the midsection of a calico kitten. It hung in midair, all four legs hanging limp. When Underhill turned his other hand palm up and deposited the kitten in it, the little creature flopped onto its back. Jane could have sworn it had a smile on its face.

"Niice," Selleck called from the other side of the parlor, then feigned a *meow* and leered at Jane while he pretended to lick the back of his hand.

Underhill glowered at him. "If you're sure all those machines work," he said, "you can head back downstairs. There's no need for you to come back this way at all." Selleck left, and Underhill returned to the topic of the kitten.

"I raised her with an eyedropper, and I don't mind telling you I'm attached."

"Well, she clearly feels the same way," Jane said and ventured a pat to the furry skull. At her touch, the kitten nosed her finger and gave it a lick.

"She likes you," Underhill said. He paused. Frowned. "The thing is, Mrs. Prescott, there's a problem up here over on the empty side. I've set lots of traps, but there's still too many mice. So I told Ma—Miss Dawson—what she needs is a good mouser. And Patch here, she's little, but she's a champion at it. The thing is, if she doesn't feel welcome up here. . .you know cats. She'll take off. I can't keep her in the dormitory, and I'm not home enough, even if I wanted her. But if she's up here on third—what with me helping out up this way, I'll get to see her, and you ladies won't have to spend the winter with traps everywhere you look. She'll take care of the problem. I know she will." Without warning, he held his hand out, clearly expecting Jane to take the cat in hand.

She didn't want to tend a cat, but neither did she want to disappoint Martin Underhill. She liked the idea of his staying close by as much as possible. At least for as long as Adam Selleck worked here. So she took the cat. It sprawled across her forearm, nestled its head against her, and began to purr. She smiled in spite of herself.

"Miss Dawson says I can give her a bit of cream in the mornings just like I been doing, only I'll set it over there by the first sewing machine. That'll encourage her to feel right at home. I'll bring the box she sleeps in up when I come on post tonight, and it won't be long and there won't be a mouse in the house. I'm obliged to you, Mrs. Prescott." He reached out and, with one forefinger, stroked the white patch just above the cat's right eye. It nuzzled his finger and purred louder.

"You really think she'll stay up here?"

"She likes you. I can tell. She'll stay."

"Patch," she said. "Good name."

"There's something happens when another living soul takes an interest in you," Underhill said. "Even when it's just a cat." He smiled. "Kinda patches things up sometimes. Patch's been doing that for me since I started feeding her." He smiled at Jane. "Thank you for taking her on. If it doesn't work out, I'll think of something else. I just hate to let her go."

As promised, Mr. Underhill delivered the box he said Patch had been sleeping in later that evening. There was a spirited discussion about where that box should be placed. As it turned out, it didn't matter. Jane had just drifted off to sleep when her nose began to itch, almost as if someone had tickled it. She scratched her nose. Patch wiggled her way up beneath her chin. Jane put her back on the floor. She jumped back up onto Jane's cot. Purring.

The box was never used again. . .at least not for the cat.

CHAPTER 18

Jane grasped a clod of earth and crushed it. Closing her eyes, she bent to inhale the aroma of prairie soil, reveling in the warmth of the sun across her shoulders, the morning breeze, the sight of the beetle crawling along the underside of a blade of grass curled at the edge of what was soon to be a flower bed. She smiled over at Patch, who had scampered after the women as they left the dormitory. When Miss Dawson saw how intent the creature was on keeping up with Jane, she'd given permission to bring her outside with them. Now, the kitten sat like a sphinx, intent on something in the grass, ready to pounce. When the grasshopper she'd been stalking jumped, Patch launched a successful attack but then didn't seem to know what do with her catch.

"Isn't that just the way?" Jane said to Agnes. "She doesn't know what to do with the mice, either."

"Sure she does. She brings 'em to you."

"The least she could do is kill them first."

"She wants you to watch and be impressed." Agnes nodded at the cat mincing toward them through the tall grass, a grasshopper dangling from its mouth. "See?" She took a pinch of dirt between forefinger and thumb and took a taste. "Smells good, tastes better." When Jane shuddered, Agnes nudged her. "Don't criticize what you

163

ain't tried. Tastes like freedom." Rocking back on her heels, Agnes stared off toward Lincoln.

Jane chucked Patch under the chin, praised her hunting trophy, and went back to work without comment. Now that Agnes could read and do sums, she seemed to be thinking more and more about her release date next year. But Jane didn't want to think about freedom today. Today, she wanted to plant flowers.

It was nice to *want* to do something within reach, nice not to be the object of Miss Dawson's worried glances and Sergeant Underhill's concerned gazes. And amazing to realize how Patch's affection seemed to have helped her find her way through the dark clouds of depression. When Patch curled up next to her at night and began to purr, it made her smile. When presented with a catch, Jane supplied the expected praise. And at some point in the recent past, things had begun looking less bleak.

She glanced up at the sky and closed her eyes. Fresh air, sunshine, a purring kitten, and flowers to plant. Jane smiled as she realized she was following Miss Dawson's example. Listing *thankful*s.

She and Agnes worked together, breaking up all the earth in their section of the flower bed. Miss Dawson had divided the women into teams and assigned each team to a section. They planted bachelor buttons and zinnias, dahlias, asters, and stock.

Mrs. McKenna and Georgia were here, too. Mrs. McKenna's wide-brimmed straw hat shading her flawless skin from the sun, even as she wielded a hoe. Georgia wore a calico bonnet—as did they all—products of the new sewing industry. It occurred to Jane that if it weren't for the guard towers and the knowledge that men with rifles were up there keeping watch, they could be a group of women working on some municipal beautification project.

Jane had just bent to dig up a particularly stubborn weed when a shadow fell over the earth. She recognized the tip of the boot planted right where she was weeding. Adam Selleck had come outside under the guise of taking a smoke a few minutes ago. Jane had heard him compliment Miss Dawson on how nice things were going to look once the flower beds she'd designed were in full bloom. He'd lingered, standing just beneath the arched doorway, watching the women work, drawing on his cigarette, and blowing smoke in a lazy fashion. Now, he seemed about to crouch down beside Jane. She nearly shied away, but before she moved, Agnes grabbed her hand and, without ceremony, practically dragged her toward the other side of the stairs where Miss Dawson stood, holding baby Grace and talking to Mrs. McKenna.

"We got our seeds planted and the weeds pulled," Agnes said abruptly.

Selleck called out another compliment to Miss Dawson, then flicked his cigarette onto the stairs and stomped it out. As he ambled back up the stairs, he began to whistle. The sound sent a chill up Jane's spine.

—✺—

As the days passed and spring gave way to summer, the cocoon Jane had attempted to pull back around herself after Max's last visit opened again.

By mid-May, in addition to tutoring some of the women, she was reading aloud for an hour every evening. She suspected some of the women actually lost sleep wondering what poor Oliver would do to escape Fagin's clutches. One evening, Susan Horst surprised everyone by offering to take a turn. She did an excellent job and later pulled Jane aside. "Nobody ever thought I had the brains for letters." She paused. "I never would have tried if I wasn't stuck in here." She forced a laugh. "So. Thanks."

What Patch and reading could not do for Jane was accomplished the first part of July when Sergeant Underhill led a parade of guards bearing several bushel baskets of remnants into the parlor. As the guards set the baskets by the sewing machines, Underhill explained. "Mrs. Reverend Irwin of the First Presbyterian Church in Lincoln organized this. She gathered things up from several women's groups." He held up a stack of new Bibles. "And they wanted you each to have your own Bible."

Agnes Sweeney was not impressed. Setting the Bibles aside, she grabbed a fistful of strips from one of the baskets and growled, "What's this good for?"

Susan Horst had a more positive reaction. She reached for a Bible and ran her hand over its cover before making a suggestion. "We could tear strips and crochet them into rugs." She looked to Miss Dawson for approval. "It'd be nice to have rugs by our cots this winter."

Agnes made a face. "As if they'd let us *keep* what we make." She sounded disgusted. "How many bouquets of flowers do you expect we'll get up here when our flowers start to bloom? You've seen the gazebo the trustees are building out front. You think we'll ever be allowed to so much as step up inside it? None of it's for us. It's all to impress the visitors about what a wonderful job the new warden's doing." She dropped the fabric back into the basket. "And whatever we make outta this stuff, you can bet it won't be for us."

"Actually," Miss Dawson said, "you *can* keep a rug if you like. Or you can sell one. Or do both. The committee I told you about has developed a business plan—for anyone interested." When the room grew quiet, she continued. "Anyone who works is to be paid by the piece. We'll keep track, and when you're released, your earnings will be waiting. The idea is to give you the opportunity to earn money toward a fresh start."

"I get out in a few weeks," Susan Horst said.

Miss Dawson smiled. "We're starting slow, with an order for rag rugs for the children at the Home for the Friendless. We don't have a loom, so obviously we'll be using your idea and crocheting strips. Mrs. Irwin suggested braiding strips and sewing them together."

"How many do you have orders for?" Susan asked. "And how big are they supposed to be?"

Miss Dawson looked down at the paper in her hand and read aloud, "Forty-two personal-size rugs for bedsides. Dimensions may vary." She looked up. "The Ladies Aid Society in charge of the Home has agreed to pay fifteen cents for each one. Either crocheted or braided will most certainly do."

"We'll need crochet hooks," Ivy said. "My vision's bad, but I can crochet. I could braid, too."

And so the industry began. Jane did her share of cutting and tearing strips, but as they sorted through the bushel baskets of remnants, she asked Miss Dawson's permission to pull some of the reds and blues out, along with some browns and tans. When she told Miss Dawson why, the matron smiled and nodded. She even let Jane stay up late some nights, seated in the parlor just beside the outer door where she could hand over her scissors to the guard on post before she retired. It wasn't long before Jane had enough strips cut to make blocks for a sizable quilt top.

Over the next couple of weeks, Susan and Agnes came alongside and helped her stitch. Harry Butler in the kitchen had begun to send flour sacks their way. Laundered and cut into squares, the sacks became the foundation for the blocks Jane called courthouse steps.

When some of the other women expressed an interest in piecing quilts, too, Miss Dawson approved. Even Agnes Sweeney stopped grumbling as she noted one day that having work helped the time go by. "I thought it was only Tuesday, but here it is Friday." She paused and glanced out the window. "I'll be out of here in no time."

As Jane's patchwork began to take form, her own spirits rose. Every block began with a red square stitched to the center of the foundation piece. Next she stitched rectangles radiating out from the center square so that two sides were blue and two sides tan. She didn't tell anyone, but to her the colors had meaning. She hoped they would for Rose, too. Hoped they would remind her of the wild rose and the bachelor's buttons growing in the earth at home. Hoped Rose would remember how Jane had always told her that no matter what Pa said, flowers weren't useless. Beauty was important. God could have made an earth that would only grow food, but He didn't. He sprouted flowers in the Garden of Eden alongside everything else. He painted sunsets and hung stars in ways that inspired ancient storytellers.

Thinking back to those days when God had seemed less distant set Jane to thinking once again about Miss Dawson's insistence that prison walls weren't a barrier for the Almighty. One day when a storm blew through, Miss Dawson said something about "grace notes in the rain." Jane realized that flowers and patchwork had been grace notes for her when life was hard. She'd spent the winter after Thomas died piecing a quilt and planted flowers outside the ranch house, in spite of Owen's sneering at the wasted water to keep them alive. And here she was in prison, tending flowers and making a quilt. Maybe God hadn't forgotten her after all.

When, by the first of July, Jane's quilt top was done, she'd gained enough weight that she had to let her skirt back out. Once again, she'd learned how to do her time. She'd learned something else, too. She was stronger than she realized. Strong enough to survive and strong enough to look forward. Not too often, and not for too long at once. But still, she began to believe in a future outside the walls. A future that included Rose.

Sometimes, she even thought about Max Zimmer.

Max wasn't sure if the feeling would last, but as the door slid shut on the freight car holding his belongings, it was as if something lifted off his shoulders. He paused before climbing aboard the eastbound train and looked back toward the town just beyond the train station. His replacement was standing in the doorway of his old office. When he saw Max turn around, he saluted a farewell. Max returned the gesture and climbed aboard. And with every mile that took him farther away from Plum Creek and closer to Lincoln, he felt lighter.

Later that day, he hurried to give instructions regarding where to deliver the freight, then made his way through the station toward home. *Home.* He hadn't had a sense of home since before medical school. Maybe he'd find it here. One thing was certain, the West wasn't for him. He only hoped the place he'd bought sight unseen was as good as it sounded.

He walked the dozen blocks east to Fourteenth and turned north. As he made his way up the street, reading numbers over doorways, the red granite house drew his eye. It was better than he'd expected. A welcoming porch, enough windows to let a lot of light into the first floor where he'd create his clinic, and a private porch off the second floor where he'd be living.

Reaching in his pocket, he drew out the key that had come in the mail, pausing before unlocking the door to look over his new neighborhood. Already it felt better than Plum Creek. He just wasn't cut out for small-town living. Lincoln made him feel energized. He loved the bustling business district and the train whistles. Loved the idea of being close to the university. . .and other things, of which he would not think. At least not at the moment.

Unlocking the door, he stepped inside.

CHAPTER 19

Mamie believed in a merciful God who poured out blessings on the unsuspecting. And wasn't that a good thing? After all, Mamie thought as she drove back toward the institution after spending Sunday in Lincoln, if the Almighty measured out blessings and answered prayer only in relation to the size of her faith, not half of what had been accomplished of late would have happened.

As the administration building came into view and a yellow blossom near the entrance caught her eye, Mamie smiled. They still had a ways to grow, but the promise of what things would look like in a few weeks could not be denied. And the blossoms weren't even the most important thing. The important thing was what those flower beds meant for the women who'd planted them.

May and June had been generous in regards to temperature and rain. Being on the north side of the walls, the flower beds were sheltered somewhat, but they would still need frequent watering. In the midst of her smiling about the promise of color and blossoms and what the fresh air and exercise had meant to the women, Mamie made a mental note about watering cans. They would need a few.

The list of things needed seemed ever-present, yet that was cause for smiling today as well. Mrs. Louise Irwin was truly an angel in disguise. Not only had she taken the Female Department

Improvement Committee to heart as a personal project, but just today she'd offered to drive out to teach a midweek Bible lesson. And wasn't that an answer to a prayer Mamie hadn't even prayed yet? She'd been too preoccupied of late with the changes in regards to Minnie's role in the department.

Thanks to Lincoln's booming population growth, Manerva was enjoying a huge increase in business. That had already meant that Minnie was less able to volunteer. But now it appeared that it might not be long before she had to quit relieving Mamie on her day off. That was a real concern. But Mamie reminded herself to not be discouraged. *God will provide. Hasn't He always?* Indeed, God had continued to provide as her list of needed things grew. Just as she pulled the buggy up at the entrance and climbed down, yet another "thankful" appeared in the guise of Martin Underhill, descending the stairs to take Jenny in hand.

"Were you watching for me?" Mamie teased as she climbed down.

Martin blushed. "I was just having coffee with Harry down in the kitchen. The table's right by that window. Couldn't help but notice a buggy headed this way. You know I have an eye for a fine horse." He patted the little mare's glistening neck. "The way Jenny's two white socks flash when she trots out, you can spot her a mile away." He tied the reins off and went back to the mare's head. "Hope you had a nice Sabbath."

"I did. Mrs. Reverend Irwin has offered to teach a Bible lesson on Thursday afternoons. And it won't be long before we have another wagonload of fabric remnants and such to bring out. The Ladies Aid wants the women here to quilt the signature quilt they're making for their Thanksgiving fund-raiser, and you'll never guess who was in church this morning." She paused to take a breath. "Dr. Zimmer. He's bought a huge house not all that far from Minnie's shop, and he's going to open a practice in Lincoln. Says he's thinking Lincoln might have need for a convalescent hospital."

Martin listened and nodded. "It's good to see you smile, Mamie. I've been worried you're overdoing." He paused. "I'll see to Jenny for you. Your sister said to tell you that, if you've a mind to stop up, Jane Prescott might appreciate having a word this evening."

"What's wrong with Jane?"

"Not a thing." Martin smiled again. "It's good news, Mamie. Your lambs are fine."

On her way up to the third floor, Mamie ran into Adam Selleck, who was also headed upstairs. "Don't you look lovely," he said. "Like a fashion plate from one of the magazines in the parlor the hens like to cluck over."

"I would appreciate it, Mr. Selleck, if you would refrain from those kinds of comments about the women on the third floor."

"Why, Mamie, I don't mean anything by it."

"If you don't mean it," Mamie snapped, "then why do you persist in such talk? It isn't gentlemanly." She bustled toward the dormitory. "You wouldn't call your lady friend in Omaha a 'hen,' would you?"

Selleck cleared his throat. "Well, I don't call her anything these days. We've parted ways." He smiled at her. "I realized there's no need to travel all the way to Omaha to meet a fine Christian woman."

They were at the barred door leading into the female department when Mamie asked, "Would you mind terribly fetching a bit of cream from the kitchen so that Patch can have a treat?" When Selleck frowned, Mamie sensed him about to refuse. "I know it's beneath the duties of a guard, but Sergeant Underhill has always been so kind to do it, I suppose we are spoiled. You don't mind, do you?"

Mentioning Martin had the desired effect. Selleck gave a terse reply and headed off.

Mamie called Minnie to the door. "Martin—Sergeant

Underhill—said Jane wanted to see me. He happened to notice me driving up from town."

"Just happened to see you, eh?"

"He was having coffee with Mr. Butler down in the kitchen."

"Just happened to be at that table by the window, I expect. Nice coincidence."

Mamie ignored her. "He's watering Jenny and walking her out. She'll be ready to take you back to town any minute. You might want to get going. It'll be dark soon."

"Oh, I'm not in that big a hurry. I'd like to hear how the day in Lincoln went. And besides, I want to be here when Jane shows you her quilt."

Just then, Jane came in from the dormitory, the quilt top folded over her arms. Mamie stood back while she and Minnie unfurled it. "Oh, Jane. . .it's. . .stunning."

"Thank you." She smiled. "It's for my daughter. Someday, I'd like her to know I was thinking of her. Even here." She cleared her throat and began to fold it back up. "I think my account has enough in it for backing and batting, if someone would buy them. I can just do a knife-edge finish. Wouldn't need any binding."

"What color backing do you want?" Minnie asked. "I'll see to it."

"Blue, I think. Dark indigo, actually. When Rose was little, I used to—" She broke off. Shook her head. "Never mind. But I would like indigo, and I've at least two dollars in my account."

Minnie nodded. "That's more than enough to purchase whatever you want in the way of batting and backing. If you want fabric for binding, I'll see that you get it."

"I don't want to cause trouble. What if every woman up here wants to make a special quilt?" She glanced Mamie's way. "You've already given me first chance at the blues and reds."

"If every woman were to make a special quilt, that would just give

173

us all a winter-long quilting bee. In fact," Mamie said, "maybe I'll suggest it." She glanced about the parlor. "Ellen and I talked about quilting weeks ago, but everything else has taken up so much time, we let that part of the plan slip away. In fact, Mrs. Irwin reminded me about it just today."

Minnie walked over to the row of sewing machines. "If you turn these perpendicular to the windows and put them two and two like so"—she gestured as she spoke—"you'd have plenty of room here by the windows. All you need is the frames and some standards."

"Martin can make them," Mamie said, even as she sent a warning glance Minnie's way. *Don't you dare tease me about Martin. I'm in no mood.* She turned back to Jane. "Mrs. Irwin spoke with me today about you quilting the Ladies Aid signature quilt. Not you personally, necessarily, but—"

"I'd love to!"

"Would a penny a foot suit?"

"More than suit. It's generous."

"Then I'll let her know. We'll put your courthouse steps in the frame first, though."

Adam Selleck returned with a bowl of cream. Patch came running when he called her name, but then, when he set the bowl down, she arched her back and took a swipe at him. He swiped back, landing a blow that sent the cat flying. Swearing, he inspected the back of his hand and cursed his way through a diatribe that included the words *rabies* and *witches*.

Mamie suggested Jane retire, and Jane scurried away. Minnie picked up the bowl of cream and followed her into the dormitory, Patch padding along behind them, tail erect, head held high.

As soon as they were out of sight, Selleck sputtered an apology. "I'm sorry, Mamie, but—"

"Please call me Miss Dawson. We are coworkers, not friends."

"It pains me to hear you say so. Over a cat."

"The cat has very little to do with it." Mamie took a deep breath. "I suppose it's only fair to let you know that when I meet with Warden McKenna in the morning, I'll be requesting that Sergeant Underhill post you elsewhere from now on. I don't believe the female department is right for a man of your. . .character."

Selleck stared at her with an expression of disbelief. When she didn't budge, disbelief became very like a sneer. "And dear Martin will be more than happy to grant that wish, won't he? He's happy as can be to dance on the end of the string for his precious Mamie."

Mamie stiffened her back and lifted her chin. "That will be all, Mr. Selleck. Your services are no longer required."

"The rules require a guard to be posted overnight."

"And the rules will be observed. Just not by you."

With a glance toward the dormitory, Selleck relented. He swept his hat off his head and gave a very deep, dramatic bow, then left without another word.

Minnie returned from the ward, locking the door as she headed through the parlor. She spoke in a low voice. "You could have heard a pin drop on the ward. What was that all about?"

Mamie sighed and shook her head. "Mostly it was about me finally facing the truth."

"Well, the women gave a collective, silent cheer when you told him he was finished up here."

"Martin's probably brought Jennie back 'round, so you can head back into town. Would you tell him what I've done, and ask him to send a replacement up? I'll wait here."

Minnie left, and Mamie took the seat Adam Selleck had just vacated. A phrase from her favorite proverb came to mind. "Favour is deceitful, and beauty is vain: but a woman that feareth the LORD, she shall be praised." It struck her that the same thing could be said of a certain man she knew. And his name was not Adam Selleck.

—⁓—

On the last Sunday in July, Ellen was already downstairs in the kitchen drinking her first cup of morning coffee, when the sun peeked over the horizon in the east.

Georgia came in yawning. As she pulled her apron down off its hook by the back door, she glanced at Ellen. "Did you sleep at all?"

"Not much. Do you think I'm insane to be doin' this?"

"I think it's a Sunday, and you already go to chapel across the way. You've spent a lot of time on the ward recently, and it's really not going to be any different from what you've already known."

"Except that I'll have the keys to everything," Ellen said. "And if anything happens—"

"Nothing will happen. And if it does, you know what to do. Mr. McKenna will likely lurk in his office the entire day in case you need anything." She stirred up the fire in the stove and began to roll out the dough she'd left to rise overnight. "You know the women. They know and like you. You'll be fine. In fact, I'd go so far as to say you'll do better than fine."

Ian appeared in the doorway. "Georgia's right," he said. "You'll do better than fine. Miss Dawson has walked you through every possible scenario *including* a stabbing, and statistics prove that's not going to happen again. At least not this year." He smiled. "I expect the biggest challenge you're going to have today involves serving meals, since Underhill will be gone, too. But J. B. knows the routine. You'll be just fine. If I had any doubt, I wouldn't have hesitated to tell Miss Dawson and Underhill they just have to postpone their Sunday together in town."

Georgia smiled. "Who would have thought. Miss Dawson and Sergeant Underhill."

"Don't let Mamie hear you say that." Ellen laughed. "She's still declaring it to be a friendship. At every opportunity."

Ian bent to kiss her on the cheek. "Isn't that what we told your father that day we went to the church picnic?"

Ellen nodded. "He pretended to believe us, as I recall. We should give Mamie and Martin the same courtesy." She set her coffee mug down. "Is Jack awake?"

"He is. The usual groaning protests about the hour and wanting to sleep." He poured himself a mug of coffee. "The growls got quieter when I told him Georgia was making pecan rolls."

Ellen tried to maintain her sense of calm through breakfast, but after two bites of a roll, she knew that if she ate any more she'd be sorry. She glanced over at Ian. "Do you think Mamie was this nervous her first day?"

"I can't speak for her, but I know I was."

"You were not. You ate a huge breakfast."

"I ate it, but I didn't keep it down." He grimaced. "Now you know the real reason I hurried out the back door."

"You mean you weren't really worried that you'd left a stall door open in the barn?"

"Heavens, no. I would have sent Jack out to check on something like that." He grinned. "I was in a hurry to get to where Georgia wouldn't take my stomach's revolt personally."

He reached over and took Ellen's hand. "You're highly intelligent, you have several weeks' experience on the ward, the women like you, and Miss Dawson trusts you. Not to mention the fact that the warden himself has said you are the best candidate he's interviewed for the position."

"I'm also the only candidate you've 'interviewed.'" Ellen smiled. "And there wasn't really an interview."

"That's beside the point. If today works out, we'll have solved the problem of the other Miss Dawson's defection to the world of business. Your taking over for her will simplify everyone's lives and create the least amount of upheaval in the female department. And after the spring and summer we've had, a smooth transition is high on everyone's list of desired things."

And so it was that Ellen McKenna spent the last Sunday in July serving as the female department matron. After chapel service, the women settled in around the quilting frame that held Jane's courthouse-steps quilt. In spite of being fitted for spectacles, Ivy Cochran didn't really see well enough to quilt, so she tended Vestal's baby. Susan read aloud for a while, and as the day wore on, bits and pieces of conversation unraveled the women's pasts, one thread at a time.

Agnes Sweeney had a son buried at the Little Big Horn.

Ivy was one of eleven children who'd survived their father's death, only to be scattered "to the four winds" when their mother lost the family farm.

Susan Horst said nothing about family, but she told how a stray dog she'd taken in once "lit in to a pack of wolves circling my campfire." She offered no details as to the why of her having a campfire, but Ellen allowed as Susan was a natural-born storyteller and told her so.

Ellen's response elicited other stories, until she finally told one of her own about a spotted mare she'd admired as a child. When she described trying to ride the pony that would not be ridden, the women laughed with her. And suddenly it was time to serve the evening meal, the day was done, and she was leaving J. B. on post for the night and descending to Ian's first-floor office.

"Well?" Ian said, as they walked arm in arm across the road for home.

"Well, I don't know. I think I may have too much of a tendency to forget they're criminals. Sometimes I'm tempted to treat Jane

Prescott more like a friend than an inmate. I might not be watchful enough when it comes time for Pearl Brand to come back on the ward."

Ian covered her hand with his. "I'm not sure what to do about Brand," he said. "But I am sure I don't want you doing anything you don't want to."

"I'd like to try it out a few more times before I decide."

Ian squeezed her hand. "Then that's what I'll tell Miss Dawson at our meeting tomorrow. Unless you'd care to attend and tell her yourself."

CHAPTER 20

August and the fierce sun seemed bent on broiling Lancaster County. As Max sat on the screened porch just off his second-floor bedroom, reading the morning paper, he read that grass fires had consumed a huge portion of the northern half of the county. He laid the paper aside and stood up, stretching and yawning before retreating into the house to shave. He'd spent the last few weeks in Lincoln visiting various churches, and today he was ready to commit. It had taken a while, but then everything seemed to be moving slower these dog days of summer, and his fledgling practice was no exception.

The four-cot infirmary he'd set up in the back bedroom of the first floor remained empty. It was just as well. In this heat it would be an unremitting challenge to try to cool the room down so the heat didn't add to a patient's suffering. As it was, Max had taken to sleeping out here on the porch, bent on catching any errant breeze that might happen to disturb the sticky, still nights. He'd expected it would be a while before his practice took off. After all, he'd hung a sign out without having so much as one connection with any of the other physicians in Lincoln. A Medical Society meeting couldn't happen soon enough. He needed some referrals.

The front doorbell rang. Taking a last swipe with his straight razor, he hurried into a fresh shirt and trotted down the stairs, smiling when the unexpected visitor proved to be none other than Dr. Aurelius Bowen.

"So this is where the mighty have landed," Bowen said and stepped inside. Shoving his hands in his pockets, he peered into the parlor-turned-waiting-room to the right of the front door, then invited himself up the hall, past the dining-room-turned-examining-room and then into the kitchen, where he stood peering into the empty infirmary.

"Well?" Max asked. "What do you think?"

Bowen shrugged. "I think I need a cup of coffee and you need some patients."

"You drink coffee when it's this hot?"

"Young man, I'd want coffee if we were standing in Hades." Bowen scowled. "However, I can see by the fresh shave and the clean shirt that you are one of those Sabbath-observing physicians, and I've interrupted your preparations for church. So I'll see myself out. Care to have lunch? I'm at the Lindell."

"I'd love to have lunch, but unless you've already checked into the hotel, why not stay here?"

Bowen responded by retreating to the front door, stepping out onto the porch, and returning, bag in hand. "That's what I was hoping you'd say." He grinned. "But I'll still buy you lunch. Meet me over at Dinah's on North Eleventh. You do know about Dinah's, I trust?" When Max shook his head, Bowen tsked him loudly. "Young man, you need some lessons in how to ferret out good cooking. Unless, of course, you've already succumbed to that disease I mentioned when last we talked."

Max laughed. "No, sir. In fact, if you're referring to 'widower's plague,' I'm not a widower, so I'm likely immune."

Bowen squinted up at him. "You joined a church yet?"

"Actually, I'm making that commitment today."

"Well then, prepare to suffer the associated strain of the virus—bachelor's misery."

"Misery?"

"No self-respecting maiden believes that a bachelor is anything but miserable, my boy. And in your case, I predict a number of them will be eager to offer a cure." He set his bag on the stairs and headed toward the back of the house. "I'll help myself to coffee and noodle about while you're gone. I have some ideas of how to get you set up as the best and brightest physician in town. We'll talk over lunch."

—✕—

Max settled into a pew at the First Presbyterian Church and reached up to straighten his tie. He ran his palm along his jaw, just to be sure. No, he hadn't left any lingering evidence of his morning shave. Why then, had those people across the aisle given him that look? It happened again a moment later. Someone came up the aisle, paused at his pew, gave him an odd look, and settled in front of him without so much as a word. He brushed his lapels and, once again, straightened his tie. Finally, he pulled a hymnal out of the pew rack and pretended to concentrate on the lyrics.

Was it his imagination, or was something boring into the back of his head? He rubbed across the back of his neck, then glanced behind him just in time to see a young woman seated next to an older woman—must be her grandmother—look away. He thought her cheeks pinked a bit, but that was probably more his imagination than anything. Still he smiled to himself. Bachelor's misery, indeed.

The organ music began, and slowly, the pews all around Max filled. Except for his. Not one person sat in his pew. He continued to study the hymnal. Finally, someone cleared their throat. Loudly. Max looked askance toward the aisle and saw the hem of a black silk skirt and a black parasol, the latter planted inches from his left foot.

"Are you going to sit there?" a voice boomed.

He looked up. The prune-faced dowager was talking to him. He rose to his feet. Bowed. "How do you do, ma'am. I'm Dr.— "

"I said are you going to sit there?"

Max glanced behind him at the pew. Across the aisle at the people who'd given him the strange look. He couldn't be certain, but he thought the gray-haired gentleman who glanced his way shook his head, almost imperceptibly. Once again, Max glanced at the pew. "Please," he said, backing away and gesturing toward the place he'd just vacated. "Be my guest."

The dowager harrumphed. "Guest? Be *your* guest?" She followed him into the pew. "And how would that be possible, seeing as how it is *my* family name on the brass plate at the end of this pew and *my* family who helped found this church in 1869 and my *own husband* who commissioned the stained glass above the pulpit?" She sat down, muttering, "Your guest, indeed."

Max offered a profuse apology, which the woman barely acknowledged. She put the hymnal he'd left open on the pew back in the rack. Lifting her chin, she rested both gloved hands atop her parasol handle and glared toward the choir loft. This was clearly not a woman to offend, even unintentionally.

As it happened, Max didn't need the flowery apology he spent half the morning planning to offer as soon as the service ended. After the closing prayer, Reverend Irwin raised his voice to get everyone's attention and, as the crowd quieted, smiled in Max's direction. "I have the pleasure this morning of introducing our newest member, Dr. Max Zimmer. He did not know that I was going to do this, and I apologize for putting him on the spot, but a venerated member of the Nebraska Medical Society stopped by my office just before the service. He wanted me to know some things about Dr. Zimmer that, he said, the good doctor would likely be too humble to share about himself. Things that are reason to celebrate his decision to settle in our fair city." He nodded Max's way.

"Dr. Zimmer has studied with some of the more preeminent physicians of our day. He took a detour of a few years between his time in Paris, France, and Lincoln, but he's seen the error of his ways, and we are honored that he's chosen to fellowship with us." The reverend paused. "Welcome, Dr. Zimmer. May the Lord bless your endeavors, and may you find rich fellowship with us here at First Presbyterian." He looked out over his congregation. "Please, let us make our brother welcome."

Before more than a few minutes had passed, Max's hand ached from all the greetings. The pastor's wife talked him into purchasing the privilege of signing the quilt the Ladies Aid would be auctioning off at the Thanksgiving fair, and solicited a promise that Max would attend—and bid. He was on his way out of the building when the dowager whose pew he'd invaded stepped into his path.

"Paris, you say?"

"Ma'am?"

"Richard said you studied in Paris?" Max nodded. Now he knew the reverend's first name. "Shall we say Wednesday next, then?"

"I beg your pardon?"

The wrinkles around her mouth deepened. "I do you hope you aren't losing your hearing at this young age, sir. I wish privacy in a medical matter. Hence, I will come to you rather than summoning you to the house. Shall we say ten in the morning?"

Max nodded. "That would be fine, Mrs.—?" He suppressed a smile. "I'm sorry, but I didn't read the brass plate on the pew." He wasn't certain, but he thought a bit of humor flickered for just a second in the old woman's pale eyes.

"You really must, Dr. Zimmer. It behooves a professional man such as yourself to understand the lay of the land." With that, she departed, leaving Max to laugh quietly as he made his way back up the aisle to read the brass plate: *Monsieur le Juge Gérard Savoie*. And on a separate line below the man's name, he read: *Madame Eugénie Savoie*.

He'd better practice his French before Wednesday.

—⚹—

For the women in the female department, August meant still air, fierce sun, clothing drenched with sweat, and no way to find relief other than to wait it out. September would come, cool breezes would flow, but in the meantime—in the meantime folks were miserable. And being miserable reminded everyone, Jane included, of what had been wrong in the past and what was wrong now with their lives.

The guards grew short-tempered, and the inmates lost their appetite. Nights offered no relief. It was too hot to sleep much of the time. Even Patch was out of sorts, eschewing Jane's cot for the bare stone floor. The women slogged through each day, not exactly sullen, but with little to say and little enthusiasm for their work. They did it, but there was little to no small talk, and when there was, it was usually about the heat.

"Never remember it being this bad," Vestal said over breakfast.

"I remember a summer that was worse," Agnes offered.

Susan glared at her. "You always think you've experienced the worst of everything."

"No, I don't."

"Yes, you do," Susan sighed. "But it's not worth fighting over. It's too hot. Hush, and eat."

"Do we have to go to chapel today, Mrs. McKenna? It's hotter than Hades in that little box they call a church."

"I'm sorry, but it's required. And the folks have come out from

Lincoln to conduct it. The pastor's prepared a lesson. We owe it to him to listen."

Jane barely suppressed a smile when Agnes said, "Well, tell that preacher to keep it short."

Mrs. McKenna laughed. "Do you really think telling a preacher to keep it short will have any effect at all?"

Agnes shrugged. "Never mind, then. Don't say anything. But if they haven't replaced those torn fans—"

"If they haven't, I'll distribute the songbooks early. You can use those for fans."

"I'll praise God for that," Agnes quipped and got in line to file down to the second floor, with Jane leading the way and Mrs. McKenna bringing up the rear, so that she could lock the doors behind them.

As Jane reached the top of the stairs, she glanced back toward the dormitory, expecting Patch to be wending her way along the line. Patch usually attended chapel with them, but apparently she was staying behind today. Jane couldn't blame the cat. No one wanted to move in this heat.

—⁓—

Ellen sighed with relief when the preacher promised a short sermon as part of his introductory remarks. She nodded when Agnes looked her way, then began to distribute the new church fans the preacher's wife had brought with her. In no time, the hot air in the chapel was moving. Ellen didn't think it improved things a bit. Her waist clung to her back, and it was only midmorning. She could almost feel her hair frizzing up in the humidity, envision the red fringe curling at her hairline.

The preacher pounded the pulpit, and Ellen jumped. Seated next to her on the pew just behind the women, Jack began to shake with laughter. Ellen nudged him and scowled when he looked her way. He sobered up, but not before rolling his eyes and wiping his brow. Ian sat beside them, alert and seemingly unaffected by the heat. Ellen would never understand how the man remained impervious to the weather. Cold didn't bother him, either. Her mind wandered back to winter and stayed there, as she tried to think her way out of being miserable.

Finally, the congregation stood. Thankfully, the preacher required only two verses of the closing hymn before praying and letting them go. The ladies had filed out of the chapel after a guard, and Ian and Jack had descended to turnkey, when the preacher's wife way-laid Ellen.

"I'm sorry to bother you, but I've misplaced a treasured bit of jewelry. I know we aren't supposed to wear valuables, but I thought—well—I just forgot to take it off." She reached up to touch her collar. "It was secreted away. No one could have known. But it's not there, and I wonder if. . .I wonder if you might take measures. I don't know the protocol, of course, but—" She looked after the line of women headed for the stairs.

It took a moment for Ellen to realize the woman was suggesting that she'd been robbed. "Did you have any physical contact with any of the inmates today? Shake their hand? Pat anyone on a shoulder?"

"Of course not," the woman said, clearly horrified by the idea.

"And you say the necklace was tucked inside your collar? Could it have fallen off on the way out from Lincoln?"

"I'm certain not. In fact, that's how I realized I had it on. As we came inside, I reached up—it's a nervous habit, really—but I felt it. I knew I should have taken it off, but we were late, and my husband—I just didn't want to make trouble."

But now you're willing to make plenty of trouble for me. Ellen paused. "I have to see to my charges at the moment. There's lunch to

187

be served. But I'll be back down as soon as possible. If you'd like to wait, we can search together. Or you can speak to my husband the warden about it."

The woman backed away. "Oh, no. I wouldn't want—Reverend Klein doesn't like it when I keep him waiting. I just thought I'd mention it to you. You being a woman and all, I figured you'd understand." Her watery eyes filled with tears. "It's a tiny thing. Just a locket. Of no real monetary value. Except it holds a picture of my little girl. Just before she died." The woman swallowed. "I'd only want the picture. I don't care so much about the locket."

Ellen's heart softened toward the little woman who seemed almost afraid of her husband. She patted the woman's thin arm. "I'll tell you what I'll do. When I can get away this afternoon, I'll come back down and make a thorough search. If your locket is in this room, I'll find it. And I'll let our sergeant know of your loss as well. He's a good and honest man, and if he or any of his staff find it, he'll see that it's returned."

The preacher's wife nodded, stuttered her thanks, and hurried after her husband, who had already groused about their being late to get back to town more than once. Ellen headed up the stairs toward the ward, alternately shaking her head and counting her blessings. What a trial to be married to such a man. What a blessing to have Ian.

—⁂—

It was late Sunday before Ellen had opportunity to return to the chapel and keep her promise to the preacher's wife. One thing after another throughout the hot afternoon made her hesitate to leave the ward, and by the time she had a chance, the shadow of the cellblock wall was lengthening along the dry grass as the sun began to set. Frustrated by how difficult her search was going to be in the half-light of evening, she asked Jane to help her.

"I know you didn't officially accept trustee, but you're the closest thing I've got." She told Jane about the little preacher's wife and her fear of her husband and the locket with the baby's picture. Of course Jane said she'd help.

As the two women pushed the dinner cart out into the hall, and Ellen closed and locked the door behind them, Sergeant Underhill arrived to take up the night post. "I thought the reason people liked promotions was so they didn't have to draw duties like this one," Ellen said, as she and Jane put the dirty dishes from supper into the dumbwaiter and lowered it toward the basement kitchen.

Underhill shrugged. "On the other hand, sometimes a promotion allows a man to draw the duty he *wants*." He smiled. "Mamie'll be along directly. You know how she is. She's always got to check on things before she turns in. You got anything to report?"

Ellen told him about the lost locket. "Jane and I are going downstairs to look for it. Other than that, the only report is heat, heat, and more heat."

Underhill frowned. "That preacher's wife should know she's not supposed to wear things like that onto the secure side."

"She apologized up and down. I told her I'd report it to our 'kind and honest sergeant,' but I also promised to have a look." Ellen paused. "We can't have the community thinking we're impervious to their concerns. And besides, I noticed this morning the place needs straightening. The cool of the evening is a better time for that."

"Just don't either of you have a heat stroke in the cool of this evening. You do know, Mrs. McKenna, that I can have some of the male trustees clean whenever you want it done?"

Ellen nodded. "I know." She glanced at Jane, then back at him. "No offense, but I just think a woman might make a more thorough search for this particular item. We'll be back up directly." Halfway down the stairs, they met Mamie on the way up. "Your favorite guard's on post, and all is well," Ellen said. Mamie thanked her and hurried past without asking what they were doing headed down to second floor. Ellen glanced at Jane and shook her head. "Not much for chitchat tonight, is she?"

Jane smiled. "Not with the sergeant waiting."

Together, the women descended the stairs and headed toward the chapel. "I don't know how we'll find a thing in this light."

"I could get a broom," Jane suggested. "You sweep beneath the pews, and I'll see what you bring out. At least we won't have to crawl around on our hands and knees."

Ellen nodded. "That's a very good idea. You go back up and have the sergeant let you into the storage side to get a broom and a dustpan. I'll go on in and get to stacking hymnals and see what I can find." When Jane hesitated, Ellen smiled. "It's all right. It's the kind of thing trustees do all the time. You're not going to get into any kind of trouble." With a promise to hurry, Jane headed back upstairs after a broom.

The still air inside the chapel hung heavy with the smell of stale sweat. Grimacing as she took a deep breath, Ellen headed to the front of the room, trying to remember where the preacher's wife had been sitting during the service. Reaching through the bars, she opened a couple of windows, then headed for the front pew. Something rustled near the pulpit. Thinking *rat*, she grabbed a hymnal and whirled around.

"Well, well, look who we've got here."

Ellen didn't need to have seen Pearl Brand to know who this was. She opened her mouth to scream, but Brand was too quick, grabbing her around her waist and clamping a hand over her mouth.

When Ellen struggled, Brand flashed something before her eyes. "You see that? Took me most of the day to sharpen one of those new church fan handles. Back and forth, back and forth, across the mortar over there under the window you just opened. See that shiny spot? That's where I done it." Her voice lowered as she menaced, "Last time it was your husband I nearly stuck. Don't think I won't stick you." She began to drag Ellen down the aisle toward. . .where?

Just as they got to the door, it opened to Jane—broom in hand. Brand squeezed tighter as she spoke to Jane. "Say one word and you'll need a lot more than a broom to clean up what I'll do."

CHAPTER 21

When Pearl told her to set the broom down and head back up the aisle, Jane obeyed, but as she walked, she scanned the room, desperate to find something. Anything.

"Sit down on the front pew," Brand said.

Jane obeyed.

"I'm going to let go of you," Pearl said to Mrs. McKenna. "But you make one sound, and I won't be quite so nice as I am right now. If you understand, grunt."

Mrs. McKenna grunted, and Pearl slammed her down onto the pew. Jane didn't really know who moved first, but suddenly they clasped hands.

"Now, ain't that sweet?" Pearl stood back, then moved to separate them, practically ripping Jane's waist as she grabbed her by the collar and hauled her to the far end of the pew.

Mrs. McKenna didn't wait to be grabbed. She scooted in the opposite direction. "Now, that's what I like," Pearl said. "Cooperation." She waved the sharpened stick at Jane. "Tell me what you're doing here."

"Cleaning. Cleaning and looking for a locket. Preacher's wife said she lost it earlier today."

Mrs. McKenna spoke up. "She doesn't care about the locket so

192

much as the photograph inside. Her child. . .just before she died."

"That is so sad," Pearl said, and wiped an imaginary tear off her face, even as she reached into a pocket and withdrew the locket. "Bet it looks just like this." She put it away. "Too bad about the kid. Life's hard." She shook her head in mock sympathy, then glanced from Jane to Mrs. McKenna and back again. "So if you two are cleaning the chapel, I've got a while to figure out what to do. You weren't part of the plan, you know."

"What plan would that be?"

Mrs. McKenna sounded almost belligerent. Jane glanced her way, trying to signal a warning. Pearl noticed. "Now, Janey, it's all right. The warden's wife wants to know the plan." She glanced back at Mrs. McKenna. "The plan it's taken me weeks to cultivate. The plan that started with stabbing a poor pregnant girl, so I could get off that cursed ward into the hole where a girl has a chance to do something without being watched every second." She smiled at them both. "When this is done, be certain you thank Miss Dawson for me. I've been waiting a long while for her to banish Adam Selleck to my wing."

"Adam Selleck is helping you escape?" Mrs. McKenna blurted the question out.

"Where do you think I got a uniform?"

"But why—why would he do such a thing?"

"Because of *love*, Mrs. McKenna." She snorted. "And believe me, he's received much more than he's given." Pearl looked back at Jane. "You should thank me, y'know. Because of me, Adam hasn't been bothering any of *you*." She looked back at Mrs. McKenna. "He was going to walk me out at shift change. Just my lover and 'the new guy' and me going through turnkey. And then, just Adam and me, heading west by the light of the moon. Now ain't that romantic?" She paused. "Imagine what he'll think when he comes to get me and I've got company."

"You can still get away," Jane said. "Tie us up. Gag us."

Pearl nodded. "Good advice. Except for the fact that people are going to come looking for you long before shift change." She sighed dramatically. "So what we have here is a conundrum of the first order." She spit on the floor and wiped her mouth with the back of her hand. "I don't really have the energy to kill either one of you in this heat, but here you are in the way of my freedom. Truth be told, I've had a belly full of your goody-two-shoes ways, and if either of you causes me any trouble, spilling your blood in this here holy place won't make me lose a minute's sleep." She wiped the sweat off her upper lip. Shook her head. "What to do. . .what to do. . ."

—⁂—

Ian stepped out on the front porch and looked across the road. It wasn't all that unusual for Ellen to be this late. Miss Dawson sometimes brought some special delicacy back with her from Lincoln, and the two of them shared it over tea before Ellen came home on Sunday nights. Still, something about tonight felt different. Then again, the heat had everyone on edge. Jack had taken to sleeping on the back porch, and Georgia—well, Ian wasn't supposed to have noticed, but Georgia only had one row of lace showing beneath her skirts these days, which meant the woman who'd been so horrified at Ian's suggestion that one less petticoat would be cooler had actually taken his advice.

He opened the screen door and went out to sit on the steps, sipping some water and listening to the coyotes yip. A rustle in the grass not far off caught his attention. There was a flash of white, and then one of Ellen's cats appeared, a small dark carcass dangling from its mouth. "Good kitty-kitty," Ian called softly. The cat ignored him, and headed around the side of the house.

He should just go to bed, but he knew he wouldn't sleep until Ellen got home. So he set his cup inside the screen door and set off across the road. The officer at turnkey was new. At sight of the warden, he sprang to military attention so quickly Ian almost laughed out loud. "Relax, son," he said. "I'm just wondering if you've seen my wife."

"Yes, sir. She and a trustee are in the chapel. Been in there nearly an hour. Mrs. McKenna said they were going to do some straightening while they looked for something the preacher's wife lost this morning."

So that was why that mousy little woman was so locked in conversation with Ellen. "You have any idea what she lost?"

The guard shook his head. "No, sir. Mrs. McKenna didn't say."

"Who's with her?"

"I don't know her name. Chestnut hair. Pretty, if you don't mind my saying so."

"I don't, and that'd be Jane Prescott."

Ian hesitated. He didn't want Ellen thinking he was worried about her, at least not in the way that said *I don't trust you to do this job.* He scratched his head. "Well, when Mrs. McKenna comes out, would you tell her that her husband is waiting in his office? Tell her I'm working on notes for tomorrow's meeting with the matron."

"Yes, sir. I'll tell her."

Ian wandered back to his office. He didn't really have anything he needed to do. *Jane Prescott.* He went to his desk, lit the lamp, and pulled Jane's file out of the desk drawer. It had been there since the meeting with Max Zimmer weeks ago. Something just kept niggling at him. Sitting down, he opened the file and began to read. But he couldn't concentrate. He looked down at his watch. *Twenty minutes till third shift.*

Enough. Ellen had no business cleaning the chapel at this hour.

If she hadn't found whatever it was, they'd have some trustees do another search by daylight.

He turned the lamp back down, put the folder away, and headed back to turnkey. "Process me through," he said to the guard. "Just don't tell anyone I spent this evening helping my wife clean the chapel."

"No, sir," the guard grinned. "Your secret's safe with me."

The kid passed him through turnkey, and Ian headed for the chapel. When he opened the door, the first thing he saw was a "guard" standing up on the podium. Ellen was sitting to the right end of one of the front pews, Jane Prescott to the left. The guard looked his way. With a shout, he charged up the center aisle, yelling Ellen's name, shouting at Jane. "Get down! Get down!"

But he was too late. He'd never get there in time.

Murderous hate and venom straight from the pit of hell transformed Pearl Brand into something that would haunt Ian's dreams as he relived the most terrifying moment in his life. Brandishing yet another homemade weapon, she screamed with fury. Spittle flew as she launched herself in the air toward Ellen, her right arm extended above her head as she plunged downward with all her strength, downward toward Ellen, who was, at the same moment, raising her hands above her head and diving for the floor.

But there was something else Ian would never forget. A flash of gray. A full-throated scream, and Jane Prescott throwing herself atop Ellen the second before Pearl Brand drove her weapon downward.

— ⁂ —

It was over in seconds. One moment Pearl was speaking in an odd, monotonous voice, detailing her plan to escape, and the next she lifted her head, glanced toward the door, and was transformed into something Ellen could only think of as *other*. Furious, hateful, murderous, yet more than all of those. Ellen wouldn't know until later that Ian's arrival had prompted the change. All she knew was someone shouted "down," and Pearl transformed, and Ellen knew she was going to die.

Defending herself was a reflex, no brave pose to fend off an attack. Her hands flew up, and she dove forward and away from Pearl. And then something landed on top of her with a grunt. The air went out of her, and the room went dark for a split second. When next Ellen was aware of what had happened, Ian had Pearl on her stomach on the floor, his knee between her shoulder blades. Guards were streaming into the room. And Jane. . .Jane had rolled off her and lay, her eyes closed, a strange half smile on her face.

Ellen sat up, screaming her name. "Jane! Jane, do you hear me?" She saw Pearl's weapon protruding from Jane's arm and reached for it.

"Don't touch that," Ian said abruptly. "It might be keeping—just don't touch it."

Two guards knelt next to Pearl Brand. While Ian held her down, one applied handcuffs, the other leg irons.

"Selleck," Ellen gasped. "Adam Selleck was helping her."

Ian glowered. "You heard her, men. You know what to do." He knelt over Jane. "And get the doctor."

"He's. . .um. . .he wasn't on tonight, Warden," someone said. "He's—"

Ian roared, "Are you telling me he's drunk again?" He didn't wait for an answer. "Pack him up and throw him out. I mean it. Now. And get me Sergeant Underhill."

Underhill came galloping in. When he saw Jane on the floor, his face went white.

"I don't think it's as bad as it looks," Ian said quickly. "But I want Dr. Zimmer. Make sure he knows it's just the arm. Tell him we've left the weapon in to control any bleeding, but it's gone nearly all the way through." Underhill headed off. "And Martin." He turned around. "Don't tell him it's Jane. We don't need him breaking his neck on the way out here. And neither does she."

That's when Ian reached out and flung his arm around Ellen's neck and pulled her close. He was trembling. "Are you sure you're all right?"

"I'm fine. Jane was so. . .brave." She blinked away the tears. "Why would she do that? To save me?"

Ian's entire body shuddered. He shook his head.

—〰—

Jane opened her eyes. Grimaced as she looked around. Where was she? Some kind of infirmary. Was that children she heard? Shouting? Playing? When she lifted her head, someone sitting just to her right moved. She blinked several times. The ceiling in this place was. . .blue? Who did that? Who painted a ceiling blue? She licked her lips.

"Here ya go. Nice and cold."

Georgia? Jane frowned.

"Yes, 'Just Jane,' it's me. Have a drink and tell me how you're feeling."

When Georgia reached behind Jane to help her sit up, pain shot through her left side. She looked down. *My arm.* Never had water tasted so wonderful. She looked over the top of the glass while she drank, taking in the rest of the infirmary. She was the only patient. Three other empty beds filled the room. Privacy screens leaned against the walls. And again. . .she heard children outside. She frowned. "Where am I?"

"You remember what happened?"

Slowly it all came back. "Ellen—Mrs. McKenna—"

"Is just fine. You took the blow intended for her." Georgia's eyes teared up. "And no one will ever forget that." She shook her head. "What a brave, foolish thing to do."

Jane tried to shrug it off, but it hurt too much. "My arm. . .hurts."

"Pearl stabbed you clean through. Doc had to do surgery, but it's not too bad. Oh, I know it hurts like fury, but you'll be good as new when it heals up." She smiled. "It won't affect your quilting arm one bit. Miss Dawson said to be sure to tell you that."

Jane smiled. "Well, I'm glad the doctor was sober Sunday night. What day is it, anyway?"

"It's Tuesday, and the prison doctor didn't do this." Georgia pointed to the bandage. "Fact is, he was in his cups again. Sergeant Underhill and that fleet mare of his raced into Lincoln and got you a good doctor. Name of Zimmer." She paused. "Here now, you take another drink of water, and I'll tell you the whole story."

Jane settled back and closed her eyes while Georgia talked. Max had moved to Lincoln. This was his infirmary, the first floor of a house he'd purchased. "He wants you to stay here for a few days, just to make sure the wound heals up and doesn't get infected. But he said to tell you he hasn't forgotten what you said, and you don't have to worry. He'll leave you alone." Georgia paused. "He seemed to think it was very important you hear that last part about his remembering."

Jane nodded. Weariness washed over her.

"You get some more sleep. You think you might want a little lunch when you wake up?"

Jane nodded again.

"All right then, I'll leave you to rest, and I'll see to it." Georgia smiled. "Anything sound particularly good? Something you haven't had in a while?"

"Pie," Jane murmured. "Any kind. Just. . .homemade. . .pie."

—⁓—

Max kept his word. Jane heard his voice a couple of times out in the hall, but for the most part it was as if she was being treated from a distance. Georgia's nursing skills were obviously excellent. The first time she unwrapped Jane's arm and Jane saw the results of Pearl's attack, she shuddered.

Georgia spoke up. "Why'd you do such a fool thing?"

"I don't know. I just. . .did." Jane winced. "She was going to hurt my. . .friend. I know she's not really my friend, but it seemed like she was Sunday night." She paused. "She's always been. . .kind."

Georgia nodded. "Yes. She is. Always."

"And she didn't make me feel like I was 'less than' because of where I am. You know?"

"Yes. I do." Georgia held out her hand. "To Mrs. McKenna, that's just a hand. Same as hers." She chuckled. "Although it's a hand that makes much better piecrust than her dainty little white ones ever will."

"You wouldn't think she was quite so dainty if you'd seen the way she faced up to Pearl." Jane shook her head. "She got her to talking, got her to reveal the whole plan. I never would have thought of that."

"Adam Selleck was trying to steal Mr. Underhill's horse. Because of what Mrs. McKenna had found out, they knew to chase after him. Underhill caught him in the act when he went to get Betsy to ride after the doc for you. Coldcocked the man. Broke his nose."

"Martin Underhill!"

"I know." Georgia shook her head from side to side. "Just goes to show: do not mess with a man's woman or with his horse. It does not pay."

"Selleck didn't hurt Miss Dawson, did he?"

"No, no. I was thinking of the warden when Mr. Underhill dragged Selleck in." She shook her head. "Way I heard it, it took four guards to hold the warden back."

Jane took a deep breath. "I'm so glad no one else was hurt." Georgia studied her for a minute. "What?"

Georgia shook her head. "Nothing. You get some rest. I'll have Jack see to getting you some pie. Don't imagine it's nearly as good as mine, but the doc speaks highly of a place called Dinah's."

Jane was almost asleep. Without opening her eyes she said, "Jack? Ellen's son? How—"

"Jack stops by every day after school to check on you before heading home." Georgia paused. "Said it's the least he can do." Jane heard her chuckle. "I imagine he'll take kindly to the idea of fetching a pie for a good cause."

Rose

Aunt Flora stood at the foot of the stairs, holding Rose's doll quilt by one corner, a look of revulsion on her face. "I don't understand you, Rose. It's worn to a rag. I couldn't believe it when I saw it dangling over the edge of your doll bed. It *smells*. It's time to throw it out." She paused. "In fact, now that I think about it, I'm quite certain we *did* throw it out. As part of our before-school-starts housecleaning *last* year."

And I'm quite certain I hate it when you send me on an errand and go snooping in my room while I'm gone. Rose closed the front door behind her, then made her way into the kitchen to put the quart of milk she'd gone after in the icebox. Aunt Flora was still waiting at the foot of the stairs when she returned. "I changed my mind," she said. "Mr. Hennessey was tending the trash bin and, when he lit the fire—" She shrugged. "I just couldn't let it burn." She reached for the little quilt.

Aunt Flora ignored her even as she pursed her lips together with displeasure. "You haven't played with dolls in a very long while. And should you take a notion to do so, you have a perfectly lovely doll quilt made in the latest fashion." She sighed. "It's no wonder they call it crazy quilting. I thought I'd go mad before I had it finished."

"I love the quilt you made for me," Rose said. "Honestly, I do. It's exquisite." Rose gazed longingly at the frayed quilt dangling from Aunt Flora's hand. She shrugged. "Please, Aunt Flora. I'll wash it."

"It will disintegrate."

"Well, I'll *rinse* it, then. Very carefully. I'll do it in my room. You won't have to. It's not like it's in your way or anything. I'll tuck it behind all my dolls. You won't even have to see it if you think it ruins the display." She gazed up the stairs toward her room. The assortment of dolls arranged atop the brass doll bed sitting below her bedroom window was little more than a monument to her childhood now. After all, she was nearly grown. Odd how the least impressive doll and the raggedy quilt were the ones she cherished most. She lifted her chin. "I like George Washington. Mother said they made that fabric especially to honor him. And I named my doll Martha. *Please,* Aunt Flora. . ."

Aunt Flora relented with a forced laugh and a shake of her head. "All right, all right. But do rinse it out."

Rose took the doll quilt in hand. Later in the day, she poured clear water from the pitcher on her washstand into the accompanying bowl and put the doll quilt in to soak. As she watched the president's face change tone as the fabric soaked up the water, the name *George Washy* sounded in her head. She swished the quilt in the water, appalled by how quickly it turned murky. "It's all right, George. I'll get you all cleaned up."

Aunt Flora appeared in the doorway to her room while Rose worked to clean the doll quilt. "I didn't realize that little rag was all that important to you."

Rose shrugged. "The one you made me is prettier." It was the truth. The exquisite little crazy quilt was embellished with literally thousands of fancy stitches. "And I'll treasure it forever."

She would, too. But it would never replace the "George Washy" Mother had made.

CHAPTER 22

On Monday morning, a week after Jane awoke in the infirmary, Warden McKenna arrived to transport her back "south of town." On the way out of the house, Jane expected Max to appear, at least to say good-bye, but he remained true to his word to let her alone. She told herself it was her imagination when she sensed someone watching her go, but once the warden handed her up into his buggy, she glanced back toward the house. Max was standing at the window to the right of the front door. She realized she wanted him to wave or nod, but he did neither. In fact, he stepped back out of sight.

The warden climbed in opposite her and Georgia, and the driver flicked the reins. They headed off to the south. Jane caught a glimpse of Minnie Dawson's shop, Manerva, and marveled at the beautiful garments in the window. Fashions had changed. She'd look ridiculous in the dress that waited for her release day. Lincoln had changed. Someone was building an impressive brick mansion at Seventeenth and South Streets.

The driver commented on it as they passed by. "Who would have ever thought the city would grow all the way down to South Street?" He shook his head.

As the buggy made its way past the last houses in town, the road narrowed to little more than two tracks leading south across the prairie, and Jane realized, with no small degree of surprise, that she was looking forward to seeing Mrs. McKenna again. And Miss Dawson. Even listening to Agnes grouse wouldn't be so bad. Maybe she was fooling herself, but she didn't think it would be quite so hard to go back inside this time.

Something in the way she was seeing things had changed, even though nothing about her circumstances had. She still had years ahead of her before she could even attempt reconciliation with Rose. But she couldn't do a thing about that, and so she would cope. Somehow, with God's help, she would cope.

God. It was strange to think of God as a help. She'd always seen Him as a kind of angry parent holding court over her behavior and always being disappointed. At some point in recent days, however, she'd thanked God for helping her ward off Pearl Brand's attack, and that seemed to have created a shift in her sense of things.

What was that term Miss Dawson had started to use since Vestal named her baby Grace? *Grace notes.* That was it. Jane realized that, if she chose to see it that way, she had grace notes in her life. A quilt to finish for Rose. Women to help learn to read. Rugs to make. Sewing to do. And there would be more patchwork quilts. Perhaps even an appliqué or two. After all, the one thing she had was time. Maybe Miss Dawson was right. If a person found a way to have a thankful heart, even when things looked grim, God felt closer. Circumstances didn't weigh so heavily on a day. Jane looked up at the blue sky and smiled.

The buggy stopped first at the warden's house. Jane had hoped to see Mrs. McKenna, but she was nowhere in sight. For a moment, dread washed over her. *Grace notes. Find them.* Georgia stepped down, then reached out and clasped one of Jane's hands between her own and said, "Be well, my friend. Be well." She blinked back tears and headed inside. The buggy lurched across the prairie to the hitching post at the bottom of the stone stairs.

A flash of blue caught her attention. The bachelor's buttons she and Agnes had planted were blooming. Jane smiled again. The warden helped her down, and she followed him inside. Expecting to be taken through turnkey right away, she was surprised when the warden said, "This way first, Mrs. Prescott. There are a few things we need to discuss." He must have noted her expression, for he smiled. "It's all right. There's nothing to worry about. I just have a report to file. A few questions, now that you're able."

Jane relaxed and followed him through the outer office, taking a seat when he pointed at one of the chairs opposite his desk. For the first time, she realized he'd been wearing a holster and gun. *Well, of course he is. You're his prisoner.* But then he did the oddest thing. He took the holster off and hung it on the back of the chair next to her. She leaned away and looked at him as if to say, *Are you crazy?*

He smiled. "It isn't loaded."

Not knowing what to say about that, she just said "Oh," and waited.

He opened a file and held up a few sheets of paper. "The clerk I sent in to take your report while you were in the infirmary wrote this after taking down your account of events. If you still feel it's an accurate record of what happened, I'll ask you to sign it."

Jane nodded, and the warden began to read. When he'd finished, he looked up. "Does that still stand as your statement of what happened?"

"Yes, sir."

He turned the folder around and pointed. Jane signed on the line he indicated. He closed the folder. Opened another. "Now I have another statement to go over."

To Jane's horror, he began to read about the night when Owen died. "Sir, please. . .I don't see why. . . ."

"Just bear with me. I have a few questions. I just need to get things clear in my own mind as we move forward."

It was agonizing listening to it again. Why was he making her go through this? Was someone—had Max tried to intervene again? Her heart lurched. He'd promised to leave her alone. She interrupted the warden again. "Dr. Zimmer promised he wouldn't do this to me anymore. Maybe he didn't tell you, but I insisted, and he said—"

The warden cut her off. "Dr. Zimmer has nothing to do with this. This is my investigation."

"There's nothing to investigate. What you read is what I said. And I stand by it."

"Still. Today? After all this time? After everything that's happened, you still insist you killed a man?"

She swallowed. "With all due respect, sir, I insist that you believe the statement as I gave it."

"You didn't answer my question."

"I have answered all the questions that matter. The trial is over. And I'm here."

"Except that questions remain in the mind of everyone who has come to know you since you arrived, and in the mind of someone who remains your champion, even though you refuse to allow it."

So Max was behind this, after all. She clenched her hands in her lap, hoping the warden couldn't see her tremble.

"That's the same gun you used." He nodded at the holster hanging next to her. "Show me how you did it."

"Sir?"

"The court records indicate that you were never asked to demonstrate how you used that weapon. It's a weakness in the prosecution's case. Such a weakness, in fact, I'm surprised there wasn't a mistrial."

The judge was a friend of Owen's. Jane barely managed not to blurt it out.

"On the other hand, I find it of great interest that, since you've been here, that name—the judge's name—has popped up on a couple of land documents." He sat back. "He took over your husband's ranch."

"And he's welcome to it."

The warden pointed again at the gun. "Show me how you did it. The holster was hanging on the back of a chair." He paused. "I just can't quite picture it. You're no Pearl Brand, Jane. I can't picture how you managed to pull a gun against a man who was, by all accounts, quite skilled at the fast draw."

"He was drunk. He wasn't fast at anything."

"Did he drink all the way home from the Bar T?"

Jane frowned. "What?"

"It says you were at a dance at the Bar T. People said he was 'tipsy.' No one said he was drunk. And then he drove a wagon through the crisp, spring night air for. . .how long? An hour? Two? Unless he drank all the way home, he would have been very near to sober by the time you two had that argument. Or you would have had to drive the wagon, because he would have been too drunk to sit up on the seat with you."

Jane said nothing.

"So you fought. And in the fury of the moment, you. . ."

Jane looked at the gun next to her. "I pulled it out and pulled the trigger."

"Exactly like that? You didn't take the time to cock it?"

"I'm a full-grown woman, Warden McKenna. There wasn't time. I'm strong enough to fire a gun without cocking it first."

The warden sat back. The stillness in the room grew oppressive. He closed the file.

"Thank you, Jane. I just wanted to be sure."

"Well, now that you're sure, would you take me upstairs? My arm hurts."

He took a deep breath. "You're very brave, Jane Prescott. Quite possibly the bravest, strongest woman I know. And I don't mean physical strength. I mean another thing entirely."

"Thank you. I'm just glad that Ellen—Mrs. McKenna—is all right, and that no one else got hurt."

"That's not what I mean, either."

He came around the desk and sat down next to her. "You didn't kill Owen Marquis. I think I know what happened that night, but you're never going to admit it. Because you love your daughter so much that you're willing to do anything—including spending ten years in prison—to take the blame for something she did." He paused. "She did it to protect you from another beating. And you're here to protect her."

Jane shook her head. "You don't know that."

He nodded. "Yes. I do." He pointed to the holster hanging on the chair. "You can't fire that gun without cocking it first, Jane. And it's clear that you didn't know that. But Rose did, didn't she? Dr. Zimmer told me that Owen used to take Rose target shooting. You hated it, but he didn't care. Said he wanted her to be able to defend herself. He even called her his 'little gunslinger.' She would have cocked that gun and fired it to protect you without giving it a second thought."

Jane closed her eyes. She couldn't look at him. If she looked at him he would read the truth.

The warden's voice trembled as he said, " 'Greater love hath no man than this'. . .to 'lay down his life for his friends.' " He took a deep breath. "You did that for your daughter, and you did it for Ellen. There is no way to thank you. Ever. If anything had happened to my Ellen. . ." He shook his head.

Getting up, he went back to his desk and opened another file. "There are two ways to do this. The first I have the power to do.

As of this minute you have served your sentence. You are done. I'm commuting the rest. The second would be better for you in the long run, and I have an appointment to see the governor tomorrow to make the case for your pardon."

"You can't do that. You—"

"It's all right, Jane. What just happened. . .no one has to know. I understand how important that is to you. For Rose's sake. My appeal will be on the basis of your overall record and your risking your life for Ellen." He paused. Swallowed. "But whether the governor grants the pardon or not, you never belonged here, and you aren't spending one more night behind bars."

The next couple of hours were a blur. Ellen had come over from the house and was waiting in the outer office for Jane with Miss Dawson. Together, they took Jane up to the third floor where the women, who had been told about the "early release," presented her with the completed courthouse-steps quilt. They'd been given special permission to work on it day and night. Leaving was awkward, especially when Patch brushed against her skirt and began to purr a welcome.

Agnes picked Patch up. "We'll take good care of the cat," she said. "She don't seem to mind me."

Back downstairs, Jane changed into the outdated dress she'd changed out of all those years ago. How odd that she'd just thought about that this morning. The clerk counted out $1.50—her earnings since the industry had begun a few weeks ago. Jane dropped it in the envelope where they'd kept. . .*the key*. She pulled it out. She would have to see Max to get the little trunk back. But not now. Right now, everything was too overwhelming.

Back outside, they descended the steps and headed across the road. The McKennas wanted her to stay with them while she made plans. *I have to make plans.* It hadn't been all that long since just stepping outside had nearly sent her into a panic. Now, the idea of freedom threatened to do the same thing.

Ellen took her hand. "It'll be all right, Jane. I know you're frightened. But it'll be all right. You don't have to do this alone. You have friends who care about you."

Together, they crossed the road to the house, where Georgia waited on the front porch—with pie.

Rose

Rose might be seated on the front porch swing, but she was mentally in Europe with Amy of *Little Women* when someone hissed her name.

"Psst, Rose! You shouldn't be out there on the porch today! It isn't safe!"

Rose looked up from her book. All she could see was the top of poor Mrs. Partain's head, barely visible above the picket fence. With a sigh, she closed the book and stepped down off the porch.

At her approach, Mrs. Partain popped up like a jack-in-the-box, complete with brightly rouged cheeks. "It isn't safe. Didn't you hear me?" She looked about her like the crazy woman she was becoming.

"Would you like to come up on the porch with me and swing for a while? I could get you some lemonade. Aunt Flora's gone, but—"

"Gone? Gone where? Did they take her?"

Rose shook her head. "No. No one took her. She's over at the church. The Ladies Aid meeting. You know. She goes every Thursday afternoon."

Mrs. Partain looked confused. "Is it Thursday? I thought—they must have taken my calendar. I've lost track. Oh dear, dear." She began to cry. "And Fluffy's lost. Did I tell you? I think I forgot to feed him."

Fluffy was buried in Mrs. Partain's backyard, having died of old age or a heart attack when Zeus cornered her once too often—Rose wasn't quite sure. But poor Mrs. Partain didn't seem to remember the cat was gone, no matter how often they told her.

"Why don't you come up on the porch with me?" Rose said. "I'll make you some lemonade, and when you've had a little rest, I'll help you look for Fluffy."

The old woman's rouged face folded into a smile. "Would you, really? Rose, you are the sweetest girl in the whole state of Nebraska. That's what I always say." Her smile disappeared, and she looked back over her shoulder. "You won't let them come here, will you?"

"Who do you mean?"

"Why, the prisoners of, course. There's been a mutiny in Lincoln. At the prison." She waved a folded paper in the air. "It's all right here. I read every word. People don't think I can read, but I can. And the prisoners have mutinied." She thrust the paper at Rose. "Read it for yourself."

"You come over and sit with me while I read," Rose said. "I'll feel better if I have a little company."

When Mrs. Partain finally agreed and minced along the fence and through the gate, Rose did her best not to notice that she was still dressed in her nightgown. Over which she'd drawn a sweater. And a jacket. A dozen bracelets encircled each wrist. She was barefoot. Once she'd settled on the swing beside Rose, a distinct and not very pleasant aroma seemed to settle onto the porch.

Poor Mrs. Partain. She leaned over and pointed to a headline. "There. There it is. That's what's got me worried."

Rose read. Escape Foiled. "It says the mutiny was foiled, Mrs. Partain. No one escaped. We're all quite safe."

"That's what they always say. Don't you know that? They don't want us to worry." She waved her arthritic hands in the air. "Lies. All lies."

Rose set the paper down. "I'll just get our lemonade. You wait here."

"What are you reading, dear?" Mrs. Partain picked up the book. "Oh, I *love* this one!" She settled back and began to read.

Rose made lemonade and came back out on the porch. Mrs.

Partain barely noticed her return. For lack of anything better to do, Rose picked up the newspaper:

Escape Foiled

A penitentiary inmate has been pardoned as a result of what Warden Ian McKenna called "bravery beyond anything I've ever seen." Considering the warden's impressive record as a member of the Fourth Missouri Infantry at the Battle of Vicksburg, the praise may seem a bit overstated.

It was a rather exciting account, containing details of violence that Rose felt a bit guilty for reading. Aunt Flora would not approve. In fact, she didn't subscribe to the newspaper because she thought it contained things "inappropriate for young minds." For some reason, that made Rose even more eager to read Mrs. Partain's newspaper. After all, it was her duty to try and calm the dear demented soul, wasn't it? Hadn't Aunt Flora done exactly that several times a week for months now?

Rose read and read and. . .stopped.

Jane Marquis.

It was as if someone had sucked the breath right out of her.

CHAPTER 23

Door's open, Jane," Georgia called from where she stood at the well out back, pumping water into a bucket.

Feeling like a fool, Jane opened the McKennas' back door and headed outside.

Georgia grasped the bucket handle and, hoisting it, headed toward the garden. She paused on the way to douse the petunias spilling out of a broken crock by the barn. "It's all right," she said. "Been a long time since you could open a door on your own. One of these days you'll remember the other way of living." She set the empty bucket down and handed Jane one of the two hoes leaning against the barn. "Until then," she chuckled, "I don't mind telling a white girl what to do now and then."

Jane smiled and shook her head even as she made her way to the opposite end of a row of beans and began to hoe up the threatening weeds. She might not have "open the door" quite figured out yet, but she'd stopped being so panicky about all the space. In fact, she actually liked working with Georgia in the garden, although her arm still couldn't handle hoeing for very long.

"Your arm starts to bother you, Mrs. McKenna can always use help around front with her flowers."

Jane nodded. But she kept hoeing. Something about those flower beds out front just felt. . .wrong, somehow. Especially at this time of day, when the women from the third floor might be out across the road. Nothing felt quite right, yet. Eventually, she would learn how to be free again. But for now, for now she was content to concentrate on this square of earth tucked behind the barn.

—⁓—

Mamie's first day off in early September required extra prayer. She had an extended conversation with the Lord for most of the morning as she rose and made tea, shed her nightgown, and donned her dark blue walking suit. She was taking Jane into town to Minnie's and, unbeknownst to Jane, who thought they were just having tea, Minnie was going to do a fitting. Three dresses, they thought. And a job, if Jane wanted it. And an apartment above Manerva.

When Minnie first suggested it, Mamie praised her. "It's so good of you to do this."

"Good of me?" Minnie shook her head. "You mean good *for* me. I need the help, and she's an excellent seamstress. As to the apartment, it's so tiny I won't be surprised if she doesn't want it."

"Tiny might be a good thing right now," Mamie said. "What little I know of transitions, freedom can be terrifying. A smaller space means more control. That could be comforting. But that'll be up to Jane to decide." And here they were, on the day when Jane would have opportunity to decide. If she actually followed through and came into town. She'd changed her mind twice before. Mamie wasn't worried yet, but she would be if things didn't change soon.

Martin joined her for breakfast, exclaiming over her scrambled eggs and making her blush like a girl with his compliments about her ensemble. "This old thing?" she protested. "Minnie made it last year. You've seen it a hundred times."

"Doesn't matter," Martin said. "It's pretty, and so are you.

Neither will ever change."

"We'll see how you feel about that statement five years from now—if we're both still working here."

"I'll still be here, and I'll still feel the same, Mamie."

His expression was so. . .something. . .that Mamie blushed. "Well, thank you." She hiccuped.

"I love that about you."

"What?"

"That little hiccup. You do it when you're nervous. Although I can't quite understand why an ugly old bird like me giving you a compliment would make you nervous."

"Martin Underhill." Mamie's voice was stern. "I will not have you speaking of my dear friend and coworker in such a manner. Beauty is vain. The Bible says so. God looks on the heart, and yours is generous, kind, and noble." Something about his expression was concerning. "Have I said something to upset you?"

He shook his head. "Of course not, Mamie. You're. . . everything. . ." He didn't finish.

"Am I really. . .everything?" She hiccuped again. He nodded. She looked away. "Eat your eggs, Martin. Breakfast is the most important meal of the day."

—⁓—

"You can't be serious." Jane stood in the middle of Minnie's shop, staring at the bolts of fabric, the dresses in the window, the drawers of buttons and trims. . .and repeated herself. "You can't be."

"Don't tell me what I can or can't be." Minnie laughed. "I *am* overwhelmed with work, and I *can* be serious about offering you a job. I promise you it will be very boring at first. I need someone to create order in the back room. That alone may take a month. I have no idea what's back there, which is the problem. Hopefully there are no uninvited guests too intent on staying. I'd also want you to sweep the shop—clean up at the end of the day so that back room never again becomes what it is. Once that's taken care of, you'll be hemming. Very basic, and, as I said, very boring. But I've miles of hems. As time goes on, we'll see."

Jane crossed the shop and brushed her palm across a bolt of cloth. "This is wonderful."

"Glad you like it," Minnie said. "Take it down." Jane hesitated. "No, really, take it down. We'll make your first dress out of it." She pointed toward the dressing screen in the corner. "Step back there. I'll take your measurements." Still, Jane hesitated. "Don't be shy. If you're working for me, you can't wear that. . .thing." She pointed at the dress Jane was wearing.

"But I can't pay—"

"Of course you can. In small increments. I'll take it out of your salary. I didn't get this place by not keeping proper accounts. I'm not offering charity. I need help. You need work. Oh, and did I mention the apartment upstairs?"

"It isn't really an apartment," Mamie chimed in. "It's more of a large room with a stove just big enough to heat a teakettle."

"True." Minnie grinned. "Care to see it?"

"Can I have a cat?"

"A cat." Minnie repeated the word.

"You know, Minnie," Mamie said. "About so high. Four legs. Fur. Makes a sound like, 'meow.'"

Minnie glowered at her sister. Glanced back at Jane. "As long as you keep it off my fabric. I won't have an animal shedding all over my merchandise."

"I give you two weeks before you've made a patchwork chaise for it so it can greet your customers," Mamie said.

"Would you care to wager on that?"

"I would, but I'd win and that's not fair."

Jane called from behind the screen. "Are you two always this way?"

"What way?" they said in chorus.

"I'll take them."

"What did we offer?"

"A job, an apartment, and the promise of a cat. I'll take all three."

Minnie came around the corner of the dressing screen, tape measure in hand. "You will probably live to regret your enthusiasm," she said. "I can be a witch."

Jane smiled. "You just hired me to wield a broom. I believe your powers will be limited."

—⁓—

Only a few days after Jane had accepted Minnie's offer of a job and a room—it really was just a room, but all she needed—Jane lay awake worrying. What had she done? She couldn't move into Lincoln. Lincoln meant crowded boardwalks and streets busy with horse-and-buggy traffic. Dusty streets and. . .oh my. . .*customers.* Women who would come into Manerva expecting small talk and chitchat, and what on earth would Jane say when they asked about her family, her background, her anything? No, she could not move to Lincoln. She'd want to go to church. Might even want to join one. They'd ask all kinds of questions. Had she belonged to a church before? Had she been baptized? If she told the truth, they wouldn't want her. If she lied, they shouldn't.

Her heart racing, sweat rolling down her back, her chest hurting, Jane sat up in bed. Was she having a heart attack? A breeze rustled the white lace curtains hanging at the window by her bed. She reached out and swept them back, closing her eyes and breathing deeply. Someone had cut hay today somewhere. Coyotes yelped. Far off. A cat yowled. *At least they're letting me have a cat.*

Slipping out of bed, she knelt by the window and looked out. In the moonlight, the building across the road really did look like a castle. Someone was awake in the second-floor apartment on the east side of the building—that, or they'd left a lamp burning. *A lamp in the window.*

When Rose was a baby and Thomas had to be gone until late at night, Jane had always kept a lamp burning in the window for him. The first time she did the same for Owen, he scolded her for wasting kerosene. And how stupid did she think he was, anyway? He didn't need help finding his way home on his own ranch. How had she ever thought—

Stop. You cannot remake the past. You have to look to the future now.

Of course the future held its own—mid-thought, something flashed in the sky. Jane leaned forward, looking up. Another flash.

Look, Mama, another one! Look, Mama! Look!

Getting to her feet, Jane slipped out of her nightgown and into her outdated waist and skirt. Barefoot, she padded downstairs and out the back door. Standing by the well pump, she looked up.

Look, Mama! Look!

With a glance back at the house, she walked toward the horizon, her attention fixed on the sky.

See that, Rose? Just there? Doesn't that look like the dipper that hangs on the pump by the barn? That's what it's called. The Big Dipper. There's a little one, too. Over here. . .

When another shooting star streaked across the sky, Jane smiled. *All this space and I'm not afraid.* She lay on her back and looked up. *The heavens declare. . . .* Again, a streak of light seared the sky. Jane caught her breath.

Look, Mama, look! What was that one's name?

The indigo backing on her courthouse steps meant this. A

reference to the times Jane and Rose lay side by side, staring up at the night sky.

Your grandpa sailed the seas, and he taught your first papa to read the sky. And Papa taught me, and someday, you can teach your children.

Jane sat up. No. *I can teach Rose's children. I'm free. There's nothing stopping me. . .but me. There's no reason to fear the memories anymore. I can reclaim them, savor them, relive them, take joy in them.* Suddenly her present reality took purchase. Freedom was no longer a thing to fear. If she didn't like the noise in town, she could move. If she wanted a cat, she could get one. If crowded boardwalks bothered her, she could go out earlier or later or not at all. If she wanted tea, she could make it. Her heart pounded with joyful possibilities.

If she wanted to, she could get on board the train for Nebraska City tomorrow and knock on Flora's front door and demand to see her daughter. That wasn't the way to do it, but still. . .*I am free.* Springing to her feet, she lifted her face to the skies and twirled about. *Free to laugh, to dance, to make a fool of myself on the prairie at night.*

She stopped twirling. Motionless, she looked toward town.

Max, I am free.

—⁂—

Jane began her first day of true freedom sitting at the McKennas' breakfast table, staring down at her plate. Melted butter oozed out of every crevice in the still-warm breakfast roll on the plate before her, and if the aromas of rising yeast and baking bread, cinnamon, and fresh coffee weren't enough to make a woman nearly swoon, the caramelized pecans were. "This has to be sinful."

"Happy to help you eat it, if you just can't manage." Jack McKenna stepped into the kitchen. He poured himself a glass of milk and drank it down, then wiped his mouth with the back of his hand before flashing a smile. "Really. I live to serve."

Jane laughed. "Thank you. I appreciate your thoughtfulness, but I think I can manage."

"If you change your mind, I'll be back in after I do my chores."

"I'll remember that."

Jack left, then ducked his head back in the doorway. "Mother said you're leaving today?"

"Yes. Miss Dawson's offered me a job in town. And a room over her shop. The Miss Dawson from across the road is driving me in this morning. She'll be here in just a bit."

"Well. . .I hope. . . ." His face turned red. "Is it all right to say good luck?"

"It is definitely all right."

"Good luck then." He nodded at her plate. "Don't forget my offer to help you out. I don't even mind if you start in and just can't finish it. I'm not picky." He gave a two-fingered salute and was gone.

Ellen swept into the room. "Did I just hear my son trying to wrangle an extra roll for himself?"

"You did. And he just might have succeeded." Jane stared down at her plate. "I don't know if I can eat."

Ellen slid into a chair beside her. "I don't blame you, and I don't know what else to say. I mean, I could say 'you're going to be fine,' which I do believe is true, but it seems arrogant for me—as if I know the first thing about what you're feeling." She paused. "How does one thank someone for saving their life, Jane?"

"You already did that."

"It isn't enough."

"Then I suppose we are at an impasse. Unless you'd want to promise a lifetime supply of these rolls—and Georgia's raisin cream pie."

"You say the word, and it will be done," Georgia said.

"Then we have an understanding, and I can go." Once again, the truth of what Jane had just said rolled over her. *I can go.* Tears threatened. "Don't mind me. I'm having a bit of trouble getting accustomed to the idea that I actually can. . .go. I mean, I can just say that and. . ." Her voice trailed off. "But before I do, I need to get my things. Miss Dawson, uh, Mamie—goodness, it seems strange to call her that, but she insists—should be here any minute."

Back upstairs, Jane gathered her few belongings into the carpet-bag Georgia had brought down from the attic. She was halfway back down the stairs when she heard the buggy roll up to the front door. She called to Mamie that she'd be right out, then retreated back to the kitchen to say a tearful good-bye. As she headed up the hall, Warden McKenna descended the stairs.

"Jane."

She looked up at him.

He reached into his coat pocket and withdrew an envelope. "I—" His voice wobbled. He coughed and looked down at the envelope. "There's no proper way to thank you." He blinked. "No proper way to apologize, either. For what you've gone through." Again, he cleared his throat. "You take this and. . ." He shook his head. Looked at Ellen. Inhaled sharply. "If you ever need anything—I don't care what—if it is in my power to give it. . ."

"I've already taken care of that," Jane said. Forcing a smile, she looked at Georgia. "I've demanded raisin cream pie for life."

"And pecan rolls," Georgia added.

The warden thrust the envelope at her. "Then you're all set." He offered his arm.

Mamie headed out, but just when they'd turned into the road, Martin Underhill appeared at the top of the administration building stairs, hollering something and waving.

"What on earth—" Mamie reined the mare in, and Martin

galloped down the stairs, a picnic basket tucked under his arm.

"Almost missed you!" he gasped, trotting around the back of the buggy to reach Jane's side. He took a deep breath. "Wanted you to have—heard you wanted—" He gulped. "She's Patch's sister," he said of the white kitten that popped its head out of the basket. "And she's just as sweet as Patch."

Jane reached in to scratch behind its ears, and the kitten leaned into her, purring.

Martin smiled and bobbed his head. "See? A match made in heaven."

Mamie leaned over. "Martin?"

"Now, Mamie. I know what you said. It's a terrible time to force a pet on a woman. But I just think maybe they need each other." He looked up at Jane. "But if you don't want her—"

"I want her," Jane glanced at Mamie and gave a little nod. "Really."

"Well, of course you do," Mamie smiled. "Obviously, I was wrong about the timing." She peered at Martin.

"Oh. Well. All right, then." Martin released his hold on the basket and stepped back.

"But that wasn't what I was going to say just now," Mamie called out as he headed back around the rear of the buggy. She followed his progress until he came alongside her.

"I'm listening," Martin said.

Mamie cleared her throat. "You are the kindest, noblest, bravest, most compassionate, smartest man I have ever known. All of that rolled into what I will not deny is an unconventional package, because after I drive away you are going to wonder about what I'm about to say, and I want you to know that I have thought about exactly what it means, and whatever you decide to do with the information is up to you. I just need to inform you of something."

Underhill gulped audibly. "What—what is it, Mamie?"

Mamie hiccuped. Twice. "I love you, Martin Underhill." And with that, she flicked the reins and urged Jenny into a smart trot.

CHAPTER 24

Jane stood motionless just inside the back door to Manerva. Carpetbag in hand, she hesitated on the threshold. To her right, the stairs led up to her little room. To her left, the disaster known as "the back room" waited. Straight ahead through the doorway, the long surface of the counter in the main shop was partially hidden by three new dresses.

"Toodle-oo-*hoo*-hoo," Minnie called, bustling into view and waving Jane and Mamie into the shop while she hung the CLOSED sign on the front door, rattling on about how that dark brown with the pink accents would compliment Jane's chestnut hair and how she just loved those chrome yellow accents in this season's indigos. As for the cadet blue that was just. . .well. . .a practical color for everyday use.

"Of course you'll need a nicer ensemble for church and such, but I wanted you to have time to look through some of the fashion plates before we got into anything like that." She paused. "Don't take this the wrong way, dear, but you're so thin. . .and I thought it likely you'll put on a bit of weight. I allowed for that in the seams with the calicoes. Silks are so much harder to adjust that way. So I thought we'd wait a bit."

Jane swallowed. "I—I don't quite know what to say."

"After you're around Minnie a bit more"—Mamie laughed—
"you'll realize it really isn't required to say much of anything. Minnie's
not one for silence, comfortable or otherwise."

Minnie glowered at her sister even as she disappeared behind
the folding screen in the corner. "I took the privilege of shopping at
Herpolsheimers for a few unmentionables. I hope you don't mind.
The fit won't be perfect."

Jane reached into her bag and pulled out the envelope the warden
had given her. "I've enough to reimburse you. . . .and to pay the first
six months' rent."

"And I'll let you," Minnie said, "but not today. I haven't had time
to do the calculations yet." She motioned toward the dressing screen.
"You'll want to try them on. Although if you'd prefer, there's a mirror
in your apartment. I also took the privilege of putting a few things
in the icebox. . . ." As she talked, Minnie was gathering up dresses
and unmentionables. Draping them over her arm, she reached in her
apron pocket, withdrew a key, and handed it over. "Lead the way,
Mrs. Prescott. And welcome home." She and Mamie followed her
out of the shop.

At the top of the stairs, Jane fumbled for a moment before
managing to unlock the door. The first thing she noticed was the
light. Streaming in the south-facing window, it pooled on the floor
in a pattern of small squares. *No bars.* The narrow bed boasted crisp
white sheets and a woven coverlet. Minnie moved past and spread
her clothing on the bed. Mamie put the picnic basket at the foot
of the bed and opened one side. The kitten popped its head out,
content to sit and look around for a moment. When Jane reached in
to stroke its head, it leaned into her, then shook its head and, peering
over the edge of the basket, scrambled out onto the bed. It explored
from stem to stern before curling up next to one of the pillows.

Jane smiled. "One of us already feels at home." When she looked toward the north windows, she took in a quick breath. Past the rocker, past the little table with the lamp sat a small trunk. Crossing to where it sat, she sank to her knees and ran her palm over the marred surface, then looked up at Minnie and Mamie. "Where. . .how?"

Mamie smiled. "Martin remembered something you'd said to Dr. Zimmer about a trunk. It was his idea. He drove into town yesterday and fetched it."

"What a nice thing to do."

"That's my Martin."

"*Your* Martin?" Minnie nudged her sister. "Somebody's been holding back."

"Nonsense," Mamie said. "You knew I loved the man before I did. How is that holding back?"

While the two sisters bantered, Jane reached into her bag for the key and unlocked the trunk. But she couldn't bring herself to lift the lid. Not yet, anyway. *I won't bother you again. You have my word.* Why did Max choose *now* to be so agreeable to what she'd said? And what did it mean that he hadn't written a note? Blast the man. When she didn't want to see him, he insisted on visiting. Now. . .she was free. And he was. . .*finished.* That was probably it. She was free and, with the returning of the trunk, Max was free, too. He'd met all his obligations, both to his conscience and to her. There was no more need to champion her cause. Thinking on it that way made sense. It also made her sad. How odd to be sitting here looking at a trunk of things she'd feared losing and still feel a sense of loss. What did that mean?

Mamie cleared her throat and said something about needing to talk to Minnie downstairs. Female Department Improvement Committee business, she said. "We'll just give you a few minutes to settle in, and then, if you'd like, we thought we'd take you to Dinah's for a nice lunch. It's just around the corner."

"Homey atmosphere," Minnie chimed in. "Lunch rush is likely past. It shouldn't be too crowded."

Jane hesitated for a moment before saying yes. This was no time to spin another cocoon. It was time to fly.

—⚌—

The one thing Jane hadn't expected was that freedom would be exhausting. Emotions rolled in uninvited and without warning. One moment she felt almost euphoric—capable, hopeful, and able to do anything. The next she was sorting through the memories represented by the things in her little trunk, longing for Rose, and wondering how on earth any of that would ever be resolved. And then. . .there was the topic she understood least. Max Zimmer. He knew she was free. Had he really moved on?

On her second Sunday in Lincoln, Jane woke to the blessed quiet of Sabbath accompanied by church bells. She lingered in bed, petting the cat she'd named Liberty and thinking about Rose. Where did Aunt Flora go to church? Did Rose behave during the services, or was she restless? Did she enjoy the hymns? Thomas had had a rich tenor voice. Had Rose inherited her father's talent for music?

Even though she and Rose weren't reunited yet, things were different now. Jane feasted on a combination of memory and anticipation. Tears combined with joy when she went through the little trunk's contents, remembering. Three cabinet photos portrayed the two of them together. Another showed Rose in her christening gown. Yet another pictured a young Thomas Prescott. Jane held that cabinet photo for a long while, remembering their youthful courtship. . .their exuberant love. . .and the passion. She'd kept the program from the literary society meeting where they'd met, looking forward to telling Rose that story one day, knowing it would make Rose laugh to think of a gangly boy trying to look sophisticated, failing. . .and still winning Jane's heart.

As Liberty tiptoed through the things spread out on the carpet, Jane fingered one of her monogrammed handkerchiefs and remembered how Thomas had kept it in his coat pocket. A cool breeze wafted in the open windows, and joy began to erase Jane's tears. The mementos began to symbolize what Mamie called "thankfuls." *Grace notes.*

God had played a symphony of such notes over Jane in recent days and weeks. She had so many things to be thankful for—among them, Minnie's understanding her not wanting to brave church quite yet. Jane would visit the Ladies Aid quilting first. That was coming up, but this morning she planned to put her teakettle on and finish binding Rose's quilt.

She'd just opened both north and south windows to capture the breeze, settled into the rocker, and taken up needle and thread, when a knock sounded at the door.

"Jane, are you all right? It's Max. Max Zimmer."

How many Max's did he think she knew in Lincoln? Feeling self-conscious, Jane reached up to smooth her hair. "I—just a minute." She didn't own a wrapper. She got dressed as quickly as she could. *Had something happened to Minnie during the church service?* There was no time to pin her hair up. She answered the door in her bare feet. "What is it? What's happened?"

"Minnie said you weren't coming to church again."

The teakettle sputtered. Stepping back from the door, she hurried to get it off the burner. The rag she grabbed to insulate the handle wasn't quite adequate to the task. As quickly as she grabbed the kettle off the burner she let go. It landed on the cool side of the stovetop. She dropped the rag and shook her hand.

"Let's have a look."

"It's fine. Just—" She blurted out the question: "What are you doing here?"

"I told you. When you didn't come to church again, I thought. . . ." He shrugged. "Are you avoiding me?"

"Why would I avoid you? I'm avoiding crowds. That's all. I'm just not ready."

"Is that really all? I mean. . .you aren't upset with me. . .that I haven't. . .I wouldn't want you to think I—" He broke off. "I'm babbling. Forgive me. I should go."

"No," Jane said abruptly. "Come in. Have tea." She blocked the door open with Liberty's basket, then pointed to the rocking chair. "I'm afraid I haven't acquired furnishings for entertaining, however. Would you mind bringing a chair up from the shop?"

While Max fetched a chair from downstairs, she fumbled her way through making tea, all the while thinking of how frightful she must look with her hair going every which way. As to the apartment, the things from the trunk were still scattered on the rug where she'd sat this morning going through them again. And Rose's quilt lay where she'd left it when he knocked at the door. *It looks like a train drove through an hour ago.* She hurried to gather things up and return them to the trunk.

Max came back upstairs and settled a straight-backed chair on the braided rug by the windows. Jane served him tea, feeling self-conscious. "I'm so sorry for. . .the mess. I wasn't exactly expecting a caller."

He grinned. "I'm the one who should apologize. It's unconscionable to barge in on a lady the way I just have. You'd be well within your rights to send me packing."

"And I will—as soon as you tell me about your moving here and the clinic."

He nodded. "Agreed. But first. . .you."

231

"What do you want to know?"

"Everything. Anything. Whatever you want to tell me."

Liberty jumped up into her lap. As she stroked the cat's silken fur, she related the first few days cleaning the back room—and how Minnie, who'd forbidden Liberty from entering "the shop," had violated her own rule and installed a basket in the front window because, she said, having a "shop cat" got ladies to talking about Manerva.

"You like the work, then?"

"I do. It's. . .predictable. That's very helpful." She paused. "It's been hard getting used to regulating my own time instead of having bells do it for me. I'm surprised how much I miss them. Vestal and Grace. Agnes and the others." She shook her head. "Owen never let me go visiting. It's very strange to say it, but I had more friends in prison than I ever had in Dawson County. In fact, when it comes right down to it, you were my only friend there." She smiled at him. "You've always been what Mamie calls a grace note."

"A rather out-of-tune one at times."

"I didn't make it easy." She reached for her teacup. "Your turn."

"There's nothing much to tell. I don't belong out West. I like it here. Although"—he laughed—"for a while I thought I'd made a terrible mistake. But things are picking up." He told her about the old woman from church and how his consulting with her—in French—had resulted in an unexpected number of referrals. "Really, her main illness was loneliness. I prescribed some powders to help elevate her mood and told her she had to 'take the air' on a daily basis. She seems to think I've worked a miracle."

Liberty jumped down and, proceeding across the braided rug, began to nose about Rose's quilt. Jane shooed her off it, explaining as she did so, "It's for Rose. I—I wanted her to know I never forgot. . . . I was always thinking of her. Even when I was away." She paused.

"I don't know how to handle that yet. I think about it all the time. It seems like I should know what to do, but. . .it's a muddle." She swallowed. "So many things are like that right now."

"Let me help you."

His voice had changed. She met his gaze. Something flickered. Something that set her heart to racing. He held his hand out to her. She took it.

"It's too soon, and I know that. You need time, and Rose has to come first. That's as it should be." He kissed the back of her hand. "And now I should go."

She rose to walk him to the door.

He descended the stairs, then called back up to her. "I should probably warn you. I'm not staying away any longer."

She nodded. "Good."

CHAPTER 25

I'm Rose Prescott." Rose bent down to scoop up Zeus. Shushing him, she stood, peering through the screen door at the man standing on her front porch, a white envelope in his hand. Something about him seemed familiar, but try as she would, Rose couldn't decide what it was.

The stranger smiled. "You don't remember me, do you?" He removed his hat.

Zeus growled low in his throat. Nothing about the well-groomed hair, the square jaw, the way the stranger looked her in the eye with those gray-green eyes said anything but honesty and goodness. Still, Rose didn't unhook the screen door. She shook her head. "Should I?"

"I suppose not. You were young the last time we saw each other." He brushed his hand across the brim of the hat, absentmindedly shaping it as he spoke. "I'm Max. Max Zimmer. I knew you when you lived in Plum Creek." He shook his head. "And here you are, about to have a birthday and looking so grown-up." He held the envelope out. "I'm delivering something for your mother."

Rose's heart thumped. Her throat went dry. "You knew. . .my mother?"

The stranger nodded. "I had a medical practice in Plum Creek."

Rose hesitated. How did he know her birthday was coming up? And why would he come all the way from Plum Creek just to deliver a letter? If he knew where Rose lived, why not just mail it? It didn't make sense. "I'm Rose Prescott, but my mother. . ." She shook her head. "You've made a mistake." She stepped back and started to close the door.

The stranger spoke quickly. "Your father's name was Thomas. You don't remember him because he died when you were very young. Your mother remarried, and you called Owen Marquis, *Papa.*"

Rose swallowed. Her mouth went dry. She stared at the letter.

"Please, Rose. I know this is something of a shock to you, but if you'll only open and read it, I don't think you'll be sorry."

Rose's voice wavered. "I don't know what you're up to, but you should leave now." She reached for the inner door, but for some reason she didn't shut it in the stranger's face.

He looked away for a moment. His expression changed. He clenched his jaw. Finally, he took a deep breath. "Please, Rose. I don't mean you any harm. Just read the letter." He held it up. "My name really is Dr. Max Zimmer. I knew you when you were a child, and I mean you no harm. Dr. Bowen knew me. We'd planned to have him help us meet you, but—"

"Dr. Bowen passed on."

"Yes, I know. He had wonderful things to say about you. And your aunt Flora. I'm sure she had her reasons for letting you believe a lie, but your mother's a friend of mine, and whatever you've heard— she isn't dead."

"If what you're saying is true, then why are you here with a letter? And where's my mother?" Even as she said the words, Rose remembered the newspaper article that had so frightened Mrs. Partain.

The man glanced toward a buggy out at the street. "She's there.

Waiting. She wanted you to have a minute to decide whether or not you'd see her today."

Rose's knees went weak. She grasped the edge of the door as she looked toward the street. Other than a blue calico skirt, one gloved hand was all that was visible of the woman hiding in the buggy. Rose shook her head. "I don't—I don't know who you are, or what your game is, but—"

"There's no game," the stranger insisted. "She's been. . .away. She's living in Lincoln, now, and her fondest wish is to see you again. To make up the lost years. Won't you at least read the letter?"

He might as well be thrusting a hot coal at her face. Rose took a step back. She opened her mouth to order him away, but no words came out. Her heart pounded. Angry tears began to spill down her cheeks. All she could think of was to get away from that unwelcome letter, the stranger holding it, and the woman in the buggy. With a last glance toward the street, Rose closed the door. She felt dizzy. Sick to her stomach. The room receded into a gray fog as she pressed her back to the door and slid to the floor.

—⁂—

Max didn't pull away from Flora's house right away. Instead, he climbed up beside Jane and reached for her hand.

"We should go," she said, patting his hand in an awkward way that warded him off.

"No. We should wait. She might change her mind."

Jane shook her head. Her voice wavered. "This was a mistake. I should have talked to Flora first. She might have been willing to help me explain." She cleared her throat.

"Explain what? That you've spent years of your life protecting the daughter *she* tried to steal away?" He looked back at the house. "At least you can have the peace of mind knowing she can't try to pack up and disappear. Rose knows you're alive, now, and she's old enough to decide what she wants to do about it."

"Right now," Jane said, her voice breaking, "she doesn't want to do anything. She just wants me to go away." She took a wavering breath. "Please, Max. I can't just sit here waiting."

"At least let me take the quilt up to the house." When Jane hesitated, he turned to look at her. "I don't pretend to know how this is all going to work out, but you poured a lot of love into that quilt. Give her a chance to see it. To remember you."

"Flora could find it first and throw it out." She closed her eyes. "But maybe. . .maybe you're right." She bit her lower lip. "I don't know that I want it lurking in my apartment now, anyway."

Max tucked the note Rose had refused beneath the string tying the quilt box closed, then carried it across the road and up onto the porch. He could hear the little black dog yapping inside, but there was no sign of Rose. She had to be in there, though. Watching. Leaving the box on the porch swing, he hurried back to Jane.

When he climbed up beside her the second time, the look on her face made him want to gather her in his arms. Instead, he gathered up the reins and urged the horse into a smart trot. They really hadn't needed the rig just to make their way here from the station, but now that things had gone the way they had, Max was glad they could take a drive instead of just slogging back to the train station.

—⁓—

Dog. . .barking. . .whining. . .licking my face. . . Rose regained consciousness with a start. When she opened her eyes, she was face-to-face with Zeus. The dog licked her nose and yapped. Wagging its tail, it backed away, spun in a circle, and yapped again. The second Rose sat up, he leaped into her lap, then bounded back to the floor and, dancing on his hind legs, scratched at the door.

"All right, Zeus, all right." With a groan, Rose got to her feet. Before opening the door, she peered through the lace curtain mounted over the oval glass. The buggy was gone. Rose opened the door just far enough to let Zeus out in the fenced front yard. He scampered across the porch and tore across the grass and around to the side he always used to relieve himself, but instead of doing so and coming back, he began to bark again. Rose sighed. Called his name. He came to the steps, but refused to come in. Instead, he did his "I've got something cornered, and you have to come see" spin-about and then charged back around the corner of the house. If it was Mrs. Partain's new cat, they'd never hear the end of it.

Rose opened the door a little wider. No sign of the buggy. Zeus barked louder. A cat yowled. With a sigh, she stepped out onto the porch. Someone had left a pasteboard box on the swing. A box. . .tied with string. . .an envelope tucked beneath the string. Ignoring the package, she descended the stairs and hurried around the house. Scooping Zeus up, she shooed the cat out of the yard. She'd just stepped up on the porch when she heard Aunt Flora call her name.

Spinning 'round, Rose saw her hurrying toward the house, her hand holding onto her bonnet, her right hand clutching the ever-present handkerchief. When Rose glanced at the box on the swing, the stranger's words came back. *She's living in Lincoln.* Somewhere deep inside, in a place Rose had successfully ignored for years, the questions she'd stored flickered. And for some reason she didn't take time to understand, she set the dog down and snatched up the box.

Taking advantage of the fact that Aunt Flora wasn't quite tall enough to see over the hedge that ran inside the picket fence, Rose hurried inside and up the stairs, where she slid the box beneath her bed. Back downstairs, she scurried into the kitchen and poured a glass of lemonade, and just as Aunt Flora opened the door with a question as to why on earth Rose had left the dog in the yard, Rose was handing her a glass of lemonade.

"Well, aren't you just the sweetest thing," Aunt Flora said, and before she could complain about Rose's leaving the dog where he might escape through the gate, Rose was entertaining her with an imaginative rendition of the dog's encounter with Mrs. Partain's cranky new cat.

—⚇—

"Did you know," Max said, as he drove the buggy past the station and toward the edge of town, "that tears are precious to God?" When Jane didn't answer, he went on. "Reverend Irwin mentioned it in last Sunday morning's service. His text was 'Jesus wept.' The reverend said it's ridiculous for people to think that tears are a sign of weakness. They are, according to him, gifts that express empathy, compassion, and caring—things that make human beings unique. He also said that God treasures them. He referenced a verse in the Psalms that says God Himself collects our tears and that they are ever before Him."

As he talked, Jane began to weep. He kept driving. A small cemetery came into view. He pulled the buggy up beneath a massive cottonwood tree. Finally, he said quietly, "She'll come back to you, Jane. She'll remember your love. And she'll come back to you." He reached for her hand. When she gave it, he pulled her into his arms, and held her until, finally, her sobs subsided.

They drove back into town in silence, returned the rig, and walked back to the station together. Thankfully, the ticket agent named Simon who seemed to want to know everyone's business, wasn't on duty.

"Thank you for coming with me," Jane said as they sat on a bench just outside the station, waiting for the train.

Max covered her hand with his. "I can't think of anywhere on earth I'd rather have been today than with you."

She gave a sad little laugh. "Things are looking up, Dr. Zimmer. You don't have to endure being searched when you want to see me. Now you just have to put up with brief bouts of hysteria."

Because it was the wrong time to say what he wanted to, Max just shook his head as he smiled. Halfway back to Lincoln, he reached for Jane's hand again. Again, she gave it. By the time they pulled into the station at Lincoln, she'd put her head on his shoulder and fallen asleep.

—⁓—

It seemed to take half the night for Aunt Flora to finally fall asleep. Rose lay in the dark staring at the ceiling for a long while. Finally, she slipped out of bed and padded across the room to the window that looked down on the street—and the place where the buggy had waited earlier that day. She'd been so distracted, so irritable since Aunt Flora came home that her aunt had threatened to take her up to see the new doctor who'd taken over dear Dr. Bowen's practice. The only thing that avoided that was Rose's suggestion that she might be "becoming a woman." That had gotten her a dose of Lydia Pinkham's pills washed down with cod liver oil and an afternoon nap with a hot water bottle. Aunt Flora was nothing if not thorough.

Now, as moonlight silvered the picket fence and Rose waited to hear Aunt Flora's outrageously loud snoring, she gazed down on the spot where the buggy had been earlier today. She tried to envision the face that went with that gloved hand. . .and failed. Standing up, she crossed the room to her dressing table and leaned close, peering at her reflection in the moonlight. Did she look like her mother? A knock sounded at the door, and in a flash Rose dove back beneath the comforters on her bed.

"Are you all right, dear? I thought I heard you up." Aunt Flora stepped into the room.

"Hmmm?" Rose put her hand to her mouth, stifling a counterfeit yawn.

"I thought I heard you up. Shall I heat up some water and refresh the water bottle?"

"I'm fine. No need," Rose said, and snuggled deeper into her comforter.

"If you're sure?"

Rose pulled the comforter away from her face. "I'm sure. Besides, if I need the water bottle heated, I can do it. I can take care of myself."

"I know." Aunt Flora sighed deeply. "But that doesn't mean I like the idea." She paused. "I just don't know where the years have gone."

"Let's get some sleep. Whatever you've got up your sleeve for tomorrow, I want to be rested enough to enjoy it."

"I don't know what you're talking about."

"Neither do I," Rose assured her. "But there'd better be cake and ice cream involved, or I'm going to throw a fit. I worked really hard to win that competition."

Aunt Flora chuckled. "Well, it was a lovely speech. The literary society was very impressed. I'm so proud of you, Rose." She said good night.

Moments later, snoring finally sounded from across the hall and Rose slipped out of bed again. She pulled the box from beneath the bed, grateful for carpet to cushion the sound. Lighting the lamp on her dressing table, she positioned it so the reflection from the mirror bathed the room in golden light. For the first time ever, she took the skeleton key down from its resting place atop the molding above the door. Wincing as the tumbler moved into position with the turn of the key, she waited, but Aunt Flora was sound asleep now. Leaving the key in the lock, Rose turned around. She stood motionless, staring down at the box.

Finally, she bent down and, with a trembling hand, pulled the envelope from beneath the knotted string. Seated on the needlepoint bench at her dressing table, she held it up to the light, then tapped one edge to make sure she didn't tear the letter inside when she opened it. Finally, she tore away just enough of one end to gain access. It wasn't much of a letter. Only one page.

She looked at her name on the envelope and wondered at the hand that had written *Rose Elisabeth Prescott*. Finally, she removed the letter and read:

> *Dearest Rose,*
>
> *Dr. Zimmer has convinced me to come with him to Nebraska City, but I don't expect that you will want to see me. I do understand. At the same time, I hate the years we've been separated and the reason it had to be. Don't be angry with your aunt Flora.*
>
> *She did what she thought best. She loves you. She probably thought my letters would be too confusing.*

Rose frowned and looked up from the page. She tried to remember back to her first year with Aunt Flora, but it seemed like it was so long ago. She remembered Aunt Flora's soothing voice offering comfort when Rose cried because she missed her mother. Mama wouldn't be coming back, but Rose would have all the love she needed, as if she were Flora's very own child. When had Rose decided that "Mama's not coming back" meant that Mama was dead? Had Aunt Flora actually said the words, or had Rose just assumed it? Either way, the idea of Mama in prison and Aunt Flora's pretense sent a wave of emotion through her. Anger? Fear? Dread? She wasn't certain what to feel.

She looked at her reflection in the mirror again, trying to

remember life before the train ride with Aunt Flora. Only flashes of memory remained, and Rose honestly didn't know whether she was truly remembering a gunshot. . .a sheriff. . .a ride into town with someone. . . .*Max Zimmer.* He'd taken her into town. She thought she remembered his soothing voice. Or was she just remembering that from earlier today?

She remembered a kindly woman and a lot of children. Warm milk. . .and a pallet on the floor by a fireplace. She must have stayed there for at least a few days. She thought Dr. Zimmer might have come by more than once. How long would it have been before Aunt Flora came for her? Had she ever seen Mama again? She couldn't remember.

She looked back down at the letter. *She probably thought my letters would be too confusing.* Rose looked toward Aunt Flora's room. There had been letters? Rose didn't know about any letters. She'd thought Mama was dead. A knot began to form in her midsection as she read further:

I've made you something, and I hope you like the colors. They used to be your favorite. Perhaps they still are. I have a friend who's been making a crazy quilt mantel cover and adding all manner of adornment in the way of beads and tatted lace. While this isn't a crazy quilt, I've decided to borrow the idea of embellishment. I hope it will make you want to open the lock it fits. Perhaps you will remember it. You used to call it the "treasure box." Dr. Zimmer kept it while I was away, and now it waits for the day when you come to visit. I pray that the key on the quilt will bring you back to me.

With all my heart,
Mama
1040 O Street in Lincoln
Above Manerva

At some point in the reading of the letter, tears began to course down Rose's cheeks. Sniffing, she laid the letter atop her dressing table and sat, her palms resting on her thighs, staring at the box that still waited on the floor beside the bed. Finally, she swiped her tears away and crossed to the bedside carpet. Crouching down, she untied the string. With trembling hands, she lifted the lid. The quilt would be even more spectacular in the daylight, but lamplight was enough for now.

Stifling a sob, Rose sat back on her haunches, hugging her knees to her chest as she stared at the thin rectangles of blue fabric marching away from a red center square. Tan strips made the blue and red even more intense. Rose remembered brown, thirsty earth and a straggly red rosebush surrounded by blue bachelor buttons. She'd pulled a handful of those blue flowers, hadn't she? Or was that later, for Aunt Flora?

Reaching for the quilt, Rose pulled it out of the box and crossed the room to sit down at her dressing table with it spread across her lap. The ornate brass key sewn to the center block shone golden in the light of the lamp. She traced its outline, and another memory flashed through her mind. A key like this on a ribbon. . .around Mama's neck. What did it open? One thing was certain. The key on the quilt had had the desired effect. Rose was curious. Yet for all her curiosity, she couldn't overcome the sense of dread she felt when she pondered the idea of meeting the woman who'd penned the letter, who'd been waiting in that buggy. If Mama wasn't dead, then what had happened that night when Papa died?

The longer Rose thought about that, the more she feared the answer. Yet it had to be. Mama had committed murder. That explained everything. Didn't it? Aunt Flora was protecting her. Wasn't she?

CHAPTER 26

For a few days after the quilt arrived, nothing changed. Rose left it beneath the bed and pondered. She went through the motions of pretending to be surprised at the party she'd known Aunt Flora was planning and helped with deadheading the rose arbor and agreed with Aunt Flora that October breezes were much to be preferred to the sweltering heat they'd endured this past summer. But through every day, the knowledge that she had a letter from Mama was never far from Rose's thoughts, and the box with a quilt and a key called to her, almost as if a faint light beckoned from the dark space beneath the bed. And then, one cool October night, Rose woke with a start when Aunt Flora shook her awake.

"You were sobbing, dear girl. What broke your heart so?"

The words tumbled out as Rose sat up, swiping her tangled hair away from her face. "It's dark. I can't see it, but I hear a loud noise. I think it's a gun. There's a flash. And then I'm in my bed, but I can't sleep. Not this bed. Another one. And Mama's talking, but I can't quite hear what she's saying. I just know she's talking. And then flowers. Lots of flowers on the ground. And a white fence." She shuddered.

Aunt Flora sat down on the edge of the bed and held out her arms. Rose snuggled close while her aunt murmured, "That must have been horrible, but it was just a dream. You're safe. No one's going to hurt you. I would never let that happen."

"I can't remember things," Rose murmured. "I've been trying to remember back before the train ride." She paused. "What was the name of the town where we lived?" Was it Rose's imagination, or did Aunt Flora stiffen just a little when she answered the question?

"Plum Creek. I came for you as soon as I heard about the accident. And it's no wonder you don't remember. It was a terrible, terrible thing for a little girl to go through, and I'm glad you've forgotten it." She paused. "The flowers on the ground and the white fence are probably what you remember about the cemetery. But that's over now. We've a happy life here in Nebraska City. You don't have to worry about the past, dear." She took Rose by the arms and encouraged her—strongly—to lie back. "Now, I'm going to make you some chamomile tea to calm your nerves." Aunt Flora left the room.

Rose didn't ask any more questions about the past, but as the days went by and she kept dreaming, Aunt Flora took her to see the new doctor. "She'll be fine," he said. "She's growing like a weed. Her body's under stress. That can cause emotional outbursts. It'll pass."

Except that it didn't. When Rose realized that telling the dreams upset Aunt Flora almost as much as dreaming them did her, she stopped the telling. If she cried loud enough in her sleep to awaken Aunt Flora, she said she didn't remember the dream, even though she did. She began to write the dreams down on waking. And as time went on, she either dreamed in greater detail or she began to remember more. She reread Mama's letter, and she began to pull the quilt out of its box on occasion, rolling it up and hiding it beneath her covers so that she could sleep next to it. She remembered red roses. And blue flowers. And lying on her back, looking up at the stars. She thought she remembered a voice. *The stars have names.* Slowly, she began to be able to tell the difference between the distortions of dreams and true memories.

And then, as a result of events connected to sweet old Mrs. Partain's decline, Rose remembered everything.

—✺—

A fall breeze tumbled fallen leaves past as Jane and Minnie made their way toward the corner of Eleventh and J Streets and Jane's introduction to the First Presbyterian Church Ladies Aid Society members via their weekly quilting. When Jane hesitated a few feet from the side door that would lead them inside, Minnie reached out to her. "You quilt twelve stitches to the inch. They'll welcome you with open arms."

Jane swallowed. "It's not the quilting I'm nervous about. It's that newspaper article. And the chitchat."

"That all happened to Jane *Marquis*. You're Jane Prescott now."

"What if they realize. . . ?"

"Well, if they do, they'll know that you're very brave and that you've modeled love like few people ever do." Minnie smiled. "Give them a chance. They're good women. You'll like them."

Jane looked back in the direction of Manerva. Every single instinct told her to run for cover while she had the chance. She wasn't ready for this part of real life. Not yet. She'd just opened her mouth to thank Minnie before heading back to the shop, when the side door to the church opened to reveal a severe-looking woman dressed in a simple green calico dress. Jane stood rooted to the earth, feeling like a schoolgirl about to be inspected for head lice. But then, the woman's green eyes crinkled at the corners and, smiling, she called out a greeting to "Minnie and the woman we've all heard so much about."

What had they heard? A new wave of dread washed over Jane, but then the woman introduced herself. "I'm so *glad* you've finally decided to join us. May I call you Jane? I'm Louise. Louise Irwin."

Oh dear. The pastor's wife. Jane stammered a greeting.

Mrs. Irwin reached out and gave Jane's hand a little squeeze, holding on as she said, "I can only imagine how much courage it's taken for you to come this far today. I've been praying my heart out while I watched for you and Minnie. I was afraid you'd change your mind."

Jane glanced back toward the shop. "I—I think I had. Changed my mind."

Mrs. Irwin nodded. "I understand how you might. Believe me, the first day my husband stepped into this august pulpit, I felt like I was being stared clean through." She patted Jane's hand. "I've been watching for you so that we could get some business out of the way. Of course I know your previous name and some of what's happened to you, but only because of my involvement on the committee with Miss Dawson and Mrs. McKenna. No one else needs to know a thing about any of that unless you decide to tell them. I just wanted to reassure you about that. Your privacy will be respected." Mrs. Irwin let go of her hand. "I also wanted to tell you that, in my opinion, you're quite heroic."

Jane stammered her thanks. She didn't feel quite like running off, but she still wasn't convinced about facing a group of church women. She thought about Vestal and Agnes and wondered how they would fare in situations like this. *Without the caveat of the preacher's wife calling them "heroic."* Would either woman so much as think of attending a church with stained-glass windows and a pipe organ, a church where prominent citizens supported aid societies and projects for "the friendless"? She couldn't imagine it. She couldn't imagine ever feeling like she really belonged here, either. Mrs. Irwin might think her heroic, but Jane felt very much like a woman with a shadowed past.

Mrs. Irwin motioned for Jane and Minnie to follow her inside. "I suppose I should confess to an ulterior motive in wanting you to stick with us." She paused. "There's something of a competition between us and the Methodists and the Baptists when it comes to our quilting—and our pie baking, truth be told. At the moment, the Baptists are the uncontested best pie-bakers." She smiled at Jane. "I'm hoping *you'll* help us get ahead in the quilting competition. Minnie says you're a master quilter. We're working on our state fair entry for next year as soon as we get the present project out of the frame, and I don't mind telling you the Methodists have a few quilters who are giving us a run for our money. Their holiday bazaar last year was the talk of the town. We're determined to best them— in a completely loving manner, of course." She laughed.

As she talked, Mrs. Irwin was leading them inside. She paused on the landing just inside the door. Jane glanced up the wide stairs toward the massive double doors above.

"Of course the sanctuary is at the top of those stairs," Mrs. Irwin said. "We're just beginning a Sabbath school. The rooms are off up this hall." She pointed straight ahead. "But we quilt down in the basement. The light isn't the best except at midday, but it's cooler in summer and warmer in winter, so we make do by meeting over lunch on Tuesdays when the light is at its best. Some of the ladies come on Thursdays, too, but this is our official. . ."

Her voice trailed off as they descended the stairs. An uninvited chill made Jane shiver a bit at the memory that came with the faintest aroma of damp basement. The floor was smooth, gray concrete. Today, though, sunshine streamed in the half-windows level with the sidewalk outside, glancing off the bright white walls and making the room much more cheerful than the prison dormitory had ever been. They made their way past a table laden with sandwiches and luncheon foods, pitchers of water, and a stack of plates and napkins.

249

Two layer cakes vied for the place of honor at the middle of the table: one with white frosting sprinkled with coconut, the other boasting pink frosting garnished with strawberries.

Mrs. Irwin raised her voice just a little as she called out, "Here, here, ladies. Minnie's brought us a visitor and hopefully a new member." The room grew quiet.

Jane forced herself to smile and meet each woman's gaze, hoping she looked more confident than she felt. She also hoped they couldn't see how she was trembling as she clasped her gloved hands in front of her.

Minnie spoke as she removed her own gloves. "Jane's worked at Manerva for a few weeks now, and I can guarantee you are all going to be happy she's chosen First Presbyterian for her home church." She chuckled. "*We'll* be winning the blue ribbon at the fair next year. You're going to *love* having Jane in our group."

Jane thought she recognized the woman in the gray silk, and she was right. The willow-slim woman looked up with a smile. "Blanche Gordon. I remember seeing you last week. I was in Manerva for a fitting."

"Thank you for the advertisement," Minnie quipped as she smiled at the other women. "And you're all welcome to follow the good Mrs. Gordon's example and come by the shop. Jane's helped me catch up and get organized. We can turn out the latest styles more quickly than any of the other dressmakers in Lincoln."

"Don't let the Thornburns hear you say that," the brunette at the far end of the quilting frame laughed. She held up the book in her hand. "Eliza Carver. I'm terrible at handwork, so I've been designated the entertainment committee. We're reading Mr. Twain's *Innocents Abroad* at the moment."

"Eliza also keeps us apprised of changes in fashion," Mrs. Irwin said. "She wears the latest styles."

"Now, Louise." Mrs. Carver smiled as she tucked an errant curl behind her ear. "That's flattery, and your husband just preached a sermon on the dangers of vanity."

Mrs. Irwin smiled and pointed to the next woman seated at the quilt. "Next to Eliza is Betty Lyman, who directs the Ladies Missionary Band, has perfect pitch, and sings like an angel. And then there's Sarah Tower. She keeps us all on task and generally has us committed two or three quilts ahead."

"Which aren't going to get finished before the snow flies if we don't get down to work." Sarah punctuated the implied scolding by snipping her thread and unwinding a new length from one of the spools lying atop the quilt.

Mrs. Irwin pulled out a chair for Jane between herself and Minnie. As she sat down, Jane studied the current project. She'd thought the church was going to have the women at the prison quilt their fund-raising quilt. Apparently they'd decided against it. She wondered why but didn't dare ask the question. She'd never seen this particular block before. Turkey-red-and-white strips created a fan in each corner of the square blocks. The white strips bore signatures, while business names and advertisements filled the spaces at the edges of the fans. A block near Jane touted Singer sewing machines. Jane glanced at Minnie. "Did Manerva sponsor a block?"

"Over here." Sarah Tower pointed to the block in front of her. "Individuals donated fifty cents to sign in a fan blade. Most businesses donated two dollars."

Blanche Gordon adjusted her glasses as she said, "Dr. Zimmer insisted I accept a dollar the day he signed. He said it was for a worthy cause." She swept her palm across the surface of the quilt. "I think there's a very good chance we'll add at least a hundred dollars to the band fund once this is raffled off." She glanced at Mrs. Tower. "You can remind Dr. Zimmer that he promised to buy an entire book of raffle tickets as soon as we have them printed up."

"That man." Eliza Carver practically sighed. "What a catch he'll be."

Betty Lyman scolded, "Eliza Carver, you are a married woman."

Eliza agreed. "Happily, permanently, and joyfully. But not dead, Betty. And don't sit there and pretend you haven't enjoyed the view from the choir loft since the good doctor joined First Pres'."

Betty laughed and shook her head, even as she blushed crimson.

Sarah Tower spoke up. "Don't let Madame Savoie catch you all giggling like girls. She'd be horrified. Besides, you know good and well she has Dr. Zimmer's romantic future planned." She held her needle up to the light and squinted in a vain attempt to thread it.

"Can I do that for you?" Jane asked.

"Thank you, dear."

Jane concentrated on threading Mrs. Tower's needle while the women teased and bantered about Max and how the church women with daughters of marriageable age were competing to have him to dinner. By lunchtime, they were practically taking wagers on whether or not Madame Savoie, whoever that was, would succeed in her plans to match Dr. Zimmer with her niece, who was apparently due to arrive in Lincoln any day now.

Over lunch, Jane learned that Blanche Gordon and Sarah Tower carried on a perpetual competition as to whose cake was the best, and Eliza had very specific opinions regarding what was and was not appropriate reading material for Christian women. They might be reading *Innocents Abroad* at the moment, but the author's novels were not on Eliza's approved list.

"Don't look now," Minnie murmured at one point. "You're being reviewed." She glanced toward the quilt. Jane couldn't help but smile as she realized that, while they were discreet about it, each of the women made it a point to look down at the place where Jane had been quilting as they passed by to take up their own stations.

That afternoon, as she and Jane made their way back to the shop, Minnie leaned close and said, "You passed inspection with flying colors, Mrs. Prescott."

"You think so?"

Minnie nodded. "When Blanche Gordon compliments a quilter's stitches, that's as good as getting an engraved invitation to the inner circle of the Ladies Aid." She grinned. "Although they may falter a bit when they see you sitting with Max Zimmer in church on Sunday. I noticed a couple of Sundays ago that the Lymans had taken to sitting in a new row that puts Betty's daughter in the line of sight between your Dr. Zimmer and the pulpit."

"He is not *my* Dr. Zimmer," Jane protested, "and there is absolutely no reason for anyone to be jealous. Max and I are friends. I hardly think we'll be sitting together in church."

Minnie rolled her eyes. "Fine, Jane. Have it your way."

"Did you hear what I just said? Max and I are friends. And besides that, don't you think Dr. Zimmer should have things *his* way when it comes to where and with whom he sits in church?"

"Absolutely. Which is why he'll be sitting with *you*."

Jane said nothing. She didn't think Max would be parading their friendship in public. What if her past became known? That would likely happen at some point, whether she'd taken back Thomas's name or not. Max should avoid ruffling feathers while he was building his practice. Earning people's trust took time. Besides that, this Madame Savoie the women talked about was obviously someone prominent. It wouldn't do to offend her. Not if it could be avoided—and it could. Jane would be a good friend. She'd encourage Max to be friendly with the woman's visiting niece. Friends did that for one other, didn't they? She would be a good friend. She told herself so over and over and over again until, finally, she fell asleep.

CHAPTER 27

Mamie Dawson stood at her turret window, looking out on the browning prairie as shadows lengthened. Tugging at the shawl about her shoulders, she set her jaw and "took herself in hand," intent on speaking to the Lord about the past few weeks—in their entirety, whether what she talked about made her sound like the fool she was or not. As was her habit, she began with "thankfuls."

There was much for which to be thankful. The ladies had adjusted to Jane's absence and settled into a new routine that kept them busy with profitable work. They'd taken to Ellen's reading lessons well. Agnes Sweeney had found ways to spoil Patch, thereby revealing a nurturing spirit that began to shine past her rough exterior. Baby Grace was thriving, and Vestal had asked for help with finding work once she was released early next year. Ellen was making inquiries, and a possibility in the small town of Normal just outside Lincoln looked promising.

All in all, the Lord had done "exceeding abundantly beyond" all that Mamie had expected in regards to the female department. All in all, if it wasn't for her foolishness over Martin Underhill, life would be satisfying. The Lord had called her to a strange mission field, but the harvest was beginning to look promising. If only she hadn't ruined everything with Martin.

Blinking away tears, Mamie finished her list of thankfuls and took up the topic of foolishness. She'd always known that words were powerful things, but she'd had no idea that only three words spoken out of turn could ruin a friendship. Martin had been. . .odd since the day she'd said them. Well. Odd*er*. He was still there to help serve breakfast every morning, and he still treated the ladies with studied kindness. But then, then that was all. No invitations to supper down in the kitchen, no smiles, and this morning when she'd invited him to drive into Lincoln with her for Sunday church—to see how Jane was faring, of course—he'd mumbled about possibly having something else to do. On the Sabbath. When he didn't have to work.

Mamie hiccuped as she turned away from the window. Tears gathered. "Why couldn't I just let things be? I made a fool of myself talking about love, and now I've lost a good friend." Tears slid down her cheeks as she murmured her misery to God. "What did I expect the poor man to do? Be waiting on bended knee when I came back to work on Monday? I probably frightened the daylights out of him. No *wonder* he's been avoiding me." She hiccuped again as she slumped down into the rocking chair. "Why couldn't I have just let well enough alone?"

Miserable, Mamie stared around her at the room that had always been her refuge. A rocker, a soft quilt, and God's Word. This evening it felt almost barren. She looked at the Bible again. *I just don't feel like it tonight, Lord. You understand, don't You?* Just allowing the thought caused a pang of regret. She couldn't let personal disappointment have this much power, could she? No. She would not. But what to read?

Thinking about love led her to the familiar passage in 1 Corinthians. *"Though I speak with the tongues of men and of angels. . .and have not charity. . ."* As Mamie read, she began to beg for help. *Keep me from being a clanging cymbal, Lord. Help me to continue to be patient and kind. I'm sorry I sought my own. Help me to look out for Martin's good.*

She would do that. With God's help, she would take herself in hand and stop her nonsensical mooning about. She would humble herself and apologize, and Martin would understand. And even if he couldn't understand, he would try. He had to, because if things didn't get put right between them, she was going to have to quit her job. It was just too painful to be around Martin without the warmth of friendship she'd grown to love as she grew to love Martin. Taking a deep breath, Mamie leaned her head against the back of the rocker and closed her eyes.

Help me know what to say. I will humble myself. Help me know how to do it. Please give my friend back. He doesn't have to love me, but please, Lord. . .let him be my friend.

She'd just dozed off when a knock sounded at the apartment door. Rising, Mamie pulled a shawl about her shoulders and went to the door. *Martin. With. . .roses?* Robbed of words, Mamie stared up at him.

He bobbed his head. "I know you said you like wildflowers best, but October's just not good for wildflowers. So I rode into town, and I just thought—"

"They're lovely." Mamie invited him inside, grateful when he accepted.

"I guess you've wondered what became of me."

Oh dear. She wasn't ready to be put in her place, but if this was the Lord's way of answering her prayer, she would manage. Somehow. "I believe I know what became of you," Mamie said, taking the bouquet and heading into the kitchen in search of a vase.

"You. . .do?" He sounded genuinely surprised.

"I made a fool of myself with all that talk of—" She broke off.

Concentrated on arranging the flowers in the vase. "I'm sorry."

"You are? You mean—" He gulped. "You want to take back what you said." It wasn't a question.

Mamie looked up at him. He was blushing. He glanced behind him toward the apartment door, looking like he was ready to flee.

"What I want—most sincerely—is to prevent that romantic nonsense I blurted out from standing in the way of our friendship. If you're willing." Mamie swallowed. "I've missed you. . .terribly." She set the vase of flowers on the dining table.

"You have?" He seemed honestly surprised.

"Well, of course I have. You're a dear, dear man and—" *There you go again. More romantic nonsense.* Taking a deep breath, Mamie began again. "We've been good friends, haven't we? Goodness, you saved my life. You've helped me get the female department organized and—well—I just hate thinking I've lost. . ." She took a deep breath. Shook her head.

"You haven't. I've been—I haven't known quite how to act, is all." He cleared his throat. "I'm just not used to getting attention from such a fine woman as you, Mamie. At least not *nice* attention."

Mamie smiled. "Well then, that just goes to show how foolish women can be." She retreated back into the kitchen. "I've a pot of soup on if you can stay for supper." She turned her back on the dining room to retrieve spoons and bowls. When she turned back around, Martin, his face crimson, had gotten down on one knee. At first Mamie thought the poor man was having an attack of some kind. He sputtered and bobbed and started to speak, then stopped. Finally, Mamie realized what was happening. Her heart fluttered. She set the bowls and spoons down on the table and waited, her hands folded.

"I. . .uh. I haven't thought about much else besides what you said." He swallowed. "And it wasn't nonsense. I just. . .I. . .I mean. . .I'm. . ."

He shrugged and hung his head as he whispered more to the floor than to Mamie. "Nobody's ever wanted me, Mamie. My own ma left me on the steps at a church. They took me to a foundling home." He looked up at her. "I know I'm a sorry sight. But you said—and I was hoping. . .maybe." He shrugged. "I was wondering if you'd think about. . .maybe. . .marrying me?"

Mamie hiccuped as she bent down to cradle his misshapen face in her hands. She looked into his eyes and said, "You dear, dear, man. I thought you'd *never* ask."

———⁂———

Poor Mrs. Partain had been in steady decline all summer long, and no one knew it better than Rose. Whether it was because Rose was one of the few people who treated the old woman with sincere kindness, or because Rose reminded Mrs. Partain of the married daughter who ignored her, or just because Rose was right there next door, whatever the reason, on days when Rose settled on the porch swing to read, more often than not at some point Mrs. Partain ended up sitting next to her. Some days Rose read to her. Some days the old woman grabbed the book away so she could read it for herself. Some days she worried about the imaginary "them" who threatened her safety, and on others she seemed content.

As summer faded into fall, Rose began to notice that less of what Mrs. Partain said made sense. It grew more difficult to know how to have a conversation. Rose didn't want to be rude, but how did a person answer a question like, "Did you remember to have Fluffy feed the owls in the attic last night?" Finally, midway through October, Mrs. Partain's married daughter, Hermione, arrived to—as she put it when she spoke to Aunt Flora—"take things in hand."

Aunt Flora called Hermione "a dynamo," even as she expressed some doubt as to Hermione's method of child-rearing. After all,

Aunt Flora said, children should be children. Hermione seemed to consider her three boys as her personal labor force. At seven, nine, and eleven years old, the boys spent the first two weeks of their stay in Nebraska City weeding, scrubbing, and sorting through the contents of what their mother called "that horror of a cluttered mess endangering Mother's health."

Rose did notice that, in regards to Mrs. Partain, some things improved right away. The old woman now smelled of rosewater and soap instead of. . .something else. She stopped wearing too much rouge and the odd collections of mismatched garments. While the improvement was obvious, so was the fact that both Mrs. Partain's penchant for bangles and her smile seemed to disappear at about the same. When asked why she felt sad, the old woman sighed. "Oh, well. . .you know." And so they sat on the porch swing, and Rose held Mrs. Partain's hand while, just on the other side of the fence, carpets were beaten, bedding aired, and floors scrubbed.

As the work slowed and Hermione began to give "the boys" more time to themselves, they began to get into trouble. First, they targeted Zeus with their slingshots. When Aunt Flora bustled over and "had words" with Hermione, the boys presented written apologies and an offer to do chores for Aunt Flora. They washed windows and weeded the rose beds and ended up lunching on the back porch, savoring Aunt Flora's home-baked gingersnaps.

One afternoon shortly after the reconciliation, Hermione asked Rose to "keep an eye on the boys" while she "took Mother to the doctor for an evaluation." That afternoon, the three boys introduced Rose to a fantastical world that made her deeply regret she didn't have any brothers. Sporting battered cowboy hats discovered in their grandmother's attic, they played "cattle rustler" and "train robber." Rose came up with the idea of turning barrels on their sides and tying ropes to the back porch railing to create horses, and momentarily forgot her mature status as an almost-fifteen-year-old in favor of riding the trail with Billy the Kid, Jesse James, and Sheriff Cody.

When it came time for the inevitable gunfight, "the Kid" disappeared inside his grandmother's house for a moment, returning with a pair of broken pistols. Rose reached for one, expecting to be a deputy to Sheriff Cody. But the boys insisted she be the captured "bonnet." Sheriff Cody—Rose suspected he had a crush on her—seemed bent on a dramatic rescue scene.

After another ride into imaginary canyons, Jesse James grabbed her and dragged her into a cave—or Mrs. Partain's back porch, depending on one's ability to imagine. When Jesse growled, "Yer—gonna—come—with—me—er'else," Sheriff Cody answered the call and came to the rescue, brandishing a broken pistol and shouting, "Stop that! Let her go! I won't let you hurt her!"

Something felt. . .odd. Rose blinked. The front door of the house slammed. Hermione and Mrs. Partain returning? Whatever the source, something about that sound and the sheriff's shouted words combined with the view of his brandishing a broken gun transcended the moment.

Reality faded. *Stop that! Let her go! I won't let you hurt her!*

Rose frowned. No longer was there a broken gun in a boy's hand. No longer was the sound just a screen door slamming closed. A flash of light accompanied a loud bang. The words echoed. The gun. . .was in Rose's hand. Not the pretend sheriff's—not Mother's, either. In *Rose's*.

She heard Mother's voice. "It's all right, Rose. Mama's taking you to bed. You've had a bad dream. That's all it is. Do you hear me, honey? You've had a nightmare. You remember that. *It's just a dream.* Mama will take care of everything. You stay here in bed. Everything will be all right. Mama will see to it. It was just a dream."

The color seeped out of the world. Rose blinked. Looked from the sheriff to Jesse James and toward Aunt Flora's house. . .and crumpled.

—⚏—

Rose didn't open her eyes right away. Instead, she lay still while flashes of light glimmered against the dark veil behind her closed eyes. When the buzzing sound in the background proved to be voices, she listened just enough to realize that whoever was talking wasn't close by.

She took a deep breath, and the faint scent of lavender and lemon oil calmed her racing pulse. She opened her eyes just enough to realize she was in her own bed, the dark walnut footboard silhouetted in the golden glow of the lamp on her dressing table. She glanced toward the door, listening to the conversation taking place just outside in the hall.

"I gave her something to calm her. She'll likely sleep the night through. Are you certain she hasn't shown any signs of illness?"

Aunt Flora sounded weary. Rose could imagine her shaking her head as she spoke. "Other than some bad dreams the last few weeks, there's been nothing. They seemed to have stopped. She was playing with those boys, and she just fainted away. Mrs. Partain's daughter witnessed it. She said one minute Rose was being rescued from an imaginary horse thief, and the next she was on the ground."

"Let her rest. If she's hungry, offer toast and tea. I'll stop by again in the morning." Obviously, Aunt Flora had summoned the doctor. After prescribing toast and tea, he asked, "Is there a history of anything like this in the family?"

Aunt Flora sounded afraid when she answered. "Her father died when Rose was four years old. His heart, they thought. There was no warning."

"And her mother?"

"Healthy, as far as I know."

"She's still living?"

Aunt Flora must have pulled the doctor away from the door, because Rose couldn't hear the answer to that question. She didn't need to hear it, though. She knew the answer. Mother had been in prison. Aunt Flora had *pretended* she was dead, but Mother wasn't dead. She'd been in prison. She been in prison, but she hadn't done wrong. *Ever.* She'd never hurt anyone. In fact, she'd done everything she could to protect Rose. Always.

Rose blinked tears away as she remembered the newspaper article Mrs. Partain had brought over that day. Even in prison, Mama had saved someone's life. *Mama.* Rose curled onto her side. *Mama kept me safe. She saved someone else. And I made her go away.*

The doctor's footsteps retreated down the stairs. Rose turned over, her back to her bedroom door. When Aunt Flora came in to check on her, she breathed deeply, evenly, pretending to be asleep. She felt the mattress sag and the coverlet tug across her shoulders as Aunt Flora perched on the edge of the bed and combed through Rose's hair with gentle strokes. "Poor baby," she murmured. "Sleep... You're safe....Aunt Flora's here...."

Rose stirred a bit, burrowing into her pillow. *Please go away. Just—go—away.* It seemed to take forever for Aunt Flora to finally lean down and kiss Rose's cheek, to get up and turn down the lamp, and finally, to leave the room.

Once alone, Rose opened her eyes. Aunt Flora had left the door cracked. As she lay quietly, waiting for the sound of snoring, resentment seethed. *You lied to me. You let me think Mama was gone. How could you lie to me that way, for all this time. How could you?* Her mind raced, connecting flashes of memory, asking questions of the absent Aunt Flora, crying tears of regret and longing until, at long last, soft snores sounded from Aunt Flora's room.

Trembling, Rose scooted out of bed. Lying on her stomach beside the bed, she reached for the box. When she'd finally managed to wriggle it free, she lifted the lid and took up the letter.

Afraid to light the lamp, she tiptoed to the window and held the letter up in the moonlight. This time, the words held different meanings. *Dr. Zimmer has convinced me to come with him to Nebraska City, but I don't expect that you will want to see me.* Mama had let everyone believe *she'd* done something terrible. She'd even made Rose believe it. She'd gone to prison to pay for something Rose did.

Rose shivered. What did they do to girls who killed their fathers? The thought was too horrible. She looked back down at the letter. *I don't expect you'll want to see me.* It was no wonder she'd thought that. She must have assumed that Rose believed the lie. And then Aunt Flora had lied, letting her believe Mama was dead.

Don't be angry with your aunt Flora. She did what she thought best. She loves you. She probably thought my letters would be too confusing. Rose supposed that could be right. After all, if Aunt Flora believed Mama had done murder, she'd want to protect Rose. Rose's anger against Aunt Flora diminished a bit. Still, if there were letters from Mama, she wanted to read them. Would Aunt Flora have kept them?

I've made you something, and I hope you like the colors. They used to be your favorite. Perhaps they still are. Rose looked across the room at the quilt in the box. She realized now that the blue bachelor buttons and the red roses were real childhood memories. She'd picked those flowers for Mama. Just outside the front door of the house out West. Rose didn't remember the house very well, except for her own room. She remembered Papa shooting a gun at a can and calling her. . .Rose frowned. *He called me his little gunslinger. Mama didn't want him to teach me, but he didn't pay her any mind.*

Rose still wasn't positive which of her recollections about that night were memories and which were bad dreams, but she'd known shouting and loud noises in the night. And crying. She remembered Mama crying for what seemed like a very long time. And then voices. Footsteps. And more anger in still more voices. Fresh tears threatened, and Rose looked back down at the letter:

> *I have a friend who's been making a crazy quilt mantel cover and adding all manner of adornment in the way of beads and tatted lace. While this isn't a crazy quilt, I've decided to borrow the idea of embellishment. I hope it will make you want to open the lock it fits. Perhaps you will remember it. You used to call it the "treasure box."*

Rose looked up from the letter again and out the window to where the buggy had waited that day, the buggy with Mama in it. She didn't remember a treasure box, but she remembered the key. *On a yellow ribbon around Mama's neck.* She crossed the room and, taking the quilt from the box, took it back to the window seat and traced the brass key, disappointed when the feel of it didn't help her remember anything more.

> *Dr. Zimmer kept it while I was away, and now it waits for the day when you come to visit. I pray that the key on the quilt will bring you back to me.*
>
>
>
> *With all my heart,*
> *Mama*
> *1040 O Street in Lincoln*
> *Above Manerva*
>
>

Rose touched the word *Mama*. Mama. . .who had taken the blame and gone away to a terrible place. A shiver ran up Rose's spine. What would they do to her when she admitted to killing Papa? New fear clutched at her midsection. She wrapped her arms around the quilt and looked out the window as tears spilled down her cheeks. Papa had been good sometimes, but he'd been bad, too. Sometimes he hurt Mama. All Rose had wanted that night was to make him stop hurting Mama. Would anyone believe her? Would Mama ever forgive her for sending her away?

Suddenly, Rose was more tired than she'd ever been. Tired and afraid. Afraid to tell Aunt Flora what she'd remembered and yet afraid not to tell. . .someone. Rose sat at the window for a long time, looking out on the moonlit yard and wondering what to do. Aunt Flora loved her, but Aunt Flora's love was the kind that fussed and flustered. Aunt Flora had let her think Mama was dead rather than face the questions Rose would have had if they'd gone to visit Mama at the jail. Aunt Flora would wish Rose had never remembered.

With a sigh, Rose placed the quilt with the key in the box and shoved it back beneath the bed. Tucking Mama's letter beneath her pillow, she slid beneath the coverlet and closed her eyes. Remembering. Finally, she slid back out of bed and retrieved the "George Washy" doll quilt from the doll bed beneath her window. Clutching it in her hand, she curled onto her side and whispered, "Do You hear me, God? I don't know what to do. Please help me know what to do." Tears spilled onto her pillow until, finally exhausted, she slept.

CHAPTER 28

Seated across from Aunt Flora at the breakfast table, Rose prodded the soft-boiled egg on her plate with disinterest. Finally, she laid her fork down. "I'm sorry, Aunt Flora. Tea and toast is all I think my stomach will abide right now." She took a sip of tea.

Clucking her concern, Aunt Flora reached over to put her palm to Rose's forehead.

"I don't have a fever. I'm sure of it. I just don't feel able to go to church is all." Rose feigned a cough. "I don't think I'm contagious, but it wouldn't be right to take a chance."

With a sigh, Aunt Flora leaned back in her chair. "Well, I suppose I'll stay with you. In case you need something."

"I won't need anything," Rose protested. She forced a smile. "Really. I can manage by myself." *I'm really trying not to lie, God. Could You make her stop asking questions?*

With a long look in Rose's direction, Aunt Flora sighed. "If you're sure."

Rose nodded. "I am. I'm sorry I'll miss your solo."

Aunt Flora waved a hand in the air. "Oh, posh. It's only half a line. It's nothing."

"Well, Mr. Vandemeer is counting on you to sing it, so you'd best get going." She stood up. "And I'm heading back upstairs to bed." *For now.* She forced herself to mount the stairs slowly, even as her heart pounded. Today was the day.

When she slid back into bed, she closed her eyes, feigning sleep even as Aunt Flora fluttered back and forth, bringing water and some of the new doctor's powders, second-guessing herself, and threatening to stay home until Rose thought she would scream. Finally, after what felt like hours, Aunt Flora called good-bye from the doorway. Rose murmured a response, then lay still, listening to Aunt Flora's footsteps retreat down the stairs and waiting for the door to close. Finally, she slid out of bed and went to the window, watching as Aunt Flora made her way up the street and around the corner. Only when she was out of sight did Rose pull the quilt box out from beneath the bed to wrap one of her belts around it, both to hold it closed and to create a kind of handle. She hurried to dress, slipping into a simple calico day dress and sturdy shoes.

Last, she retrieved a change purse from where she'd secreted it among her dolls. She re-counted the money. Exactly enough. From beneath her pillow, she extracted an envelope. She'd written the note a few days ago. Pausing to read it again, she crossed the hall and laid it on Aunt Flora's bed where Zeus lay, curled up and shivering.

"Don't tell me it's going to storm," Rose said to the dog, who only lifted his head momentarily, then whined and proceeded to burrow beneath the pillows on Aunt Flora's bed. "I'm sorry, Zeus. I can't stay. You'll be all right. She'll be back before too long."

Turning her back on the dog, Rose descended the stairs, carrying the quilt box much like a suitcase. She went to the front door only long enough to pull her wrapper and bonnet off the hall tree. Was it her imagination, or did she hear thunder in the distance? Aunt Flora had taken the best umbrella. Rose reached for the older one, but it was in such sad shape, she decided she'd just have to brave the weather and hope for the best.

Please, God. Could You hold the rain off until I get there? And could You help Aunt Flora not be too angry with me? It seemed odd to be worrying over Aunt Flora after what she'd done. But in recent days, Rose had read and reread Mama's letter. Mama said she shouldn't be angry with Aunt Flora. Rose wasn't quite certain that was right, but then if anyone had a reason to be angry, it was Mama. If Mama could forgive, Rose thought she should, too. Maybe she would. But today. . .today she was angry. And determined.

Stepping outside, Rose looked around the backyard. She glanced over at Mrs. Partain's back porch, where she'd been the day everything started to come back. The house looked forlorn, what with Mrs. Partain's daughter having taken the old woman off to some "home" in Illinois where she would receive "proper care." Rose wondered if the people at that home let Mrs. Partain wear bangles. She hoped so.

Thunder rolled. A train whistle sounded. And, quilt box in hand, Rose took off running for the station.

—⁓—

The October Sunday after she attended the Ladies Aid Society quilting, Jane rose shortly after dawn and made tea atop the tiny stove across from her narrow bed. The skies were overcast, and as church bells began to ring across the city, Jane gazed toward the south, thinking about the women in the female department and how dismal the ward could be when skies turned gray.

She wondered if Ellen McKenna had returned to minding the ward on Sundays yet, or if Pearl Brand's violence had frightened her fully and completely away. Jane hoped not. Ellen was doing good work the women appreciated. Agnes Sweeney loved being able to read and do sums, and whether they admitted it or not, the women all liked being around a real lady who cared about them. . .and Ellen McKenna was nothing if not a real lady.

Thinking about Ellen roused the memory of Ian McKenna descending the stairs the day Jane left for Lincoln, thanking her, insisting she accept an envelope with money in it to help her get started on a new life. Insisting with a trembling voice that barely managed not to crack with emotion. Thinking of Ian and Ellen McKenna's love for each other made Jane glance across her tiny apartment toward the box of mementos she'd kept for Rose. The few things that had belonged to Thomas seemed even more important in light of what Rose might remember someday about Owen.

As Jane steeped her tea and nibbled on a cold biscuit, she made her way to the box and opened the lid. Settling on the floor beside it, she took out the cabinet card of Thomas. Remembering Thomas made her smile. He'd cherished her the way Ian McKenna cherished Ellen. As she put the portrait back atop the mementos in the small chest, Jane thought of Max Zimmer. Was he enjoying his morning coffee out on that screened porch of his? Did he have to mind patients in the infirmary, or would he be at church this morning? Had he hired a city version of the Widow Mabry, who'd minded the office in Plum Creek? The thought tempted a flicker of jealousy.

Closing the lid to the chest, Jane took the last bite of biscuit and another gulp of lukewarm tea, even as she scolded herself. *You have far more important things to ponder in life than romantic notions of Max Zimmer.* Thoughts of Rose were never far away, but somehow she was managing to wait. To give Rose time. She had done what she could to reconcile—for now. At least that was what Max said, and somehow she thought Max was right. *Max.* What a dear man. What a faithful friend.

Setting her teacup aside, she unbraided and brushed her long hair, then smoothed it back into a neat bun. Church bells rang out again. She felt better about venturing out today. Thanks to the

Ladies Aid quilting, she'd encounter familiar faces. She really was hoping that one of those familiar faces would be Max's.

She smiled as she donned her blue dress. Black jet earbobs would do. At the last minute, she reached for her only brooch, a tiny mosaic of forget-me-nots inlaid into the center of an oval piece of polished onyx. She'd received it in the wake of Thomas's sudden death from a woman she'd tended who was convalescing after a bad fall. Jane had tried to refuse the gift when the woman fished it out of an overflowing jewelry box. This morning, as she pinned it on, Jane saw the brooch as a symbol of the grace notes she'd missed hearing in the past. The blue flowers glimmered, accented by the cadet blue of the dress Minnie had stitched.

Donning her black bonnet and taking up Thomas's small Bible, Jane inspected herself in the mirror. Thunder rolled across the sky, and she chuckled at the idea of God raining literal grace notes down on her first Sunday morning. As she made her way downstairs and out the back door, Jane thought about Rose off in Nebraska City, safe and well loved; the women down south learning to read and involved in an industry; Max here in Lincoln; and herself. . .blessed to work at Manerva, learning what it meant to be free.

—⟊—

"You didn't tell me to expect a welcoming committee," Jane said as she and Minnie rounded the corner and the church building came into view. She nodded up ahead.

"Don't look at me," Minnie said. "Uh-oh."

"Uh-oh?"

Minnie stopped. "I knew it. I knew those roses meant something was up." She laughed aloud. "He's done it. Martin Underhill has proposed, and Mamie's said yes."

"Are you sure?"

"Am I sure? Look at them. Look at Mamie. It's written all over her face." Minnie didn't wait to be told. Instead, she bustled up to Underhill and held out her arms. "Let's do make a scene. Hug your future sister-in-law." Blushing furiously, Underhill complied, even as Mamie protested.

"You could at least have had the grace to pretend you didn't know. And how did you know, anyway?" She glowered at Martin.

"Now don't look at your intended," Minnie said. "He didn't say a word. If you must know, the florist told me Martin bought roses. There could only have been one reason." She kissed her sister's cheek. "And I've just about gone crazy waiting to hear."

"And you still haven't heard," Mamie said. "You didn't give me a chance to say a word."

"Say a word, Mamie. When's the wedding?"

Martin answered, "We thought Thanksgiving."

"Thanksgiving!" Minnie glanced at Jane. "We're going to be busy." She turned back to her sister. "You'll have to come to the shop after church so we can get started." She looked up at Martin. "I don't suppose you're planning on getting married in that, are you?" She eyed his somewhat rumpled suit.

"And what if he is?" Mamie sprang to his defense.

"Settle down. It's a perfectly fine suit. But you've a sister who sews. Why not take advantage?"

The two sisters bantered as they climbed the steps to the great double doors, and in the banter, Jane relaxed. Louise Irwin greeted her at the door with a warm smile. Betty Lyman tried to get her to sing in the choir, and after she was seated in a pew, Sarah Tower came across the sanctuary and, perching next to her on the pew, said, "Minnie said you're a master at drafting patterns. I saw a quilt at the Congregational church spring bazaar. I've a sketch of it in my bag. . . ." As she spoke, Sarah was pulling a folded piece of paper out of her bag. "The girls think I'm insane, but it's the prettiest thing I've ever seen." She held it out. "I'm hoping you'll agree to help me draft a pattern. If I were better at geometry. . ."

Jane looked down at the piece of paper. The block was a hexagon, which wasn't all that difficult to draft, but inside the hexagon a few dozen intersections inside a circle created what looked like the compass at the edge of a map. "That's going to be. . .challenging."

"But won't it be beautiful?"

"Stunning. But. . .how many dozen pieces are there in each block?"

"I'm not sure. Will you help?"

Blanche Gordon passed by, glanced down at the drawing, and shook her head. "Sarah Tower, you are insane." She smiled at Jane. "I told her she was insane to try that. Are you going to help?" When Jane nodded, Blanche just shook her head, but she was grinning as she did so. "Heaven help us all. The Ladies Aid has another crazy quilter." She laughed. "Welcome to First Pres', Jane. We are especially happy to have you take Sarah in hand."

Sarah feigned offense as she folded the paper and put it away. "We'll talk more at quilting," she said to Jane. "I'm making Boston cream pie this week." And she was gone.

Jane had just turned to say something to Minnie when a familiar voice sounded from the aisle. "Might I impose on you to make room for one more?"

With an expression that said *I told you so,* Minnie slid over, pulling Jane along with her to make room for Max.

—⟞∞⟝—

Max had barely settled in his place next to Jane when Madame Savoie arrived. She paused uncertainly when she reached her pew, looking over the congregation. Finally, she waved the young woman with her into the Savoie pew, then took her usual place. Max smiled to himself as the dowager assumed her usual posture, chin held high, hands resting atop the ornately carved head of the cane she'd finally admitted to needing, but only after she realized how much better she felt if she followed her doctor's advice and "took the air" on a daily basis.

When Martin Underhill and Mamie Dawson came to join them, Max leaned over and said to Jane, "Do I detect an unusual amount of. . .enthusiasm on Underhill's face this morning?"

"You do." Jane nodded. "He's proposed, and Mamie's accepted."

"That's wonderful."

Minnie Dawson leaned forward, grinning as she said, "Don't make any plans for Thanksgiving Day, Dr. Zimmer. The wedding is at the McKennas', and I'm quite certain you and Jane will be on the guest list."

You and Jane. He didn't dare to look at Jane to see how she'd reacted to their names being thrown together that way, almost as if they were already a couple. The organist sounded out the first notes of the call to worship, and when the congregation stood to sing, Max shared his hymnal with Jane, reveling in the way their voices blended.

When Pastor Irwin stepped to the podium to deliver the message, Jane reached into her bag and withdrew a small New Testament. Max realized that he'd never thought of bringing a Bible to church. He rather liked the idea of he and Jane being joined in their mode of worship. He determined to tuck his own New Testament in the breast pocket of his shirt next Sunday.

It was when he went to hand the offering plate to the usher in the aisle that Max caught Madame Savoie's eye—and that of the slight young woman seated with her. The girl smiled at him with an unsettling amount of boldness, then whispered something to

Madame Savoie, who smiled at Max. He nodded. She returned the unspoken greeting.

At the conclusion of the service, Max was just about to invite Jane to lunch at Dinah's, when Madame Savoie crossed the aisle. She spoke first to Jane. "I wondered why the good doctor had abandoned his usual pew," she said and held out her hand. "Eugénie Savoie."

"Jane Prescott." Jane returned Madame Savoie's handshake.

"Ah. . .the new member of Louise's aid society. I've heard good things." Without waiting for Jane to respond, Madame Savoie reached for the young woman who'd been waiting at her side. "I have the great joy to introduce my niece this morning." She smiled down at the young woman, slipping effortlessly into French as she said, "*Permettez-moi, Monsieur le Docteur. . .ma nièce, Mademoiselle DuBarry.*"

The girl didn't wait for Max to respond. Instead, she trilled, "*Enchantée,*" and poised her hand in exactly the correct position for Max to bow and offer a continental kiss.

Smiling, Max indulged the expectation, then took a step back and offered Jane his arm.

"What a lovely brooch," Madame Savoie said, indicating the onyx oval Jane was wearing.

"Isn't eet charming," Mademoiselle Barry squinted as she inspected the brooch, then with a lilting little laugh she looked up at her aunt. "It reminds me of ze one Ariana insisted on buying when we were in Rome last year." She rolled her eyes. "Can you imagine? Choosing to wear a petite mosaic of St. Peter's? How droll." She pointed at Jane's brooch. "Yours is so much more attractive. It is proof that one need not spend a great deal of money to find something amusing." She squinted at the brooch again. "It is a floral design, *non*? Ze little blue smudges are meant to be flowers, *oui*? But then some artisans simply don't do nice work, do they?"

Max saw Jane's cheeks flush. There was a moment of odd silence, during which Jane dropped Max's arm. Madame Savoie frowned and, in a low voice, scolded her niece, who merely fluttered her eyelashes as she waved the scolding away with an insincere "*Pardon, Madame*," directed at Jane.

Jane nodded. "If you'll excuse me." Disengaging from Max, she slipped up the aisle toward where the Dawson sisters and Martin stood, chatting with Pastor and Mrs. Irwin.

—⚬⚬—

Don't let her steal your joy. She's a spoiled little girl, and her flirting clearly embarrassed her aunt. And Max. While Minnie and Mamie, Martin, and the Irwins discussed a Thanksgiving wedding, Jane did her best to pretend to listen, but she could not seem to keep her eyes from straying toward Max and the domineering woman who'd taken control of him the moment the organ music died away.

"Jane."

With a start, Jane looked at Minnie, who'd just called her name. "You will come with us, won't you?"

"Come with you?"

Minnie laughed and shook her head. "We're headed to Dinah's for a celebratory lunch. You'll come, of course. And bring Dr. Zimmer?" She glanced toward the front of the sanctuary. Frowned.

Jane followed her gaze just in time to see Max retreating toward the side door, the dowager on one arm...and the little French snippet on the other.

"Oh dear."

Jane forced a smile. "I'd love to come." She glanced at Mamie. "As long as you promise to tell us all just exactly how your beau proposed." She smiled up at Mr. Underhill, who flushed crimson even as he grinned.

"It wasn't all that much. I took flowers. And I stuttered a lot."

"Well, obviously you managed the most important words," Jane said.

Mamie nodded and took Martin's arm. "That he did." She smiled up at him with unabashed affection.

Together, the foursome made their way out into the foyer, down the broad stairs leading to the street, and then to Dinah's, where, in spite of the welcoming aroma of roast beef, Jane discovered that she didn't have much of an appetite.

CHAPTER 29

Max escorted Madame Savoie and her niece out the side door of the church and toward their waiting coach. The ladies had just ducked inside when the skies opened, and with screeching laughter, Mademoiselle DuBarry clutched Max's sleeve and hauled him in after them. He landed on the bench next to her, flustered and more than a little embarrassed.

"It is fate," the girl said. "You must join us for lunch."

Max hesitated, looking back toward the church, but there was no sign of Jane, the Dawson sisters, or Martin Underhill.

"Please, *Monsieur le Docteur*. When my aunt speaks of the handsome doctor and his great gift for *le médecin*, I do not believe her. But I visit, and she has returned to such great health. I wish to thank you."

Max glanced at Madame Savoie. He didn't know how to interpret her expression, but when she echoed her niece's invitation, he decided that pleasing the woman who'd helped him so much was a small thing to ask. He could endure an hour with a vapid girl for Madame Savoie's sake.

The brooding Savoie manse lurked at the end of a wide thoroughfare that connected to O Street and then led south. As the driver turned between two brick columns, lightning flashed and, with a sharp whinny, the horses broke into a trot. The girl at Max's side gave a shrill cry and grabbed his arm.

"Claudine! Comport yourself with some measure of dignity!"

Madame Savoie's severe tone had the desired effect. The girl let go of Max and, leaning forward, peered toward the house. "What do we have for lunch, *Ma Tante*?"

"Roast guinea, glazed carrots, escalloped potatoes. . .and hopefully, a renewal of good manners."

Beneath her aunt's angry stare, the girl seemed to shrink. As soon as the phaeton stopped beneath the portico extending from the east side of the grand house, she opened the door and descended, leaving Max to assist Madame Savoie.

"She is young and foolish," Madame Savoie said as Max helped her down.

"And lovely," Max said.

"Yes. Dangerously so. My sister is hoping to see the dawning of some level of maturity after Claudine's time with us." She sighed. "She's been here only a few days, and already I despair."

Together, Max and Madame Savoie mounted the stairs to the side door. At the top of the stairs, the older woman turned and called out to her driver. "The doctor will need to be taken back to his home after lunch."

"That's not necessary," Max said. "I enjoy walking."

Madame Savoie nodded toward the lane, which was obscured by the pouring rain. "I know that quite well. I do not, however, require my dinner guests to swim home through such as this."

"Touché, Madame," Max said and followed her inside.

"Genie!" A booming voice called from up the hall. "What's this I hear about company for lunch? Claudine says—"

Max hesitated inside the door and looked in the direction of the voice. A tall, broad-shouldered man sporting unfashionably long white hair and a drooping mustache approached, stopped dead in his tracks, and peered at Max. "I know you," he said. "But for the life of me I can't recall how." He paused. "Ever been on trial for anything?"

"Gérard!" Madame Savoie's beaming smile belied her scolding tone. She glanced at Max even as she removed her gloves and hat and handed them to the uniformed maid waiting with outstretched hands. "Pay him no mind." She looked back at her husband. "Dr. Zimmer is to be our guest for lunch, dear. Try to live up to your reputation as a civilized gentleman."

Savoie grunted at his wife and rolled his eyes at Max. "Women. Ruin all a man's fun, sometimes." He paused. Tilted his head. "You asked my advice. At the capitol. About a pardon for a woman."

Max nodded. "Yes, sir. I did." He glanced at Madame Savoie. "A friend of mine. A victim of injustice."

"Ever get that worked out?" the judge asked.

Max nodded again. "Yes, sir. She. . .well, I suppose you could say she took things into her own hands. She's free."

Claudine DuBarry descended the stairs like a cloud gliding down from above. She'd changed into a diaphanous ensemble in a color that made her skin glow and her dark eyes glimmer.

"Zounds!" the judge exclaimed. "You're the prettiest thing I've seen since my Eugénie was your age." He held out his arm. "Come along, *ma chère*. Humor an old man."

Max offered Madame Savoie his arm, and together they went into the dining room, where servants waited to serve what proved to be an astounding series of courses.

"We take our main meal at noon," Madame Savoie explained as Max pulled out her chair and then took his own seat next to Mademoiselle DuBarry.

"I do hope you have come with an appetite, *Monsieur le Docteur*," the young girl said as she spread her damask napkin across her lap.

It rained throughout the meal. In spite of Mademoiselle's flirtations, Max found himself enjoying himself. The judge proved to be an erudite gentleman of no small intellect and no pretense. The combination made for delightful dinner conversation.

After lunch, Max declined Mademoiselle's invitation to join her in the library. "I really do need to attend to some business in town this afternoon."

Madame Savoie smiled knowingly and, after her niece left the room, said quietly, "Mrs. Prescott seems very nice, Dr. Zimmer. Do give her my best, won't you?" She glanced toward the library. "And please forgive my niece her foolishness."

—⚍—

Back in town, Max had the Savoies' driver turn right on O Street and drop him at Manerva. The heavy rain was little more than a misty drizzle now, but when he looked up at Jane's window, it was obvious she still wasn't home. He stood for a moment, looking up and down the street. When the Savoies' phaeton turned the corner in the distance, he walked toward the end of the block and then up the alley toward the back door. There was no light in the rear apartment window, either, but movement near the door caught his eye.

A pasteboard box, nearly falling apart but held together with a belt, and a girl drenched and shivering. At sight of Max she burst into tears. "You're Mama's friend. You brought her to see me." She gestured toward the box. "I've got the quilt here. . .and the key. . . and. . ." She shuddered. Max shrugged out of his coat and threw it around her shoulders. "Do you know where. . .where Mama is? I came. . .I came to tell her—" She began to sob. "I remember—I remember everything. And. . .and—" Her voice broke. "I'm sorry. I'm so. . .sorry."

All through lunch, Jane did her best to rejoice with Mamie and Martin. The skies opened, and the rain poured, and the crowd at Dinah's hunkered down and ordered dessert. When the rain didn't let up, they pulled the checkerboard down off the shelf in the back and ordered coffee and more dessert. Finally, the rain stopped, and together, the Dawsons and Jane and Martin hurried toward Manerva for an afternoon of measuring and selecting fabric and planning wedding clothes and a trousseau.

Mamie blushed at the word *trousseau* and declared herself "too old for such nonsense."

"I beg your pardon, dear," Martin said firmly, "but my wife deserves the very best we can afford, and I will thank you to stop pronouncing her decrepitude." He reached for one of Minnie's fashion magazines and pointed to a lovely traveling suit. "This," he said. "In that." When he pointed to a bolt of claret fabric, Minnie and Mamie exchanged glances and dissolved in laughter. Martin blustered an apology for his faux pas, and Minnie told him the story of Mamie's war with claret.

"Told me she didn't care to look like a bottle of wine walking down the street," Minnie said.

Martin grinned at his fiancée. "It'd be fine wine."

"Oh, you—" Mamie dismissed him with a wave. "You take your jacket off and let Minnie take your measurements." She glanced at her sister. "A nice charcoal?"

Minnie nodded. "And a black overcoat."

"And a nice derby."

And so it was that Martin Underhill, the ugliest man in town, ended up in the middle of a dressmaker's shop being fussed over by two women who loved him and a third who thoroughly admired him, although she herself wasn't quite ready to love. Yet. Not quite yet.

—⁂—

The storm clouds moved on, and the sun emerged late in the afternoon. Martin and Mamie headed back to the penitentiary, and Minnie went home, leaving Jane to climb the stairs to her room and wrestle over what had happened at church this morning. She'd just put the kettle on when someone pounded on the door.

"Jane! Jane Marquis. Are you in there!"

Just the name sent a chill up her spine.

"Open up. It's Flora. I know you're in there. Open up or I'll be forced to go to the police."

Jane opened the door to a bedraggled, frantic woman waving a piece of paper as she blustered. "I was here earlier and no one—and so I walked—" She thrust the paper at Jane. "Read it. Where is she?"

Jane took the proffered paper and read:

Dear Aunt Flora,

I am sorry I deceived you, but I knew you wouldn't let me do what I must. I am going to see Mama. I don't understand why you let me believe she was dead, but she isn't. She came to see me. And she's very brave and wonderful. I didn't know that at first, and I wouldn't talk to her. But then on that day when I fainted, I remembered. I remembered everything. And I have to see Mama. So I am going to Lincoln. She lives above Manerva at 1400 O Street, and I can find that without any help at all.

Thank you for taking care of me while Mama was in prison. I will always be grateful. I have taken the doll I had when I was little and the George Washington quilt Mama made with me.

If you don't want to keep my things until I get out I understand. But I hope you will. And I hope you'll come and see me.

Your loving niece,
Rose Elizabeth Prescott

The instant Jane looked up from the letter, Flora demanded, "Where is she? What have you done with her?"

Jane stepped back. "I don't—I haven't seen her." A knot formed in her midsection as a thousand horrific scenarios involving what could happen to a young girl traveling alone flitted through her mind.

"How could you have gone behind my back?" Flora began to weep.

Jane pulled her inside, led her to the rocking chair, and made her sit down. While Flora wept, Jane made tea. Flora didn't calm down until she'd drunk half a cup of the steaming brew.

Jane perched atop the small trunk beneath the windows. "I came without telling you because I was afraid you'd take Rose and disappear. I was terrified that I'd never see her again." She swallowed. "That seemed to be what you intended."

"You murdered a man," Flora snapped. "Whatever you did to get free, that fact remains."

More footsteps sounded on the stairs. Another rap on the door. And this time, joy as Jane opened the door. A sobbing Rose flung herself into her arms, while Max stood in the doorway. "Mama. Oh, Mama. . .I remember. I'm sorry. I'm so sorry, Mama."

Flora stood up.

Rose saw her, and her eyes grew wide.

"How could you?" Flora began to cry again.

Rose glared at her. "You lied to me. You let me believe Mama was dead. You didn't give me her letters. You never took me to visit."

She swallowed. "You should have taken me. You shouldn't have lied."

"I did what I thought best."

Rose blinked. Looked up at Jane, then back at Flora. "That's what Mama said. She said not to be mad at you. That you did what was best. That you love me."

"I do—" Flora's voice broke. "Oh, Rose, I do love you. I only wanted to protect you from—" She glanced at Jane.

"You thought Mama killed Papa."

Flora nodded.

"She didn't," Rose croaked. "I did." And she burst into fresh tears.

CHAPTER 30

Y ou—!" Flora grasped the back of the rocking chair.

Even now, Jane couldn't bring herself to say it. She put her arm around Rose, but remained mute.

"Papa called me 'his little gunslinger.' He taught me how. Mama hated guns. I never saw her so much as touch one." She began to tremble.

Max stepped up. He put his hand on Rose's shoulder. "It's all right, Rose."

Rose shook her head. "It isn't." She blinked. "I killed him. He was going to hurt Mama again. He was always hurting Mama." She began to sob. "And she never did anything. She just tried to make him happy. He used to get so mad. . . ." She shuddered. Croaked, "I couldn't let him hurt her anymore."

Dear God in heaven, help us. Forgive us. Help us. Tears spilled down Jane's face as Rose talked and Flora stared, and a cloud of emotion descended over the apartment.

Flora spoke first. "When you said you hoped I'd come visit you. . ."

"When I go to jail," Rose said.

Jane frowned. "Sweetheart, you aren't going to jail." Her voice wavered. She couldn't remain standing, or she was going to collapse.

Max moved to her side. His arm encircled her waist. "You need to sit down," he said, and spoke to Rose, "Come and sit down over here by your aunt Flora."

Flora sank into the rocking chair. Jane and Rose sank to the floor beside the little trunk, and Jane reached for Rose's hand.

Max cleared his throat. "Any physician worth his salt would prescribe rest and quiet to give you three some time to recuperate emotionally." He glanced around the room at the three women.

Rose took a ragged breath. "I don't want to go to jail."

Jane pulled her into her arms. "You aren't going anywhere. At least not tonight." She gazed across the room at Flora. Flora seemed to hesitate, but then she nodded.

Max spoke up. "If you ladies can manage on your own for a while, I'd like to retrieve something that will help you all rest. With your permission?"

Jane stroked Rose's hair. It seemed the girl had already fallen asleep. She spoke to Flora. "Why don't you stretch out on the bed?" Flora did. Max smiled down at Jane, nodding at the sleeping Rose.

"That's a beautiful sight. I'll try not to take too long." He bent to kiss her cheek. With that, he was gone.

—⁂—

Rose started awake and, lifting her head, stared across the room toward the bed where Aunt Flora lay snoring. She sat up and, looking at Mama, smiled. "Yes," she said. "Every night." She giggled, but then she remembered. . .and the laughter melted away.

"It's going to be all right," Jane said.

"I don't see how."

"You were very brave. And you were defending me. Max knows how Owen was." She reached out and tucked a curl behind Rose's ear. "I'm so sorry I didn't find a way for us to get away." She took a

286

ragged breath. "But you—you were defending me. There's a legal term for that, Rose. *Justifiable*." She paused. "And besides that, you were only a child. You hardly realized what you were doing. There are so many reasons why it's going to be all right." She paused. "Is that what you meant in the note you wrote to Flora? When you said you hoped she'd come and visit? You thought you'd be going to jail?"

Rose nodded.

"And you were hoping she'd write to you."

"She's kind of a fussbudget. But. . .she always took good care of me." Rose glanced at Jane. "Except for lying. And not letting me read your letters." She took a deep breath. "I hope she still has them."

Jane leaned over and, lifting the lid of the little trunk, she reached in and produced a stack of letters tied with string. "Flora returned these. They kept them for me until I got out."

"The key," Rose glanced across the room at the pasteboard box by the door. "The key opens this trunk."

Jane nodded. "I haven't locked it since I put the key on the quilt."

"You said you hoped it would bring me back to you." Rose got up and crossed the room. She opened the box and pulled out the quilt. "I remembered, Mama." She settled down next to Jane and spread the quilt across their laps, touching the pieces as she said, "Blue for the bachelor buttons and red for that scrawny rosebush by the house. And tan for the earth."

Jane reached over and turned up an edge. "And indigo. . ."

"For the night sky." Rose nodded. "The stars have names. You used to take me outside, and we'd lie on our backs and watch the sky. And one time I saw a shooting star. And you said that even that star had a name, and it might have gone out, but God hadn't lost it." She reached up and tugged at an errant curl. "Just like He doesn't lose count of the hairs on my head."

As she sat listening to Rose remembering, something deep inside

Jane took root and blossomed. Tears gathered.

Rose whispered. "I didn't mean to make you cry."

Jane shook her head. "It's joy, sweetheart. . .pure joy."

—⁂—

Flora had awakened, and Jane had served up tea and bread and jelly before Max returned. But he wasn't alone. Jane saw panic flit across Rose's face as he introduced Judge Gerard Savoie.

"The judge has helped me in the past," Max said, "and he's agreed to listen to your case, Rose."

Savoie perched atop the trunk, his arms folded, his white mane of hair glowing white like a halo as the setting sun broke through the storm clouds outside. Max brought two chairs up from the shop below. Flora settled in the rocker, while Jane and Rose took seats side by side.

"All right, Rose," the judge began. "Tell me how old you are."

"She's only fourteen," Flora said.

The judge smiled. Nodded. "All right, Rose," he repeated. "Tell me how old you are."

"I'll be fifteen on my next birthday, sir."

Max came to stand behind Jane. "And you were how old the night Owen Marquis died?"

"Nine."

"And you had no recollection of that night until recently?" When Rose nodded, the judge asked her to explain.

And so it went. The judge asking questions, Rose answering. Finally, he nodded. "All right. I believe I have a good understanding of the crime."

Rose clenched her hands before her and waited.

Savoie cleared his throat. "The real crime, Rose, is that a man was allowed to terrorize a good woman and her child. To beat the woman to the point that she suffered broken ribs. To finally become so violent that a child felt forced to take action to protect her mother's life." He paused. "That, dear child, is the real crime. When your mother couldn't defend herself, you acted on her behalf. It is my considered opinion that there is not a judge or jury in the universe who would seek to punish you for doing something so brave as to stand up to a drunken, violent man bent on murder. Owen Marquis is dead, and the court does not take human life lightly. But that event has been judged and the sentence served. And you, young lady, may rest assured that justice has been done and the only thing that remains now is for Owen Marquis to meet the Judge of all the earth, whom we pray will have mercy on his soul." He waited for Rose to meet his gaze. "It's over, dear girl. The price has been paid. Let it be."

Rose sat so still for a moment that Jane wondered if she understood what was happening. But then she raised her hands and covered her mouth for a moment, almost as if to smother a shout. "I. . .don't have to go to jail?"

The judge shook his head. "No, dear. Your mama already did that. There's no reason to repeat the mistake of punishing something that was justifiable."

Rose blinked. She looked at Jane. At Flora. And she began to cry.

—◊◊◊—

Max walked the judge back downstairs and out to his rig. As the older man swung up to take a seat, Max thanked him. Again.

"Like I told the girl, Doc. A man in my profession doesn't get to make people happy all that often. It's a singular story. I was glad to be a part of helping that young woman." He gathered up the reins. "You gave my wife a new lease on life, Doc. Don't know if you realize it, but she's always struggled with melancholia. I love her with all of my sin-soaked heart, but it didn't seem enough. Whatever you did. . .I've got my Genie back, and I thank you."

Max shook his head. "All I did was prescribe a walk. Truly. That's all."

The judge laughed. "Well, she thinks you're a miracle worker." He winked. "Although she is more than a little disappointed that her plans for you and Claudine aren't going to work out."

"I. . .don't know what to say."

"Nothing to say, son. You've a fine woman up there." He nodded toward Jane's apartment. "Claudine's got a ways to go. She's spoiled. A good girl, but never had a heartbreak. Always gets what she wants." He grinned. "Until you." He chirruped to the horse and headed off, his booming laughter ringing out as he headed for home.

—⁓—

Aunt Flora went home on the morning train, but not before she begged—and received—Mama's forgiveness for everything. In the days that followed the judge's pronouncement that Rose bore no guilt for which she had to pay, Mama took Rose to speak with Reverend Irwin in private, and finally—although Mama said that the old feelings of guilt might resurface sometimes—finally, Rose began to believe that what Jesus said about forgiveness was true, even for what she'd done.

Rose helped Mama in the shop downstairs, and when she showed a natural talent for matching colors and selecting trims, Miss Dawson declared her a "born designer" and even let her help with sewing her own sister's wedding dress.

In the evenings, Rose and Mama spent hours with the things stored in the little trunk. Dr. Zimmer joined them a couple of times, and when Mama told stories about Papa Thomas, Dr. Zimmer listened as if Papa Thomas had been his own friend.

One evening, the doctor took them to dinner at the Lindell

Hotel, and then they walked over to his infirmary and sat upstairs on his private porch. He made Rose chamomile tea, and when she got chilly, he took off his very own coat and draped it across her shoulders. Rose decided that one day, when she grew up, she would marry someone like Dr. Zimmer.

And then, the week was over, and Mama said it was time to go home to Aunt Flora, because Rose must finish school and then come to live with her in Lincoln while she attended the university. Mama would work hard over the next year to "get established," and by the time Rose was ready to move to Lincoln, she would have a home for them instead of the little room over Manerva.

As the train pulled out of the Lincoln station headed for Nebraska City, Rose smiled and waved at Mama. And Max. He'd said to call him Max and teased her about keeping "that ferocious dog of your aunt's in hand" when Mama came to visit next weekend.

Rose promised.

CHAPTER 31

Jane watched the train until it was out of sight, oblivious to everything else around her except, of course, for Max, who waited, unmoving, at her side. She dropped her eyes from the horizon and followed the line of the tracks back to where she stood beside Max. Other passengers moved around them. At the far end of the siding, a couple of men transferred crates from a wagon onto a freight car. Farther still, someone was leading an impressive black horse off another car, down a ramp, and toward a group of men who, by their smiles and gestures, seemed pleased with the animal. It seemed odd that life was continuing on for everyone when such a momentous thing had just happened.

Former penitentiary inmate, Jane Marquis, had just put her *daughter* on a train. . .and prior to boarding, that daughter had flung her arms around her and hugged her tight and made her promise to come to Nebraska City next weekend.

Seamstress and upstanding member of First Presbyterian Church, Jane Prescott, was standing here at the Lincoln railroad station, and she wasn't alone. Next to her. . .waiting, unmoving. . .Max. *Dr.* Max Zimmer. Who'd waited for years and, when he did move, had moved with her in mind. At least it seemed that way.

When she finally looked up at Max, he smiled. "I don't know where you've been just now, but it seems to have been somewhere pleasant. You look. . .happy."

She took a deep breath. Shook her head. "I was just thinking about what Mamie calls grace notes in life." She nodded toward the horizon that had swallowed Rose's train up. "There were times when I didn't dare ask God for that. I talked to Him all the time about Rose, but I didn't dare ask Him to bring her back to me. I thought I had to make that happen all by myself." She blinked back tears. "I have so much to learn. And so much to be thankful for." She looked into Max's gray-green eyes. "Have I ever thanked *you* for being such a good friend?"

A muscle in his cheek twitched. For a moment, Jane thought he was going to take her in his arms. She wished he would. But then he winked at her, and once again, she was aware of the busyness around them—the noise and activity that, for just that moment when she stood looking up at Max, had all seemed to fade away.

He offered his arm. "You just did thank me. But I'll believe it's sincere if you join me at the Lindell for a late supper."

—◊◊◊—

It all started at quilting, the second Tuesday after Jane and Max dined at the Lindell. . .and the first Tuesday after Jane traveled to Nebraska City to spend Sunday with Rose and Flora. The teasing. The double entendre. The sense that she and Max were the leads in a play being watched by everyone who knew them.

First, Blanche Gordon said something about "a certain doctor" who seemed to have made a permanent move to a new pew on Sunday mornings. "He looked positively forlorn this past Sabbath in that empty pew." She looked meaningfully at Jane.

Minnie, seated to Jane's right at the quilt, nudged her and said,

"You must understand, Jane, that new members of the church—and especially new members of the Ladies Aid—are required to report their whereabouts on Sunday mornings—unless, of course, they have an excused absence. In writing. Signed by God." She paused. "And you are probably going to have to get used to the idea that the women at the Ladies Aid feel it their personal responsibility to monitor all courting and potential pairings in the congregation. I believe the duty is outlined in paragraph three of the organization's constitution." She leaned close and in a stage whisper said, "I am on very thin ice with this group. They may have to excommunicate me since I unabashedly refuse to be paired up, married off, or otherwise encumbered with anyone who would provide fodder for quilting conversation."

Sarah Tower scolded, "If you aren't careful, Minnie, I am going to have to tell that sister of yours to take you in hand."

"Well, that will most certainly work." Minnie slapped a palm to her chest in mock panic. "Everyone knows I'm terrified of Mamie."

Sarah glowered at her. "Were you always this incorrigible?"

"Define *always*," Minnie quipped.

"How many times did you have to sit in the corner at school with a certain pointed hat on your head?"

"Only once. It took me exactly ten minutes to get the rest of the class laughing so hard, poor Miss Ferguson decided I was incorrigible, assigned me to the back row, and ignored me for the rest of the school year."

"That," Sarah said, "explains a great deal."

Minnie agreed. "But I learned a lot on that back row."

"Did you, now?"

"I did. How to organize, for example. Four of us sat on that back row. We named ourselves The Incorrigibles and terrorized the other students for the rest of the year."

Sarah shook her head. "I almost believe that of you, although I cannot quite imagine Mamie Dawson taking part in such a venture."

"Who said anything about Mamie? She was teacher's pet. Up on the front row."

Much to Jane's relief, thanks to Minnie's clever interruption, the subject shifted to youthful escapades, but it wasn't long before someone spoke of Eugénie Savoie's disappointment in regards to certain plans regarding a certain visiting relative. Blanche, it turned out, had a daughter about the age of Claudine DuBarry, and Claudine had made no secret of her opinion of Lincoln, Nebraska. Provincial. Without merit except, of course, for her darling aunt and uncle. And with a distinct lack of "qualified prospects."

Betty Lyman spoke up. "You wouldn't believe the way that young woman scans the crowd on Sunday. It's distracting for the whole choir. She's like a she-hawk looking for prey. I don't think there's any possibility she's heard a single word of Pastor Irwin's sermons."

"Now, now," Louise demurred gently. "Let's not forget that we were all young once." She chuckled. "As a matter of fact, when I was Miss DuBarry's age, I was something of a she-hawk on occasion."

When no one said anything, Jane glanced up. The women at the quilting frame were staring, aghast, at their pastor's wife.

Louise laughed aloud. "If you could see your faces!" She knotted her thread and popped it between the layers of the quilt, then reached for another needle and began to stitch. "Happily for *this* she-hawk, her prey proved easy to capture. That was nearly thirty years ago, and I've still got him held firmly in my clutches." She glanced over at Sarah Tower. "Tell us again, Sarah. Who are we quilting this for?"

As quilting day drew to a close late that afternoon, Jane drew Sarah Tower aside and invited her to lunch at Dinah's the next day. "Other than taking Tuesdays for quilting, we've been working long days at the shop. Minnie said I could take a bit more time at lunch on occasion, and I've a few questions about that quilt block drawing you showed me a couple of Sundays ago. I got the impression you don't want it to be a group project."

Sarah nodded. "You're right. When I showed them that drawing, they just shook their heads. Called me crazy for wanting to try anything so complex." She shrugged and lowered her voice. "And. . .well, Betty is a lovely woman and such an accomplished musician, but sometimes her quilting stitches—I want this to be my masterpiece." She smiled a conspiratorial smile. "Lunch at Dinah's tomorrow would be lovely."

—⁓—

Jane was pedaling furiously, completing a row of stitches on the claret silk that would be Mamie's wedding dress, when Minnie appeared in the doorway between the shop and the workroom.

"Goodness, girl, you can make that thing fly."

Jane kept pedaling, although she slowed down. "Can you believe we used to do all of this by hand?" When she came to the end of the seam, she stopped pedaling and looked up. "It only took us forty-nine hours to finish Martin's suit. If our foremothers had had one of these"—she patted the machine head—"women would rule the world."

Mamie waved a hand in the air. "Do not get me started on the topic of how we have been kept back by men's refusal to apply engineering and industrialization to women's work." She took a deep breath. "I've put the CLOSED FOR LUNCH sign on the front door. You want to join me out back? I think it's still warm enough to get away with al fresco dining, and I want to take advantage of it before the weather turns once and for all."

"Thanks, but I'm meeting Sarah Tower over at Dinah's today."

Minnie arched an eyebrow. "If the two of you are planning a

quilting mutiny, I want to be included."

"Nothing nearly that exciting." Jane laughed. "I've taken another look at that impossible quilt she wants to make, and I think I've managed to draft the pattern." She paused. "Sarah seems to want to do it all on her own, though. She said something about the group calling her crazy and her wanting to surprise everyone with a masterpiece." She grimaced. "So I guess that'll be impossible now that I've just—"

"Not to worry, Mrs. Prescott," Minnie said. "One thing a good dressmaker learns is to hear but never remember." She swept the air with her hand. "Want to join me for lunch?"

Jane laughed. "Thanks, but I've made plans."

Minnie grabbed the cretonne fabric bag she used to carry her lunch from home to the shop every day. "See you later. Same time, same place." She hesitated in the doorway. "We need to decide on the buttons for Mamie's dress when we get back from lunch. She refused to tell me what she wants, and if we have to order something, I need to let my notions man know. He's due in tomorrow." She smiled. "You will love it, by the way. It's like Christmas when he starts pulling samples out of his case."

Jane stood up, grimacing and stretching from side to side.

"I'm telling you, Jane, you have to make it a point to get up and stretch every so often or you are going to end up permanently bent over and in pain. And I do *not* need a certain someone blaming me for crippling the woman he loves."

"I thought you said dressmakers hear but never remember."

"We do. And I haven't heard a thing. But I'd have to be blind not to see the expression on that man's face every time he looks at you."

"I don't know what to say when people hint about Max and me."

"You don't have to say a thing. They can see the same things I see." She winked but then grew serious. "Jane. I know you need time to be you. To find your way. To embrace. . .your new life. Anyone would. But don't wait too long. *He's* been waiting nearly five years, all told." She scooted out the door without waiting for a reply.

—⁓—

As soon as she and Sarah Tower were seated at a table at Dinah's, Jane reached into her bag and pulled out a piece of paper. "I've had a night or two where I haven't been able to sleep," she said as she unfolded the paper, laid it on the table between them, and pointed to the first of two drawings.

Sarah pulled it closer and, with the tip of her finger moving around the circular design, counted each section. She looked up. "Sixty?"

"Sixty-four," Jane said. "It's stunning, but that's a lot of piecing. And I hate to say it, but I think you'd have to have at least nine blocks to keep it from looking like they were just floating." She pointed to the other drawing on the paper. "I realize this sashing carries the entire project to an entirely new level of insanity, but my mother had a quilt she called her New York beauty. It had sashing like this. Sadly, it was lost in a fire when I was a girl."

Sarah looked up from the paper. "A fire? I'm so sorry."

"When I grew older I seemed to remember Mother being more sorrowful over the quilt than she was her own widowhood. My father died in that fire, but they'd never been happy. He was—difficult." *He was like Owen.* The realization sent a chill up her spine. She'd repeated her own mother's mistake. How. . .odd.

"Your mother," Sarah said. "Is that who you visit in Nebraska City?" When Jane hesitated, she said quickly, "I'm sorry. That was. . .indelicate of me. I didn't mean to pry."

"You weren't prying. You were making conversation. And showing concern. I appreciate both." Suddenly, Jane realized that she'd come to a new place in regards to her past. What was it Mamie had said about the women? *They're good women.* And they were. Sarah wasn't prying, and Jane didn't need to feel defensive. In fact, she felt safe, not only with Sarah but also with the other women she'd come to know through quilting.

"My mother died a long time ago. Long before I married." She paused. "I was visiting my daughter in Nebraska City. Her name's Rose."

"You must bring her to quilting if she's ever here on a Tuesday," Sarah said. "And of course, church on Sunday."

Jane nodded. Swallowed. "There's something I should probably tell you about Rose. We've been—estranged since she was a child. It's a long, involved. . .and not very nice story, I'm afraid."

"It seems that it has a happy ending, though."

Jane blinked back tears. "Yes." She nodded. "But if you knew—"

Sarah reached over and squeezed her hand. "Dear woman, don't we all have 'not very nice' in our past? Isn't that why our Savior had to die? Goodness, did you think everyone in those pews on Sunday is all shiny and clean?" She chuckled. "Even our pastor's wife has a shaded past as a she-hawk." With a pat, she released Jane's hand and took a sip of coffee. "My mother used to say that if we ever found a church full of perfect people, we must never join because we'd ruin it." She took a sip of coffee. "You don't need to explain anything for me to share your joy over the happy ending."

"Rose is coming to live with me when she attends the university in a couple of years. Of course I'm hoping she'll want to join the Ladies Aid."

"That would be wonderful. Praise God, from whom all blessings flow. I shall look forward to meeting her." Sarah turned her attention back down to the drawing. Shook her head. "It *is* a bit insane to attempt it." She traced the sashing sketch with her index finger, tapping the space where a setting square would be required. "A small compass would be lovely there. And unify the overall design." She looked up at Jane. "Don't you think?"

Jane chuckled and shook her head. "I do. . . . But *Sarah.*"

Sarah shrugged. "Anything worth doing is worth overdoing." She laughed. "Which brings me to lunch. Let's start with dessert. You must never tell her I said this, but Dinah's lemon meringue pie rivals mine."

Over pie, the women discussed the upcoming fall bazaar and what Sarah pronounced Louise Irwin's "good work" on the Female Department Improvement Committee. "I so admire her for taking that on," Sarah said. "Those poor women. . .I can't imagine." She took a sip of coffee before asking Jane about the coming fashion season and how to update a favorite walking suit, and the two women were just about mid-pie when the bell on the door gave a jingle.

"Goodness," Jane said, with a glance at the watch she'd taken to wearing pinned to her waist. "It's nearly two o'clock. Mamie's coming in for a fitting this afternoon, and I promised to help Mamie decide on buttons for her wedding dress."

Sarah folded her napkin and reached for her bag. "This is my treat," she said. "You go on back to the shop. I don't want Minnie taking me to task for keeping you too long." She smiled. "You've been a great encouragement in regards to my compass quilt, Jane. Thank you."

Jane laughed as she stood up and reached for her parasol. "Just remember you said that when you're laboring over adding piece number twenty-two to the first block."

And then she heard a familiar high-pitched titter and realized who'd just come into the diner. Claudine DuBarry. Her aunt and uncle. And Max. Her Max. With that. . .child. . .on his arm.

CHAPTER 32

Standing before her dressing mirror, Ellen gave her hair a quick brushing, then twisted it into a chignon and pinned it into place. Stepping into her petticoat, she pulled it up and buttoned it, then paused to glance over at Ian, still lounging on the bed. "Shouldn't you be getting back to the office?" She crossed the bedroom and peered out the windows toward the garden. "And Georgia will be back inside any minute. There isn't that much left to pick."

"Georgia," Ian said—and hooked a finger in the waist of Ellen's petticoat to draw her close—"isn't really out there to pick the fall produce, although maybe she'll end up with an armful of something. The truth is, I asked her to give us a little more privacy than just a closed door. I think she said something about going over to the flower beds at the entrance and gathering seeds." He wrapped her in his arms. "Do you know how adorable it is that you still blush?"

Ellen relaxed in his arms for a moment, then kissed his chin. The clock in the hall chimed noon. "Lunch was delightful, Mr. McKenna, but if I don't hurry and get dressed, I'm going to make Mamie late for her fitting in town." Ian collected another kiss, then released her.

"Lunch?" he chided as he reached for his shirt. "I must be losing my touch. Time was you called these clandestine meetings *dessert*, Mrs. McKenna."

Ellen tied on her bustle, then donned her skirt and, turning away from the mirror, looked over her shoulder as she adjusted the skirt into place. She'd just buttoned the top button of her waist when a soft knock sounded at the door.

"Sorry to bother you two," Georgia said through the door, "but I thought you'd want to know that Miss Dawson's just driving across to fetch Mrs. McKenna."

"I'll be right down," Ellen said.

Ian frowned. "You aren't taking our rig into town? I thought the Dawson sisters shared and traded out over the weekend."

"Martin bought a new rig," Ellen said. "And the prettiest little mare. Chestnut with four white socks. Mamie says he drove her crazy with it. Was this buggy all right? Did the springs cushion the ride enough? Was the step too high? Too low? Did the horse seem a big fractious?"

"Reminds me of me when I was trying to win you," Ian said. "I used to stand in front of the mirror trying on vests and retying cravats like some fool."

"Just for the record, you never got the cravat quite right."

Ian stared at her in mock horror. "Surely you jest."

"No, but it didn't matter. I thought it added to your boyish charm." She pinned her hat in place, blew him a kiss, and headed for the door. Opening it, she paused and looked back. "I love you, Mr. McKenna." Her face flushed as she said, "Let's do lunch again. . .tomorrow, if you can find the time."

"I'll find the time. Now get out of here before I send Georgia on yet another meaningless errand and tell Mamie you are. . .indisposed."

———

"Now, Jane," Sarah said, as soon as they'd left the diner, "don't jump to conclusions. It's no secret that Eugénie Savoie has a soft spot for Dr. Zimmer. She's suffered from melancholia for years, and whatever the doctor did, there's been a remarkable improvement. Everyone who knows her realizes it—and they've all heard her give Dr. Zimmer credit. It would not be wise for him to offend one of his most influential supporters."

"You're right," Jane said, hoping she sounded convinced.

"The fact that they are having lunch doesn't mean anything but that. They are having lunch."

"I'm sure you're right."

"Dr. Zimmer is clearly very fond of you, Jane. Everyone knows that. That's why we had such fun teasing you at quilting the other day."

"I know." *He's fond of me. But he hasn't kissed me. And I wanted him to at the train station. But he didn't. He winked at me like I was his buddy.*

They had rounded the corner and were out of sight of the diner when Sarah stopped in her tracks. "Jane. Are you listening to me? Don't jump to conclusions. Give the poor man a chance to explain."

Surprised when tears welled up, Jane merely nodded. She cleared her throat. "I—I have to get back to the shop. Thank you. . .for everything." She watched Sarah make her way toward her home, then hurried off, but when there wasn't a rig outside Manerva, she decided to walk a bit more to calm her nerves. It wouldn't do to be in a state when Mamie and Ellen arrived for the fitting. Mamie deserved a relaxed afternoon and a chance to chat with her sister. As for Jane, she'd been looking forward to hearing the news from the third floor. Whether or not Max was spending time with a French snippet shouldn't affect any of that.

Her feet unwittingly carried her past Max's combination house/ infirmary, where the sign in the window informed patients that *Dr.*

303

Zimmer will return at 4:00. Jane wondered at the hour. Apparently the Savoies and Miss DuBarry had more than lunch planned for *Monsieur le Docteur.*

Jane stifled a sob. What was it Mamie and Minnie called it when they needed to help their mind control their emotions? She must take herself in hand. *And concentrate on thankfuls. And rejoice with Mamie this afternoon, and not distract anyone with my troubles.*

She listed thankfuls all the way back to Manerva, calmed by the idea that she had so many. Among them. . .Max Zimmer, whatever form their relationship might take in the coming days.

—⁓—

"Back-door customers are best!"

Ellen McKenna's voice sang out from the back door as she and Mamie stepped inside. Jane held up one hand signaling "just a minute" and kept pedaling until she'd finished the inner seam on the second of the claret sleeves for Mamie's ensemble. Ellen and Mamie went on into the shop. Jane heard Minnie order her sister behind the dressing screen, even as she lifted the presser foot and snipped the threads. Reaching inside the sleeve, she grasped the bottom edge and gently turned it right-side out as she asked Minnie if she should press it.

Minnie shook her head. "That won't matter as much for a fitting. We'll do fine." She draped the sleeve over the dressing screen, then went to retrieve the pin cushion she'd fashioned to fit around her wrist. Draping a measuring tape about her neck, she took up her station by the dressing mirror, waiting for Mamie to emerge. While the women waited, Minnie asked Ellen how things were on the third floor.

Ellen, who was scanning the bolts of fabric on the far side of the shop, pulled out a rich burgundy paisley wool and laid it atop the cutting table. She spoke to the folding screen. "Shouldn't Mamie answer that question?"

"Mamie's buried in truly unmentionable unmentionables," Minnie said, then added, "I've made a few purchases on her behalf."

"Minnie!" Mamie called out from behind the screen. "You don't have to shout it to the entire population."

"Who's shouting? You don't think your friends know a lady needs certain appurtenances for her wedding trousseau?" She paused. "If you need help with those ribbons, let me know. It can be tricky for the uninitiated."

"Are you telling me *you're* initiated? Because if that's the case, it has the makings of a scandal."

"For goodness' sake, Minnie. I'm a professional. Dressmakers have to know all about the many layers of fashion. All layers, dear. And we have to be able to discuss them without blushing, so"—she peered around the screen—"you've got it, dear. And you look lovely. Martin will be speechless."

"Martin doesn't need lace and ribbon to render him speechless. Most anything does, you will recall. Now go away and leave me be until I'm decent."

Minnie reappeared and looked over at Ellen. She nodded at the bolt of cloth. "That's become quite popular for men's dressing gowns. I've an order to make one for Judge Savoie."

At mention of the name, Jane excused herself to "look in the back for another selection of buttons for Mamie to consider." But searching for buttons didn't keep her from hearing the conversation in the shop as Ellen ordered a dressing gown for her husband, then selected another pattern for Jack. In the midst of selecting styles and discussing whether to put fringe or tassels on the sashes, Ellen gave a report about the women that quickly drew Jane back into the room, button drawer in hand.

"Mrs. Irwin has been to Omaha twice now, and next week I'll be going along," Ellen said. "Mamie has decided—and both Vestal and Agnes agree—that it would be easier for them to get a fresh start someplace new. There's a church interested in providing a house as lodging for women like Vestal and Agnes. And"—Ellen smiled at Jane—"there is the promise of a job for them both. Working in a small store."

"That's because they can read and do sums," Jane said and nodded Ellen's way. "Which is thanks to you."

Ellen deflected the compliment to "Ian and Mamie's shared vision."

Just then, Mamie stepped out from behind the dressing screen. Ellen clasped her hands in front of her. "Exquisite."

Mamie minced her way to the full-length mirror. Paused. Swallowed.

"Well?" Minnie leaned over and met her gaze in the mirror.

"It isn't what I expected when you showed me that fashion plate." She ran her hand along the nipped-in waistline and down to the edge of the fabric that fanned out over her hips, ending in a V at both center front and back.

Minnie adjusted the three-way mirror so Mamie could see the back of the skirt, a cascade of silk poufs ending in a two-foot train bordered with eight-inch-long box pleats.

Mamie returned to studying the front, from the square neckline accented with a wide collar of exquisite lace to the panel of brocade that ended with a band of box pleats at the hem.

"I know the fashion plate didn't show box pleats in front, but it echoes the train." Minnie was beginning to sound concerned. And still, Mamie continued staring at her reflection.

Minnie moved to slip one of the sleeves on and pinned it in place. "The V over the back of your hand echoes the line of the bodice." She pinned the other sleeve on, then stood back and glanced at Jane. "I think it's a nice fit."

Jane had never seen Mamie at a loss for words.

Finally, Minnie said, "We can change it. We can take it apart and start over if you don't like it. I remember what you said about not wanting claret. Martin won't care if—"

"I love it." Mamie turned to face her sister.

"You do? Really? Because you don't have to—"

Mamie began to cry. "I—I never thought I'd feel this way. I don't know what to say."

Ellen suggested she and Jane make tea and give the two sisters some privacy.

"No," Mamie protested, waving a hand in the air as she accepted a handkerchief from her sister. "I mean, tea would be lovely, but you don't have to. We don't need privacy." She glanced at herself in the mirror as fresh tears spilled down her cheeks.

"Mamie Dawson," Minnie scolded. "If you stain that silk with tears, I won't be able to sell the dress." She glanced at Jane. "Make tea. I'll get my sister settled down and out of that contraption, and we'll make a new plan."

Jane had headed for the door and the back room and the small stove tucked into a corner when Mamie said, "Do I have to take it off?"

Minnie sighed. "You don't have to do anything, Mamie, except tell me what in tarnation is going on!"

Mamie turned to look at herself in the mirror again. She glanced over her shoulder to view the back of the ensemble. Then she turned to look at her sister. "I never expected to feel. . .You've made me feel. . .beautiful." She dabbed at fresh tears with the handkerchief. "I don't know how to thank you."

Ellen leaned over and murmured to Jane, "Mark this day. Minnie

Dawson has been rendered speechless."

Jane chuckled.

But Minnie's speechless state didn't last long. "You don't have to thank me," she said. "It's my job to make women look beautiful. Remember?" She cleared her throat. Glanced at Jane and then back at her sister. "So, have you decided? Wedding veil or hat?"

"Hat," Mamie said without hesitation.

"Excellent." Minnie reached for the magazine lying on a nearby chair, opened it, and pointed. "I was thinking something like this."

"It's lovely. But no dead bird."

"It's the latest thing."

"Not for me."

"Feathers?"

"Feathers are fine."

"You do know that feathers come from dead birds."

"I try not to think about that," Mamie sniffed. "And at least it isn't quite so obvious."

Minnie laughed even as she shook her head. "All right, then. No birds, but feathers. Let's get you out of that so Jane and I can finish it. And are you certain you don't want to pick out the buttons?"

"Well. . ." Mamie glanced one last time in the mirror. "Maybe I would like to see what you have in mind." She slipped behind the screen.

"We have definitely earned some celebratory tea." Minnie turned to Jane and Ellen. "In fact, why don't you two ladies slip out to Dinah's and bring back a pie? We'll have teatime and then move on to men's dressing gowns." She winked at Ellen.

The minute they'd retreated to the workroom, Jane said, "I'll be forever grateful if you'll fetch the pie on your own."

Ellen nodded. "Happy to. Are you all right?"

"Fine." Jane grabbed the teakettle and retreated to the water cooler in the corner. She concentrated on watching the water trickle into the kettle.

"I'll be right back," Ellen said and slipped out the back door. She returned and served up pie without comment. It wasn't long before the four women had drawn the overstuffed chairs Minnie had placed around the shop into a circle and were chatting, pie plates balanced on their knees, teacups atop a small table that usually displayed fashion magazines. Minnie had just pulled a second bolt of soft wool challis out and broached the topic of a dressing gown for Martin Underhill when someone knocked at the front door. "It amazes me," she groused, "that people cannot seem to believe a sign that clearly says c–l–o–s–e–d." She glared at the door.

"It can't hurt to see who it is," Ellen said. "He sounds. . .insistent. I mean. It sounds firm. Like a man knocks."

Minnie spoke to Jane. "Would you mind? We'll be quiet so they think you're here alone. Just make whoever it is go away."

Jane paused with her hand on the doorknob and took a deep breath. *I'm sorry, but the sign tells it all. Miss Dawson is unavailable until first thing in the morning, and I'm not authorized to open up without her being on the premises.* That sounded professional, didn't it?

All thought of professionalism fell away, though, when Jane opened the door and saw the man standing on the other side, hat in hand, gray-green eyes troubled.

—⁂—

"It was lunch," Max said. "That was all. Claudine wanted to apologize for her behavior."

"Claudine," Jane said.

"She's barely older than Rose, Jane. And it seemed a way to. . . state the obvious."

"The obvious."

He shook his head. "You don't make it easy on a man. Do you know that?"

"I don't know what you mean."

"I'm trying to wait. To give you time. To let you. . .just. . .I don't know. Enjoy your freedom?" He shook his head again. "But I— blast it, Jane, I—"

"You. . .?"

The muscle in his jaw twitched. He glanced off up the street. "I'm trying to wait," he said again.

"Waiting is highly overrated, Dr. Zimmer," a voice trilled from behind them.

Minnie Dawson. I will never forgive you, Jane thought.

Max flushed. "Who else is in there?"

"Mamie," a voice called.

"And Ellen McKenna, Dr. Zimmer. We're sorry. We didn't mean to eavesdrop."

"But it's been fun," Minnie's laughter filled the room as she walked to Jane's side and peered through the door. "We're going to retreat now. Out the back door. For home." She nudged Jane. "I'll come in early and help you clean up tomorrow morning." She looked pointedly at Max. "No eloping."

And just like that the other three women were gone, and there they stood, alone in the dress shop, with such a cloud of unsaid words between them Jane wondered if they'd ever manage to find a way through them to the only three that mattered.

The back door closed, and Max cleared his throat. "What did I interrupt?"

"Mamie's dress fitting."

"It went well?"

"She cried. Said she never expected to feel beautiful."

Max nodded. Swallowed.

"Did Ellen McKenna say something to you at Dinah's?"

"Ellen was at Dinah's?"

"She fetched the pie we were eating."

"I didn't see her. I saw you. And the look on your face. And I wanted to run after you, but I was afraid—" He broke off. Tossed his hat toward a chair. It missed and rolled across the floor. "I was afraid this would happen. That I'd stand here like a tongue-tied dolt." He took a deep breath. "I have loved you since that night at the Bar-T when we danced together. I shouldn't have loved you then, but I did. And I still do. More than ever. And I know you need time to wait, and I'm trying, Jane. Believe me, I'm trying. But—"

"Stop."

"Stop?"

Jane nodded. "Stop waiting. I hear it's highly overrated." She stepped into his arms, closed her eyes, reveled in the warmth of him.

And finally. . .they kissed.

And the sweetest of all grace notes played love.

AKNOWLEDGMENTS

Book ideas can spring up in unlikely places. *The Key on the Quilt* is a combination of an account I read many years ago that lauded the bravery of the warden's wife during an early escape attempt at the Nebraska State Penitentiary, and a lecture I attended in Phoenix, Arizona. Undoubtedly, part of the reason the history of corrections intrigued me is that both of my husbands (Bob, who graduated to heaven in 2001, and Dan, God's blessing for this season of my life) have worked in corrections.

I was researching another story in a county archive when I came across the mug shot of a woman who served time in Nebraska in the late 1800s, and eventually, the "what ifs" of an imaginary woman's story combined with the historical account and the Arizona lecture. Mamie Dawson, Ellen McKenna, and Jane Prescott came to be, and together we learned that what Mamie said is true: prison walls can keep a person in. . .but they cannot keep God out.

Researching this book involved dozens of hours at the Nebraska State Archives, a visit to the Iowa State Penitentiary, and phone calls and searches aided by Mr. Winn Barber, public information officer at the Nebraska State Penitentiary, and Mr. Doug Hanson of the DCS Engineering Division, who answered many questions about "the early days" in Nebraska corrections. When answers couldn't be found in the historical record, I did my best to create scenarios that were reasonable given the available documentation. *Any errors in the historical foundation to this story are mine alone.*

Readers of historical fiction seem to enjoy knowing "what's real" and what isn't. In the real world, Ellen and Ian McKenna would have inhabited an apartment in the castle-like main building. The separate warden's residence didn't come into being in Nebraska until the 1920s. I was never able to locate the original architect's plans for the building constructed in 1876, and so the actual configuration of the third floor, which housed the female department, is my design based on Sanborn fire maps of the penitentiary from 1884, 1886, and 1891. Lastly, I do not know the exact year when gas lighting and a telephone line arrived at the penitentiary, which was about three miles south of the city limits when constructed in 1876.

I owe thanks to many. Thank you, Rebecca Germany, for believing in quilt stories. Thank you, Becky Durost Fish, for your editing expertise. Thank you, Kansas Eight, for helping me brainstorm. Thank you, Nancy Moser, for going above and beyond as a critiquer. And always. . .Daniel. Thank you for all the sacrifices you willingly make in the real world that enable me to create imaginary ones.

Stephanie Grace Whitson
August 28, 2011

Stephanie Grace Whitson, bestselling author and two-time Christy finalist, pursues a full-time writing and speaking career from her home studio in southeast Nebraska. Her husband and blended family, her church, quilting, and Kitty—her motorcycle—all rank high on her list of "favorite things."

DISCUSSION QUESTIONS

1. For the person who chose this book for book club discussion: What made you want to read it? What made you suggest it to the group for discussion? Did it live up to your expectations? Why or why not? Why do you suppose works of historical fiction are so popular with readers? What appeals to you the most about these types of books?

2. The story introduces three very different women, Jane Prescott, Ellen McKenna, and Mamie Dawson. Which woman did you identify with? Why? What would you say is each woman's greatest strength? Her greatest weakness? Her greatest challenge?

3. Share a favorite passage with the group. Why did it resonate with you?

4. Talk about the time period in which the story is set. Is this a time period that you knew a lot about before you read this book? If so, did you learn anything new? If not, did you come away with a greater understanding of what this particular time and place in history was actually like? How well do you think the author conveyed the era?

5. What do you think each of the three women fears the most? How would you encourage them?

6. Mamie says that prison walls can't keep God out. What events prove or disprove her belief? What kinds of barriers do people erect today to keep God out? Share a time when you have seen evidence of God's moving in spite of difficult circumstances.

7. If you were casting the film version of *The Key on the Quilt*, who would you have play the various roles? Where would you BEGIN the film? Describe the setting. Where would you END the movie?

8. Among the minor characters, who is your favorite? Why?

9. Choose one of the couples (Ian and Ellen, Martin and Mamie, or Max and Jane) and share what you think their life will look like in 1885 (five years after the conclusion of the book).

10. What do you think will be your lasting impression of the book? What spiritual lesson will stay with you?

Coming Spring 2013

Hidden in Plain sight

The Quilt Chronicles
Stephanie Grace Whitson